Sleuth of Sherwood

A ROBIN HOOD MYSTERY

Also by Jay Ruud

THE MERLIN MYSTERIES:

Fatal Feast

The Knight's Riddle

Lost in the Quagmire

The Bleak and Empty Sea

The Knight of the Cart

To the Great Deep

Sleuth of Sherwood

A ROBIN HOOD MYSTERY

JAY RUUD

Encircle Publications
Farmington, Maine, U.S.A.

Paperback ISBN 13: 978-1-64599-372-8
Hardcover ISBN 13: 978-1-64599-373-5
E-book ISBN 13: 978-1-64599-374-2

Encircle editor: Cynthia Brackett-Vincent

Cover illustration by Jennifer Hrabota Lesser
Cover design by Deirdre Wait

Published by:

Encircle Publications
PO Box 187
Farmington, ME 04938

http://encirclepub.com
info@encirclepub.com

INTRODUCTION AND ACKNOWLEDGMENTS

Unlike the King Arthur legend—which flourished in the courts of medieval Europe, and drew the attention of major writers composing for the aristocracy—the legend of Robin Hood was fostered among the common people, and so there are no great medieval epic compilations of the entire Robin Hood tradition, with any kind of coherent story arc from the beginning to end of his career. There is no Malory to create the "whole book" of the legend of Robin, and so there is no subsequent Tennyson or T. H. White. We do have Howard Pyle, whose *Merry Adventures of Robin Hood* in 1883, aimed chiefly at boys, made the first coherent narrative using most of the pieces that had survived from medieval and early modern times, and his book has been the starting place for many modern retellings of the story.

The story of Robin Hood comes down to us in fragments, mostly in separate incidents told in early folk ballads dating from the fifteenth century, and later in folk plays from May-day celebrations, and then in later broadside ballads and a few influential Elizabethan dramas. Many of these ballads were collected in Thomas Percy's *Reliques of Ancient English Poetry* in 1765; then more exhaustively in Joseph Ritson's *Robin Hood* collection in 1795, to which Ritson added a fanciful "biography" of the hero; and then much more definitively in the later 19th century by Francis James Child in volume 3 of his monumental *The English and Scottish Popular Ballads.* More recently and more readily available, Stephen Knight and Thomas Ohlgren produced a thorough collection of *Robin Hood and Other Outlaw Tales* in 1997, where you can check out all these medieval and early modern sources for yourself.

What you will learn from such a perusal is, first, that there is no definitive story arc for Robin Hood. The longest, and one of the earliest, of Robin Hood tales is the mid-fifteenth century *Gest of Robyn Hode*, a long (1,824-line) ballad in seven loosely connected "fits" relating several interconnected episodes featuring Robin and Little John. In these earliest ballads, Much the miller's son and Will Scarlet or Will Scathelock join Little John as part of Robin's meinie, or band of men. The Sheriff of Nottingham is Robin's chief adversary from the beginning. Friar Tuck, Alan a Dale, and Maid Marion appear somewhat later.

Second, you learn quite quickly that modern depictions of Robin as a fallen nobleman, especially one who supports the "true king" (i.e., Richard the Lionheart) against his usurping brother Prince John (supported by the sheriff) have virtually nothing in common with the original tales of the outlaw of Sherwood. These developments have been influenced mainly by the highly popular 1938 Errol Flynn film, the premise of which stems ultimately from two Elizabethan plays by the hack writer Antony Munday, called *The Downfall of Robert, Earl of Huntington* and *The Death of Robert, Earl of Huntington.* But these are fabrications—an attempt at appropriation of a legendary hero of the common man. For Robin is from the beginning identified as a man of English yeoman stock—a term whose meaning has shifted somewhat across the centuries but that always refers to the common man, never to a member of the noble class. And Robin is from the beginning an outlaw: one who deliberately sets himself against those in power who uphold the law, the status quo. Though generally portrayed as especially devoted to the Virgin Mary, the Robin of the ballads is violently opposed to the rich princes of the Church and to all authority figures. There is always a political undercurrent to an outlaw like Robin Hood, and the later attempts to tame him and bring him into the fold of royal service have the effect of de-politicizing him. I've not allowed that to happen here: my Robin is strictly a yeoman, and his men are all peasants or working class characters with a variety of backgrounds. I *have* thrown in Sir Palomides as one of Robin's meinie, partly to placate those who want to see a fallen nobleman here, and partly to make that connection with the crusades and the Muslim world that a number of modern Robin Hood stories have made use of.

Third, you should be able to see by these ballad sources that there is really no question of an historical Robin Hood. Since the fifteenth century, and especially more recently, chroniclers, scholars, and others have sought for some real historical personage as the source for the popular legend. Read my lips: there is none. A historical Robin Hood certainly did not live during the reign of Richard I in the late twelfth century. The early ballads seem to allude to a time in the thirteenth or early fourteenth century: the *Gest* refers to the good King Edward, but whether this is supposed to be Edward I, II, or III is impossible to tell, so the lines may refer to any time between 1271 and 1377. The first written reference we have to Robin is in William Langland's *Piers Plowman* from ca. 1370, in which Langland's personification of Sloth declares that he may not know much about theology but he knows a lot of "rymes of Robyn Hode." But there are mentions of "Robin Hoods" as outlaws in judicial rolls dating back to 1230. This does not necessarily mean that the petty fugitive of 1230 is the source of Robin Hood ballads, but that tales of the outlaw were already known by that time so that thieves and outlaws might take on the name as a pseudonym.

Because the historicity of Robin is so doubtful, I've placed him in the same kind of Neverland in which medieval romances place King Arthur: a world that mirrors the actual world of England in the early thirteenth century, but in which no historical king reigns. Indeed, I have located the time of Robin directly after the fall of King Arthur, and have given some of the characters (including Robin himself) an origin in that world (Robin, Marion, Palomides, and a few other characters are characters from my previous Merlin Mysteries series, now graduated to a series of their own). In this I am wildly changing tradition, but I hope I am preserving the spirit of the original outlaw ballads, including the theme of their political resistance.

In this novel, the story of Robin's friendship and assistance to Richard at the Lee, as well as Robin's, Sir Richard's, and Little John's thwarting of the Abbot of Saint Mary's Abbey, and the bilking of the Bishop of Hereford, all are suggested by the *Gest of Robin Hood*, though the conspiracy of the abbot, Lady Abigail, and Hugh Peveril against the Countess of Chesterfield is my own invention. The ballad of "Robin Hood and Little John" sung by Sir Palomides I have borrowed, shortened, and modernized from the version in Child's ballads (vol. 3, no. 125). The closing ballad sung by Palomides is borrowed (and slightly modernized) from the ending of a ballad of 1632 by Martin Parker called "A True Tale of Robin Hood" (Child, vol. 3, no. 154). Will Stuteley's ballad in chapter eleven is a modernization of "The Maid Freed from the Gallows" (Child, vol. 2, no. 95). The "Abraham and Isaac" play performed by Robin's company in chapter fifteen is based loosely on the late medieval biblical play known as *The*

Brome Abraham and Isaac, and some of the lines of that play are modernized and included in our outlaws' play. Friar Tuck's story of the walking corpse of Robert of Boltby from Kilburn comes from an early fifteenth century manuscript compiled at the monastery of Byland—you can read more about it in Maik Hildebrandt's "Medieval Ghosts: the Stories of the Monk of Byland," available online.

I should add that the Peveril family did indeed own both Codnor Castle and Peveril Castle in the high Middle Ages, and were a vastly powerful family in the north of England whose founder, the first William Peveril, came over in the Norman Conquest and was rumored to be the natural son of William the Conqueror himself. He was granted 162 manors in Derbyshire and Nottinghamshire. I admit that my interest in the Peveril family stems from my discovery that one of my ancestors was a Peveril—Mellette Peveril, said to be the daughter of that first William. She married a knight, Guy Le Strange, and their son, Roland Le Strange, is my 26th great grandfather. And careful readers will notice that I've made Lydia Peveril's mother Lady Margaret Le Strange. However, there is no evidence that either Peverils or Le Stranges were ever involved in the kinds of nefarious activities engaged in this book. But Hugh and Maude are legitimate Peveril names, though there were never any real Earls of Chesterfield until the 17th century.

As for the abbot, there *was* a Robert de Harpham who was abbot of Saint Mary's Abbey in York from 1184 to 1195, and who ended up being deposed. Incompetence and infirmity were the reasons given, rather than the kinds of high crimes and misdemeanors committed by the abbot in this book, but the name seemed appropriate for my own dear abbot.

Finally, there was a real Skipsea Castle, the ruins of which still exist on the Yorkshire coast. It was actually owned by William de

Forz, Count of Aumerle, in the early 13th century (so, not quite a true contemporary of the aforementioned Abbot Robert). William joined in a rebellion against King Henry III, and royalist forces captured Skipsea Castle and destroyed it. Hence, those aforementioned ruins.

PROLOGUE

The young woman stood atop the tall wooden tower that served as the castle keep, looking eastward across the sea where the rising sun was awakening the earth to another new day. "Twenty-five," she said to herself. "And no end in sight."

The brisk spring wind off the sea made her dark free-flowing tresses dance with abandon across her face and shoulders. Her deep brown eyes glared at the horizon, darting from left to right in the forlorn hope of seeing a ship that, in answer to her prayers, might be coming to carry her away.

She breathed a dispirited sigh and slumped forward, leaning on the low parapet and wondering if there was any chance she could ever escape this place. The castle had the sea on one side, and treacherous marshes on the other, and as if that weren't enough there were guards or spies around her at all times. Even the women who acted as if they were there to attend her were, she knew, really there to report her every move and remark to her keepers.

Of course, she could simply give in to her captors' demands, and then she would be set "free." But giving in meant acceding to their mandate that she marry the man of their choice, and so in fact it meant enslaving herself for the rest of her life to a man she found intolerable. Her choice was one prison or another, and she preferred the one she was in, which at least left her the freedom to say "no."

When she heard the shuffle of feet on the staircase behind her she did not bother to turn around. She knew what she would see: a young man with a thin face like one carved from stone, notably sporting an eyepatch from which a scar protruded above and below. The face was ruggedly handsome, though the uncut, oily brown hair was hardly attractive. He was in his early twenties, and dressed as a nobleman in a blue tunic with a surcoat bearing his family's coat of arms. But his voice was hardly courteous when he demanded, "And so you are here again, my lady? Do you think you're going to see something different from what you saw yesterday? Or the day before? Why do you watch the sea so intently?"

"It's peaceful," she answered. "And it keeps me from having to look at things within that appall my sight."

"And do you include my own visage among those appalling sights, my lady?"

"I didn't say that," she replied, still not turning around. But to the smile she imagined was beginning to spread on his thin face, she added, "But I don't deny it either."

"This stubbornness will not last," he told her confidently. "You will stop this nonsense and do as you're told, and agree to wed me. Women haven't the fortitude nor the stamina for a long siege, and I intend to besiege you until you say yes."

"Such a romantic proposal, I can't imagine any woman resisting that kind of charm. I suppose I would have this kind of gentle persuasion to look forward to after we are married, then, as well?"

"Women were made to serve their men, and if they resist it is perfectly acceptable to force them into submission," the man answered.

"Oooh, now that's a lovely thought. Is that what Antony told Cleopatra to make her fall so passionately in love with him?"

"Pah!" he spat. "Your head is full of these classical ideas. Your grandfather wasted his time providing you with tutors. Educating women only creates problems for their men."

"Well, one of 'my men' you will never be, that I can promise."

"You will come around," he predicted. "It is inevitable." And with that he turned and stomped down the steps.

She was left to continue her perusal of the sea, and she smiled fleetingly to herself. "Don't count on it," she whispered.

CHAPTER ONE

"Mmm, do that again, Robin dear," Maude cooed, licking his earlobe. "I haven't had a fit like that in years."

Panting heavily, Robin groaned, stirring from the exhausted stupor he'd been in for the past several minutes. "I swear, Maude, we've gone around twice already, and one more time's like to be the end of me. And what will your husband say then, when he comes home and finds my corpse in your bed, eh?"

The sheriff's wife scoffed as she rolled over, pulling the sheets with her as she curled away from him, covering her soft nakedness and murmuring, "He'll probably thank me for ridding him of the notorious outlaw of Sherwood."

Robin lay on his back, naked atop the sheets with his forearm resting across his brow and squinting through the sheer curtain surrounding the bed. It was too thin to keep out the chill morning draft, whose effects he was beginning to feel all over his exposed flesh. Maude opened one eye and glanced down at his shrinking manhood, chiding, "The little feller's hiding himself away, I see. Was it something I said?"

"You've humbled his pride, that's for sure," Robin agreed. "But don't worry, he'll raise his head again before too long, or my name isn't Robert fitz Ooth of Locksley..."

"Your name *isn't* Robert fitz Ooth, fool, as you know I'm well aware. But when that head does rise up again, you bring him over here and let me humble him some more."

The other thing the sheer curtain didn't keep out was the sun that Robin now noticed was raising its own unwelcome head over the eastern horizon and streaming through the bedroom window he'd left open crawling through it at midnight. And when that first beam hit his eyes, Robin sat up with a start. "Best be off, Maudie dear," he told her, giving her generous bottom a sound smack through the bedclothes as he hopped out of bed and began to pull on his brown hosen and his Lincoln green tunic. "You did tell me your great oaf of a husband was due back from Oxenford early this morning, did you not?"

"I did," she said with a sigh. "Anyway, he's not *that* great of an oaf…" her voice trailed off, having gone about as far as she could with her half-hearted defense of a man she abhorred, but whom the Church told her she was matched with for life.

"Oh please!" Robin scoffed as he buckled on his belt from which hung the scabbard of his short sword. "John of Oxenford, Shire Reeve of Nottingham, is as great a thief as anyone in this land has ever seen, the worse for it because he does it under the auspices of a royal appointment. He takes bribes, commandeers goods and services under his right of purveyance, claiming they are for royal use but lining his own pockets at every step. As if there even *is* any royal authority anymore! That's laughable in itself. Why the…"

"Shh!" Maude warned him.

"What…" Robin began, then he heard it too: the snort of a horse, followed by the slow clop-clopping of the gentle palfrey returning from a long ride overnight.

"That's Daisy! That's John's horse," Maude exclaimed, now sitting up with some urgency. "What are we going to *do*?" Her voice rose till it bordered on a shriek. "He'll find you!"

"Not with an open window in the house," Robin flashed her

a smile. He was fully dressed now, with boots and brown hood, and threw Maude a farewell kiss as he pulled himself through the window, whispering, "Until next time, wench!"

As Maude got up to close the shutters, he held on to the windowsill with his hands, letting his legs hang down from the second-floor window, then let himself drop. The sheriff's house was a newer waddle-and-daub construction with sleeping rooms on the second story and a kitchen, hall, buttery, and storage room on the ground floor. The door was on the front side, while the master bedroom's window was in the back (an arrangement that allowed the sheriff to evade the new window tax imposed on casements facing the Nottingham street). As he dropped lightly onto the grass behind the house, Robin was congratulating himself on having successfully avoided discovery when he heard horse hooves scuffling along the side of the building and remembered that the sheriff kept a small stable behind the house where he naturally would be bringing Daisy for her breakfast and a good rest.

The sheriff did employ a slow-moving greybeard named Giles who acted as stable boy, groundskeeper and general factotum, and Robin knew it was too early for the old man to be stirring yet, but thinking quickly he pulled his brown hood up so it obscured his face, bent his head down and shuffled slowly in the direction of Daisy's amble. When the sheriff appeared coming round the corner of the house, Robin gave his best impression of the old servant and croaked in the back of his throat, "I'll take her, sir," casually snatching Daisy's reins and turning as if to lead her toward the stable. The sheriff, tired from a long ride in the dark and eager to get inside to his wife and his own breakfast, barely noticed him, turning around and shouting back, "Mind you brush her well and give her some oats" as he stepped tiredly back toward the front door.

"Sir," Robin acknowledged ambiguously.

Robin's own steps shuffled more and more slowly as he listened for the sheriff's boots striding around his house until, at the sound of the front door opening, Robin swung into Daisy's saddle and, with a kindly stroke of her neck, whispered into her ear, "A few more miles, Daisy, and I'll make sure you get a delicious breakfast in Sherwood."

As the sheriff entered his door, coming face to face with Giles, just risen from a sound sleep in the great hall of the house, he heard the clatter of galloping hooves growing fainter and fainter as the horse disappeared down the road.

"Bastard," he whispered to himself as the dawn came.

* * *

The Great North Road, a long highway dating back to Roman times that led from London town all the way to York and connected there to a route heading into Scotland, passed through Nottingham and cut through Sherwood itself, and this was the road Robin and Daisy trotted along that early spring morning. Small oaks and silver birches appeared along the road and before long they had passed into the thicket of ancient oaks that formed England's largest forest. As he rode in the quiet shade of morning he could hear about him the high chirping of chaffinches moving down the scale to the lower, quicker chirps as they ended their songs, and here and there he saw several of their rusty breasts in the branches above him, where he could also hear the brittle rat-a-tat-tatting of small black and white woodpeckers who contributed their own shrill monosyllables to the choir all about him in the trees. He loved this place.

There were perhaps another two miles before Robin would need to turn off the main road and cut into the depth of the forest to find the Great Oak that marked the clearing where lay the campsite of his meinie, his retinue or band of comrades, and Robin let Daisy amble now, lulled into a kind of reverie by the soft breeze and the birdsong and the beauty of the great trees. He was enjoying all the splendor and freshness of the bright April morning when he heard a rustle of leaves and the soft, almost imperceptible crack of a dry twig and before he could blink, a large red hind dashed into the road not thirty feet in front of him. The deer stopped suddenly and looked at him, her placid eyes staring as if suddenly entranced by Robin's face. He cursed himself for not bringing his long bow with him on this trip. The game in Sherwood—particularly the deer—were technically all the property of the crown, and so if one wanted to act strictly within the law, it might be interpreted as illegal to shoot a deer in this forest. But the crown had been up for grabs ever since the death of Arthur, and Robin wasn't even sure who was wearing it right now. But whoever it was he was a long way from Sherwood and was certainly not likely to begrudge a poor yeoman forester like himself a little venison. The sheriff, of course, had other ideas, but the sheriff could go whistle as far as Robin was concerned. "Need has no law," was the motto of Robin and his men, and who had more needs than they? They had to eat. Every day. And they lived in the wood. Ergo, the wood must needs provide.

"Zing!" Robin heard a whistle and felt the breeze of an arrow passing barely six inches from his right ear. With a solid *thwock*, the arrow buried itself in the hind's breast close to her heart, and the animal fell dead in the road, killed by a single shot. Robin jerked his head around and reared Daisy up, the scowl on his face auguring no happy outcome for the man who had loosed that shot.

"Have a care, there, Robin old boy," came a loud, nasal voice from the branches of one of the larger oaks behind him along the road. "You nearly ruined my shot with your great looming pate poppin' up there between me and the quarry!"

Robin heaved a sighed as his brow softened. "And what if I'd turned my head at the last instant and put it right in the path of that arrow?"

"Well," came the reply as Much the miller's son dropped down out of the tree, shouldered his bow and strode toward his quarry. "I suppose me and the boys would have had to get by with just your stringy carcass for dinner in place of this fine venison feast I've just secured us." Much's broad smile was infectious, even though only about half of his original teeth remained in his head. But his round face with its generous sprinkle of freckles across his pug nose held a pair of twinkling brown eyes whose high spirit could not be ignored.

"That *would* have been disappointing, for sure," Robin admitted, swinging down off his newly acquired horse. "Come, I'll help you dress this deer and we can fling it over my Daisy's back to carry it to the camp."

"*Your* Daisy?" Much raised his eyebrows. "I don't recall you leaving with a horse last night…"

"She's my Daisy now," Robin told him. "A gift from my good friend the Sheriff of Nottingham himself."

"John of Oxenford gave you that beast?" Much replied dubiously. "A little early in the day for you to have drunk *that* much wine already…"

"It's true!" Robin replied, holding his hand up as if taking an oath. "Put her reins right in my hand. I swear it by the Blessed Virgin herself!"

"And now he's adding blasphemy to his list of sins. Oh Lord, let me get this deer dressed quickly, before the blackguard corrupts me too with his iniquitous lies!"

* * *

There was a good deal of rejoicing when Much and Robin brought the day's venison into the bright clearing around the Great Oak in the midst of Sherwood. Here fifteen of Robin's meinie, all dressed in the Lincoln green that was his livery, met them and lifted the hind's carcass from Daisy's back to ready it for roasting over the open fire now roaring to life in the center of the clearing. A few of the men's wives who lived with them here in the woods helped see to the cooking, and one of the men, who wore a scarlet hood over his green tunic, whistled low as he took the reins of the newly acquired horse.

"Treat her kindly, Will," Robin said. "Brush her coat and give her a nice bucket of oats if you can. She's been kept in the dark dungeon of the sheriff's stables for the past few years. She'll need some gentle handling in her new home."

Will Scarlet flashed his white teeth and laughing blue eyes at Robin, tossing his own blond mane aside as he led the horse away, calling back, "I'm sure she was grateful to be sprung from her prison, Uncle."

Robin turned from the horse. By now Much had joined the group readying the venison on a large spit for roasting, and Robin looked over the clearing without spying the man he was looking for, but he called to a fellow in a hooded brown homespun wool habit tied with a white cord with three knots: "Tuck! Is Little John not about?"

Friar Tuck turned toward Robin, his fleshy jowls quivering as he did so, beads of sweat glistening on the bald spot of his tonsure. "Gone early this morning with four other lads, meaning to patrol the Great North Road and waylay any visitors coming south. But Will Stutely's just come back to warn us John's coming with some rich prelate he's invited to dine with us. It's why I'm carrying this great skin of wine," and at that Tuck lifted up the heavy wineskin from under his arm. "I want to pour out a few nice flagons to welcome our guests."

And as Tuck finished, Stutely himself, a slight young man whose face was tanned a deep brown, but who still may have been the handsomest of all Robin's retainers stepped shyly toward him. "Sir," Stutely addressed him, as he always did, with deference. Robin would have been annoyed if any of his other foresters had addressed him so, but he could never be annoyed with Will Stutely. The boy was so charming and so open, but at the same time with a mischievous streak that could be contagious, that Robin never had any wonder why Little John loved him more than any other man. "Little John sends greetings that he is bringing a fat bird to dine with us, ready for the plucking. It's a purple-clad prelate, riding with two yeomen archers and a string of five horses. We ambushed them as they were coming down from the north: John sent an arrow thumping into a heavy wooden chest on the back of one of the horses, and that stopped them right quick. We had them surrounded and approached with longbows at ready and arrows notched, so they surrendered their crossbows and swords readily enough. But the proud one's quite adamant that he's too important a personage to be touched by the likes of us, being, as he says, the Bishop of Hereford himself. He seems to have agreed to sup with us, though. I suppose the choice between that and an arrow through his fat guts wasn't so difficult to make. I rode one of the bishop's horses back to bring the news, and John and the others are walking the bishop and his boys back here at a nice casual pace." And at that Stutely grinned broadly, his brown eyes sparkling and his freckled nose wrinkling with amusement.

It wasn't long before the sound of several horses could be

heard moving noisily through the woods from the direction of the Great North Road, and the substantial form of John Naylor of Hathersage strode confidently into the clearing, leading by the bridle a fine white horse on which sat a purple and white clad, middle-aged prelate with a deep scowl on his face. Naylor, dressed in Lincoln green like his fellows in Robin's meinie, was better known as Little John, an ironic epithet drawing attention to his great height, approaching six and a half feet, and his muscular bulk, exceeding some twenty stone. Most people were so impressed by his size that they didn't notice his face, which was their own loss, since he was ruggedly handsome, with piercing blue eyes and a well-trimmed beard under a shock of blond hair bleached by the sun.

The bishop, on the other hand, had dark eyes that blazed at anyone who came within his gaze as he ranged around the clearing, his face bright red with a fury ready to flare out at whoever he might decide was responsible for this outrage. Robin smiled as he came toward John and the bishop, his arms outspread in a good-hearted welcome.

"You!" the bishop raged at the sight of the green-clad woodsman. "Are you the one in charge of this rabble? Do you have any idea who I am? I am Edward of Worcester, Lord Bishop of Hereford, on my way to Nottingham Castle on important business. Let me tell you, this mischief will not go unanswered! You think you can treat prince of the Church in this manner with impunity?"

"My lord," Robin began, bowing to hide his impudent smirk. "I regret your rough handling, if indeed such has occurred. Sometimes Little John forgets his manners. Comes from ill breeding, I imagine."

At the name, the bishop's face lost its angry red and grew suddenly pale. "Little John you say? Then…this is that notorious outlaw band of Sherwood that people speak of? The band of that foul scourge…Robin Hood?"

At the name Robin smirked more openly, bowed once more and responded, "Foul Scourge, at your service, my lord."

By now Little John had halted the bishop's fine horse and had extended his hand to assist the prelate to climb down from his mount. Bishop Edward, fuming but resigned to the indignity of supping in the greenwood with a band of outlaws, swung his own not insubstantial bulk out of the saddle and allowed himself to be guided to a place of honor on the turf beneath the huge spreading oak that marked the place while trying to maintain his princely dignity. Dressed in his everyday garb for riding, he wore a purple cap that just covered his tonsure, and a cape-like purple mozetta that draped his shoulders and reached down to his elbows. It was buttoned in front and had a small hood at the neck, which he had not been wearing, and it covered a white, long-sleeved alb, reaching to his ankles now that he was off his horse. On his feet he wore leather boots rather than his bishop's sandals and liturgical stockings, in deference to the long ride through the forest. David of Doncaster, youngest of Robin's crew, and Wat o' the Crabstaff, the former tinker, were helping the bishop's two yeomen down from their own horses, since the two guards had their hands tied behind them. Finally, the lanky Will Scathelock was guiding in the train of five ponies the bishop's men had been leading. The horses carried several large bundles and, on the last and sturdiest horse in line, a heavy wooden chest.

By now Much's deer was well roasted over the open fire, and Robin called for a fine helping of the venison to be placed before Bishop Edward, served on a round trencher of hard brown rye bread and a wooden cup of good Nottingham ale, which Robin's men stocked by the barrel from their favorite Nottingham tavern at the sign of the Blue Boar.

"I fear your excellency will have to dine with your fingers," Robin apologized as he dropped down to seat himself on the bishop's right hand, and took a trencher and helping of venison of for himself from the dwarf Thorvald who had taken it on himself to slice and serve venison from the spit for this meal. "We have no fine plate or cutlery here in our humble forest home."

The bishop, having softened enough to accept the food, which gave off a savory aroma that was hard to resist, scoffed at that. "Your 'humble' forest home seems to provide you with meat fit for the richest table in Britain," he observed, adding, "I see that you do not scruple to kill and serve the king's own deer," before sinking his teeth into his own portion of that forbidden meal.

"No scruples at all," Robin acknowledged between mouthfuls of his own meat. "But tell me, my good Lord Bishop, since you've piqued my curiosity," and with that Robin paused for a long draft of ale. "Who, then, *is* the king these days? I've heard widely varying reports. Perhaps we'll want to send the venison to the king the next time we have the luck to shoot one of his deer. Where should we send its remains?"

The bishop scowled again. "You should not be so flippant concerning your betters, nor concerning your crimes. Poaching the king's deer is a serious offense, subject to large fines once the Sheriff of Nottingham catches up with you and your fellow ruffians," and with that he took another large mouthful of savory meat, followed by a good swig of the Blue Boar's ale.

"John of Oxenford has been looking for me for a good long time," Robin replied contemplatively. "I suspect he'll keep looking for a while yet, with the same success. Frankly, my lord, I don't think the sheriff could find me if I were hiding in his own house, bedding his own wife!" The other outlaws in his hearing guffawed at that, as if it were in fact hypothetical hyperbole. Then Robin sobered for a moment and added, "But I notice you avoided my question as to who actually sits on the throne as we speak."

"What does a Sherwood poacher and outlaw like you know or care about court politics? You need to leave such questions to your betters, and return to a law-abiding life in whatever villeinage you were born to. That is my advice to you." He'd finished his venison and, disdaining the dark rye as beneath his notice, fit only for pigs and peasants, tossed his bread trencher onto the turf, where young David of Doncaster picked it up an began gnawing on it with some appetite.

"That's your good Christian advice, is it, my Lord Bishop?" Robin answered him, "I'm a freeborn Englishman of good yeoman stock, and even if I were the villein you suggest, I would be as much the king's subject as you are. As for the doings of the court, it might interest you to know that, in the days before this current anarchy, I served the late King Arthur, in those glory days, as chief of his palace guard, commanding his loyal archers."

The bishop scoffed at that idea. "Such airs you give yourself, you and your lying tongue. I'll have the sheriff cut it out of your churlish mouth when he catches you. You, in Arthur's court? Poppycock! And I suppose you have Sir Lancelot here among your rustic band."

Robin looked down, pursing his lips, before replying. "They called me Robin Kempe in those days," he finally said, shaking his long blond locks. "Because of the bounteous hair, you know? But now, I wear my green hood most of the time, so…"

By now Bishop Edward's two bodyguards had been seated and their hands freed to allow them to partake of the meal as well, a meal they attacked with some relish, so that Robin wondered how well fed the bishop kept his servants. It was still Lent, after all, and he wondered if the bishop kept them fasting. Judging from Bishop Edward's own bulk, he was not much given to fasting himself, but his unsolicited pontificating toward Robin suggested that the bishop might be a "do as I say, not as I do" kind of master.

"But I am an ill host," Robin changed the subject. "I should be providing entertainment for my guests, to make their banquet more memorable. Now what will it be, my lord? We can either have an impromptu archery contest, say two of my best archers against your two guardsmen, marking a target on a tree some hundred paces or so from here," and at that he raised his eyebrows at the bishop's two men, who by now were fairly comfortable at their meal, and well into their second cups of ale. They were unenticed by the sport.

"Or," Robin continued, "we can have a merry ballad from our resident minstrel. What is your pleasure, my lord? True arrows or poetical barbs?"

The bishop, losing some of his gruff edge, spoke with a bit less ill humor. "I think," he said with what was almost a twinkle in his voice, "that we have seen enough of your fellow outlaws' skill with the bow when one of your devils buried a shaft into my trunk that last horse was carrying. Let there be music if any of you has a voice worth hearing."

"Ask for music, and music you shall have!" Robin responded with a short laugh. He clapped his hands and called, "Palomides! Are you in camp?"

"Where else would I be?" came the answer from a tall, stately figure who was walking across the clearing to Robin, from where he had been chatting and drinking ale with Will Scarlet, Friar Tuck, and Skipper Haakon, a retired Viking raider who continued his thieving ways on land with Robin's outlaw band. Palomides had a large chest and a mellow baritone voice, and was better dressed than anyone else, including the bishop. He didn't wear the Lincoln green livery in which the other outlaws were dressed, but a dark blue doublet covered with a fur-lined black cape, green breeches and fine brown hose with leather boots.

"My Lord Bishop, you asked whether Sir Lancelot of the Lake was among my meinie, and I now can answer that he is, sadly, not among our group. This, however, is Sir Palomides, late of the Round Table. Palomides, may I present to you Bishop Edward of Hereford."

Palomides bowed slightly toward the prelate in deference to his title, but the bishop was so taken aback that he forgot all courtly manners and simply stared at Palomides with his mouth open. It was difficult to know whether he was more astonished that one of King Arthur's own former knights would be here among this rabble, or that said knight was a Moor.

After an uncomfortable moment or two, when the bishop tried and failed three times to address the knight, Sir Palomides took matters into his own hands. On the principle that one should always respond as if the other party had behaved and spoken in an acceptable manner, he spoke to Bishop Edward smoothly, as if continuing a briefly interrupted conversation. "Yes, my lord, I was a knight of the late king's great Table. After the fall of the kingdom I found I had lost my taste for the demands of chivalry. I knew of no other king I could have been satisfied with serving under after that most honored of monarchs was no more. Besides, I have lost all of my closest friends: my brother Sir Safer, my great and respected rival Sir Tristram, my beloved Sir Gareth, the great Lancelot…all gone. Besides," he continued, waving off the melancholy mood he had invoked. "I did not think it would be easy finding another lord who would take me as a vassal on first sight. You may have noticed, I am a Moor."

At that the bishop coughed and sputtered. "Y…yes! Of course. So you are. How is it that you…I mean, how did you come to be in this kingdom? And are you a worshipper of that heretic Mahomet?"

At that Palomides gave a great laugh that echoed among the trees in the surrounding forest. "No Moor worships Mahomet, my lord. Where *do* you people pick up these things? A Moor's first tenet of faith is that there is no god but God. Mahomet is God's prophet."

"Nonsense," answered the bishop. "Your Mahomet was a Christian bishop who wanted to become pope, and when he was denied the election, he began a schism by starting his own church, of which he made himself pope and god in one. This is well known."

Palomides laughed again. "Well, my lord, I can see there will be no denting your tight shell of absolute certainty, but I thank you nonetheless for explaining to me the basics of the religion I was born and raised in. I have been baptized now, I should inform you, so you needn't worry I will be spreading heresy throughout the land."

Robin broke in before the exasperated bishop could insult Sir Palomides further, and remarked, "Sir Palomides is our resident minstrel I was telling you about..."

"I prefer 'troubadour,' master Robin," Palomides objected. "A minstrel I consider a mere wandering jongleur, like our friend Alan a Dale, who, I am sure, is here somewhere. A minstrel is a wandering teller of tales, often singing rhymes others have composed. I compose my own verse, and accompany myself in my poor way upon this lute."

It was only then that the bishop noticed the pear shaped instrument slung over the knight's shoulder, where in the past he might have slung his emblazoned shield. "At your request, my good Robin, let me sing a verse I made the other day—one I'll teach Alan a Dale himself to sing in taverns all around the shire. I call this merry ballad 'Robin Hood and Little John.' Hark now!" Palomides spoke the last words with some volume, and heads turned toward him as he moved slightly toward the center of the large circle of diners around the clearing. Then, plucking the strings of his mellow instrument, he began in a clear, strong voice to sing:

Bold Robin Hood said to his jolly bowmen,
"Pray tarry you here in this grove;
And see that you all observe well my call,
While through the forest I rove."

Then did he shake hands with his merry men all,
And bid them at present good-bye;
Then, as near a brook his journey he took,
A stranger he chanced to espy.

They happened to meet on a long narrow bridge,
And neither of them would give way;
Quoth bold Robin Hood, and sturdily stood,
"I'll show you right Nottingham play."

"You talk like a coward," the stranger replied;
"Well armed with a long bow you stand,
To shoot at my breast, while I, I protest,
Have naught but a staff in my hand."

Then Robin Hood stepped to a thicket of trees,
And chose him a staff of ground-oak;
Now this being done, away he did run
To the stranger and merrily spoke:

"Lo! see my staff; it is lusty and tough,
Now here on the bridge we will play;
Whoever falls in, the other shall win
The battle, and so we'll away."

"With all my whole heart to thy humor I yield,
I scorn in the least to give out."
This said, they fell to't without more dispute,
And their staffs they did flourish about.

And first Robin he gave the stranger a bang,
So hard that it made his bones ring:
The stranger he said, "This must be repaid;
I'll give you as good as you bring.

So long as I am able to handle my staff,
To die in your debt, friend, I scorn."
Then to it both goes, and followed their blows,
As if they'd been thrashing of corn.

O then into a fury the stranger he grew
And gave him a damnable look,
And with it a blow that laid him full low
And tumbled him into the brook.

"I prithee, good fellow, O where art thou now?"
The stranger in laughter he cried;
Quoth bold Robin Hood, "Good faith, in the flood,
And floating along with the tide."

At that, Palomides ceased and his conclusion was greeted with uproarious laughter from all sides, as all in that warm circle of companionship had drawn closer and hung on every word of his ballad. Little John himself had moved over behind Robin and placed a great beefy hand on the outlaw chief's shoulder, laughing harder than any of his peers. With his characteristic good humor Robin was nodding and smiling, slightly abashed, and held up his hands, saying, "All right! All right! I admit you've told the story pretty accurately, Palomides, I can't deny it. But you've ended it too soon. You should add the truth about how the story ends: how John agreed, after our little squabble, to become my man and to join our band, so impressed was he by my courage…"

"Impressed by the inordinate hardness of that block you call a head, rather. I figured anyone who could withstand those blows and suffer no damage to his brain either had no brain at all or led a charmed life, so I threw in with the luck of a hard-headed forester."

At that, young Will Stutely pushed his freckled countenance into the circle and crowed, "Add the part about how the band rechristened him that night, and how I thought to name him Little John because, you know, he's such a puny little fellow!" And overcome with his own wit, he rolled on the ground laughing.

Aware that the party might be getting a bit too boisterous for the fastidious taste of the bishop, Robin judged it was probably time to end their jest with the bishop and send him on his way. "My lord," he said, taking advantage of the lull in the general revelry that followed the conclusion of Sir Palomides' ballad, "you and your guards have finished your dinners, and I see that the sun is well past its height. You must be on your way presently if you are to reach Nottingham before nightfall. And so, reluctantly, we will have to bid you adieu."

"And not a moment too soon!" Bishop Edward replied, rising from the turf on which he sat. "You're saying I am free to leave, and you and your men will hinder me no more?"

"Hinder you?" Robin answered with mock alarm. "And on your

important visit to the sheriff? Nothing could be further from our intent. We merely wanted to treat you to a fine dinner. You must admit, it was a fine dinner was it not?"

The bishop lowered his brows and glared at Robin. "It was an illegal dinner of the king's own venison."

"Exactly!" Robin replied. "A dinner fit for a king! And you must admit, such a dinner is quite costly. I'm sure that you wouldn't mind leaving us some fair payment for our trouble in its procurement and preparation. You know, as you would have paid had you supped at an inn on your way—an expense that we've spared you, I might add!"

A light began to burn behind Bishop Edward's eyes as he realized that the time had indeed come for the reckoning, and that he was not going to escape this forest with his purse as full as it had been when he entered. His face reddened considerably as he noticed Robin's eyes fixed on the leather purse that hung invitingly from the rope-like cincture the bishop wore as a belt. Edward cleared his throat theatrically and answered the outlaw's polite demand.

"My good man, I am but a poor servant of Christ. What wealth I have belongs to the Church itself, or is intended for charitable causes. Surely you would not imperil your immortal soul by extorting money from the body of Christ? What little coin I carry with me is intended simply to defray expenses that might occur on my journey. I have barely enough to ensure that my companions and I reach Nottingham without incident—perhaps twenty shillings, no more."

At that Robin held out his hand. "Let me see your purse, my lord," he said. "If what you say is true, if you have twenty shillings or less, then we will not touch your poor pittance. Never let it be said that Robin Hood or his band ever stole from a poor man."

The bishop, now seeing some hope for himself after all, took his purse and held it toward the outlaw, his hand shaking with hopeful anticipation. Robin untied the purse string and held the small bag upside down, spilling its contents into his left hand. Little John and Palomides bent slightly to look into Robin's hand as he eyed the small pile of coins. Sixteen shining shilling coins sparkled in Robin's hand. Both of the other outlaws nodded at Robin as he returned the coins to the purse and handed the purse back to its owner. "Your purse is even skimpier than you guessed, my good bishop. You shall certainly keep this leather sack and all that is in it. No one will touch these coins, and you have our leave to carry them with you through Sherwood."

The bishop, sweating profusely, nearly dropped to his knees in relief, and was letting out a great sigh of deliverance when Will Stutely and the dwarf Thorvald came running up to Robin, carrying between them the arrow-pierced wooden chest that had been on the hindmost horse in the bishop's procession. "Master Robin," Thorvald cried. "Here's another beast that seems to have been felled by one of our bowmen. What do you suppose could be inside?"

"Well now, I can't say, Thorvald old sot. Let's break that lock and see, shall we?"

Now the bishop, white with fear, reached out his hand in vigorous protest. "No! You can't! It's…it's…it belongs to the Church!"

"I suppose," Little John suggested, picking up a good sized rock in his ham-like fist and smashing the chest's puny lock, "that this belongs to the Church in the same way that our venison dinner belonged to the king. That is, it is for our use under the benevolence of its generous owner."

The lock broken, the chest fell open, revealing tall, neatly stacked piles of glittering gold pieces. Thorvald and Will immediately fell to their knees and began counting.

"A miracle, my lord!" Robin cried as the exasperated bishop fumed with inarticulate fury. "Where can it have come from? You gave us your word that you had but the sixteen shillings in your purse, and look at the bounty that God has provided, it would seem, out of thin air!"

"For...for charity, you villain! This money is for the Church to distribute to worthy charitable causes..."

"Perhaps the Sheriff of Nottingham is one of those worthy causes? And who else...some of the other greedy lords and prelates you are meeting with there at Nottingham Castle? Well..." Already Thorvald and Will were finishing their quick assessment of the wealth that chest contained. "Considerate of our Lord Bishop to have packed the gold in such neat piles. What is the final tally, my lads? Is there more than sixteen shillings here?"

"We count 1,500 gold nobles, master Robin," Will said, in his excitement his voice an octave higher than normal. With all the band's success in assessing tolls from travelers on the Great Northern Road through Sherwood, Will had never seen this much booty in one place.

"But you can't..." Bishop Edward protested again. "What kind of godless pagans are you churls?"

"Yeomen, sir, yeomen. And why do you object so, my good bishop?" Robin asked with his most impish smile. "You said yourself you had no more than what was in your purse. Surely this is a great windfall. Friar Tuck!"

At that, the rotund, curtal friar appeared at Robin's elbow. "Do you think you might be able to find a good number of poor folk, widows and orphans and the destitute in Nottingham and its environs who could use some of this windfall?"

The friar rubbed his round jawline, his eyes twinkling. "I can think of several right off, Robin. I can certainly find many who can make good use of this gold."

"Then here's what we do," Robin decided. "This gold will be divided into three piles, with five hundred nobles each. One pile shall go to Friar Tuck to distribute among the poor of the vicinity, just as you intended, my Lord Bishop." By now Edward was trembling with rage. "Another five hundred we shall keep for our own use, my good men of Sherwood. It will help with our own upkeep, and keep us in victuals and clothes over the next year." A small cheer went up from around the clearing at that.

"The other five hundred nobles, my good bishop, I give freely to you. What a great bounty for you, my lord! You came into our camp with but sixteen shillings, and you leave with five hundred gold nobles you did not dream you would have! And oh, by the way, that last horse in your train must not have been yours at all, since he carried this chest that you said was not yours. So we will keep the horse. Friar Tuck can make good use of a pack animal like that one when he traverses the shire distributing these monies among the poor. And now best be on your way, my lord Bishop Edward of Hereford. You can still make Nottingham by dark if you do not tarry on the road."

By now some of Robin's men had brought round the bishop's horses and were helping his two guards into their saddles. As the bishop mounted his horse, making sure that his five hundred gold coins were made safe in a pack on one of his other horses, he turned haughtily to Robin and spat out a venomous farewell: "I shall remember this, Robin Hood of Sherwood. Don't think you have seen the last of me."

"Farewell, my good lord," Robin answered cheerfully. "May our next meeting be as mutually profitable to us both as this one has been. Oh, and when you get to Nottingham, greet the sheriff for me, will you? And thank him for his horse."

CHAPTER TWO

It was several days later when a small band of Robin's woodsmen had the good fortune to shoot two more of the king's precious red deer, and brought them dressed back to Robin's camp, all ready for roasting. But Robin was feeling restive and uneasy, having had word from Nottingham that the sheriff, his nose out of joint over the robbing of the Bishop of Hereford, was planning to put together a significant force of hand-picked men to move into Sherwood to keep up the pursuit of Robin and his meinie until they had the outlaws in chains. And in his agitation, Robin had declared that he would not sit down to a venison feast that day until he had a fitting guest he could welcome to it.

And so Little John, Much the miller's son, and Thorvald the dwarf were hiding along the Great Northern Road, waiting for some likely prey to come along. They'd had little luck so far: only an elderly friar in a threadbare habit, accompanied by a wandering minstrel he must have met on the road, both on their way north toward York, and neither one likely to have two pennies to rub together. By the time the sun had reached the height of midday, Little John was ready to give up on the enterprise and head back for the feast, and Robin could go whistle if he wasn't content to eat yet. But as he was about to say as much to Thorvald and head home, the dwarf pointed north to where a lone rider was approaching, just now coming into sight some three or four furlongs off.

He was certainly a knight, as he rode a powerful war horse and was dressed in rich blue garments of fine quality and bore a well-kept arming short sword at his side, but he rode without squire or attendant of any kind. Furthermore, the knight's demeanor seemed lethargic. His shoulders drooped and his head hung low, so that he paid no mind to the road on which he traveled, trusting his horse to amble along at its own pace while the knight was lost in his private thoughts. The horse was caparisoned as simply as his master, his harness being of the wholly utilitarian kind, as if the knight had fitted him out as cheaply as possible without losing the necessary functionality of the gear. As he drew nearer to where the three outlaws awaited him at the side of the road, they could see that despite his fine clothing, the knight wore no chain or other jewelry. A shield was hanging from the right side of his destrier, with a noble device—a lion couchant in gules (or red), on a field sable. He was muscular but quite thin, and the grey of his hair and beard seemed to have seeped into his face, giving it an unhealthy pallor. Even his destrier walked with head down, as if sharing in his master's grief. When Little John stopped him, standing in front of the horse with his hand outstretched, the lugubrious rider looked up slowly, evincing very little interest in this obstacle, as if it were just another small indignity he would have to endure.

"I crave your pardon, my lord," Little John began. "But my master, the lord of Sherwood, has decreed that no one can pass this way without paying a toll—in return for which, he offers you a roasted venison dinner with our humble band of foresters. Will you come, my lord? Shall I lead you and your horse to our camp, or do you plan to put up some kind of resistance to our waylaying you?"

At that the knight scoffed. “Resistance? Why, what should I resist? A venison dinner would be most welcome, master forester, and I am not in so much of a hurry to get where I am going that I can’t spare an hour at table with your master. As for the toll, though, I’m afraid you may be disappointed. There is little enough in my purse to keep my body and soul together, let alone pay your master any sort of toll.”

Little John looked skeptical. The rich, he had noticed quite often in his thirty-odd years on this indifferent earth, had a quite different way of measuring poverty than did the folk he was used to. He’d seen gentlemen lament their hard lot when they had a mere thirty gold pieces on hand, or great ladies baffled when seeing a poor child out in the snow without wearing a warm fur coat—how could his mother have let him out of the house dressed so ill? And so he merely took the knight’s horse by the bridle and began to lead him into the woods to the outlaws’ camp at the great oak tree, muttering reassurances to the knight to the effect that he was sure they could work out some arrangement, while Thorvald and Much followed behind, glad that they finally had a guest of honor for Robin’s feast, and smiling that they had snared the knight without struggle of any kind.

“Oh, I say, my good man,” the knight called out after they had walked a furlong way or two into the forest. “Do you think my horse can get some water and perhaps a few oats when we reach your master’s lodge or manor house? We’ve come a long way today, and he’s a faithful and uncomplaining beast. I’d really like to see him made comfortable.”

Thorvald chortled a bit at that. “M’lord, you’ll be searching a long time before you find our master’s manor ’ouse. The forest is our ’ome, and our master’s, and our roof is God’s good blue sky.”

The knight looked back over his shoulder and, seeing who had spoken, answered, “But lad, what do you do when it rains?” At that Thorvald raised his head until the knight noticed his long beard with the streaks of grey in it, and sputtered, "Why…you're no lad at all, are you?"

"Not for some years now," Thorvald replied. "But t'answer your question, we do 'ave tents or pavilions that we set up to sleep in, at least in the nastier weather. But many of us prefer to sleep under the stars when the nights are fine in the summer and early fall. It ain't 'alf bad, that."

"No, I dare say," mused the knight. "Close to the hand of God, through the heaven and earth He created, eh? Might not be such a bad life for a fellow in his prime, I'll warrant you." And then he looked thoughtful again, the way they had seen him look on the road, before shaking his head and muttering, *a propos* of they knew not what, "But not for one with so many winters on his bones as I have, I'm afraid. So that's no answer."

"As for your horse, my lord," Little John said, "we'll take right good care of him, you can be sure of that. Now look up ahead, you see the light of our cooking fire between the trees there. I'd guess that deer is well roasted by now! Time to meet our good master."

As the horse burst into view in the clearing, Robin bounded up, almost leaping into the air with delight. How sweet it was, he thought, to live free and easy in these woods, and to be able to entertain the occasional rich guest in his forest home. The sheriff's vow to clear him and his meinie from their greenwood refuge seemed wholly unjust to him. After all, he never took money from anyone who didn't have a significant amount to spare, and he always helped out those in need, so where was the harm? As for the king's deer, let the king come and hunt them if he wanted them. Because he wasn't sure there even *was* a king now, so the deer were just going to waste in that case. Like the excess money of those rich nobles and prelates. Waste, Robin thought, was perhaps the greatest sin of all. He'd have to discuss that with Friar Tuck.

"Robin Hood of Sherwood at your service, my lord!" He greeted his guest. "Come down from your horse and sit with me here on the turf under our great oak and enjoy some well-roasted venison and a bit of bread and ale from our larder. We cater to noble travelers like yourself. Pass a pleasant hour and rest your bones among us denizens of the forest before continuing on your journey, won't you?"

With a rueful smile the knight did as he was asked, dismounting and turning toward his host with a slight bow that came as something of a surprise to the yeoman Robin, who knew full well he was the nobleman's social inferior. "I am called Richard at the Lee, for I hail from the village of Lee in Verysdale," the knight introduced himself.

"Well, sit beside me, Richard at the Lee," Robin invited, seating himself against the trunk of the Great Oak. "And Much, bring our noble guest some dinner!" The miller's son took a few trenchers, one for himself and one for their guest, to where Sir Palomides, the only true gourmet among them, was dishing out slices of venison.

"Now tell me, good Richard of Lee," Robin broached after his guest had been provided his meat, bread, and cheese, and after Will Scathelock had brought him a wooden cup of hearty ale. "For I know you have not been completely honest with me. I see the blazon on your shield, so I know you bear the arms of a noble house. Tell me what your true title is, for I know it is not simply 'Richard at the Lee.'"

The rueful smile flickered again across the worn grey face of the knight. "My title is indeed Sir Richard of Verysdale, and I am lord of those lands around the village of Lee. Indeed, I have a castle on those lands that has been in my family, along with the noble title, for seven generations."

Robin slapped his knee and cried out, "I knew it must be so!

And now that you've broken bread with us and shared our meat and ale, I must insist that you pay your toll. Come, come, Sir Richard, let us see what you have in your purse!"

A short, bitter laugh escaped the knight's lips as he reached to his belt and untied his leather purse, tossing it cavalierly toward the leader of the outlaws. "I would not grudge you a fair bill for the dinner and entertainment you've given me, master Robin, but as I tried to tell your agents when they waylaid me, my purse is virtually empty. I have ten shillings in it, and no good prospect for adding to that fortune. Indeed, what little I have will soon be gone, I'm sure, so it might as well go to you and your men in payment for this meal."

Robin, having dumped the contents of the purse into his hand, saw that the knight had in fact overestimated his treasure. Indeed, there were but eight shillings in the leather bag, and Robin looked at Sir Richard with disbelief, then glanced toward Thorvald, who had taken the knight's horse to be seen to. If Sir Richard had any funds secreted in any packs on the horse, Thorvald would have found them. But the dwarf merely frowned and shook his head at his master.

"It seems you are quite as poor as you claim to be, my lord," Robin said. "But sit awhile yet and tell us, if you would, how you came to be without any fortune at all, you who come from seven generations of landed gentry? There must be a tale to it."

The old knight sighed and raised his eyes heavenward. "Oh, there is, good master Robin, there is. But I fear it may be tedious to listen to such a tale here in this pleasant wood, among so many merry men," and with that his eyes, tearing up, gazed around the clearing to where the two dozen members of Robin's party, decked out in their Lincoln green livery, were laughing and singing, and where a few of them, led by Haakon with his braided Nordic hair, had gathered to watch Alan a Dale and Will

Scarlet test their prowess with the longbow by shooting at a small wreath nailed to a narrow tree fifty yards off, the loser obligated to clean up the detritus of the feast from the campsite.

"No, let us hear your story, Sir Richard," said Little John, moving toward Robin and the knight. "If you look around this camp site, every man you see here has, one way or another, lost something that he built his life around, or suffered some sort of oppression from some bloody noble or other, saving your reverence my lord. Otherwise we'd be in our native town or village, warming ourselves at our own hearth. So let us hear of your own miseries, Sir Richard, for we're an audience what can truly appreciate them."

And Friar Tuck, who had moved in from the other side, added his own encouragement. "Besides," he said, "the Apostle Paul tells us to bear one another's burdens. Share your troubles with us and they'll feel lighter. I know from experience that confession is good for the soul. So tell us, my lord, and if nothing else we'll weep with you."

"All right," Sir Richard said, "if you'll have it so, here's my story. First of all, you should know that I was married once, quite some time ago, and that my dear wife died giving birth to our only child, a son whom we named Peter. I loved him well for his mother's sake. And because he was to be my sole heir, and because I wanted him trained up well in arms, I had him fostered with my friend, Sir William of Derby, whose lands bordered on my own. William trained him well, and for a time he acted as squire to Sir William's son, Sir Walter, but the two young men had a falling out—I never knew what it was about. Still, Sir William knighted my son, who at the age of nineteen became Sir Peter of Verysdale. Not long after the boy's knighting, Sir William died, and Peter returned to my castle at Lee to help me in the running of my manor. But he had a taste for chivalry, and often would leave to take part in tournaments if they were not too great a journey from our lands. Six months ago, he went to fight in a tournament held by the lord of Sheffield Castle, and that was where our troubles truly began."

"Did he take some great harm in the tournament?" Friar Tuck asked.

"In a manner of speaking," Sir Richard allowed. "It was in the melee. The sides were divided between knights fighting under the banner of the Earl of Derby and those under the banner of the Earl of Lincoln. Peter fought for Lincoln, while his former master Walter, now his bitter rival, fought on the side of the Earl of Derby, whose vassal he was. Seeing Walter on the other side, my son thought he would take that opportunity to strike a blow to his enemy, and rode at him, challenging him to joust. The two came together in a mighty collision of lance, horse and shield, and Peter's lance shattered to splinters on Sir Walter's shield on the first pass. But Walter seemed stunned, jerked back on his horse, then fell suddenly to the ground, where he lay motionless. The heralds rushed to the body and saw that a splinter of Peter's lance had flown up into Walter's right eye—his helmet had an eye-slit wide enough to allow that freak occurrence. They carried Sir Walter from the field. The tournament continued, and Peter bore himself well, helping the Earl of Lincoln's knights to claim victory.

"But at the celebratory banquet that followed the tournament, Lady Abigail of Derby, my old friend's widow and Sir Walter's mother, came before the two Earls at the head of the table and announced in a raw, rasping voice that her son was dead. The splinter, she claimed, had pierced Walter's eye and reached to his brain, killing the lad. The news struck my son like a thunderbolt. You understand, he had only wanted to test his prowess against his former master, to show him he was as good a man as he and worthy of his respect. The shattered lance, the freakish piercing of the eye, these were circumstances so bizarre as to seem part of some demonic curse."

"But no one could blame your *son*, surely," Robin said. "Accidents like these happen all the time in tournaments. They're a part of the chivalric culture."

"So I should have said," the old knight replied. "And so should all reasonable people. But you do not reckon on the wide vindictive streak in Lady Abigail's soul. I swear, that must be where her son had taken his character. Because this Lady Abigail complained and implored the Earl of Derby so incessantly to demand restitution for the loss of his vassal, Sir Walter, that at last the Earl gave in and brought a case for manslaughter against my son. In the absence of a royal court, it was decided between Derby and the Earl of Lincoln (who demanded my son receive a just hearing, since Peter had been fighting in his retinue) that the case would be brought before the Abbot of Saint Mary's in York. We all thought he would be an impartial mediator in the case."

"Let me guess," Robin said. "He wasn't."

"Not a bit of it!" the knight cried, for the first time betraying raw anger. "He ignored my son's pleas, and my own appeal to the laws of chivalry, saying in effect that the laws of Christ trumped the laws of chivalry, that my son had held a grudge against his old master, and that the death blow was delivered in anger and so was a sin particularly heinous to the Holy Spirit. In God's eyes, therefore, my son was guilty of murder, had violated the sixth commandment and for that must make his reckoning with God. As for the secular charge of manslaughter, he fined my son six hundred gold nobles, to be paid immediately to the lady Abigail, Sir Walter's next of kin—or, failing that, to forfeit his life."

Robin let out a dismissive scoff, and Little John grumbled, "Outrageous! For what any impartial observer could only deem an unfortunate accident? Who had suborned that villain of an abbot?"

Sir Richard shrugged. "I have no evidence to prove it was a dishonest verdict," he admitted. "Misguided as it may have been. And the abbot did ultimately show my son some mercy. I told the abbot that I was not a wealthy knight, that I could scrape together perhaps two hundred nobles, but had no means of obtaining the other four, and petitioned him to reduce the fine. He told me he could not do that, but for pity's sake he would lend me the additional four hundred nobles from his own purse, so long as I would put up my ancestral lands for surety on the loan."

"Well," Robin responded, not without irony. "What a fine act of Christian charity from our good prelate. Where do you stand now?"

"As you see," Sir Richard gestured toward his hollow purse. "I've sold what I can—jewels, furnishings, livestock—so that my castle is bare and my lands virtually empty, but that only secured me the two hundred nobles I expected to raise. My son, to escape the scorn of his peers and hoping to restore his reputation, has taken himself off to the Holy Land to take the cross and do battle with the heathen Moors..."

At that point the knight's eyes came to rest upon Sir Palomides' face near the open fire and, taking in what he was seeing, stopped in mid-sentence, his mouth frozen open. Palomides' eyes glared at the knight with undisguised contempt, and the campsite had become suddenly still. In low tones, and without taking his eyes from Sir Richard's face, the Moor spoke: "I have no reason to love crusaders," he began. "I was present at the siege of Jerusalem and witnessed their slaughter of the entire population—Muslims, Jews, even Christians who were not from their own lands or of the same complexion as they. Yes, Sir Richard, I am a Moor. But not a heathen one. Forgive me if I do not wish your son success in his desire. Tell us more about your own troubles, and, I beg you, do not stray into the troubles of my own native lands."

"I, uh…" the old knight was tongue tied, until Robin stepped in as Palomides strode off proudly, to hold a private conversation across the clearing with Will Scarlet, Haakon, and Alan a Dale.

"Palomides is one of us," Robin began. "But don't ever bring up 'crusaders' to him. Please, go on with your story. You've nothing left of your fortune, you say, and your land is given in surety to this abbot?"

"Uh, yes, yes," Sir Richard blurted, returning with difficulty to his narrative. "And the worst of it is, I have been given until the Feast of Saint Job, one week from today on the 10th of May, to repay those four hundred nobles to Abbot Robert of York or forfeit my lands forever. And that is where you find me today. And that, my friend, is why I have only ten—no, eight shillings in my purse to pay you for your hospitality."

Robin, Little John, Thorvald and the Friar, who had all been listening to the tale of Sir Richard's woes, were silent now, until Robin, with a wan half-smile, tossed Sir Richard's purse back to him and waved it off. "No, keep your widow's mite. We've no need of it here. We take nothing from those who cannot afford to sacrifice what we demand. But do this for me, my lord knight: spend the rest of the afternoon here with us. Get to know our little band and accept our friendship. Who knows? It may be that, in our poor way, we can find some means to help you in your troubles. Here, go with the friar, he knows where the ale is flowing. I plan to go off and think a bit. Here, Friar Tuck, got him? Good."

* * *

On the other side of the great oak tree that marked their permanent camp site, most of Robin's men had pitched their tents and pavilions. Some slept two or three to a tent; a few, like Alan a Dale, slept with their women. None had children here: The life was too hard—to be precise, it was too dangerous—for the men to have their families with them. A few—Alan of Winchester for one—had a wife and children living in nearby villages, who claimed, when pressed, that their husbands had abandoned them and so lived on the charity of their neighbors, but once a month they would receive secret nighttime visits from wanted fugitives from the forest, and for a week or so after that visit those families would eat very well.

The land here sloped down to a clear running stream, whose water sustained the outlaw band. Brown trout were common and were good eating. The outlaws also caught dace, which were less appetizing but could be eaten in a pinch. But Robin was not here to fish. In the middle of the current a huge, rugged boulder split the stream in two, and, removing his leather shoes, Robin waded out to it, the water reaching only to his knees. With some effort, he pulled himself up onto the boulder, which was neck high. Panting, he sat for a moment, his feet hanging down as he rested on the flat top of the great stone. Then he swung his feet up and felt around the rock's edge until he felt the crack the men had made when with blacksmith's tools they hollowed out a good section from the interior of the stone, and used this flat section to close the hollowed space and hide it from prying eyes. Robin removed the stone cover and looked inside the wide storage place, pulling out the heavy chest in which lay 500 of the Bishop of Hereford's gold nobles. After a few minutes' contemplation, Robin removed a hundred of the coins from the chest and placed them back into the hollowed stone. Then he replaced the cover, took up the chest with its fortune in gold, and slid back down into the stream. With slow but determined steps, he started back toward the outlaw camp.

CHAPTER THREE

There was a family of larks nesting in the great oak tree who all began to sing their melodious welcome to the dawn sometime around four a.m. Robin, sprawled on a mat inside his small pavilion, opened one eye, failed to see any hint of sunlight, hugged to his breast the small chest he'd been using as an extra-firm pillow, and after an incoherent grumble or two drifted back to sleep.

After what seemed just a few more moments, he was awakened by his own snoring to see that the sun was peeping over the horizon and into the flap of his tent, and he sat upright with purpose in his spine. He knew what he was going to do.

Clutching the chest, he crawled out of the pavilion and stood up, stretching the kinks out of his back. Then, picking up the box, he held it beneath his arm against his hip and stepped over to the tent Little John shared with young Will Stutely, his particular friend. "John!" he whispered at the tent door. "John, get out here, you great hulking bear!"

Rubbing his eyes and grumbling audibly, Little John emerged. Whispering lest he disturb Stutely, John glared at Robin and said, "What am I doing up this early? Have you lost what was left of your wits?"

"Probably," Robin answered honestly. "I've got something to do that I don't want everybody in the camp to know about right now, but I didn't want to do it without a witness. Will you swear to keep to yourself what you see me do this morning until I tell you it's all right to go ahead and reveal it?"

Little John ruffled his hair and sniffed. "I'm not sure any promise I make while I'm still half asleep and before I've had any breakfast is binding, but if you insist, I'll swear it. What is it you're planning on doing?"

Robin didn't answer, just placed a finger to his lips and stepped lightly to the foot of the great oak where Sir Richard at the Lee, a bed of moss beneath him and his warm blue cloak over him, slept with his head—no doubt feeling unusually large this morning after a good many portions of Nottingham ale imbibed the previous evening—resting on his right arm. Robin kicked the old knight lightly in the ribs until he stirred, objecting even more sincerely than had Little John. "Oh, my head," Sir Richard complained, sitting up gingerly and closing his eyes to the unwelcome sun. Then, as if any movement at all was a torment, he winced and reached for his spine. "Oh, my back!" he exclaimed and then, as he rose slowly to his feet, he continued to bend at a forty-five-degree angle from his waist, reaching down to massage his knees. "Oh, my joints! How can you people sleep like this on the ground and out in the open? Good lord, to think I actually entertained notions yesterday of chucking all my worries and joining you here. Well, gentlemen," he nodded to Robin and Little John in turn, "you may be good company, but I'm afraid I'll never be one of you. Don't know how you youngsters do it. If I do lose my castle, I'll have to hire on with some other lord where I can sleep indoors on a bed or cot or at least a pallet. I say, what is it you're rousing me for when the others are still sleeping?"

"I've something to discuss with you that I didn't want them to hear. Keep your voice down, will you? And when I've had my say, I think you ought to be on your way."

Sir Richard's expression grew immediately serious, and he stood up, donning his cloak, and looked Robin in the eye. "What is it then? Is there a problem?"

Robin rolled his eyes. "The problem is yours, Sir Richard, as you well know. I'm trying to solve it. Listen," and with that Robin held out the chest to the knight. "In this box are four hundred gold nobles." Over Little John's gasp of surprise, Robin continued. "I want you to take it. This will pay your debt to the abbot of York and save your lands from forfeit. No, take it, I mean it," he continued, pushing the chest into the old knight's hands. "We obtained this money from one greedy prelate. Let it be used to thwart the plans of another."

"Are you completely mad?" Little John rasped, exasperated but remembering his promise not to awaken any of the band. "That money was for the maintenance of our men. What are they going to say when they hear of this?"

"Well," Robin shrugged. "You promised they *wouldn't* hear of it, at least not until I'm ready to confess. And besides, there's always more where that came from, in the purses of the rich who travel the Great North Road. We'll fill our coffers again."

"Now wait a bit," Sir Richard interrupted. "I haven't said I'll take your money. I certainly would not accept this as a gift, and with my land already pledged, I have nothing to put up for surety against this loan. No, I don't see how I can accept it..."

"I don't want your land, or your castle, my lord—and, if you'll forgive me for saying so, you're being a twit. Consider it a loan if you like. I'll accept your word that, when you are able to repay it, you will do so!"

"Well, let me make this pledge," the knight answered after a moment's contemplation. "I swear, by the Blessed Virgin Mary herself, that I will repay this debt at my earliest convenience. If I have my lands and my tenants to tend them, I feel certain

I can make good this pledge."

"So be it. I take Saint Mary as your surety. Now take the chest, Sir Richard, and be on your way before the others wake up. But first tell me this, to satisfy my own curiosity: You said that your lands bordered on those of the lady Abigail of Horsley. Tell me whose lands border yours on the other side?"

The old knight looked puzzled for a moment. Then, his face looking skeptical for a moment, he answered, "Why, those lands belong to the Abbey of Saint Mary in York. But surely that is mere coincidence. I can't believe there could be any connection between that fact and the abbot's verdict in my case."

"Believe what you want to," Robin answered. "But for myself I intend to do a bit of snooping in this affair. Something does not smell right. But be off, be off, Sir Richard. Take this chest and pay off your debt. Keep your ancestral lands. And go with God."

"Now wait just half a minute here, lads, I'm not overly happy with this little arrangement," Little John broke in, his whisper reaching the heights of alarm.

Robin snapped, "It's decided, John. We're doing this."

The big man held up his hands to placate the outlaw chief, asserting, "No, no Robin, I'm not trying to be a fly in the buttermilk. I'm right on board with helping out our friend here," and with that he placed a heavy arm on the old knight's frail shoulder. "I'm well aware that we don't take treasure from them as can't afford it, and we don't keep relief from them as needs it. And this poor soul needs it bad, as far as I can see. What I'm worried about is the cash itself. Our friend needs to take this payment all the way to York, to this Abbot Robert of Saint Mary's, and to do it by the Feast of Saint Job, now six days hence. I've got some concerns, some serious concerns, about his getting there with the money safely. As we saw for ourselves, Sir Richard is unattended."

"I ride as my fortune dictates," the old knight explained. "When my money fled, so did my retainers. But I have sword and shield, and a serviceable helmet. And my horse still can give a good account of himself. I'm still a considerable threat for anyone bent on challenging me along the way!"

Little John bowed slightly, deferring to the old knight's claim, but he argued, "I've no doubt of your prowess when faced with a single foe, my lord. But it may not have escaped your notice that there are outlaws in these woods. Lots of 'em, and not all paying homage to the good yeoman Robin Kempe, better known as Robin Hood. Now here's what I've got in mind: Let me come along with you—say I'm your squire or your servant or what you will. I'll bring along a sword and a staff and any band of thieves fewer than a dozen will think twice about bothering the two of us, right? We'll make a pretty fearsome team, you and I. I'll give 'em a false name when we get to York. Say, Reynold Greenleaf. How do you like that one? I've used it before."

"All right, all right," Sir Richard nodded after a moment's hesitation. Robin noted a fleeting wave of relief that seemed to pass over his face. "I'll go and ready my horse and we'll be off. Will you have a mount, master Greenleaf?"

Little John pursed his lips and glanced at Robin questioningly from under lowered brows. Robin could see the sense in Little John's proposal, though he didn't like the idea of yielding up one of the band's few horses for the duration of Sir Richard's trip to York and back. But after a moment he relented and said, "Yes, of course take one of the horses. You'll never get there if you have to walk to York and back. Just don't take Daisy…"

"It's all right, I'll take that sturdy fellow we took from the Bishop of Hereford's train. If he could carry fifteen hundred gold nobles, he ought to bear my weight without too much difficulty." John bit the cuticle on his right thumb as he looked thoughtfully toward Sir Richard, who with the help of Will Stutely, one of several of the outlaw band who'd now risen, was getting his horse saddled and preparing to exit the camp. "I'll just pop over to get him, and to take my leave of Will, and I'll be off then."

"John," Robin spoke quietly, laying a hand on the big man's arm. "I'm uneasy about all of this. There's something about this plight of our good Sir Richard that smells to heaven. Surely that abbot was in league with this widow and grieving mother. Our knight is too honest himself to suspect dishonesty in others, or else he feels it's not the gentlemanly thing to do to accuse them. But those two are in cahoots to steal his land, or I'm a hedgehog."

"Well, you *are* a prickly creature of the forest…"

"Save the jokes, this isn't the time," Robin chided. "Listen: Keep your eyes open when you get to the abbey, and see if you can learn anything more about this situation. There may be more to it yet that we're just not aware of. And remember, Little John, the sheriff has launched a wave of new hunters into the woods, with *us* as the expected prey, so keep your head down and act your part as Sir Richard's servant meekly, all right?"

"Ain't I always meek?" Little John said with a wink. "I figure it's around eighty miles from here to York, and if we don't want to strain the horses, we can go twenty miles a day pretty comfortably. That'll get us to York with a day or two to spare to pay the abbot by the feast of St. Job, and another four days back from York. Look for me in nine or ten days, right? If it gets to be more, you might start worrying. But I'll find out what I can about this business." With that he grasped Robin by the hand, and Robin gave his chief lieutenant a hoarse, "God be wi' ye," and they parted, Robin with a chill down his spine.

* * *

Left to himself, Robin stood a moment on the edge of the clearing as the rest of the outlaw band arose and prepared for breakfast. Everyone knew his assigned tasks for the day: who was to do the cooking and fetch the water, who was to watch the road for likely marks looking fat enough to be good for a few quid by the day's end, who was to fish in the stream and who was to have a go at the king's deer, or look for rabbits or grouse, or even geese depending on the time of year. Still others stayed around the clearing to guard the camp all day, and now that they knew the sheriff was hunting them with a vengeance, Robin had doubled the guard.

But his mind was not on the sheriff this morning. The injustice of Sir Richard's plight was eating at him, and he would not feel content until he had uncovered whatever plot lay behind this effort to take the old knight's ancestral lands. He knew that Horsley Castle, the estate of Sir William, Richard's old friend, was only about twelve miles due west of his camp in Sherwood. It would be but the work of a morning to take Daisy and pop over to the castle, where it should be a fairly simple matter to cajole, coerce, or bribe a servant or two to reveal what they knew about this situation. And in the blink of an eye, he'd decided.

"Will!" he called to Scathelock, who was one the older woodsmen here and tended to be at least relatively responsible. "Little John has gone off with Sir Richard to see he makes it to York without incident. He's going to be gone several days."

Will's long face grew longer as he frowned at Robin. "Kind of unusual gallantry on John's part, that. He think there's money to be made from the old knight after all?"

"Just the goodness of his heart," Robin answered, keeping his voice light and downplaying the significance of Little John's journey. "That and an itch to get a look at York Minster. They say it's one of the greatest in all England."

"Never knew John was so gung-ho about churches," Will mused, scratching his chin.

"It doesn't matter," Robin said, with some frustration. "I'm just telling you in case anybody asks. As for me, I've got some business to conduct over at Horsley this morning. Can you get Daisy saddled for me while I grab a bit of bread and cheese for breakfast?"

"Horsley? Whatcha want to go there for? Nothing there but old Sir William's castle, that's now in the hands of his lady. She's not likely to be much of a friend to us yeomen of the forest."

"I'm just going there. Saddle Daisy, will you?" Robin was almost shouting now. This was the problem with being the nominal leader of a group of independent-minded yeomen who had each taken on an outlaw's role in the forest rather than serve any master. They all thought they had a right to question what you were doing.

"All right, all right, nothing to get impatient about, criminy." Scathelock said, and moved languorously off.

So after quickly devouring half of a small portion of bread and half a wedge of cheese, Robin put the remainder inside his cloak to serve as his lunch. His leather purse hung from the side of his belt in case a bribe was necessary, and a cross-hilt dagger from a sheath on the other side in case that was what was wanted. He mounted his pretty new palfrey and started off at an ambling pace on a path that swung westward through Sherwood, and that he knew in a few furlongs would join the wider road toward Horsley, where he should arrive in just two hours or so.

Horsley Castle, he found, was about a mile south of the small village of the same name, and it was a modest structure positioned on a raised ground or motte, surrounded by a deep protective ditch. A wooden palisade perhaps five meters high encircled the space above the ditch, creating a wide bailey or courtyard there within the castle. And there was a gatehouse with a barbican for a guard tower atop it of the sort that Robin used to man himself when he'd served in King Arthur's palace guard. At the moment, since it was mid-morning, the gate was open and a drawbridge spanned the ditch outside the palisade. Within he could see the tower of a rectangular stone keep, rising to a height of perhaps ten meters, and within which he assumed whatever guards the lady Abigail employed were housed. He imagined that within the small castle must be a chapel, living quarters for Lady Abigail and all her household servants, a kitchen, storage rooms, and probably an armory of some sort, though that might be located in the keep or barbican as well. Beyond the walls at the rear of the castle he could see a small churchyard and pens for keeping animals, including a stable for horses. The problem he now faced was how to enter the castle and talk to one or more of the unsuspecting servants without drawing too much attention to himself.

But as Robin stood next to Daisy, giving the horse a rest after the morning's ride, he saw that the stars were still in his favor, for coming down the road between Horsley village and the castle itself was a small wagon being pulled by a smiling little man dressed in a tunic that at one time must have been brown but which now bore so many patches of various colors that he seemed to be wearing a patchwork quilt. The mustard-yellow hood that covered the fellow's head was still in one piece, though, if somewhat threadbare, and as he came nearer Robin could hear him whistling a lively tune, though without any true melody, like birdsong itself. As he drew closer to Robin on the path, the outlaw could see that the wagon was hung with a variety of metal pots, plates, and utensils, and he quickly hatched a scheme to get himself into the castle without suspicion.

"Ho there, Tinker, a word with you if I may?"

"Time's money, young fella," the tinker replied, continuing to trudge along, pulling his wagon.

Robin swung into a walking pace beside the tinker, holding Daisy's reins while keeping pace with the old man, now noticing the grizzled white whiskers on his rough and weathered face, which looked like a turnip with squinting eyes. "I'll pull your wagon for you, if you like," Robin offered, "and tie my horse behind it, if you'll tell the folks in there that I'm your new apprentice. You fix their old pots or sell them new ones, just let me stand with you and chat them up for a while. What do you say?"

"I say, that and your horse's apples won't buy me any breakfast. You get what you want—a way into the castle without raising any suspicion—and what do I get? An unskilled apprentice for an hour and a headache from listening to you jaw with the natives. You'll 'ave to do better than that my lad."

Robin had to admit the man had a point. He reached for his purse and held it up so the tinker could see it and revised his proposal. "I've got five gold nobles in here," he told the fellow. "I'll give you two now if you agree to my plan, and three more when I've got what news I want inside the castle. Does that work for you?"

The tinker set down his cart and held out his hand, squinting up at Robin. "It will when I see the color of your money, boy!"

With a little close-lipped smile, Robin opened his purse and shook out two coins, dropping them into the tinker's outstretched hand. The old man snatched the money, slipped it into a pocket inside of his tunic, and then beamed up at Robin, shifting the wrinkles of his face into a grotesque smile, in which only four of his front teeth were visible. "That'll do, young man. Let me now bid welcome to my new apprentice! Your first job is to pull this wagon for me. Off you go, now. I'll just take a load off my poor feet and ride this 'ere 'orse of yours." And with that he hopped up into Daisy's saddle.

Robin, a bit taken aback, decided not to worry that the tinker would steal his own stolen horse, since he did not think Daisy would trust this new rider far enough to let him lead her away from her adopted master, and he also figured that the tinker was not likely to ride off and leave his entire livelihood in Robin's hands. Besides, if he was to play the part of the tinker's apprentice, it would not look right for the master to be pulling the load while his lowly apprentice rode the horse. Though truth be told, Daisy looked like too fine a horse to belong to a wandering tinker. Robin hoped it wouldn't be enough to make anyone in the castle suspicious. He positioned himself between the two thills or shafts of the little vehicle, lifted them up, and began to pull the wagon, while the tinker ambled behind on Daisy's back.

"So tell me, Tinker, do they know you well in this castle?" Robin asked as they made their unhurried way toward the castle's gate. "Do you visit here on a regular basis?"

"Part of my usual route," the tinker answered. "I make a monthly round up and down the Derwent valley. Always spend a good three or four days in Derby, then make my way north here to 'Orsley village and castle. Make stops at Duffield, Belper, up to Matlac, Baslow, 'athersage and Bamsford, and end at the village of Derwent itself. Then I branch off and head over to Sheffield, spend a good three/four days there and turn around and head on back down to Derby again. Been doing it for a good twenty years, I reckon, and folks along the way know me and save up their repairs for when they know they'll be seeing me again. So it's gonna look a bit strange me having a new apprentice and all, but I wouldn't worry, lad. They all know I'm not getting any younger, and it'll be no great surprise for them to see I've got some new fella in training to help me with the route and to take over when I've 'ad enough. And more important than that, I'm pretty sure nobody cares all that much what I do, so they're not gonna give it a second thought. Now keep your trap shut; we're coming to the gate."

Robin bent his head as he huffed his way over the drawbridge, hoping to draw as little attention to himself as possible, and there was no challenge from the barbican—either the guard was sleeping up there, Robin mused, or this tinker was so well known at the castle that no one remarked upon his presence. "This way," the old man said, gesturing to his left as they entered the bailey, to an open space near a low building that smelled of smoke and grease and so, Robin thought, must be the castle's kitchen. "Set the wagon up here, turn it so's they can see the wares 'angin' off the sides." Then, dismounting, the tinker tied Daisy's reins to the rear of the wagon, and told Robin in a low voice, "There ain't many as live in this castle, and them that'll be hinterested in our wares are likely to be the kitchen crew."

Then, without further warning, the tinker called out in a loud voice, "Pots and pans and all utensils, get 'em repaired here, or see what I'm selling that's new!" A few heads turned, but there was little traffic here in the bailey as few guardsmen or servants crossed the yard going about their business, and none gave the tinker a second look. "Give 'em a little time," he whispered again to Robin. "Nobody ever wants to come up too quickly. If they seem too eager to see me, they're afraid I'll charge 'em more. Which, I must admit, I would."

And so they waited. After about ten minutes of standing silently and watching the castle's residents walk by without glancing at them, Robin, never the most patient of men, broke out of his quiet, humble demeanor, grabbed the largest metal basin on the tinker's wagon, and carried it over to the well that stood in the midst of the bailey, halfway between the gate and the keep. He felt a few eyes on him as he pulled a bucket of water from the well and emptied it into the basin, and as he carried the pot of fresh water back to the tinker's wagon, he called out to anyone who might be listening, "This horse thinks she is the queen of all beasts, and will only eat and drink out of the most precious vessels in Christendom. Fortunately, my master's pots are the highest quality pots in all of England!" And when he set the water in front of Daisy, thirsty from her long morning walk, she guzzled it with great appetite. And Robin was rewarded with a few snickers from the castle folk, and a sarcastic muscle-straining eye roll from the tinker himself.

Amid Daisy's great gulping, Robin glanced toward the kitchen where the clanging of many pots could be heard above a busy din of voices preparing for the mid-day meal and saw a young kitchen wench holding out a brass pan with a broken handle. Like every other woman of her class, she wore a white smock beneath a brown woolen kirtle that laced down the front. She approached, looking at the tinker, and challenged him, "Can you make anything of this, then? I'd have thrown it out but Cook said he expected you'd be here sometime this week." Her voice was brash, and when the old man took her pan she stood with hands on her hips and struck a cheeky pose, watching Robin with a sidelong glance and trying to suppress a slight upturn of the corner of her mouth. She was about sixteen years old, Robin guessed, and if you scraped the kitchen grease off her and washed her hair, she might look halfway decent, with those laughing brown eyes and that turned-up nose on her saucy face.

"I can give you a new 'andle for that pan of yours for, say, four pence, and do it in a quarter of an hour," the tinker offered. The girl looked at him askance and crossed her arms, but the tinker held firm. "New one'd cost you a good two shillings from my wagon, so look what you're saving!"

The girl relaxed and said, "Go on, then. I'll just wait here for it…" and with that she turned to Robin with that half smile and gave him an audacious wink. Crossing her arms again and leaning against the wagon, she asked, "And how long have you been on the road with this old swindler? Learning his tricks, are you? Seems to me you'd do better as a wandering player or minstrel, you seem so to like putting on a show."

"Just joined him a few days ago in Derby," Robin lied. Then he embellished, "Maybe if it doesn't work out, I'll take your advice and turn juggler."

"*Hmmph*," she responded. "And what do they call you when you're at home?"

"Usually they call me 'knave' or 'scoundrel,' but I like to answer to the name Robin," he told her.

"Well, Robin," she made his name sound like a tasty morsel from her kitchen. "I'm called Agnes. You know, like the young virgin martyr." And with that she batted her long eyelashes at him. "What's the news in the wide world? We don't get visitors here as often as some of us might like. What's the news from Derby or Sheffield or Nottingham?"

"Well," Robin said, adopting a pose similar to hers and leaning against the wagon himself, "I have heard that the Sheriff of Nottingham has reached the limit of his patience with the outlaws of Sherwood, especially after they fleeced the rich and powerful Bishop of Hereford, that he's hired a whole crew of mercenaries to flush them out of their holes."

"Ha!" Agnes snorted. "From what I've heard, that dull-witted sheriff is as likely to catch those outlaws as your master here has as of getting a kiss from me along with his four pence!"

The tinker grunted without looking up from the work he was focused on. "You want a kiss, it'll cost you extra!" he deadpanned.

Agnes shrieked with laughter at that, but when she'd stopped, Robin casually raised the topic he was really interested in. "And what's the news here? I remember hearing not long ago about the lord of this castle being struck down, isn't that right? In a tournament up Sheffield way wasn't it?"

"Young Sir Walter?" The girl responded. "Oh, that's old news, that is. Must be, oh, two months ago now. Killed when the splinter of his rival's lance went into his eye. Such a freak accident, that. And such a fine, handsome lad to lose," she pouted.

"Right, right, that's how I heard it," Robin answered with some animation, letting his sincere interest energize him. "Very much a freak accident. But then didn't I hear as how the young fellow that killed him…what was his name again?"

"Sir Peter of Verysdale," Agnes responded on cue.

"Yes, Sir Peter, that he was found to be guilty of manslaughter, and forced to pay some ungodly fine as a result?"

"That's how the rumor went, anyway," Agnes agreed. "Not that any of us were there—but our mistress, Lady Abigail, took Sir Walter's death so hard that she forced the Earl—that's the Earl of Derby, her liege lord—forced him to bring young Peter to trial with the Abbot of St. Mary's as judge in the matter."

"Impartial judge, was he?" Robin hinted.

"Him? Not bloody likely!" Agnes scoffed. "Old family friend, more like. And when they finally came back here for Sir Walter's funeral, the abbot returned with her to do the ceremony. There were folk here that would have liked to have seen the young master, that were really going to miss him," and with that she dropped her eyes downward. "But he'd been dead awhile by then, and the coffin was nailed shut. They buried him in a Christian service behind the chapel, in the churchyard outside the palisade on that side of the motte," and with that she made a gesture with her head.

"Well," Robin said, making as if the subject had just about exhausted its interest for him. "It's too bad the household didn't get to pay their last respects to the corpse. Seems to me that's what you need a funeral for. But I suppose the old lady was distraught, eh? Prostrate with grief and all that?"

Agnes looked at him and winked. "Funny thing that. She hardly seemed broken up about it at all. Maybe she'd done all her grieving before—it was two weeks after he died that they finally brought the body home for burial. I guess she was comforted by those six hundred nobles she'd collected as compensation from poor Sir Peter after the abbot's verdict. But who am I to talk about my betters this way, eh?"

"If you don't talk about 'em, who will?" The tinker asked drily, without looking up. "Anyway, 'ere's your pan, Miss, good as new and twice as shiny." And indeed, he had buffed the pan as well while she and Robin had been talking and, pleased with his work, Agnes gave another of her half-hearted smiles as she took the pan from him.

With a twist of her head and a flick of her skirt, she told him, "I'll just have to get your four pence from Cook. Be right back!" With that promise, she winked at Robin and sauntered back toward the kitchen. As she left, though, Robin glimpsed another figure, this one older and more stately, dressed in a red silk gown with long sleeves and accompanied by two attendants, one of whom was carrying a metal object of some sort. The woman was coming across the bailey from a low building Robin assumed must be the main hall or the family living quarters, and quickly muttered to the tinker, "That, I assume, is Lady Abigail coming our way?"

"That's 'er," the tinker confirmed. "Mistress of the castle. She's usually got some work for me..."

"But not for me," Robin said. "I've got my own reasons for not meeting the lady, at least not right now, so…" Robin took the tinker's hand and bade him farewell. "It's been an honor being your apprentice for an hour, my good man. Perhaps we'll meet again someday, but right now, I need to disappear." And without another word, Robin tore his purse from his belt and tossed it to the tinker with the three gold coins he still owed the old man, leaped up into Daisy's saddle and trotted her straight out the castle's front gate before Lady Abigail could get a good look at him, leaving the tinker scratching his head and wondering what it had all been about. To the guards in the barbican he called, "My master's sent me on to Duffield to get us a place to stay tonight!"

Certain that there was some mystery at Horsley Castle that affected his new friend Sir Richard at the Lee and preferring not to let Lady Abigail know quite yet that someone was looking into that mystery, Robin moved off as quickly as he could without raising any alarm in the castle. Something about this situation and his friend's part in it was not right, and he vowed to himself that he would return to Horsley Castle. But not, he said to himself, through the front gate.

CHAPTER FOUR

The Great North Road was a well-traveled route that largely followed an old Roman highway that started as far south as London and kept going, or so Little John had been told, to the far north beyond the old Roman wall that had been built as a barrier for the fierce Picts who still held much of the land of the Scots. Well-traveled, but certainly not well-patrolled, particularly in these lawless days since the fall of the true king had left thugs like the Sheriff of Nottingham in control of large tracts of the country—and had left honest men like Robin Hood and Little John, who only stole a little bit, pursued as outlaws in the forests of England.

For John, the ride was not completely pleasant. He had never been a man of property and was unaccustomed to riding long distances on horseback. He needed a break from riding fairly often, and would dismount to walk his horse, a tall chestnut whom he had named Bishop, a good mile for every five he rode. Still, he and Sir Richard were making progress in fine weather their first day on the road, and, having brought his bow along, he had been able to provide them with a couple of rabbits for lunch. Sir Richard knew of an inn on the road west of Lincoln where they could stay the night, and tomorrow Doncaster would be a reasonable stopping point, according to the knight. John himself had never been that far north, nor had he been south of

Coventry. "Born and bred in the Midlands," he had been telling Sir Richard as they chatted—and argued—on the road.

"I would think a man your size might have been recruited for his lord's wars at some point. You were born in a village on some lord's estate, were you not?"

"Yes," Little John answered cautiously. "Actually, my father worked on land belonging to a monastery. He was bound to the land and I was expected to follow him. To spend my life eking a living out of the land and spending my labor in another man's service."

"But isn't that the way of things?" Sir Richard said, unmoved.

"You sound like my father," Little John scoffed. "I worked the land with him all my life, till I was sixteen, and the abbot who owned the land took the bulk of what we raised, and we had barely enough to eat for ourselves. And when my father cut one of the monks' old dead trees for firewood one winter, he was fined."

"This is the world God has ordained," Sir Richard argued. "There are those who fight, like my own class—those whose task it is to defend the commonwealth against its enemies and to protect the citizens. There are those who pray—priests and monks like your abbot, whose task it is to see to the spiritual needs of the citizens, to ensure that they and the commonwealth as a whole are on a right footing with their Maker. And there are those who work: those who, like your father, grow the food, raise the animals, and produce the goods needed by the commonwealth and its citizens."

"Ordained by God, you say?" Little John replied. "I've heard the stories they tell about Adam and Eve and the Garden of Eden, and I don't remember anything in that story about some men being made to be servants to others. The priests say so, but how do I know what they say is true? I never went to no school, because 'those who work' apparently aren't supposed to. But I heard something once that made me think twice: 'When Adam delved and Eve span, who was then the gentle man?'"

Sir Richard frowned and shook his head. "But my boy, we aren't in Eden anymore. Mankind sinned, you know, and because we are born to sin, we must have a ruling class in society that keeps sin from corrupting the commonwealth."

"Ah, well then, answer me this," John said, heaving himself back in Bishop's saddle. "How is it that those of us whose lot it is to work see so much less of the food we grow, the meat we raise, the goods we make than those who fight or those who pray? If you don't do any of the work why do you get twenty or thirty times more of the goods than those who do the work to make them?"

"Well, that's because our job is so much more important," Sir Richard said, though he was not completely comfortable with that answer. "Where would you be if there were no one to protect you from marauding brigands who would steal your goods?"

"I'm a marauding brigand myself at this point," John answered. "And I don't take half as much from the rich 'uns I rob as they steal from the poor folk that work for 'em. And what about these abbots and bishops, then? You say they keep us in God's good graces do they? That abbot who owned my father's land, all I ever saw him do was fine my father when he tried to keep his family warm and beat him when he didn't pay his church tithes on time. Do you think God needed those tithes? What was He gonna do with 'em? They went to build the abbot a fancy new chapel at the monastery and give the abbot and his praying monks a big feast once a week while we ate oats and barley. What about this abbot of yours we're on our way to see? How honest was he with your son's mishap? Sounds to me like he was just out to get your lands. If God hears their prayers sooner than ours, what are they praying for then? It sure isn't for my father or anybody else in that village, or they wouldn't be sick, poor, or starving."

Sir Richard had never heard anyone question the principles on which he had always assumed society was based. If everyone felt the way Little John did, he could only imagine chaos would be the certain result. And yet Robin Hood and his men of the forest, it had to be admitted, were a species of man that fit nowhere in his accepted scheme of the estates of Christendom. But if it were not for them and their four-hundred-noble loan, his own position in the society he believed in would have come tumbling down. And, too, perhaps what Little John was saying about the Abbot of Saint Mary's had a ring of truth to it as well. It was all very confusing.

"I don't understand this," he finally told Little John. "I have never been aware that any of my own tenants have these kinds of complaints about me. I believe I have been ordained by God to be their good lord, to protect them and to ensure their livelihood for the sake of the commonwealth. My estates, as I see it, are a microcosm of the kingdom itself, and as the king must consider the welfare of all of his people, I must concern myself with that of my own serfs, and to apply the law fairly and justly to all."

John scoffed at that. "And suppose your son had had an argument with one of your serfs, and the serf had blinded him with a blow to the head. How would you as judge punish that serf?"

"Why," Sir Richard seemed surprised that anyone would have to ask such a question. "The serf must hang, of course, for striking his master."

"And suppose it had gone the other way, and your son had blinded the serf?"

"Why, he, um…"

"Right," Little John said. "Is that how you apply the law fairly and justly to all? Look, Sir Richard, I'm sure that you are as conscientious a lord as any in England, and it may be that your serfs have little to complain of. And if that is indeed the case, then I am glad we are helping you to maintain control of your manor. But the law itself makes this 'fairness' you speak of an absurdity. The only place a man like me can feel free in this world is outside of that law. And so I am an outlaw, like Robin Hood and my brothers of the forest."

"I'm not so sure that 'a man like you,' as you put it, is not a mighty rare thing," Sir Richard mused. "Most men seem content with their lot, or at least are willing to accept it, seeing no other alternative. What if everyone did as you do, and took to the forest? What kind of a commonwealth would we have then?"

"A commonwealth of free men," Little John suggested. "But you're right. It is a very unusual attitude. But I found that I could not bring myself to follow in my father's footsteps. He expected me to find some local village girl and to settle down to a life like his. Forever. And first, I was not interested in any local girls. Or any girls at all, come to that. I suppose that might have qualified me for the clergy, but I had no schooling and no way to get any, and besides, the abbot who owned our land had put me off the church for good. So, when the brotherhood of the forest beckoned, I answered. And I've never regretted it."

After a moment of silence, Sir Richard said, "I can understand the attraction of that. The freedom from cares and responsibilities. But our responsibilities…"

But whatever Sir Richard had intended to say stuck in his throat as, without warning, five mounted men with swords drawn left the shelter of the woods and rode into the road before them, blocking their progress. "I say…" Sir Richard was about to complain of this high-handed treatment when he noticed that another half-dozen ruffians had slipped behind them on the road, cutting off any chance of escape.

Recalling that the whole purpose of his traveling with Sir Richard had been to safeguard the small treasure he carried with him, Little John cursed himself for a heedless sluggard for being so caught up in his debate with the old knight that he had missed any signs of this ambush, and reached for the poignard he carried at his thigh, though he doubted it would do much good against nine men bearing short swords. His heart sank at the thought of those four hundred nobles hidden in Sir Richard's pack, and he began to consider the feasibility of a dash through the forest itself, a terrain he was sure he was more at home in than his assailants.

But to John's surprise, and somewhat to his relief, the leader of the mob pointed his sword and addressed his first comments not to the knight but to himself. "You, the big man in the green livery! Hold your hands out where we can see them! And tell us quickly where you are bound and what is your business on this road!"

Abandoning any thoughts of using his dagger, Little John slowly extended his hands, fingers spread wide and palms up, and considered his answer. But before he got beyond a simple "Uh…" Sir Richard, bristling with the affronted dignity of the slighted aristocrat, had begun to harrumph his answer: "My good man, what gives you the effrontery to address my servant in this manner? You have the manners of a villein. If you have legitimate concerns, address them to me. Who are you and on what authority do you detain honest men on this public road? And who is your master, that I may inform him of the boorish behavior of his underlings to their social betters? Boorish I call it! Villainous! Well, sirrah, have you no answer?"

The captain of the band, taken aback by this aggressive response from one that had at first glance seemed not even worth his notice, now relaxed his aggressive stance, pulled back his sword, and glanced, a tad sheepishly, at his fellow riders on his right and his left, who were themselves hemming and hawing with chagrinned uncertainty as they awaited their leader's response. Sir Richard, meanwhile, had swung his shield, bearing his coat of arms, from his shoulder down to where they could all see it, and he drew his own sword with what looked like absolute confidence.

"Well, my lord," the captain, a ruddy, round-faced man, began. "We are hired men in the retinue of the Sheriff of Nottingham. We…er…he has charged us with ridding the environs of Sherwood and the Barnesdale area of the poachers and bandits who use these woods as their, uh, their base of operations. We are to arrest all those we find, and…and…"

"And we're ordered to kill any of 'em who resist us, so the sheriff said!" added the thin-faced man with the sparse, scruffy beard on the leader's right hand. "This 'un," he added, pointing his sword tentatively once again at Little John, "is dressed in the colors of that rogue Robin Hood, the worst of all the bandits of Sherwood."

"We thought," added the red-faced captain, running his fingers through the wisps of his hair that fluttered in the breeze, "that this fellow might even be Robin's notorious lieutenant, Little John himself."

Sir Richard scoffed at that. "Ha! A man *this* big, you thought might be this 'little' John? Has the sheriff been reduced to hiring half-wits now? This is my servant Reynold Greenleaf, who's been a member of my household for, I dare say, as long as anyone currently in my employ. He accompanies me on a necessary journey I'm making to York, to the Abbey of Saint Mary. It is imperative that I make this journey with as much speed as possible and so it is just the two of us. As for these bandits of whom you speak, I can say with absolute assurance that no one has robbed me or taken any aggressive stance toward me anywhere on this road until I have met you 'gentlemen.' So as far as I can see, the only danger on this road comes not from any outlaws but from the sheriff's own hired brigands. And you can tell him so from me, Sir Richard at the Lee. Now if that answers all of your questions, sirrah, my man and I will be off now. We have a long way to go and we are losing daylight as we speak. I bid you good day."

And with that Sir Richard rode on without a backward glance. Little John, his head drooping down in the pose of a humble servant, trotted along in his wake, while the sheriff's men, cowed and humbled, sat on their horses gazing after them for a few moments before turning and riding back in the direction of Nottingham. When they were well out of sight, Little John allowed himself a pleased chuckle. "I may not think much of the noble class," he said. "But that display certainly got me out of a tight spot!"

"You're welcome, Master Greenleaf," the old knight answered good-humoredly. "Stick with me and you'll be all right, I'll wager. Now unless I'm mistaken, our inn for the evening can't be more than a mile or two off. I'll be glad to get out of this saddle—as, I'm sure, will you."

* * *

Little John had never been in a city larger than Nottingham, and the sight of York took his breath away. The stone walls that completely surrounded the city and dated, Sir Richard told him, to Roman times, made his heart pound, stretching as they did as far as he could see on all four sides of the city. He was on foot and walking Bishop, taking his time and letting the sights and bustle of the great northern capital sink in, as he glimpsed the spire of the cathedral rising higher than any man-made structure he had seen. Then, drawing closer to the spire as they moved northward outside the city's western wall, they crossed the bridge over the River Ouse and there, in front of him, was the richest monastery north of the Humber: Saint Mary's Abbey.

The abbey, built on a gradient west of the city sloping down to the river, had its own walls, which Little John judged must be a good six furlongs around. They entered the abbey grounds through a tall gatehouse, manned by an armed coterie who were certainly not Benedictines. Inside the gate, though, they were met by a Benedictine porter, whose task was to welcome visitors and who listened to Sir Richard's explanation of his business there.

Robert Longchamp, Abbot of Saint Mary's, was to be found conducting abbey business in the chapter house, they were told. He did this, according to the porter, each morning after terce, and since it *was* a business meeting, this was probably the proper time to approach him—at least in the opinion of the somewhat superannuated porter. Leaving their horses with a groom at the gatehouse, Richard and John strode with purpose into the cloister, along which they knew they would find the abbey's chapter house and the abbot. Abbot Robert, they were certain, would be quite surprised to see them, especially two days early. Little John held the chest, following Sir Richard and admiring the Gothic stone arches of the cloister and the fruit trees planted within the cloister's circumference. When they reached the large archway near the church on the eastern side of the cloister, from which they could hear the buzz of voices where the monks sat in session, Richard turned to John and whispered, "Let me do all the talking, and follow my lead.

I'll ferret out this abbot's true colors, see if I don't!"

John could do nothing but nod, and followed Sir Richard through the elaborately carved archivolt that framed the entrance into the meeting chamber, humbly inclining his head like an obedient servant. The room was a large octagon, with an arch-shaped stained-glass window directly across from the entry arch, which depicted Christ as the Good Shepherd, and through which the morning sun lit up the chamber. Beneath the window, on a dais raised above the stone floor, the abbot sat in a large wooden chair resembling a throne. His black Benedictine robes were not simple worsted but fine woolen tiretaine cloth, which John could see was trimmed at the sleeves and lined in the hood with black sable fur. While all the other assembled monks wore their hoods over their heads, this chapter meeting being a formal occasion for them, the abbot himself wore a miter, like his rival the archbishop of York Cathedral, because he was considered one of the peers of the realm and the chief Benedictine in the north of England. A large solid gold crucifix hung from a pure gold chain around the abbot's neck, and on either side of him on the dais, each in his own wooden seat of power, sat the abbey's other two highest-ranking officers, the prior on the abbot's right, and the cellarer, or chief steward, on his left. Along the other six sides of the room, from the dais to the doorway, each panel decorated with a fresco depicting a scene from the life of Sant Benedict of Nursia, the other hooded monks, at least fifty of them, sat on stone benches built into the walls.

When John and the old knight entered, they interrupted a reading from a pious text that lay on a lectern before the prior, who stopped his reading and looked up at the sight of them. Sir Richard, the model of courtesy, went down on his knees before the abbot's seat and Little John, taking his cue from the knight, knelt as well, behind Richard and to his right.

"My Lord Abbot," Sir Richard began, modestly keeping his eyes lowered rather than boldly meeting the abbot's angry glare. "Forgive my disturbance of your chapter meeting. I was told by your guard that this would be the proper time to bring my business to you."

"After chapter would have been a better time," the abbot intoned nasally, raising his eyebrows and sighing as if this were just another cross to bear. "But since you are here, and have already disturbed our session, state your business now. And briefly, if you please. You are, if I am not mistaken, Sir Richard of Verysdale, and if memory serves, you are bound to repay a fairly significant debt in some very few days or forfeit to me your lands, is that not so?"

"Indeed, the debt comes due the day after tomorrow, on Saint Job's day. But on my knees here before you, and in the presence of your fellow monks, I am bold to request an extension of the loan for another six months. Give me, say, until the feast of Saint Gregory of Tours, on November 8, to raise the money I owe you. That will give me an entire growing season for my lands to produce what they can, and I should be able to pay you in full on that day, and I pledge further to give you an additional twenty-five nobles on that day in interest for the privilege of the half-year's respite. Lord Abbot, your generosity in loaning me the sum to pay my son's fine gives me the hope that you will not deny me this plea." As he finished, the knight hung his head in reverent humility. Little John followed suit, though he was puzzled why Sir Richard would play this charade when he had the necessary funds in his hands.

Abbot Robert de Harpham glowered down at the old knight with an imperious glare. Before he could speak, the prior on his right, in a conciliatory tone, spoke deferentially to his superior. "Lord Abbot, surely this is a reasonable request. The knight promises to redeem the loan. Does not our Lord Himself tell us to ask his Father to forgive our debts, as we forgive our debtors? Would it not be a Christian act to forgive this debt completely? Would that not be Christian charity?"

His eyes bulging like a toad's, Abbot Robert turned a scarlet face on the prior and seemed about to burst with rage, when an unctuous, insinuating voice from the cellarer on his left side stopped him. "Ah, but Prior Stephen, does not the Apostle say in his letter to the Romans that we are to 'pay to all what is owed them'? Surely our abbot is within his rights as a Christian gentleman to expect payment from this debtor? Besides," the cellarer continued with a glint in his eyes that came not simply from his love of scripture, "if what this knight says is true, his lands can yield four hundred nobles a year in profit. It would be foolish for the abbot to give up our claim to those lands now simply in six months' time to collect that sum as a one-time payment, when we could gain that much in income annually by holding on to the property. What profits the abbey profits Christ's church, remember. So does not true Christian charity consist of keeping the lands for ourselves?"

The prior looked doubtful at this logic, but the abbot was quite pleased with it. "You are quite right, brother cellarer, though let me just mention in passing that the sum I lent to this knight came from my own coffers, not those of the abbey, and so the property reverts not to the abbey but to myself on its forfeiture." And now the prior opened his mouth, ready to object that for Abbot Robert to hold such substantial property in his own right was contrary to his Benedictine vow of poverty, but held his tongue when he remembered that the abbot was his superior, and that there was also a Benedictine vow of obedience. He allowed the abbot to continue.

"Therefore, Sir Knight, your request is hereby denied. Unless you deliver to me, here in this same cathedral, the sum of four hundred gold nobles by noon in two days' time, your lands and castle in Verysdale are mine. And I will expect you to have evacuated the castle and be off my land before my agents take possession. Now, do we understand each other?"

Little John could not see Sir Richard's face from where he knelt, but studied the corner of his visage he could make out in profile, and noted the stiff restraint with which the knight bore this answer, and saw Sir Richard's jaw muscle tighten with unreleased resentment. But Richard bore himself with courtesy the while, rising slowly from his knees and clearing his throat before he responded. "I understand *you* perfectly, my Lord Abbot," he began. "I understand you to be an avaricious old hypocrite, feigning Christian charity to mask your own plots. I understand at last that your 'generous' loan to me, coupled with the excessive fine you laid upon my son for his innocent mishap on the field of valor, was simply a deceitful scheme to lay hands on my property by fraudulent means.

"You, however, are far from understanding *me*, my Lord Abbot." With that Sir Richard turned and took the treasure chest from Little John, who had risen to stand along with his purported master. "Since you insist on payment now, you shall have it." Richard opened the box, stepped toward the abbot, and dumped all four hundred gold coins in the abbot's lap. The prelate's mouth opened in shock and anger, but all he could do was sputter.

"There are four hundred gold nobles, and I call on each monk present to witness that this debt has been paid. Had you been in truth as full of Christian charity as you pretend, you would have had an even greater reward. But since you are what you are, you will receive only what you deserve. Now my land is redeemed, and I shall expect to receive from you in writing a receipt, under your own seal, my good abbot, that exonerates me of this debt and ensures that my lands are now my own." He leaned forward, lowering his voice so that he could be heard only by Abbot Robert and the mild-mannered prior, and added, "And I expect to receive that deed immediately after this chapter meeting ends, before I leave the abbey. My man and I will wait here in the cloister until I have received the quittance I have come for."

The fuming abbot was still unable to articulate even his rage, but the prior, trying to pour oil on the waters, laid a hand on Sir Richard's arm and whispered, "You shall receive it, sir. You have my word." And with that, Sir Richard turned on his heel and strode out into the cloister, followed by a buoyant Little John, doing his best to contain his merriment.

* * *

The old knight had an unmistakably self-satisfied manner as he and Little John strolled along the cloisters of Saint Mary's, enjoying the mild air and the songs of the skylarks and starlings singing in the fruit trees of the enclosed garden.

They had taken their leisure in the cloister for less than half an hour when they were pleased to see the gentle prior coming toward them, his hood now pushed back onto his shoulders and his gray tonsure revealed. He took from his sleeve a rolled piece of parchment from which hung an almond- (or mandorla-) shaped seal of red wax on which was engraved the abbey's patron saint, the Virgin Mary, enthroned with the Christ-child in her lap and crowned as Empress of Heaven. She held in her left hand, a staff from which sprouted a burgeoning fleur-de-lys. Around the circumference of the seal Sir Richard could make out in Latin the mottos of the Benedictine order: *PAX* (i.e., "Peace") at the top, and around the sides *in omnibus glorificetur Deus* (which is to say, "in all things may God be glorified"). The irony of these mottos as displayed by Abbot Robert was not lost on Sir Richard.

The deed itself, when the old knight unrolled it, was also in Latin and was fuzzily worded, stating only *lator huius libellum tenendum est, nulla antea poenae debitum incurrit, vel in dicione subditos*, which Sir Richard, silently thanking God for the clerical tutor who had drilled his Priscian's grammar into him as a boy, meant something like "the bearer of this certificate is to be held free of any debt or penalty previously incurred in my jurisdiction." The old knight smiled grimly. The abbot did not want to put into writing anything specific that would come back to incriminate him in his plot to strip Sir Richard of his ancestral lands. Richard handed the parchment to Little John, to whom the ink scratchings were so much gibberish, and told him to put it in a safe place, and John, at a loss for a safer place, folded the parchment and shoved it into the inside pocket of his Lincoln-green tunic.

The friendly prior, having delivered his charge, now held out his arms in a welcoming manner and said, "Now this awkward business being finished, let us show you better hospitality, if you will allow us. Please call me Brother Stephen. I am prior of this monastery, and so second in rank to Abbot Robert. The brothers are now filing into the abbey church for the office of sext, after which we will be sitting down to a fine dinner, to which you and your attendant here are invited," and with that he gave a nod to Little John, who nodded back in thanks.

"I thank you for the offer," Sir Richard answered with a demurring shrug. "But I think that my words in the chapter would hardly have set me in good stead with your abbot. Sharing a meal in your refectory with your abbot at the head of the table is sure to make things awkward for everyone involved."

"Not so!" Prior Stephen responded with a scoff that was not completely convincing. "Our rule of Saint Benedict states very clearly *Omnes supervenientes hospites tamquam Christus suscipiantur, quia ipse dicturus est: Hospis fui et suscepistis me*, or as we would say in English, 'All guests who present themselves are to be welcomed as Christ, for he himself will say: I was a stranger and you welcomed me.' And Saint Benedict specifically puts this requirement on abbots, saying 'the abbot's table must always be with guests and travelers.' Abbot Robert is, first and foremost, a Benedictine, and he will, he must, welcome you to dinner. Besides, we have a few other travelers who are staying with us today, and have, as well, a few important high-ranking visitors who will be sharing the meal. You needn't worry that you will be seated next to the abbot and have to engage him in small talk throughout the meal." And he ended with a knowing smile, causing Little John to laugh outright, and Sir Richard to give in with a smile of his own.

* * *

The large refectory was quite crowded for the midday meal, for not only were the fifty monks of the abbey in attendance, but so were the forty or so students who studied in the minster school. Add to that the dozen travelers, all of them fellow religious, currently accepting the hospitality of the Benedictine house, and there were more than a hundred diners in the hall. Prior Stephen had certainly been right when he said there would be no reason for Sir Richard to interact with the abbot at that dinner.

And the prior, perfunctory in his cordiality, met them at the door of the refectory and welcomed them with a pleasant demeanor. Little John got the impression that the prior, embarrassed and appalled by his superior's lack of courtesy, was determined to leave them with the impression that the Benedictine order was, after all, an institution dedicated to the theological virtues of faith, hope and particularly charity. It was almost as if he had connived with Sir Richard to demonstrate for Little John the embodiment of the role "those who pray" might play in the ideal commonwealth they'd been discussing on the way here—as the abbot had already demonstrated the justice of Little John's views on the matter.

"You might sit anywhere you like," the prior told them. "I suppose you might be more comfortable here at a back table somewhere," he motioned them to his left as they entered. "Your attendant—Reynold is it?—is welcome to dine with you, or if it would be more comfortable for him, he might eat in the kitchen with the abbey servants and the lay servants who attend our minster students. There is far less formality at that table, I can tell you. Especially with the abbot's noble guest here today."

"And who is that, if I may ask?" Sir Richard asked.

"It's the Bishop of Hereford, my lord. One of the most powerful prelates in the land—nearly as powerful, I might say, as our own abbot." And with that Prior Stephen gave a light laugh, as if he had made a joke.

But Little John saw no humor in the situation. His heart had plunged abruptly into his stomach at the name, and he looked up in horror, staring at the front table where, mitered and blustering, he did indeed see that same bishop that he and his companions had robbed of fifteen hundred nobles not long before. Of all the bloody luck, John grumbled to himself. Didn't that bishop ever spend any time in his own diocese?

John could not take a chance of being spotted by the bishop. It would be disastrous for himself, and dangerous for Sir Richard, if he were to be found harboring a notorious outlaw of Robin Hood's band. And so Little John did the only thing he could do.

"Oh, by all means, let me go eat with the servants, Master," he exclaimed, as the old knight turned a puzzled look upon him. "Sounds like that's where the real fun is in this place!

Which direction do I go, now, Brother Stephen?" And under Sir Richard's confused frown he followed the prior's gesturing arm toward the kitchen, where he could hear a far more raucous crowd than he had seen dining in the refectory.

In a few moments, Little John was seated at a table with several servants of the minster students, enjoying a frothy mug of ale and a trencher of mutton slaughtered for the occasion of the bishop's visit. The other four fellows at the table, all somewhat younger than John, were a lively crew who were friendly enough and easily accepted John's vague account of himself as an attendant to a knight who had stopped at the abbey on business of his own. They were too involved with their own affairs—concerning, as far as John could make out, their respective masters' relationships with a certain Brother Michael, who taught logic in the minster school.

"My master says that in his lecture the other day, ol' Brother Michael gave his students to consider the proposition 'God was not justified in creating women.' Tol' them to prove or disprove it," the tallest of the diners remarked. "Have ye ever heard such a thing?"

The youngest of them, a fat-cheeked blond boy, mused, "My mum would take a hickory branch to that old bugger, see if she wouldn't!"

"Well, what do you expect from these cloistered religious, anyway?" Little John felt the need to join in the conversation himself. "They're cooped up here like a bunch of bantam roosters, and they keep harping on what evil creatures women are. Why should it surprise anybody if they teach such things to these students of theirs, your masters?"

"You've said it, old man!" John blinked with surprise at being so addressed by the teenager with the thin growth of hair on his upper lip. "My master for one is going mad being penned up here in this cloister when York is teeming with sweet young ladies ripe for the plucking."

"Well now," the baby-faced blond protested. "I think my mum would come after *you* with that hickory stick if she heard you a-talkin' that way!"

And amid the laughter the downy-lipped youngster continued. "So, my master says, here's Brother Michael's first proposed syllogism." And here the boy assumed a pontificating voice intended, Little John supposed, to approximate the pompous tone of the monastic instructor: "'Major premise: God should not create anything that leads men into temptation. Minor premise: women lead men into temptation. Therefore, God should not have created women. QED.'"

"QED?" Little John queried.

"*Quod Erat Demonstrandum,*" the lad said, and after a beat explained, "My master tells me it means 'that which was to be explained.' In other words, when you put it at the end of a statement, it's like you're saying, the proof is done and indisputable."

Little John thought about this for a moment. He was himself never tempted by women but saw the logic in the argument as regarded the majority of men he knew. But in fairness, he was hardly convinced by such specious reasoning. "But how can such an argument be convincing? What if I say, 'God should not create anything that leads women into temptation. Men lead women into temptation. Therefore, God should not have created men.' Isn't that just as plausible?"

"My mum would say so!" the blond boy was quick to answer.

"Nay, nay, the problem with it is that Adam was created before Eve, so the monks tell us," the tall young man objected. "So the question as you put it couldn't arise. But here, according to my master, is what one of the students countered Brother Michael with: 'It was not good for man to be alone, so God needed to create a helpmeet for him. Woman was made as a helpmeet for man. Therefore, God needed to create woman.'"

"A fine solution that!" blond boy cried.

"But no," he of the downy moustache countered. "My master says Brother Michael deflated that argument this way." Again he adopted the officious voice: "'Man needed a helpmeet who was equal to himself. Woman is not the equal of a man. Therefore, woman is not the helpmeet man needed.'" And after a brief pause he added, "QED."

"Ow!" cried the blond boy, pounding the table in exasperation.

"But it didn't end that way," interjected the dark fourth youth, who up to now had simply listened and watched the others with quick, clever eyes. "Brother Michael could not allow his class to end on such a note because it is in fact blasphemous to assert that God had been 'wrong' in any aspect of his creation. My master, as I recall, summed up Brother Michael's final solution to the question this way: Major premise: God's first commandment to men was to 'be fruitful and multiply,' so he had to create men with the potential to fulfill that commandment. Minor premise: The only way for man to be fruitful and multiply is with woman. Therefore, God had to create woman for man to fulfill His first commandment." The dark lad looked around the table at the thoughtful faces of his comrades, and then added, with a sly smile, "QED."

"By that reasoning," Little John mused. "Women are created for only one purpose: to breed." They would, in that case, certainly be of no use at *all* to *him*, John reasoned, if that's what God intended.

"I know!" the blond one agreed. "And that ain't right in my mind! Nor would it be in my mum's!" And after another pause, he jumped to his feet and pointed a finger at the dark lad's chest shouting, "QED!"

"Hey," the clever fourth boy protested, putting up his hands. "These aren't my words, they're Brother Michael's. Just goes to show what kind of strange things these monks get up to, locked away in these cloisters year after year without ever *seeing* a woman."

"Oh, I don't know," the tall boy disagreed. "They see nuns and such, you know, holy women. *They're* not for breeding. And what about the Virgin Mary they're always going on about?"

"And then there's the abbot himself," downy lip added. "I think there's some woman of his acquaintance that he thinks is pretty important, not for breeding but because of some land deal."

Little John's ears pricked up. "What?" He blurted. Here was some gossip that might be of real use to him, and to Sir Richard as well.

"You heard!" moustache said knowingly. "I heard it from one of the servers at the abbot's table just before we sat down here."

"But what...what exactly did he say, can you remember?" Little John prodded.

"Ask him yourself, here he is," the boy replied. "Nicholas! Come here once, will you?"

A lad of about the same age as John's four companions, only dressed in the simple brown tunic and wearing the stained white apron of a kitchen boy, came over to them. He was breathing hard from the exertion of trying to keep his portion of the hundred guests in the refectory happy, and his face was flushed and his hair hanging in oily clumps from the kitchen grease. Nicholas seemed glad for this moment's respite from his busy tasks, and slumped forward, leaning with both hands on their table.

The lad with the thin moustache, his mouth curling up on one side in a bemused smirk, encouraged the newcomer to tell his tale. "Nicholas, tell our diminutive friend here, nodding in Little John's direction, "what you told me you heard the abbot tell that visiting bishop at the beginning of the meal."

"Oh, that," Nicholas said, shrugging as if it was of no importance. "It was when I was a-pourin' the wine that the abbot keeps in reserve for the high table, when all the others was just a-comin' into the room. Our abbot, he turns to the lord high bishop and he says to him, 'Well now my plans have hit a snag, they have. I'm not so sure the girl is likely to get the whole inheritance we planned for her,' and the bishop says something like, 'My Lord Abbot, don't tell *me* your troubles. I've got enough problems of my own lately,' or some such thing. Anyway, they stopped talkin' right about then 'cause the rest o' their table was a-fillin' up."

At that point, a shrill cry of "Nicholas, where are you, you lazy git?" filled the kitchen and the boy, giving them a comic grimace and a wink, rushed off to resume his duties, and the moustached lad looked at Little John smugly, saying, "So there it is. Our abbot apparently knows at least one woman he's interested in for other than breeding purposes," triumphantly adding, "QED!"

So he does, Little John thought to himself. And pursing his lips, he turned it over in his mind. Who was this mysterious girl, and how was her fate tied up with the fate of Sir Richard's lands? And what were these "plans" the abbot was talking about? And did this mean the assault on Sir Richard's patrimony was still not over? It was too much of a mystery for him now, but he vowed to himself that, having picked their side in this battle, he and Robin and the others would see to it that Sir Richard's interests were kept safe. From what, he wasn't sure.

CHAPTER FIVE

Robin looked back into the cart and shushed his companions once again. This was serious business they were about, but he could not seem to convince Will, Alan, and Friar Tuck to think of their mission as anything but a lark.

The moon was bright tonight, but clouds had begun moving in from the west shortly before sunset, and Robin was certain that, before they began their night's work, moon and stars would be invisible, ensuring that their work would remain invisible as well to prying eyes.

Thorvald had offered his cart to transport Robin and the others back to Horsley Castle, where Robin felt he had unfinished business. No, not the kitchen wench Agnes, though admittedly that thought had occurred to him more than once in the week since he'd first visited that place. It was the curious story of young Sir Walter's coffin that had kept Robin awake and wondering during those nights, so much so that at last he had determined to get to the bottom of this mystery by digging up Sir Walter's corpse. In secret, of course. He didn't imagine that Lady Abigail of Derby would be especially sanguine about the idea. But Robin was burning to know why the young master's coffin had been nailed shut, why Lady Abigail had been so quick about burying it and had refused to give any members of her household the chance to bid Sir Walter farewell. And why, for that matter, had the Abbot of Saint Mary's Abbey come all this way just to bury the young man? What was he to the abbot? The answers, Robin guessed, might lie inside that nailed coffin.

Naturally, digging up a coffin in the middle of the night was more than a one-man job, and Robin had tapped two of the younger and stronger members of his crew—his nephew Will Scarlet and the boisterous young jongleur Alan a Dale, to help him with the project. They both had readily agreed, finding the prospect a novel challenge, something that provided a welcome diversion from the usual fare of shooting the king's deer and robbing his prelates on the road. But it was hard to get the two lads to stop their anticipatory nattering as they rode toward Horsley, and Friar Tuck was not much better. Considering what he was about to do—that is, desecrate a newly consecrated grave—Robin figured he probably would need all the spiritual support he could get on his side and had begged the friar to come along.

"I'll come," the friar had agreed. "If only to pray for your soul. If nothing else, you'll need me to re-consecrate the grave after you've blasphemed all over it." But now all he seemed to want to do is pass the time on the road to Horsley telling ghost stories about corpses rising from the grave and feasting on the brains or the entrails of the living, much to the delighted terror of the two young lads.

As for Thorvald, the dwarf had volunteered to bring his cart, the one he had originally used to transport criminals and, later, the goods he sold in the days before the fall of the old king. None of the foresters were skilled horsemen, Thorvald reasoned, and they would have trouble keeping four or five horses quiet as they stood outside the castle. His cart was drawn by a single horse, and a quiet and reliable one. They could park the cart far enough from the castle wall that it would not be heard approaching, and Thorvald could wait in the cart until their return, keeping the horse quiet and keeping her, too, from running away. Besides, Thorvald added, they would need to bring several shovels and a good length of rope as well as at least one oil lamp or lantern, not to mention a heavy hammer and iron crow to open the casket once they found it, and it would be easier and safer to bring such items in a cart, rather than having them bang around on the backs of several horses.

Robin sat next to Thorvald, bent forward and whispering to his old chestnut mare that she was almost at her destination and could rest for a few hours. From the back of the cart, the voice of the good friar drifted up to them as he entertained Will and Alan with another tale of the walking dead.

"Now this story I swear is as true as the gospel itself, for I heard it from a certain monk I know from Byland Abbey up in north Yorkshire. This monk tells me that a certain Robert of Boltby, from the village of Kilburn up that way, was dead and buried in the abbey's cemetery, and yet refused to stay put in his tomb. Every night the dead lad would rise from his grave and carry on in the village, frightening the townsfolk and spooking the dogs, so they'd chase after him barking and howling and what not. It got so nobody in the village could get a decent night's sleep, what with the noise and with the never knowing when they were going to come face to face with young Robert's corpse. All of the young men of the village said they'd had enough, and they vowed to wait at sundown right at this Robert's grave, and pin him down and make him stop his hauntings."

"Can you do that?" Alan broke in. "Aren't ghosts spirits of some kind?"

"Who's telling this story, you or me?" the friar snapped back. "This was a walking corpse, you see? Not one of your run-of-the mill spiritual haunts. Anyway, as soon as it got dark and the stars came out, so did Robert, bursting out of his grave like one possessed. Which, come to think of it, he was. He burst out of his tomb shrieking madly, 'You flimsy weaklings, you think that I, who come here from the scorching flames of Purgatory, can be contained by mewling bull's pizzles like yourselves?' All those brave young men of the village took one look at that rotting, walking corpse, and they all bolted. All but two of them, and that was the brave Foxton twins, Caleb and Joshua. The brothers each grabbed one of the ghost's arms and held on no matter how loud he roared or how wildly he squirmed, and they dragged him to the churchyard gate and pinned him against it. Now Caleb hops over the gate and holds the corpse tight by both arms while Joshua shouts at it, 'Hold fast until I come back to you!' and then he tells his brother he's running to find the parish priest, and Caleb yells to him, 'Make it quick, brother, I don't know how long I can hold him!' And off runs Joshua."

"I'd've taken off, too!" Will cried. "And not bloody likely that I'd be back. I'll see you, Caleb! I wouldn't want to *be* you, Caleb!"

"I hope we never have to rely on you in a dangerous situation, Master Scarlet!" the friar said, regaining control of the story from Will. "Fortunately, Joshua was not of your ilk, and though Robert of Boltby's corpse strained and struggled against Caleb's grip, so that he had very nearly separated his moldering flesh from his arm bones and slipped away that way—and *then* where would those twins have been?—Joshua got back with the priest just in time. And being a priest, he knew just what to do, and begins to conjure the ghost in the name of the Holy Trinity until he compels this Robert's corpse to answer his questions, and finally he convinces him to confess his sins. The corpse gives in, and spends an hour confessing to the priest all of the heinous deeds he committed while alive—by the way, his mouth and lower jaw are rotted away, so he talks through an open hole in his guts—

and the priest absolves him, and he goes back to his tomb and never rises again. So let that be a lesson to you, my boys!"

Alan and Will looked at each other, neither one completely sure just what specific lesson they were expected to learn from this, when Robin turned around and said, "Hist, now, not another word! We're at the castle."

Thorvald had halted the cart nearly half a mile up the road from the Horsley Castle, so that the sound of cart or the clunk of tools could not be heard from the fortress itself. They were behind the structure now, on the other side of the motte from the gate through which Robin had entered a few days earlier. Since the churchyard was outside the palisade, it should be possible for the four outlaws to approach Sir Walter's grave without raising suspicion from any guards stationed in the barbican. Robin did not know if any would be stationed permanently on the back-palisade wall, but was gambling that, in a time of peace, the castle guards would send only a single guard to the back wall a few times during the night for a cursory look. Still, the grave robbers needed to do everything possible not to draw any attention to themselves, and that meant not only making as little noise as possible, but also working in the dark for much of the time.

They would need to move toward the castle, climb into the ditch that surrounded the motte, which was a good eight feet deep, and then climb the side of the motte itself, which here stood about twenty-five feet high, by Robin's estimation. That would get them to the flat top of the motte, and into the graveyard. As they left the cart, Thorvald held his old chestnut mare to keep her calm as the others leaped out, grabbing their gear: Will held two wooden spades (wood made less noise than metal) and carried a strong length of rope coiled around his right shoulder. Alan carried a heavy sledgehammer and an iron crowbar. Friar Tuck brought up the rear, carrying an unlit copper-alloy oil lantern and, in a small pocket inside his habit, a flint, curved steel striker, and a charcloth in order to light the lantern to look into the grave. Thorvald was to stay with the cart until the others came back, or until dawn, at which time he must assume they had been captured and should return to the outlaws' camp to arrange a rescue.

Robin led the way. He could see better than the others in the dark, and it was quite dark now that it was past compline, and clouds had moved in with the evening breeze to block the moon and stars. As noiselessly as possible the four outlaws clambered down the edge of the ditch, Will and Alan trying to keep their tools from knocking together, Friar Tuck trying to keep the oil from spilling out of his lamp. Feeling his way, Robin was relieved to see that the motte on which Horsley Castle was constructed was a natural hill, flattened on the top, rather than a man-made structure that would have had sheer walls. The side of this hill would be relatively easy to scale, and he waited for the others to gather around him before he whispered, "I'll lead the way up here, but follow close behind, one at a time. Try not to lose sight of the man in front of you!"

They climbed slowly up the steep, weed- and bramble-covered side of the motte. The slope was uneven enough that there were plenty of footholds and no one slipped on the way up. Most opportunely, there was, some five feet below the flattened top of the hill where perched the churchyard and the castle grounds, a sturdy ledge wide enough for all four of them to stand before hoisting themselves over the cliff's edge and into the graveyard itself. Here they crouched and rested for a few moments to catch their breath, and Robin whispered almost inaudibly, "Now let me poke my head up over the edge and see what I can see!"

There were only shadows and darkness visible when Robin tried to focus his eyes on the scene before him. He was eventually dimly aware of different concentrations of blackness: The wall of the palisade stood out like a deep black barrier between them and the castle's residents, and that was perfectly fine with Robin. He wanted no interaction with *them* tonight. Well, maybe Agnes… No, no, no, he told himself, concentrate on the job. There was no light apparent on the palisade, making it unlikely that a guard was on duty there, at least at this point. Nearer his gaze, Robin could see several hulking grey objects that he knew must be tombstones. And he could make out ragged tufts of rough grass and weeds, level with his eyes along the plane he was surveying, but also what appeared to be a smoother area, a very shallow mound, just six feet or so to his left, and ending no more than eight feet from the edge of the motte.

Ducking down, he whispered excitedly to his companions, "I can see it! Fresh dirt on a new-made grave just six feet to the right. We know that Sir Walter was the last person to be buried in this churchyard. It's got to be his!"

"So…" Will began tentatively, holding up the spades he'd been carrying, "we go over the top and start digging?"

Robin scowled for a moment, and then hissed to the friar, "Tuck! Can you get that lantern lit? I want to get a good look at the grave before we go to all the trouble of desecrating it. Let's see what we're up against."

Anticipating Robin's decision, the friar was already gripping his flint between the thumb and forefinger of his right hand, and he was holding a woven piece of char cloth under this right thumb as he sat, legs apart, on the ledge, with the metal lantern open between his knees. In his left hand he held his steel striker and, with quick downward motions of his wrist, struck the flint with glancing blows, causing sparks to fly and, before long, to ignite the char cloth with a small glowing blaze.

Deftly, Friar Tuck pushed the cloth into the lantern and lit the oil-soaked wick, and then closed the lantern before the light breeze could blow out the flame. "Ask and ye shall receive," he said, handing the lantern to Robin by its handle.

"Ha!" Robin whispered. "They're going to make you Saint Tuck for your fire-starting miracles!" Again, he stood to his full height and peered over the edge, holding the lantern above his head to shine its light on the ground before him. He looked ahead for a moment, then moved along the ledge six feet or so, stepping over the seated friar as he moved, then looked before him, nodded his head, and ducked down again. Holding the lantern out to the friar, he hissed again, "Don't put it out, but cover it so nobody from the castle can see the light. We'll work in the dark!"

The friar was briefly flummoxed, then decided to pull off his cowl and hide the lantern under it. The night was pitch dark again, and Robin, taking one of the wooden spades from Will shoved the spade into the side of the hill just above the ledge on which they stood.

"Dig here!" he whispered sharply to Will and Alan. "We'll dig a narrow tunnel straight into the motte from here."

"What…you mean you want to dig to the coffin from the side, instead of from the top?" Alan asked with a scratch of his head.

"The head of Walter's grave is on this end, and it's straight in from here, eight feet at the most." Robin, a little bolder, was speaking quietly but loud enough for them all to understand. "If we stand in the churchyard and dig down, it may be faster, but we can easily be seen from any guard who happens by on the wall. Nobody from the castle can see us if we dig from down here. Not only that, nobody will ever know the grave was opened, unless they come to the edge of the motte and look here on purpose. So let's get at it, before the sun comes up and Thorvald drives his cart off without us."

They took turns in twos, digging horizontally into the hill until they were so deep that only one man could be in the tunnel at once. Then they took turns, one at a time, each man digging about a foot of tunnel until he was exhausted. In the end the man digging had to lie on his belly and pass dirt out to another man behind him. After five hours of hard work, Alan felt his spade strike against a hard, wooden barrier. It was the head of Sir Walter's coffin.

"The lantern! Give me the lantern!" Alan whispered behind him, and Robin, who was clearing out the dirt Alan was passing back, retrieved the light from the friar and passed it up to him. "It's the coffin all right," he told Robin quietly. "Let me clear away more of the dirt, and we can break open the coffin's head and pull the…pull him out from here."

"Keep the lantern there if it's not in your way," Robin advised. "Best to be able to see what we're doing now, and if the light's in the tunnel it can't be seen from the castle."

"Right!" Alan said, and Robin could hear more scraping and see more dirt being pushed back toward him to be removed from the tunnel. After a good twenty minutes of this, Alan wanted to come out, and he and Robin exited the tunnel. Now it was Will's turn. With the hammer and crowbar he crawled through the tunnel to the head of the coffin. Robin heard a few half-hearted blows of the sledgehammer before he heard Will's harsh whisper declare that he could find no way to swing the hammer to any effect inside the narrow tunnel but thought he could pry off the head of the casket with the iron crow. Now came wrenching sounds of metal on wood, and of nails creaking and bending, and Robin was grateful that the earth surrounding Will's efforts also smothered their sounds. Then there was a final screech of timber giving way, and a subdued and muffled cry of triumph from Will, followed by a sudden darkness in the tunnel and

Will's voice trailing off into a moan of despair. "The lantern's gone out!" he hissed.

"The oil's burned up," the friar moaned. "It's taken so long to dig our way to the casket that there wasn't enough left to see us to the end!"

"Can we get the body out of there without being able to see it?" Robin asked, then added, "Come on out of there, Will, let me see what I can do. Where's that rope?"

"Here!" Alan found the rope where Will had left it on the ledge and handed it to Robin while Will backed out of the tunnel, dragging with him the hammer, crow, and broken pieces from the coffin's head.

"Right! Now listen," Robin said in a husky whisper. "I'll crawl in there with one end of the rope, and the two of you wait out here holding on to this end. I'm going to tie the rope around our Walter's neck, and when I say 'pull,' I want you to give it a good yank, see if we can't budge him from in there. I want to see the body, to see what it is they're hiding. If it seems a normal corpse…I suppose we'll leave it in the tunnel and bugger off!"

"Except we won't be able to see it well without the lantern," Friar Tuck pointed out.

"Oh, bloody hell, you're right," Robin admitted.

Alan a Dale cleared his throat. "Well, you may not have noticed, but there's a bit of a glow on the eastern horizon. We've been at this so long it's going to be dawn soon. In another half hour we're going to be able to see the corpse well enough."

"And the guards are going to be able to see us," Will added.

"We're still hidden below the edge of the motte," Robin whispered, realizing they'd all been talking too loudly. "We'll get the body out, get a quick look at it, leave it in the tunnel, and light out for Thorvald's cart as fast as we can move. We'll leave the tools if we have to. Friar Tuck, you make your way back to

Thorvald and tell him we'll be on our way and to wait for us. I'm going in there with the rope."

And as Robin crawled back into the tunnel, Tuck felt his way down the slope, murmuring to himself, "'Behold, I send my messenger before your face, who will prepare your way before you.'"

"Okay, I'm here," Robin called back to Will and Alan in muffled tones. Feeling blindly inside the coffin, his hands found a hard, round object. "I've found the head!" he called back. "I'm tying the rope around it now!" And as carefully as he could, Robin slid the rope toward where he guessed the chin must be, and looped it around, finding the best purchase if he pulled the rope end back up toward himself and tying a knot on what his blind hands told him would be the top of the dead man's skull. Giving the rope a few quick jerks, he was satisfied that he had a good hold on the head, and he hissed behind him, "All right! Let me back out of here quickly, and be ready to give the rope a mighty pull!"

Robin scooted back as fast as he could, and just as he left the hole, Alan and Will counted "One, two, *three*," and yanked the rope with all their might. But their pull was far stronger than they needed, and both fell backwards, rolling down the slope, as the rope came flying out of the tunnel, bound only around a single round object.

"It's the corpse's bloody head!" Alan cried out, far louder than was prudent, "His ghost is going to haunt us, like Robert of Boltby's in the friar's tale! It'll eat our entrails!" Will shouted, and the two of them scrambled up the ditch wall and were off before Robin could utter a word. "Oh, Tuck," Robin muttered under his breath. "Not especially helpful, you with that story."

Behind him, Robin heard a shout from the palisade wall. "Who is out there? Guards! Guards! We have intruders at the rear wall of the castle!" But Robin, knowing he could not be seen from the wall where he was, and knowing that any pursuing guards would have to issue from the castle's gate, on the other side of the fortification, was confident he could get away if he ran now. But the sun was starting to rise, and somebody was almost sure to see him flee. Grabbing the rope and its captured spheroid, he slid down the embankment and up the other, and took off at full speed across the field where Thorvald's cart stood waiting, with Tuck, Will and Alan already aboard, and Thorvald waving him on calling, "Haste, Robin! Hustle! They won't be long in getting after us!"

The cart started moving before Robin reached it, and he threw his bundle into its bed and then leaped up as best he could, while Will and Alan grabbed onto his clothes and hauled him up to safety. They all sat and panted for a space, then looked back for any signs of pursuers.

"I think we'll be safe," Robin said, looking back over his shoulder. "They're going to look in the graveyard first, and they won't find anything there. I doubt if anyone's going to think of looking down the slope into their ditch. And if they saw me running, it will still take them some time to mount horses and pursue us."

"By the time they catch us, we'll be a mile off at least," Thorvald said. "They didn't know you had a cart parked so far off, and I'll be going at my old chestnut's pace. Just a small crew of farm 'ands up early to get into the fields. Nothin' to see 'ere."

Alan grinned, but then looked down at the tangled rope in horror. "Great horn spoon! Did you actually bring Sir Walter's head with you?"

Robin reached down into the dark corner of the cart's bed and brought up what the rope had snagged, setting it on his lap. It was a fairly smooth round boulder, about the size of a human skull. "Meet Sir Walter of Horsley," he said. "There is no body at all in that grave. Just a pile of stones."

CHAPTER SIX

Lady Maude Peverel, the discontented wife of John of Oxenford, Sheriff of Nottingham, stood in the parlor of her husband's mansion in the heart of the city with her arms folded, glaring at the two men standing before her, their caps abjectly in their hands. She was dressed in a simple but elegant gown of blue silk with unfashionable sleeves that hugged her wrists rather than hanging impractically down to her shoes—a style she considered silly and cumbersome in daily life. Her luxurious auburn hair was bound up under a linen veil held in place by a stiff linen fillet or headband that encircled her brow, embroidered with pearls in vogue with the upper classes. She also wore a thin chin strap or barbette to complete the perfect picture of the modest municipal housewife—though she was, she would be the first to tell you, not of that class, but rather a younger daughter of the younger brother of the aristocratic Peverel family that owned the estate of Codnor Castle and its environs, twelve miles northwest of Nottingham: She was immeasurably superior to these two clowns who stood before her now.

"You disappointed me in letting him get away the first time," she said, her fiery green eyes glaring at her two villeins, the nostrils of her narrow nose flaring. "Tell me why I should trust you this time, when the task will be infinitely more difficult. You couldn't manage to eliminate him here in Nottinghamshire. How on earth do you expect to track him down halfway across the known world?"

"We know 'e's set out for Jerusalem, to join with them that's defending the crusader's kingdoms against them 'eathen Mohammedans," the tallest of the two villeins explained. "So we follow him there, find 'im, and make sure 'e don't come back, see?" The shorter, stockier lout nodded vigorously, his thin blond hair flying about in agitation. Maude eyed them with distrust, taking in their broad-brimmed hats, their brown tunics and black cloaks, the scrips they bore on straps over their shoulders, and the staffs on which they leaned. Each of them bore on his hat the scallop-shell badge of Santiago de Compostela.

"So you think you're going to fool people into thinking you're pilgrims, is that it?" she asked. "Pilgrims who are going to Jerusalem—but who have the badge of Saint James on their hats? You don't think that will look suspicious?"

"No, no," the first man countered. "See, we ain't *been* to the 'oly Land yet, right? But we're avid pilgrims, 'o've been to other sites, like Santiago. It's all part of the disguise!"

"And this disguise is going to help you complete your commission?"

"Right!" replied the tall one, his goggling eyes bulging from his pale, narrow face. He was obviously the pair's designated spokesman. "We get to Jerusalem, we find 'im, and we kill 'im. Simple as that."

"You do realize he's a knight, don't you?" Maude asked. "And he'll be in the company of other knights? What makes you think you can get the better of him? Assuming you actually make it to Jerusalem? And assuming you can actually find him? And assuming he will actually talk to you if you do find him?"

"My lady, if I may," the tall rustic began, almost pedantically. "First, we 'ave never failed to complete a job once we've been hired to do it."

"Except this time," Maude corrected him.

"Except this one time, so far! We aim to correct that mistake, my lady. Second, 'e won't 'ave no suspicion of us, being's we're 'is own countrymen, from 'is own home turf of Nottinghamshire, *and* 'e'll see we're just innocent pilgrims, ya see? And third, and 'ere's where we need your 'elp, mistress," and with this the pair both took on a humble, groveling pose and looked up at Maude with pleading eyes. "We'll 'ave a letter addressed to 'im in 'er own 'and, that you'll provide us with."

Maude narrowed her eyes on the speaker. "If you think she's going to write him a letter just because I ask her to, I think you know very little of my young cousin. But…" and now she grew thoughtful, tapping her finger on her lips as she paced the room. "I can counterfeit my cousin's hand close enough, I'd wager, and give the impression that I had to dash the missive off hastily, which might be enough to excuse anything in the handwriting that might appear slightly off. More importantly, I can stamp the letter with my own version of the Peverel family seal. That may be something that actually works, assuming you can get close enough to him to give him the letter."

"Oh, we can, your worship, we definitely can. Now, when can we expect to 'ave this letter? I 'ope it may be soon, being's 'ow the sooner we can be off, the sooner we might be able to take care of this business. It's a long road to Jerusalem. A long and *expensive* one…"

"I have already paid you a substantial sum. You want to extort yet more from me?"

"My lady, my lady, you gave us 'alf of the five hundred nobles before the job, and you 'ave promised to pay us the remainder when we complete it. But travel to the 'oly Land is a big expense."

"You seem to think I am the king's mint, or some Italian banker. Use some of the money I've already given you to cover your expenses!"

"My lady, that may not be enough for the entire journey," the tall man complained. "We might end up in Jerusalem and 'ave no way to get back. To make this trip I think we will need the 'ole amount now. And then, since we'll be spending our entire profit on expenses to do the job, it does seem to me that we ought to get paid another two-fifty when we get back. Begging your pardon, ma'am."

Maude glared at him with undisguised contempt. "Let me get this straight," she began slowly. "I've paid you two hundred and fifty nobles, for which you have failed to do what I hired you to do. Now you are proposing that I add *another* two-fifty to that, throwing good money after bad, to help fund what looks to be a fool's errand with virtually no chance of success, sending you to a place you've never been to track down one man amongst thousands, who for all we know may never have even arrived in Jerusalem. And then you want me to pay you *another* two-fifty when you get back for finally doing the job you've already been paid for?"

The two men looked at one another a moment, then nodded, and the tall one responded, "That's about the size of it, yes ma'am."

Losing all control now, Maude screeched, "*Do you think I am a complete ass*? Why would I do such a thing?"

The tall man paused a moment until his ears stopped ringing, and then replied, grinning a ghoulish and virtually toothless grin, "All depends on 'ow much you want the blighter dead, I reckon, don't it, my lady?"

She held his gaze in her iron glare for a few moments longer, and finally relented, sighing, "All right, then. It appears you leave me no choice. Come back here on Friday. I shall have the letter for you, as well as your two hundred and fifty nobles. But listen, villein, this I demand: When you return from this pilgrimage of yours, you will bring me back indisputable proof of his death, or you get no additional payment from me."

"What, you mean our word is not good enough for you, my lady?" the tall man asked.

"Ha!" Maude scoffed. "Said the fox to the chicken farmer. No, your word is not worth the fart whose foul air it so resembles. I want proof."

"But what would that proof consist of, my lady?" the tall man persisted.

"That is for you to figure out," Maude told the exasperated spokesman. "Now void my sight until Friday. Go!"

The tall man bowed and made for the door, while the shorter man, more slowly and decorously, inclined his head toward the sheriff's wife and said, in a hoarse, gruff baritone, with an evil looking grin, "You shall have your proof, mistress."

* * *

Maude walked into her private closet, calling out to her servant, "I'm not to be disturbed, Anna," and closed the door behind her. It would be best for all their sakes if Sir Peter of Verysdale were eliminated as soon as possible. There was no certainty that the two buffoons she had hired would be able to complete the task, though she knew they had served as mercenaries in Spain and in Italy and so had some experience with foreign travel. But having them out of the country for the next several months would be an advantage in itself, since she also did not trust them not to blab her secrets throughout Nottinghamshire. She had the two hundred and fifty nobles to pay for their journey—she had had it in the expectation that the two villeins would have finished their job by now. So there would be no difficulty in paying them as they left. Where she would get another similar amount was a question she could not at present answer, but it was a question that could be put off for the several months between now and the clowns' return, if indeed that ever occurred. And by then, with her plan well under way, there would be enough for all things—perhaps enough even to get her out of this house and away from John of Oxenford, whom, it must be admitted, she was far too good for.

Maude sat down in the comfortable chair in the corner of her room and reached under it for the wooden box with the angled surface, in which her writing materials were stored. She removed a clean sheet of parchment, a feather quill and some black ink that she placed in a holder on the top of her box. She set the portable desk on her lap and, after frowning a moment in thought, began to compose this letter:

> *To my one true love (you know who you are):*
>
> *Since we have been parted, my soul has had no peace. I yearn for you day and night, without cease. I pray for your safety, and I pray for the confounding and ruin of those who endeavor to keep us apart. I have vowed that I shall not live without your love, and that if our parting promises to be for evermore, then I have no reason to live longer, and would gladly die.*
>
> *Trust, I implore you, the one that has brought my message to you. He has come at my direct bidding, and he means you no harm. Do as he says, and all will be well. I am counting the moments until I shall see you again, and I count as worthless any moment I am not with you. Adieu, my love, until you are returned to me again, or until my despised life ends at last.*
>
> *Your own, as you know her*

Maude squinted at the paper even as she waved it gently in the air so that the ink would dry more quickly. She wondered if she had laid it on a little too thick, but then decided that Sir Peter, as great a lunkhead as any young male, was bound to be as susceptible to the breathy moanings of a lady in distress as the next man. And besides, all she had to do was to get him to put himself in the hands of those two villeins for a minute or two, like a lamb to the slaughter, and the biggest obstacle to her lovely plans would vanish like the mist in the afternoon sun. She folded the paper, took a blazing candelabra from her mantle and let candlewax drip copiously onto the folded edge of the page, then took her family seal from her writing box and pressed it into the wax. There would be no reason for the letter's recipient to suspect that it had *not* come from Lady Lydia Peverel, Countess of Chesterfield.

* * *

By the time her husband returned home for the evening meal, Maude had put away her letter and her purse, had covered her headdress with a gold net-like crespine, and had put on a gold necklace and a belt of braided gold. John of Oxenford liked his wife to be adorned richly, so that he might show her off like a prized heifer, and she knew that tonight he was bringing home to dine the new commander of the garrison at Nottingham Castle, Sir Guy of Gisbourne. The sheriff was eager to secure Sir Guy as a new political ally and wanted to impress him as far as his budget could reach, and so had urged Maude to do her best.

Accordingly, she had instructed Anna, their cook and housekeeper, to prepare a sumptuous meal for three, with several courses, beginning with a thick frumenty pottage with vegetables and bits of venison, followed by second course of meats, including the rest of that venison as well as salmon and pike, the only options available in the local market this week. The main course would be a roasted capon, the sheriff's household lacking the means to secure a swan or peacock to make a big splash. A dessert course of pastries followed by a plate of cheeses would complete the dinner, which Maude felt was as good a dinner as might be had in Nottingham, outside of some noble's castle or one of the larger monasteries in the area, and if this Sir Guy expected more, he would have to go elsewhere to dine and the devil take him. She was willing to put herself out for her husband's advancement, but only so far—and, with any luck, would not have to do so much longer. For her own pleasure as well as her husband's and his guest's, she had made sure that a spiced Burgundy wine would be served with the meal. And because the sheriff's household was not a wealthy one, or not nearly as wealthy as John of Oxenford would have wished (or wanted the townsfolk to believe it was) Maude had coerced their elderly groundskeeper, Giles (their only other servant) to help Anna serve the meal and pour the wine.

"So, Lord Sheriff," Sir Guy began, flattering the decidedly bourgeois John with a promotion to the noble class, to his wife's proper class. "Even with your increased vigilance and your newly hired deputies, you have still had little success in ridding Sherwood of these outlaw bands that plague travelers along the Great North Road." He was clearly continuing a conversation the two had been having before stepping into the room.

Now they were sitting down to dinner, the sheriff at the head of the board set up on trestles for the occasion, Maude at the foot, and Sir Guy between them, as Anna was setting their bowls of pottage before them and Giles was pouring the wine. "From the left," she whispered to him. "Always from the left."

Sir Guy was a head taller than her portly husband, with dark flowing hair that reached to his shoulders and a neatly trimmed goatee. He was lean, with a thin, pinched-looking face, dark squinting eyes, a narrow nose and thin lips that curled into a sneer whenever he smiled, which was seldom.

"Ah, Sir Guy, this Robin Hood is a slippery devil! Cunning as he is brazen. Doesn't shrink from the vilest of acts. Even great princes of the church are prey to his knavery! Why just recently, his grace the Bishop of Hereford was robbed of more than two thousand gold nobles while on his way here from York. The bishop himself! Can such impertinence be suffered? I ask you sir. Is it to be borne?"

"As you know," Sir Guy said, not bothering to answer the sheriff's rhetorical questions, "Nottingham Castle is a royal residence, and I am charged with holding it in the name of the crown. The crown, as you may have heard, is—at least currently—worn on the brow of young Constantine of Cornwall, the old king's distant cousin. Constantine has sent me here to assert the royal presence in this part of the realm, and what is of most concern to me is what I have heard about this Robin and his band poaching the king's deer in Sherwood—and poaching them, it must be said, with impunity!"

"Indeed," said the sheriff, "that is of course also a concern. But what hurts us most grievously is his stealing egregiously from every merchant who comes this way, so that they have no money left with which to pay the excise taxes they are expected to pay for use of the road and for the purchase of supplies here in Nottingham. Which we collect, of course, in the name of the king."

"The name of a king whom, until I arrived, you did not know," Sir Guy reminded him, now digging into the meat course Giles had laid before them. "I wonder," he added with a sneer—or was it a smile?—where those funds have found their way to in these intervening months?"

The sheriff cleared his throat, knowing very well which of his pockets those funds had found their way into, and how much emptier those pockets had become since Robin Hood and his meinie had been lords of the forest. He changed the subject. "But that poaching! The poaching is certainly a major concern. No matter how many foresters I have set to guard Sherwood, he eludes them every time! And nothing escapes his greedy hands!"

"No," murmured Maude dreamily. "Nothing escapes them."

"So it seems," Sir Guy replied, pausing to admire the dressed capon that Anna was bringing in, on the household's one silver platter, and which Giles began to carve, standing across the table from Sir Guy and placing the choicest cuts on the guest's pewter plate. Maude had decided on the pewter for the evening meal because those plates conveyed more wealth than the bread trenchers she and the sheriff commonly used while dining alone. She lifted her own pewter tankard and drained her wine, unhappy but unsurprised at the direction the dinner conversation was taking.

"Let me make you this vow," Sir Guy continued. "Today is what? Saint Sophia's day, the fifteenth of May, is it not? Then I promise you this: By the end of the summer I will have this Robin Hood of yours in irons, in the dungeons of Nottingham Castle. Your local deputies have been impotent to catch this rascal…"

"And the rascal is far from impotent himself," Maude added, keeping up her end of the conversation.

"Indeed, he seems to rule the forest as his own domain," Sir Guy agreed. "But you should know, I have brought forty doughty knights of my own to man the castle garrison. They are battle-hardened troops, veterans of many skirmishes with the Scots in the north. They will scour the length and breadth of Sherwood Forest between here and Barnesdale…"

"That's 100,000 acres, Sir Guy," the sheriff informed him.

The new captain of the garrison blinked, but paused only for half a second before continuing, "They will comb this entire shire until every last nit of an outlaw is exterminated." Maude put down a morsel of capon she'd been raising to her lips and coughed, somewhat put off her meal. "Those who won't surrender to my guards will be destroyed where they are. And those we capture we will bring back here to Nottingham to face your justice," and with this he nodded in polite but insincere deference to the sheriff, and then flashed his sneering half-smile. "And you sir, I am quite sure, will know exactly how much rope it will take to hang them. And most particularly to hang Robin Hood."

"No doubt," Maude quietly averred, "he will be well hung indeed."

Having verbally done away with the annoyance posed by the outlaw band of Sherwood, John of Oxenford and Sir Guy of Gisbourne dallied over the sweetmeats brought in for their dessert and had Giles refill their tankards with more spiced wine in order to toast their new alliance, and passed into more pleasant conversation as they discussed mutual acquaintances among the local landholders and among the courtiers of the new king. The lady Maude Peverel, musing over her wine and licking confection from her fingers, was contemplating something else entirely: how she might get a message to the notorious outlaw king of Sherwood.

CHAPTER SEVEN

At the Sign of the Blue Boar on the outskirts of Nottingham, north of the city and close to the southern edge of Sherwood, was an inn and public house frequented by many of the town's artisan class and several yeoman from the countryside round about. Men, and a few women who were not particular about their reputations, came here some evenings after shops had closed for a late supper. Or they might come for a pint or two or three of the local ale, on holidays when work was finished early, or often on Saturday nights when they might sleep late the following morning, especially if they were planning on skipping Mass the next day—or at least sleeping through it.

Being just one quick turn off the Great North Road, the Blue Boar was also a favorite haunt for members of Robin Hood's band, and on this particular Saturday night, young David of Doncaster was sitting at a table with Much the miller's son and Arthur Bland, a huge fellow who had formerly worked as a tanner but had been convinced—after a good-natured fistfight in which Little John had knocked out a few of Arthur's teeth—to give up his trade and join John in Robin's outlaw band. David, youngest of Robin's meinie, was turning sixteen the following day, and Much and Arthur figured that milestone called for the boy to get roaring drunk. It was only natural, Much said.

No one passing by on the road that night would have seen anything remarkable about the veiled figure dressed head to foot in brown and gray, and bundled, though it was a mild evening in the third week of May, in a substantial brown cloak. She walked with a stick as if she were an aged crone, but if one bothered to glance at her hands, he would have been undeceived, for they were smooth and fair, with long graceful fingers gripping the head of the walking stick. She shuffled a furlong or two down the Great North Road and turned right after she reached the edge of the city, and made her way as unobtrusively as possible into the Blue Boar, where now, just after vespers, things were beginning to liven up.

At a table in the corner were three lads dressed openly in the Lincoln green livery she recognized as Robin Hood's colors. She clicked her tongue to herself and wondered at the brazenness of these outlaws. If the sheriff knew how impudently Sherwood's outlaws patronized the Blue Boar, he'd close the place down. Or plant some of his own deputies here clandestinely to arrest Robin Hood's men when they showed their faces. But of course, the sheriff would never set foot in here, nor would the mayor or any of the chief burgesses or guild masters of the city. Nor, for that matter, would she, if she didn't have an overriding reason for being here. And so, slouching her way across the pub's floor, she plopped herself down without ceremony at the outlaws' table and said in a low, sultry voice, "Buy a girl a drink, fellas?"

Young David coughed, shocked at the unexpected audaciousness, particularly coming from such an unlikely source, and spewing Nottingham ale over the table, but the ancient hag, undeterred, lifted her veil for an instant and winked one of her emerald green eyes at him. Much, the most seasoned member of the trio, thought he recognized in that flash of beauty the haughty bearing of the Sheriff of Nottingham's wife. Though what she was doing in this place he could not imagine.

"Sure, grandmother," he said, with only a trace of irony. "A pint of ale to keep the chill out of your bones." And with that he signaled to a tavern wench whose eye he had caught. "Although you look pretty bundled up to be worried about that now, right? Tell me then, what might a lady of your rank and breedin' be doin' here amongst us lowly folk, is what I'm wondering."

"And what I'm wondering," an affected croaking voice came from behind the veil, "is how cheeky the outlaws of Sherwood must be to sit so openly at an inn in Nottingham itself, when they know the sheriff has put on extra men just to search out those brigands and bring them to justice."

"Maybe it's because we know the sheriff to be a feeble poltroon who is all bluster and no follow-through," said David, by this time half on his way to a memorable birthday hangover.

"And suppose the sheriff heard you abusing him so?" the voice croaked with a hint of bemusement.

"Why, I'd add that he had a face as ugly as a toad, and that his wife rented her favors out by the hour..."

Much's right hand shot out and clutched David's collar, and with one quick motion brought his face smashing down onto the table, and while the lad rubbed his nose with a surprised moan, Much hissed, "*Shht*, Davy, shut yer yap! Anybody in here could be the sheriff's spy, ya yammerin' fool! Now apologize to the lady for yer rudeness and drink yer ale."

"S-sorry granny," David whispered, not quite sure what for. The lady nodded to him as she accepted a tankard from the serving wench. She lifted her veil just enough to take a sip of her drink before putting it down and leaning forward as if to take the three foresters into her confidence.

"I need you to get a message to Robin Hood," she spoke plainly and in her own voice.

Much sat up straight, now all attention. The other two dropped their jaws and Maude muttered quietly, "Don't gape like netted trout, boys; anybody here could be watching. Now smile and nod as if we're all just cozy chums, and I'm telling you the latest gossip about the bishop's concubine."

David and Arthur immediately did as they were bid, but it must be admitted that if they were ever to try their hand as traveling players, they would almost certainly starve. Much, his smile looking far less pasted on, leaned forward to meet the veiled woman nose to nose, and whispered, "We may have a way of getting a message to Robin. What is it?"

"I know you are of his retinue," she answered, and reaching into her sleeve, brought out a small, folded sheet of parchment and slipped it across the table so that it dropped inconspicuously into Much's lap. He did not immediately make a grab for it, in case any suspicious eyes were taking him in. Anyway, he couldn't read. But Robin knew his letters and would certainly be able to make sense of it.

"He will have the paper," Much said. "But give us the gist of it, if you will, madame."

Maude sighed, and whispered, "In brief it is this: The new captain of the king's guard at Nottingham Castle, Sir Guy of Gisbourne, has vowed to track Robin and all of his men down by summer's end. He means to hang you. You must take precautions. He has forty men with whom he vows to scour the forest."

Much frowned. "And we have only two dozen, on a good day."

And at that, the veiled lady surprised him by laying one of her slender, elegant hands on his own, whispering, "But you have the advantage of being in your own home! Now I must leave before I am missed. Tell your master he can expect Gisbourne's onslaught to begin immediately, and not to underestimate him." And with that word she drained the last of her cup and rose slowly, as if painfully, and walked out bent over her walking stick, as the crone she was when she walked in.

* * *

Little John had returned from his impromptu mission to York and had told Robin and all his men about the vehemence of the sheriff's deputies who had tried to arrest him—would indeed have locked him up had it not been for Sir Richard's intervention. And when Robin read aloud to them all, without revealing the identity of the source, Maude's written warning about the new and significant threat from Sir Guy's troops, there was a definite chill in the outlaw camp.

"This is unprovoked persecution, this is," Thorvald the dwarf complained. "Who do we 'urt when we shoot the so-called king's deer? Nobody! Not even the deer. The 'erd needs cullin' anyway, or the poor deer'd starve, am I right?"

There was a lot of grumbled agreement with Thorvald's point of view, but Friar Tuck, more realistically, stepped in with a more sobering opinion. "We have, it must be admitted, made a number of enemies among the rich and powerful in the land—most recently the great Bishop of Hereford, you might recall. While I will be the first to acknowledge that our charity in giving away much of the bounty our dinner guests have given us to the poor in the parish has put us in good stead with our Heavenly Father, our taking it in the first place has, conversely, gained us the enmity of some very powerful and influential figures in both church and state. Now this newly acknowledged king, Constantine, certainly wants to gain the favor of the powerful barons in this part of the realm, and he's sent this Gisbourne to make a show of strength. And what better way to demonstrate his new power than by wiping out the figure who has plagued those powerful figures for so long? We may have amongst us the most skillful archers in all of England, but we would be foolish to try to stand against an armed force from Nottingham Castle. My counsel is this: We know there are numerous caves up in Creswell Crags on the border of Derbyshire, up near Chesterfield. The northern part of Sherwood. We've talked about using one or more of those caves as winter quarters—when we need to get out of the snow and the wind and when the trees are bare and harder to use as camouflage. I suggest we make our way there now. Gisbourne's men will be focusing their attention closer to Nottingham, where the bulk of our activity has been heretofore. No one will think of looking near Creswell, and we can hunker down there until this all blows over."

There were a number of nodding heads and a general agreement with Friar Tuck's sentiments, but Thorvald twisted his face into a grimace that suggested he was thinking about something pretty hard. "I grant ya those caves'd be a fine refuge for the 'ole band, and what families we got with us as well, but you do know they've got to be a good twenty-five miles from 'ere, and we got a lot of gear to transport. 'Ow we gonna get everything moved up there then, and do it without giving every king's guard and sheriff's deputy in Sherwood a perfect shot at us while we're movin'? Might as well paint targets on our backs, it seems to me."

"Leave it to you to think of the practical questions of cartage, my friend Thorvald," Sir Palomides added, his deep baritone sounding a note of authority in the meeting. "And you are quite right. Your cart can carry some of what we need to bring, but only some. What we truly need are more horses. At present we have only your old chestnut, Robin's Daisy, Little John's Bishop, Wat o' the Crabstaff's mare Genevieve, that used to pull his tinker's wagon, and my own great destrier Zulfiqar. Five horses for what, thirty-two men and women, and all their supplies and household goods? If we want to move quickly, it's just not possible."

"Then we won't move quickly," Little John proposed. "If we truly are moving base to those caves—and I assume we are?" At that, he glanced at Robin, to see what he had to say. Robin shrugged, and John went on. "Let's do it gradually, right? We've got six of the lads' women here. Let's work it this way: Have Thorvald take the women in his wagon. They can all fit if they squeeze, I think. And carry as much bedding and cooking paraphernalia as can fit in the wagon bed with 'em. Let them head up to those caves and they can choose what looks like it will make the best headquarters for the band. Maybe make it nice and homey before the rest of us get there?"

Robin nodded. "It has the virtue of getting the women out of harm's way if we do get found out by Gisbourne's guards. They, at least, will be safe."

Ellen, the youngest of the women among Robin's meinie, but the most outspoken, stood up then, her hands on her hips. She was Alan a Dale's wife—Friar Tuck swore he had married them before she moved into Alan's tent—and kept him well in line with the kind of stance she took at that moment, her chin thrust forward, her blue eyes flashing, and her blonde hair tumbling unkempt down her back. "Oh, I see. Send the women ahead to the bare caves and expect us to make a home of them before you all move in, is that it? It's about what I'd have expected from you, Robin Hood. Never met a woman you couldn't use, isn't that your game?"

Robin looked puzzled, holding out his hands in silent plea, and said, "Little John suggested it, not me! I just wanted to get you safe. How am I to blame here?"

"Not my idea!" Little John said. "I was just…uh…"

"Never mind," said Ellen, with a prodigious eye roll. "If we can make a home in the middle of the trees, we can probably make a better one in a cave. But what happens when the sheriff's men stop us and we're six women riding in a wagon with a dwarf? What do we tell them we're doing? On our way to open a brand new bawdy house in York?"

"Helping in the fields," called out Jack Rolfe, former yeoman farmer whose small holding had lately been forfeited, swallowed up by the lords of nearby Codnor Castle, leading him to join Robin's band. "Tell 'em you've been hired as day laborers to help with the planting at the Earl of Chesterton's lands up that way." He looked around at some of the nodding heads, surprised that he'd contributed something to the conversation. Then he shrugged. "Makes as much sense as anything, don't it?"

"It does," Ellen answered for everybody. "Then we'll do it. When do we leave?"

"Better make it soon," Robin said. "Our informant here warns us that these troops are coming sooner rather than later. Take a day to prepare, and then, Thorvald, if you and your old chestnut are up to it, you can leave tomorrow morning. Meantime, over the next week or so, the rest of us can move, a few men each day carrying their gear, through the woods rather than on the road, until we've disappeared from the old oak clearing. And in the meantime, we'll double the watchers along the road, to bring the rest of us fair warning if we see them coming. And one more thing: Let's make a point of gathering up as many horses as we can, if any rich prospects show themselves on the road."

"More horses will help," Little John agreed. "More watchers helps even more."

* * *

Robin and his men were concealed in the trees along the Great North Road, awaiting the dozen armed men that were riding single file from Nottingham. They were the first of Gisbourne's mounted guard, clad in chain mail and helmets, and news of their coming had been sped to Robin's camp by some of the spies he'd had watching the road. The outlaws might have cut a number of the soldiers down with a barrage of arrows from the trees, but the men's armor would certainly have protected some of them, and an attack upon this contingent would only provoke a larger and more dangerous retaliation from Gisbourne's entire company immediately following. Besides, Robin was never a proponent of indiscriminately killing his enemies. Stealing from them, yes—even beating them black and blue if he felt they deserved some rough justice. But killing was for him in a different category.

He crouched on the branch of a sturdy elm high above the road, with Little John sitting directly below him on a thicker branch, and closer to the trunk. John's size made him a little warier of sitting in trees than Robin's average disciple, but he was comfortable enough here. The two had not had much chance to talk since John returned from Saint Mary's Abbey, and now Robin opened up to his lieutenant about what they had found in Sir Walter's grave.

"Stones," he whispered as the two outlaws stared down the road toward Nottingham, waiting for the first sign of Sir Guy's guard. "Nothing in the coffin but stones. And nobody in the castle had any chance to view the young fellow's corpse. I'm telling you John, that boy's as alive as you or me, but Lady Abigail of Derby and your good friend Abbot Robert of Saint Mary's sure have gone to great pains to make everybody *think* the poor boy is dead. Why would that be, do you suppose? He's secreted away for some evil purpose, is that it?"

"No great mystery there," John answered. "If Walter's dead, they can blame Sir Richard's son, and that allows them to charge him with manslaughter and fine him some unheard of sum that forces his father to forfeit his land."

"But why *keep* the boy hidden? Where is he now and what's he doing? If the land grab failed, why is Walter still dead?"

"There's got to be more to it than just a land grab cooked up between the abbot and Lady Abigail," Little John answered. "Who's this girl the abbot was concerned about, and what inheritance was he referring to when that serving lad overheard him talking to the bishop? She's mixed up in this whole land scheme too. It can't be Lady Abigail. Even if she's a beauty as you say, she's well beyond the age when anybody would call her a girl."

"And Walter didn't have any sisters that I have heard of. For that matter, there's no sisters of Sir Peter's in Sir Richard's family either. So 'the girl' is a mystery," Robin mused.

"A mystery, but looks like she's the key to everything else," Little John agreed. Then added, "Hush, now, here they come!"

An armored guard led the way, carrying a gold banner emblazoned with a sable lion rampant—that is, standing with both forearms raised. The Gisbourne family crest, Robin reasoned. An interesting choice for a band of soldiers protecting the *king's* castle. But let that pass. Following the lead officer, in single file, were a dozen more soldiers, all of whom were riding slowly and studying the surrounding trees. Well, if this was how they planned to search for the outlaws of Sherwood, Robin thought, he didn't have a great deal to fear. They hadn't yet figured out that if they really wanted to search for what was hidden in the woods, they probably actually needed to leave the road. But this was fine with Robin. He was in no hurry to help them learn that lesson.

Because of their searching approach, the guards were separated by at least thirty to forty feet as they moved along the road, and none of them was paying any attention to anything going on behind them, so intent were they on what might be hiding to their left or their right. The last rider, Robin could see, was trailing a string of horses intended as replacement mounts for any of the guards' horses that grew tired. There were ten fine horses, strung out for a good thirty yards behind the rearmost rider. And as Robin watched, he saw Will Stutely dart out furtively from the right side of the road, dash toward the hindmost trailing horse and with a single slick motion cut the horse's tether and lead it into the woods on the left side.

Not to be outdone, David of Doncaster, after a respectable pause, flitted out from the left side of the road and even more quickly had cut the next trailing horse from the line and ushered it over to the right side. Jack Rolfe, Wat o' the Crabstaff, and lanky Will Scathelock had all successfully snared one of the mounts, with none of the guard being the wiser, by the time the rearmost rider with the trailing mounts—now at half their original number—was passing Robin's tree.

"Well I can't be outdone by those youngsters," Robin whispered to Little John. "Wish me luck, then…"

"I'll wish you better sense," Little John replied as Robin dropped lightly down from his branch, unsheathed his poignard, and after assuring himself that the rearmost guard had no intention of turning around, glided out into the open and held the muzzle of the trailing horse, now the fifth in line. "Shh…" Robin breathed, but the horses, well aware of what was happening, were taking it all in stride, assuming this was just what was supposed to occur, and who could figure these crazy humans out anyway. Robin cut the horse's tether with a single stroke, but as he started for the trees on the other side of the road, his foot scraped on some gravel with enough of a sound to make the hindmost guard turn. It was all they needed.

"Halt! Thief!" cried the guard, and at that point the rest of the guards had turned.

"It's one of the outlaws!" another shouted, and a third called, "Grab him!" And as the whole company began to turn for him, Robin leapt onto the animal's back and turned him around, galloping in the direction of Nottingham.

"Oh, bugger," Little John grumbled, notching one of his arrows and letting it fly at the guard who had taken off after Robin most quickly. John's arrow was followed by a barrage from both sides of the road as Robin's meinie loosed their arrows at the surrounded troops, then fell back as the guards who had not been wounded attempted to rush into the trees after them. All of Robin's men slipped away, to meet up again, with their six new horses, at their home base of the old oak. They would be safe, for now, but Gisbourne's company, trudging back to Nottingham Castle with seven wounded and six fewer horses, would be far more cautious, and determined, the next time they met.

CHAPTER EIGHT

Now June had come to Sherwood there were swallows and swifts, cuckoos, robins, even a golden oriole or two singing and twittering in the branches of the oaks and birches. The scent of the trumpet-like honeysuckle, the shy violets, and the beautiful but deadly foxglove brightened up the forest along the Great North Road. Sir Guy of Gisbourne's patrolling guards were treated to all these delights as they spent the late spring scouring the woods for Robin Hood's company. It was pleasant duty, especially since, finding no sign of Robin or his men, they were never threatened with bodily harm or danger of any kind. And so the days passed. Sir Guy and the sheriff were only slightly annoyed, since, though they could not find the outlaws, the danger to traffic passing along the road seemed to have ground to a halt. Still, Sir Guy had vowed to track Robin down and hang him, and he was no closer to that goal than he had been his first day in Nottingham.

If there were any royal foresters in Sherwood—which there had not been since the death of the old king—they would have noticed a sharp reduction in the poaching of the king's deer in the southern part of the forest. But if those foresters were paying close attention, they would also have noted a sharp upswing in such illegal activity in the northern section of Sherwood. Somebody in that part of the wood was definitely eating pretty well.

It was during these relatively peaceful days promising

unmolested travel on the Great North Road that a party of young people were riding north along the highway, chattering amongst themselves as young people do. There were four ladies, the youngest perhaps seventeen and the oldest no more than twenty, dressed in light summer finery, and with their hair uncovered and flowing freely, each of them having woven garlands of fresh flowers in their tresses, one of them blonde, two with brown hair, and one whose locks were nearly black. The four ladies were accompanied by three young gallants, perhaps pages or squires from some noble household by the look of their clothing. They had trailing behind them a pack horse, who seemed burdened with too many bundles, so that it appeared unlikely that the group was undertaking a short day-trip. Whatever they were about, they would be about it for some time.

Or so it seemed to Robin, who was watching from the side of the road along with Little John, Much, Will Stutely, Alan a Dale, and Sir Palomides. All were now on horseback, since the band had so fortuitously been able to increase their stock. Palomides was mounted on his great war horse Zulfiqar. The Moorish knight seldom took part in the waylaying of travelers, finding the role of highwayman somewhat beneath his dignity as a knight, but because of the threat of armed guards from Nottingham castle, he was insistent that he accompany the road bandits on this, their first expedition since moving to their new headquarters. And he was not happy that this particular heist involved the waylaying of ladies.

"I can't even imagine what some of my old comrades in the service of chivalry would be saying if they could see me now," Palomides was grumbling.

"No doubt they'd want you to bend over backwards to make sure the ladies were comfortable while you were rifling through their purses," his jongleur Alan told him. "But if it bothers you, hang back. Maybe nobody will notice the silent Moor standing politely in the back while we rob them."

Robin was uncertain how to accost the party. The three young men were armed, two with daggers and one with a short sword whose scabbard hung from his belt. He had no doubt that youthful hormones were flowing aplenty among and between these noble youths, and could predict that the three courtiers would see it as their chivalric duty to keep their ladies from being robbed or taken to the outlaws' camp. They would not consider six forest ruffians as too many to engage in battle. And if violence did ensue, Robin could not guarantee the safety of those young men or even, he regretted to think, their ladies, who could easily, in the ensuing fracas, be caught accidentally in bowshot or sword-slash. And as he thought about the situation, he smiled suddenly, unexpectedly glad that Sir Palomides happened to be along with them on this particular outing.

"Listen," he said to the whole group. "Here's what I want: Sir Palomides, you and I will ride out in front of the party and stop them." He looked the knight over from top to toe: He was a magnificent sight on his tall, noble destrier, and he wore his chain mail in addition to his great battle sword. "I want you to address them, Palomides. Speak them fair—you know how to speak in courtly phrases. Tell them we mean them no harm, that we request their presence at a venison feast in the forest, for which we will later ask for a modest payment. And meantime, the rest of you ride out behind the party, with bows notched and ready. That way, they will not feel they are being treated rudely, but they will be certain that resistance would be very unwise."

The Moorish knight pursed his lips, but then, seeing the wisdom in Robin's plan, and intending, like Robin, to avoid violence at all costs, he agreed. And the two of them rode out into the highway, turned toward the approaching party, and held up their hands. The approaching courtiers halted and the three young men's hands went immediately to their weapons, but straightaway their mouths gaped open at the sight of the accoutered knight in their path.

"Good ladies and gentlemen," Robin began. "We do apologize for accosting you this morning, but my name is Robin Hood." There was at that word an excited buzz among the seven youths. "And I and my foresters have, as it turns out, much more food than we can possibly eat for our dinner today, and are in need of company. My colleague here, Sir Palomides, will explain to you."

The knight moved his great stallion forward a step or two, and in low, soothing tones, like a musical entertainment, began to calm the gentlefolk's fears, and as he spoke, it was unlikely that any of the youths even noticed the four horsemen who swung in quietly behind them with bows at the ready. Or if they did, they were not alarmed by it.

"Gentles," Sir Palomides began, "be assured we mean you no harm, and want nothing from you but your company, your good will, and perhaps a few coins from your purses to contribute to our coffers and help us afford the elaborate supper we will soon be preparing for our next guests. Who knows? If the meal goes well, I may even entertain you all on the lute with one of my own courtly compositions as the dessert is brought in."

But that was as far as the Moorish knight got, for he was interrupted suddenly from a completely unexpected quarter. The blonde lady, one of the older courtiers of the party, had been gawping at Sir Palomides since he'd first ridden out, and having started when Robin introduced him, now could contain herself no longer and cried out in wonder, "Sir Palomides! It really *is* you! I couldn't believe my eyes and now my ears are telling me it's true! You're really here! You're alive and well—and in an outlaw band?"

She was a lively young lady with flashing blue eyes, who sat on her white palfrey with a sprightly dignity and what seemed a boundless energy, and so delighted was she to have come upon Sir Palomides himself that she couldn't keep herself from approaching him with an outstretched hand.

The knight squinted at her for a moment until, suddenly a smile of recognition flashed across his face. "Lady Mary, is it not? The lady Mary of Winchester, lady-in-waiting to the old queen herself, are you not she?" He took her by the hand, bowing toward her courteously as she approached.

"Have I changed so very much, my lord, that you could not recognize me at sight? Have I become an old maid, as I so often feared?"

She batted her eyelashes at him with mock modesty, as the knight, slightly abashed, answered, "No, no, madame, but you have lost your girlish demeanor and have blossomed into a true woman, of great beauty and charm."

"Aha!" the lady exclaimed. "So chivalry is not dead after all."

"Not quite," Sir Palomides agreed, "though it has certainly been moribund since the old king fell."

"And you," Lady Mary turned her blue eyes at last on Robin. "Robin Hood? Robin Poppycock! I know the captain of the old king's guard on sight, Mr. Robin Kempe."

"At your service, my lady," Robin bowed and, taking hold of her horse's bridle, led her, chatting gaily between himself and Sir Palomides, into the woods toward the bandits' new camp, where one of the king's newly-felled deer was even now roasting on a spit over an open fire. The other six courtiers, chatting among themselves, trotted along behind, accepting their detainment now as if it were a simple social engagement, while Little John and the others trailed behind, not sure what had just happened.

* * *

The outlaws' new camp was not yet quite so comfortable as their old one had been, but it had far more potential. Creswell Crags was a gorge cut through limestone, with low cliff walls honeycombed with caves and a stream flowing through. They had placed their camp where the stream widened into the broad "Crags Pond." This gave them an unlimited source of fresh water flowing right past their encampment, on a narrow green meadow between the cliffs and the pond. One of the caves they were using as a stable, and the horses seemed to like the feel of safety it afforded them. Several of the other caves were deep and roomy enough to provide as capacious an area as the finest castle on offer between Nottingham and York, and many of the couples had set up tents within residential caves themselves for the sake of privacy. The casual observer would see nothing on the meadow between the water and the caves to suggest any sort of permanent encampment here; there was a fire over which the venison was being roasted, and there were blankets and foodstuffs and a barrel of ale visible where the members of the band were gathered, but all of this except the ashes of the fire could be—and for safety's sake would be—swept into the caves at night. As for what was left of the campfire, there was no way for a sheriff's deputy or castle guardsman to distinguish it from any traveler's temporary fire, and so Robin Hood and his crew remained as undetectable as a group this large could be in a place like Sherwood.

As Robin and Palomides led their guests over the rough terrain into the gorge itself, the scent of roasting meat met their nostrils, and Lady Mary smiled at the sight of a curtal friar turning the spit with a few bustling women laying out bread and fruit, and with a few stout men in Lincoln green with long bows, shooting at a row of targets set up along the shore of the pond. "That seems a bit foolish," Mary said to Robin, as Sir Palomides excused himself to rush over and supervise the preparation of the meat. He didn't want to see it ruined by overcooking or the wrong combination of spices.

"What do you see as foolish, my lady?" Robin asked.

"Well, shooting the arrows toward the pond," she replied. "If they miss the target, they lose the arrows. That can't be economical."

Robin looked at her with a wry grin, as if she were the most naïve girl imaginable. "Well, it's a real incentive *not* to miss, then, wouldn't you say?" And while she laughed, Robin said more seriously, "The fact is, my lady, that my men are the best archers in England. When they miss, it is when their arrow falls outside the red of the bull's eye. None of them even admit the possibility of missing the target altogether."

They had reached the camp by now, and Robin helped Mary alight from her palfrey, as Alan a Dale and Little John were helping the others to dismount, and Much was leading away the horses to water and feed them. Thorvald had come up and taken the pack horse as he usually did, with the intent, Robin knew, of glancing through the contents of the bundles to see what valuables might be to hand. With such a group of courtiers, Robin was anticipating a fairly significant haul.

But for the moment, he was enjoying passing the afternoon with the lovely young Lady Mary of Winchester. The other guests were being made welcome by Friar Tuck and Sir Palomides and Little John and Haakon, and while Palomides was too busy with his culinary concerns to sing one of his own compositions, Alan a Dale entertained the picnickers with a mournful ballad about a hard-hearted maiden named Barbara Allen, who spurned a knight who ended up dying for love of her. It was the sort of tale the romantic heart of Lady Mary loved to listen to, and she had tears in the corners of her eyes as she applauded Alan's efforts, and she turned to Robin with an embarrassed shake of her head.

"That's me," she said. "Always with the soft heart for a sad story. My sister always used to chide me for it. She was practical—and a bit cynical, truth be told. But I was always a sucker for a love story."

"And yet, you've never married," Robin observed. "You're still a maid, as I observe, traveling with other maidens, and a few chivalrous protectors."

Mary rolled her eyes and whispered, "Three boys whose egos need a lot of stroking, so that Lord Peveril gave them the assignment to escort four of us from Codnor Castle to Peveril Castle, the estate of his uncle, the Earl of Chesterfield. It seemed like a walk in the park, with nothing likely to molest us on *that* short jaunt. And then you showed up! From what we'd heard, the fearsome Robin Hood was only active in southern Sherwood. Weren't *we* surprised!"

"Well we do aim to entertain, if nothing else," Robin said, gnawing one last bit of flesh off his joint of venison. "But you managed to dodge the question, didn't you?"

"You never asked one, did you?" Mary asked innocently, raising one eyebrow quizzically. "But all right, I hear that unasked question loud and clear. No, I'm in my twenty-first year and still unmarried, which in my social class makes me an old maid. But maid I am. Mary the maiden. Oh, you may remember, I was plighted to the knight Sir Thomas back when you knew me. And he was young and handsome just like in a love story, but he was killed in the late king's last battle—just like in a very sad love ballad. One that your Alan a Dale might sing to his lute. And I don't have family left to arrange another marriage for me. These others," she jerked her head toward the three other ladies, sitting and flirting on the green with their three escorts, "they're all still on the market, though they all expect an arranged contract pretty soon. Not me, though."

"No prospects?"

"No money, no land, no prospects," Mary agreed. "The old queen still had some contacts when she entered the convent. Most of the rest of her ladies went with her, you probably know, but it just wasn't for me. I still have those romantic notions, you know. Anyway, she was able to get me a position as lady-in-waiting to Lady Lydia Peverel—that's the granddaughter of the current earl. It hasn't been a bad position. Might even be getting more prestigious now."

"Oh? How do you mean?"

"Well, the word is that the old earl is on his deathbed. Not likely to hold on for another fortnight. And guess who's his heir?"

"Your mistress is it, then?"

"Got it in one," Lady Mary confirmed. "She's the earl's only direct descendant, and so he's made her his sole heir. A lot of his other relatives got their noses out of joint—not the least of which was Lord Peveril of Codnor—but the earl saw to it that Lady Lydia was officially pronounced Countess of Chesterfield, and so she's the one who takes over once the old boy passes."

"And so you lot are moving up there now, in preparation for this Lady Lydia to take over," Robin concluded. "Well, best wishes to you, and to her. She's traveling separately, is she? Or is she already there, at the earl's castle?"

Lady Mary, who thus far had been chattering away like a magpie, now stopped, rearing up unconsciously as if she'd been a mare and someone had pulled up on her reins. "Oh dear," she said after a moment. "Perhaps I've been talking too much? I'm not sure that all the Peverils would be happy with my telling you these things."

Robin, taken aback, was quite unaware that he'd heard anything that could be construed as a family secret, and smiled at Lady Mary in what he hoped was a disarming manner. "Surely, my lady, the naming of this Lady Lydia to countess status is no great matter to be kept from us peasants. I've never heard of a secret countess before. Or is it not generally known that the old earl is in ill health? I am not acquainted with either one of these high personages, my lady, so the goings on in their family circle are not of special interest for me, and you needn't fear I'll speak of these things, if they are not for common consumption."

Lady Mary put out her bottom lip in pensive pout, and then looked at Robin with a furtive side-eye. "Talking to you has been like talking to an old friend," she admitted. "Even though we were never really friends back in the old days—you up there in the barbican shouting insolent jibes down at the folk who moved through the gate, me bored to death with my embroidery up in the queen's chamber. But still it's been like talking to someone from home after being gone for years and years." She shrugged her narrow shoulders and smiled at him. "That home is gone now though, and what's left of it lives on in people like you. The queen is gone, and my Thomas is gone, and my dear sister is gone too. But you are here, and what still goes on from that time goes on in you, and in me. And in Sir Palomides there," she glanced at the knight, happy at his spit over his open fire.

"And in Thorvald the dwarf there," Robin nodded, "and in Alan of Winchester, from your own home town, standing off there with Thorvald and the horses. Which reminds me…" now Robin looked at Mary and cast his eyes down, knowing that she was probably not going to like this part of the entertainment. He stood up and shouted to the dwarf, "What's the verdict, Thorvald? What's the tally of the packhorse?"

The dwarf held high a purse, and called back, "It's all in 'ere. An 'undred gold nobles, I make it."

"A hundred gold pieces it is, my lads!" Robin called out to the whole band. "And what shall we do with these? What's your pleasure, men?"

"Divide the spoils in the usual way," Little John called back. "Let these gentles pay the standard rate for their meals!"

Calls of "Right!" and "Hear! Hear!" arose from the rest of the assembled crew, and the courtiers began to look at one another anxiously. One of the other ladies stood up, crying, "You bandits are going to rob us of all our money, then?" And looking at Lady Mary, she pleaded, "Marion, don't let them take our only treasure!"

"And what do you expect *me* to do about it?" Mary called back.

"Marion?" Robin asked, raising his eyebrows.

"Just their nickname for me," Mary said. "But just how big a thief are you actually, Robin 'Hood' if I must call you that now?"

"Call me Hood and I'll call you Marion," Robin suggested. "As for your question, Thorvald is separating the spoils even now. Listen to his verdict."

The dwarf now held up a smaller bag, and called out "Thirty-three nobles for our band!" He held up another: "Thirty-three nobles for the poor!"

"I'll take those, my lad," Friar Tuck said, snatching them before Thorvald could answer. He must have a recipient in mind already, Robin thought to himself.

"And thirty-four nobles for the seven little nobles we've had to dinner," Thorvald said, holding up the last little bag, and tossing it to the woman who had complained. She was not happy, but sat down quietly anyway, thankful that the outlaws' meal tax was only sixty-six per cent, and not the whole treasury.

Lady Mary crossed her arms, miffed that Robin could treat an old friend in this fashion. "Well," she told him, "I thought you were a bit more of a gentleman. I'm sorry to see that you are just the bandit of Sherwood that everybody says you are. I would apologize if I thought you'd be offended at our taking leave of you now. But, truth to say, I don't care whether you are offended or not." And with that she made as if to rise, until Robin reached out and touched her arm in a silent plea that she might stay longer.

"My lady," he began in his courtliest manner. "If I *were* a 'gentleman,' I'd have taken all of your money and wouldn't care if I left you to beg, which is what their noble masters do to the villeins who work their lands. You can be sure, when you say that 'everybody says' I am a bandit, it is only those 'gentlemen' that you converse with who say so, not the great majority of folk that live on the land. That third of your treasure we have given to Friar Tuck will be going to help the poor left destitute by some of those fine 'gentlemen.' I am fairly certain that neither you nor your companions will starve, or even go without a single new dress over the next year, for want of that pittance you have given us today. And you have gained a fine picnic dinner in the bargain!"

Lady Mary could feel herself blushing to the very roots of her hair. Robin's words had made her recall the days of her own youth, when her father, a knight who had lost almost everything he owned, had left his daughters impoverished, until through the connections of their uncles they'd found themselves in the household of the old queen. From her own experience she could understand poverty, though not to the point of starvation. But she could also tell Robin a thing or two about gentlemen who did *not* oppress their laborers, and she knew that Robin knew of some himself. What about his own man, Sir Palomides, in whom he had an example right under his nose? Mary, who had spent nearly all of her twenty years in the habit of speaking before she thought, was momentarily tongue-tied amid her own conflicting thoughts.

Her hesitation gave Robin the opening he needed, and he pounced on it. "Dear Marion," he began, using the intimate new nickname she had allowed him. "It would grieve me if I thought you would take away only unfavorable impressions from our chance meeting. Spending this time with you in pleasant conversation and memories of happier days has been the most congenial hour I've spent since retreating to these woods. And to assure you that nothing you've said shall be bruited about, whatever it is you don't want known, let me do this: I will tell you a great secret of my own, that would cause me grave difficulties if it came out—and I will trust you with my secret, to prove that you can trust me with yours."

Marion unfolded her arms. Robin could see that his words were having their desired effect on her. And she could see that he thought as much, but was willing to let him go on thinking so because in fact she too had had a most pleasant experience at the outlaws' feast and was unwilling to let it end so abruptly without some hope of another meeting. She allowed herself a faint half smile and a coy look, saying, "And what is this great secret of yours, Robin Hood, champion of the forest's villeins?"

Robin glanced about quickly to ensure that none of his men was approaching, and lowered his voice so that Marion had to lean closer. "A few weeks ago," he began, "we had an impoverished knight to dinner. Sir Richard at the Lee. He owed a great abbot some four hundred nobles, which he had no prospect of repaying. If he defaulted on that loan, he would lose his familial estate, lands and castle that had been in his family for seven generations."

"I have heard that name," Lady Mary said. "He had a son, if I'm not mistaken, called Sir Peter of Verysdale. I know because it was said that this Sir Peter had ambitions to marry my lady, Lydia. That is before she became the Countess Lydia. But at any rate this Sir Peter has gone into exile or something, has he not?"

"Crusading," Robin clarified. "But yes, it is the same family. In any case, the secret I am revealing to you is this: Without the knowledge of the rest of my men except Little John alone, I made the poor knight a gift of the four hundred nobles from our community coffers. Well, we called it a loan, but I don't expect sir Richard will ever be rich enough to pay me back. But at least he won't lose his estates. So now you know a secret that could ruin me with my men. But I will trust you not to betray me."

Again Mary thought of her father, and her heart warmed to this brash outlaw, who had helped a knight in similar straits as her disgraced parent. And she was again struck by how little this act squared with his earlier attitude toward "gentlemen." This time, though, words did not fail her. "How generous you are to this class of people you despise," she said.

Robin shrugged. "Sir Richard was a good man," he admitted. "Perhaps the exception that proves the rule."

"Ha. Even you don't believe that," Marion suggested. "There are devils and angels in all classes. And a whole lot of everyday sinners like you and me. But listen: You've told me a secret to show your trust, so I'm going to return the gesture. You asked me whether the lady Lydia was already waiting for us all at the earl's castle. I didn't answer because she is not, and the lady's kinsman Sir Hugh, lord of Codnor Castle, has forbidden anyone to talk about it or ask about it. None of us know where she is. She disappeared a little over a month ago and none of her ladies have heard anything from her. But Sir Hugh probably knows where she is, or at least he gives the impression he does. He has told us that, as an unmarried woman in control of a significant fiefdom, Lady Lydia will be in great danger once she becomes countess, and so is being kept in a secret location until an appropriate husband is found for her, and she can rule her lands under his protection and guidance. So there, that is my secret. And honestly, like you, I would be likely to lose my position if it comes out that I've told you this. So keep it quiet."

"I...will..." Robin said thoughtfully. "But it strikes me that perhaps your Lady Lydia may not *want* to be kept 'safe' until her relatives sell her into marriage."

Marion gave Robin a startled look. "Exactly what I've been telling the other ladies," she said. "But no man I know has ever gotten that point. Maybe there's hope for you after all, Robin Hood."

"My lady," he answered, standing up and giving her an exaggerated bow, "My *only* hope is in your good wishes."

Lady Mary arose and presented her hand to Robin in her own exaggerated courtesy. As he took the hand and kissed it, she said, "I see my companions are eager to leave." Indeed, they were all standing near their palfreys, ready to mount them and be on their way, and the three young ladies were waving to her to spur her on. "I thank you for a truly memorable afternoon. Perhaps we can do it again sometime, when I will be sure to carry no money at all upon my person."

"It strikes me you are less than serious," Robin said, with more than flirtation in his voice. "But I would welcome another afternoon with you, my lady. Now tell me, before you go: You told me at first that you have remained a maid through these turbulent years. Is that a state you would wish to maintain, or might a man entertain hopes of eventually altering that situation?"

The lady lowered her head and replied demurely as she left him, "Well, I suppose an appropriate match might be made, if such a man could be found," she answered. "But for the foreseeable future, I shall most certainly remain a maid."

"Then I will always think of you as my Maid Marion," Robin replied, adding, "Until we meet again," under his breath.

CHAPTER NINE

Peveril Castle, seat of the ailing Earl of Chesterfield, was a larger and much more comfortable castle than Codnor had been, and after Lady Mary arrived late the next day and was welcomed with her charges as the new countess's senior lady-in-waiting, she was shown the rooms that would be hers and the other ladies', adjacent to the bedchamber wherein the old earl was now breathing his last. That chamber would become the new countess's private quarters as soon as she took up residence in the castle.

The rooms were rather spacious for ladies' residences, and Marion realized that this was, of course, because these rooms had been intended for the lord of the castle and the men who served as his retainers. The castle's builders had never imagined that women would be quartered here. And she allowed herself a little inward smile when she thought about that. She was pleased with the rooms: They were bright, with shuttered windows that could be opened to the sun, and they were warm, with bright tapestries lining the walls, depicting the story of a unicorn hunt. Yes, this was a place she could be quite comfortable, she decided.

What surprised Marion more than anything was when one of the pages, a thirteen-year old boy dressed in the blue and silver livery of the Peverils, announced to her that Lord Peveril had been waiting for her arrival and wanted a word with her. Marion had not even realized that the Lord of Codnor had intended to come to Peveril today, and was particularly surprised that he had arrived before she had. Then she realized that Sir Hugh must have come up the Great North Road while she and her companions had been lunching with Robin and his meinie. The thought ran through her head that it was too bad for Robin—if he and his men had waited for her and her group to pass, and had instead waylaid Lord Peveril on the road, they'd have certainly found more than a hundred nobles on his person. Bad luck, boys, she thought.

The page told Marion that Lord Peveril wanted her to come down to his own temporary personal lodgings, in a small solar on the ground floor. She realized that Lord Peveril, in the absence of the new Countess Lydia and of the control of the moribund earl, had asserted his own authority here and had begun to issue his own commands. What she didn't understand was why he hadn't set himself up in what she was now thinking of as the administrative suite. Perhaps he intended to act as de facto lord of the castle while his cousin kept the titular role—and rooms—of the countess. She followed the page without demur through the passageways in the castle until, arriving at Lord Peveril's door, he announced her as "Lady Mary of Winchester, my lord."

Sir Hugh Peveril, lord of Codnor Castle, was a man of substantial bulk, most of it clinging to his midsection. His pear-shaped face was flat with jowls that weighed down the corners of his mouth into a perpetual frown. He had a high forehead that encroached upon his hairline, for his dark hair was thin on top, though luxuriantly long on the sides and back, and curled under like a lady's. His large brown eyes stared out at her through their drooping lower lids like those of a gentle mastiff hound.

"So you've made it," Sir Hugh began without prelude. "We feared you may have been waylaid on the road!"

"Oh, it was such a lovely day that we all decided to have a picnic lunch in the woods, on a green by a wide stream there. We sported there for some time before remembering ourselves and getting back on the road." Marion was proud of herself for coming up with that innocuous sounding explanation on the spot, particularly since it wasn't really a lie. Except maybe a little, by omission. Then she thought to add, "We were quite unaware that you would be following us here, my lord. Why, if I may ask, did you bother?"

"Oh," Sir Hugh began, shifting his eyes nervously, "that's easily explained. You and your party left two days ago after terce, but even before sunrise I had received an urgent message from this castle that the old earl was not likely to survive the day. I thought that he should have some family here, at the end. After all, Earl Ranulph is my own dear uncle. There are physicians in with him now, who will keep me informed of his progress… er, his decline, and I can be with him at the end. Not that he will know it—I am informed he is completely unresponsive. A priest has just performed extreme unction on him, but he was unaware of the presence of the body and blood of our Lord. The priest remains in the sickroom even now as well. I intend to return there once our interview is finished."

Just at that moment a servant came in. Not the page who had conducted Marion to Sir Hugh's room, but a lad of nineteen or twenty, dressed in a brown tunic covered by a white apron. He was apparently a lad from the cookhouse, with a red face and hair that hung down in clumps, as if styled with kitchen grease. He carried a pewter tray with a pitcher and two pewter goblets. "'Scuse me for interruptin', me lord, but you were wantin' some mulled wine I believe, sir?"

"Right, yes, thank you Nicholas," Lord Peveril said automatically. "Set it there, will you?" And he gestured to a small circular table standing between the two wooden chairs in the chamber. "Please, be seated, my dear," and with that he continued to gesture, pointing out one of the chairs while seating himself in the other. "Care for some wine?"

"None for me, my lord," Marion replied. "We drank quite enough at our picnic. I'll need nothing else today."

The serving lad, who'd waited to hear the outcome of this exchange, nodded to himself and said perfunctorily, "If there'll be nothin' else, sir, I'll return to the kitchen," and headed out the door.

"Yes, thank you Nicholas," Sir Hugh muttered, without giving the lad another look, and then poured himself a generous serving of wine and took a healthy swig.

As he did so, Marion, having considered Sir Hugh's last comment, resolved to be bold and test her own supposition about the lord's presence. "I thought that perhaps you had come because, in the absence of my lady, the countess, you were planning to insert yourself here as the authority in the castle." After a short space in which Marion swallowed nervously, she added, "Sir."

The corners of Sir Hugh's mouth twitched upward as far as his jowls would let them, in a reasonable facsimile of a closed-mouth smile. He was choosing to give Lady Mary's assertion the most generous possible interpretation. "Certainly there must be someone on the premises to look out for my cousin's interests once the estate loses its rightful castellan, and as her closest male relative, that duty falls to me. Indeed, I expect she will expect me to stay on as governor of the castle until she marries, at which time I expect her new husband will take charge of that responsibility. But for now, I am here to make sure the estate continues to function smoothly."

Lord Peveril had begun to sweat rather heavily, and he wiped his brow on the sleeve of his tunic as he took another long swallow of his wine. He poured another cup as Marion asked, "You say you are my lady's closest male relative—after her grandfather, Earl Ranulph. Why is it you have not inherited the title of earl from Sir Ranulph, then? I've never really understood quite how you are related."

Sir Hugh's new grin actually revealed his teeth, many of which were still sound. He was quite happy to regale Lady Mary with the Peveril family pedigree. "My father, Thomas, was the current Earl Ranulph's younger brother. They were sons of the first Earl of Chesterfield, Sir William Peveril. Ranulph had one son, Stephen, a chivalrous knight who died well before his time of a fever, when his daughter was still a small child."

"That would be my mistress, then?"

As Marion asked this Sir Hugh winced for a moment, his hand moving toward his substantial belly. He suppressed a large belch, then apologized, saying, "Forgive me. I must have eaten something that disagreed with me. Perhaps some more wine will settle my stomach." With that he downed the rest of his glass and poured himself the last of the pitcher. "But yes, to answer your question. Lady Lydia was the daughter and only child of Sir Stephen Peveril and his noble wife, Lady Margaret Le Strange. Since he died young, he had no other children, so that she is the only direct descendant of Earl Ranulph."

"So you are…what? My Lady's cousin? Or second cousin?"

"Her father was my first cousin," Sir Hugh explained, once again wiping the sweat from his forehead. "Making her my second cousin, I believe."

"First cousin once removed, as I think the terminology goes," Marion corrected him primly. "So, there are no other Peverils about?"

"My own dear wife Susannah died early as well—she died in childbirth with what would have been my son, but the poor lad was born dead. I got no children with her. I did get the castle that had been in her family, Codnor Castle, so I cannot say the marriage failed. The earl and my father had a sister, my Aunt Eleanor, but she is in a convent in Hereford and so has no children of her own. That is, unless the nuns are keeping it a secret." He smiled wryly and Marion gave him a quick close-lipped half smile to humor him.

"I did have a younger brother as well, Sir Aubrey Peveril. Now he was a roisterer and a madcap. Died in a tavern brawl in York. Never married, but he did beget a child—a by-blow of some night he spent in the bed of some tavern wench in Sheffield, I think it was. Some scrawny little red-haired girl they named Maude. But he acknowledged her as his own, and before he died he sent her to me to foster her. But there it is, then, that's the lot." He wiped his forehead again and drank some more wine. "The only male relative, me. And not a chance for the earldom."

Not a chance unless you murder my mistress, Marion thought. That'd give you a clear shot at the prize. Oh no, I do not trust you, Sir Hugh. I do not trust you as far as I can throw you. And with your bulk, she thought as she eyed him fidgeting nervously in his chair, I couldn't even lift you, let alone heave you anywhere.

"But family relations aside, let me talk about why I wanted to meet with you here in my private chamber," Sir Hugh began, fixing Marion now with what looked to her like a hungry eye. He drank the last of his wine, saying as he put the cup down, "My mouth is quite dry tonight. I may have to call for some more wine. But listen, my dear. As I've told you, my wife has long since passed. As you must know—you are not a young girl any more, but a woman of some experience, I'm sure—as you must know, a man has certain needs which must be assuaged from time to time if he is to remain sound in body and mind." By now he was breathing quite hard. Marion was fairly certain she knew the cause of his labored breathing, and shrunk away from him slightly, as much as she could while remaining seated in her chair.

"I'm not sure I understand what you mean, my lord," she responded innocently, looking over her shoulder to see whether the young page was still in calling distance, or the door to the solar was open. Neither was the case.

"My dear, do not play the blushing virgin with me..." Sir Hugh pressed.

"Sir, I am not called 'Maid Marion' for nothing," she replied, beginning to rise from her chair, the better to beat a hasty retreat.

"I can make it worth your while, Lady Mary," he offered, now panting, but adopting a more formal tone. "It is not too late for me to take a new wife—a young one that might bear me sons, heirs to my estates which, who knows, might one day include Peveril Castle."

Sir Hugh reached out to take her by the arm, but as his hand reached her, he seemed unable to open or close it. Puzzled, he stared at the hand, then looked at the doorway. His eyes opened wide, as if seeing in the empty space some specter, and he cried out, "You can't say I did it! No one told me where you were!"

"What?" Marion asked, bewildered as she looked at the empty doorway. "Who are you..." But she looked back at Sir Hugh barely in time to see him wheel about suddenly in his chair, hold his hand to his head, and pitch forward onto the stone floor. Gingerly, she poked his fallen body. Then she felt for a pulse. Then she sat back in her chair, dumbfounded. Sir Hugh was dead.

* * *

The black-robed physician examining the body on the floor of the solar found no sign of life, and as he rose from his knees another black-robed figure, the castle's chapel priest, knelt to give Sir Hugh last rites, though it was hard for Marion to imagine that Sir Hugh's soul would be mounting to paradise any time soon, what with his having died in the midst of what had certainly been shaping up to be a sinfully indecent proposal. But then, God works in mysterious ways, she acknowledged and turned her attention to the physician, who was asking her as gently as he could what Sir Hugh had been doing before he had collapsed.

"Well," she began, recovering from the shock Sir Hugh's dramatic sudden breakdown had thrown her into. "He had called me to his room here and was telling me about the earl's imminent death…"

"No longer imminent," the physician informed her. "The old earl left this thoroughfare full of woe just a few moments before young Jack came to fetch us from Sir Ranulph's sick room."

Marion had learned the young page's name when he had answered her shrill scream upon realizing that Lord Peveril was dead. She'd sent him to the earl's deathbed, ordering him to bring back a physician. And, while he was at it, a priest. Doctor Phineas had arrived moments before with the chaplain. Now Jack stood in the doorway, waiting to do anything at all that might help the situation, if anybody could think of anything appropriate for him to do. She crossed herself at the physician's news, then continued: "He had just finished telling me the reason he had relocated here to Peveril Castle for the time being, how he felt a responsibility as Countess Lydia's nearest male relative to protect her interests while she was still away from the castle."

"Yes," Dr. Phineas stroked his grey beard. "It's curious that she is not here, now the earl's death puts her in charge of the estate. Where is she?"

"I don't know! Sir Hugh told me she was being kept somewhere for her own safety, but even he apparently didn't know. So who does know? It's…quite a conundrum. How do we get word to her that she is now the ruling countess if nobody knows where she is?"

The physician shrugged as if to say it wasn't his problem, and returned to the subject of Sir Hugh's sudden affliction. "So you were simply talking to him, you say? Did you notice anything strange about his manner?"

"Not at first," Marion replied. "But he began sweating, for no particular reason that I could see. He had no fire in his hearth here, and it was comfortable enough. But he seemed quite thirsty, and kept drinking wine. I remember now, he did comment that his mouth was very dry. Oh, and he complained of a pain in his stomach. He thought he may have eaten something that disagreed with him."

The physician's eyes grew round when Marion mentioned the dry mouth and the stomach pains, and he stroked his beard again, muttering distractedly, "Lord spare me from such disagreements." And he reached for the wine pitcher, which was still on the table, and stared down at the few dregs at the bottom. He sniffed it carefully, then reached into it, taking a bit of the wine onto his finger and tasted it. His lips pursed and his nose wrinkled, and then he glared at Marion and asked, "Tell me, Lady Mary, did Sir Hugh seem to you…distracted before he collapsed?"

"Distracted? You mean, like, confused? Or, what, agitated?"

Doctor Phineas nodded, but leaned forward and added, "Even mad, perhaps? Hallucinating?"

Marion recalled Sir Hugh's last words, and nodded vigorously. "Indeed!" she cried. "He looked into the doorway," and she pointed to where Jack now stood, "and he said, 'You can't claim that I was the one who did it,' or something like that. But there was no one there."

"Yes, quite, quite," Doctor Phineas nodded with an air of satisfaction. "All these symptoms are consistent with poisoning."

"Poison!" Marion cried, and at that point the priest stood up as well with a horrified expression and echoed Marion's cry.

"Deadly nightshade," the physician clarified. "Also known as belladonna. Nasty stuff. I thought I detected a trace of it in the wine pitcher. Did you drink any wine?" He asked Marion, his eyes suddenly bulging again.

"No, no, thankfully I was not thirsty," she answered. "But let me understand what you're saying. Sir Hugh was murdered?"

"Without a doubt he was poisoned, by belladonna that someone had put into his wine," Doctor Phineas pronounced.

"But...but who could have done such a vile thing? And why?" Marion stammered.

"That is a question for the lord of the manor to inquire into," said the priest, and the physician nodded in agreement. "The question of murder must come before the manor court, after a thorough investigation."

"But there is no lord of the manor!" Marion said. "The old earl has just died. Lord Peveril lies here murdered. And the countess, who should inherit the responsibilities of the estate, is being held somewhere unknown! Who is lord of this manor?"

The old physician cleared his throat. "It would appear, Lady Mary of Winchester, that under the circumstances, you are the ranking noble in this place." Then, in response to the blank stare he was getting back from her, he added, "Perhaps you might appeal for judgment to some representative of the king. The lord of Sheffield Castle, for instance, or the new captain of the king's garrison at Nottingham Castle."

"That is probably the direction to go," the priest agreed. "It certainly would promise more likelihood of success than to have a woman like yourself investigating this heinous act."

"Yes, I daresay," answered Marion, completely unconvinced as to the wisdom of this suggested course. "Well, I shall certainly ponder this. And ponder, as well, what steps might be taken to track down Countess Lydia. Thank you so much, Doctor Phineas for your help in this matter. And you, Father…uh, Father…"

"Father Thaddeus," the young priest said, giving her a slight bow.

"Father Thaddeus, I wonder if I can rely on you to see that these two bodies are taken care of and prepared for burial. And sometime tomorrow please let me know when we can expect their funeral rites. We may as well commit them to the earth at the same time, since they chose to leave us at the same time."

"I doubt that either *chose* his time," Father Thaddeus said, bowing again. "After all, 'we know not the hour,' eh? But yes, I will see them prepared, and let them lie in state in the chapel until we are ready for the commitment."

"Very well," Marion said, feeling suddenly very tired. "That will be all gentlemen," and as she said this, she marveled to herself how well and how quickly she had adapted to being The One In Charge. "Come, Jack," she said to the page. "See me up to my quarters. I have much to relate to my companions, and much to think about tonight."

As she left the room, she heard the physician and priest conversing. "Quite a successful day, I'd say," Doctor Phineas was saying.

"Successful?" Father Thaddeus answered with some surprise. "You lost not one but two patients tonight, didn't you?"

"Yes, yes," the physician said, waving off those trivial details, "but I definitely got the *diagnosis* right!"

* * *

The following morning, Lady Mary of Winchester paced about the new ladies' residence in Peveril Castle alone, the other ladies-in-waiting having gone to breakfast. She may have been the ranking noble of the manor, and might expect the servants and household retainers to submit to her decisions in the absence of any other authority—unless and until Lady Lydia, Countess of Chesterfield, arrived home from wherever it was she'd been hidden away—but in the sure and certain knowledge that someone in that castle had just committed the cold-blooded murder of the presumptive castellan of the Peveril estate, she felt nothing but vulnerable. There were a few household knights in the castle, sworn to serve Earl Ranulph, but she did not know how much she could count upon their loyalty now that the earl was dead, and she had no way of knowing whether one of them might not be behind this murder. The same was probably true of the skeleton crew of knights Sir Hugh had left behind at Codnor Castle. Could anyone in his retinue be trusted? Nor was it a great comfort to her that she might call upon the king's captain down in Nottingham, some forty-five miles distant. Sheffield, of course, was much closer, but the idea of sending to another lord to help put down lawlessness at Peveril Castle seemed inadvisable in a milieu in which royal power had waned so significantly, and where even the royal troops so recently established in Nottingham seemed so far away. Was there another alternative? Was there another source of help that she could turn to?

Marion smiled as the answer came to her. "Jack!" she called. The obliging page appeared instantly at her door. "Bring me young Giles of Huddersfield," she told him, and the young man was gone immediately. Marion went straight to a desk in the corner of the ladies' quarters, which stood directly under the woven tapestry image of a unicorn, its head lying in the lap of a virgin. In the desk was a sheet of parchment along with a pen and ink, and Marion quickly scratched out a note:

From Peveril Castle
To the hon. Robin Hood, Esquire, at Creswell Crags
Robin, I turn to you, having no closer or truer ally. Murder has occurred here at this fortress and I have no one I can trust to help me seek out the murderer. I choose to trust you. Please come and bear me up.

Now she hesitated as to how to sign the letter. Suppose someone should waylay her messenger and find the note. Calling on a known outlaw for help in such a crisis might not be seen as appropriate by any other authority, even one sympathetic to her cause. So rather than sign "Lady Mary of Winchester," she signed the note in bold letters that read:

Maid Marion.

When Jack returned with the young squire Giles of Huddersfield, Marion had folded and sealed the note. She handed it to Giles and told him that she wanted him to take it as quickly as possible to Robin Hood back in Sherwood. "You remember the place where the outlaws took us for their venison feast?" she asked the dumbfounded squire. "That is where you will certainly find him. Give him the note, and when he reads it urge him to return with you here. He will not refuse if you beg him in my name."

"B…b…but Lady Mary," the bewildered Giles stammered. "The man is a rogue and a bandit. Why would you possibly want to bring him here, and in the midst of this…this crisis?"

"It's precisely *because* of this crisis I am sending for him," Lady Mary assured the babbling boy. "Now listen Giles: I am trusting you, perhaps with all our lives. And I am trusting him to bring us aid. Now go to the stables, saddle up the freshest horse there, and ride to Creswell Crags as fast as you can. It's a good thirty miles, isn't it? So I can't expect you back here before tomorrow night at the earliest. We will tread very cautiously until you return, but return you must. Don't take no for an answer. Now go, and God speed!"

Giles strode out of the room and into the bailey with all dignified haste, and Marion sat down at the desk with her head in her hands, trying to work out a plan for what to do until Robin arrived.

CHAPTER TEN

The sheriff's wife learned of her uncle's murder less than a week after the event: The mercenaries who'd accompanied Sir Hugh to Peveril Castle returned immediately to Codnor, where they brought the story to Codnor's chapel priest, Father Mark, who was heading to Nottingham the next day anyway, and planned to stop in to see his former parishioner, Maude Peveril. And of all the people in the world, it was Lady Maude who felt the death of Lord Peveril most intensely. Maude did not remember her mother, and her father was a shadowy figure whose image floated in and out of her life without ever making any impression on her memories. Sir Hugh had taken her in, out of what might be regarded as the goodness of his heart, though in truth it was more a distorted family pride and a desire to contain rumors of bastardy that clung to the little girl like a bad smell that must be washed away. Sir Hugh was as much a father figure as she had ever had, and though he seldom showed interest in her, and never showed love, he did see that she was fed, clothed and even educated to some degree by the chapel priest, Father Mark's predecessor, Father Timothy. Sir Hugh had even arranged a marriage for her with the respectable burgher John of Oxenford, who'd been appointed Sheriff of Nottingham. Recently, Sir Hugh had included her in a complicated scheme he had going with the Abbot of Saint Mary's Priory in York, one of the most powerful prelates in England. If all went as planned, Sir Hugh had told her, he would be sure she shared in the riches that were certain to be coming the family's way. He just needed her to take care of one little item.

Well, she had done her best with that task, and sent two brigands overseas to accomplish it. Now, for the first time, she began to have second thoughts. Sir Hugh's murder could be interpreted, at least from a certain point of view, as a case of his own methods being turned back against him. Maude did not like to think of it that way—after all, the man he had urged her to eliminate was someone standing in the way of her family's advancement in the world, which, she was as sure as Sir Hugh had been, was something that God Himself had ordained. She certainly believed that. Sir Hugh had believed that. Abbot Robert of Saint Mary's Abbey had encouraged Sir Hugh in it, and he was the most powerful prelate in this part of the country, so why shouldn't she believe God was smiling on their enterprise? But God had allowed Sir Hugh to be killed. And what was she to think of that? Was it possible that God did *not* favor the use of murder to achieve political ends, and that how you treated others might just affect how others treated you?

Maude was not often given to such abstract philosophizing. She had a bias for action, and she wanted to do something about what had happened to her uncle. But to do something she needed to find out who could possibly have gained from her uncle's death. The two villeins she'd sent after Sir Peter of Verysdale could not possibly have tracked him down and completed their task yet, so there was no possibility that it was revenge for Sir Peter's murder, even if the old man, his father, was prompted to exact such vengeance. Nor was it at all likely that her two hired assassins had let slip their assignment to any of their fellows before they'd left. If that had been the case, then it was she, not her uncle, who would have been the target of any reprisal. She had never let on who was behind the plot to kill Sir Peter. Then who? Who knew of Sir Hugh's involvement in the scheme? Only his fellow conspirators. And why would they...

That thought made Maude sit up suddenly. Sir Hugh was involved in a three-way plot with Abbot Robert and Lady Abigail of Derby, using Maude's cousin Lady Lydia as the unwitting pawn in their scheme, to consolidate the largest tract of lands in the midlands, and to share in the spoils. But splitting the profits two ways would be far more lucrative than splitting them three ways. There was no question as to who profited the most from this murder. Lady Abigail, Maude was quite certain, would never have the audacity to have conceived of this tactical murder on her own. No, it could only be the ruthless monk.

It crossed Maude's mind for an instant that her uncle may have had other dubious intrigues in his past, or even ongoing. But she shut down that idea. Her uncle, bless his heart, did not really have the imagination to carry on more than one devious treachery at a time. It had to be our very reverend abbot. Now, what was she going to do about it?

* * *

Within Nottingham Castle there was a lesser hall that served as a formal meeting place for Sir Guy of Gisbourne and any of the residents of Nottinghamshire who requested an audience with him. He had seldom used it since his arrival a month earlier, and now he did not seem particularly pleased to be meeting here with the sheriff and with his attractive but bumptious wife. He was afraid they might be there to chide him over his lack of progress in bringing the notorious outlaw band of Robin Hood to justice. In fact, he had had half of his guard scouring Sherwood Forest all along the Great North Road for three weeks and they had not made a single arrest. The only incident worth reporting had been the theft of six of their horses by what had almost certainly been a party of this Robin Hood's men. His guards had returned to that neighborhood of Sherwood again and again, but to no avail. They never saw another outlaw.

Sir Guy was not looking forward to questions on the subject of the Sherwood bandits from this fat, greedy burgher or his uppity wife, and his cold sneer as he sat across the table from them was hardly welcoming. But as it turned out, the subject of Robin Hood never came up.

"Sir Guy, we do thank you for this audience," John of Oxenford began in his most pompous tone. "I know you are a very busy man—as am I myself, for that matter. So I am sure you will trust me when I say this is a matter of some moment that my wife brought to my attention yesterday evening. The affair, as it happens, is well outside my jurisdiction, concerning a foul case of murder occurring in Derbyshire, rather than Nottinghamshire. You, however, with the king's mandate, are completely within your prerogative in dealing with such a crime."

At the word "murder," Sir Guy's ears pricked up, and he leaned his narrow face forward with interest. "You have my attention," he intoned in his deep baritone. "Tell me what you know about this murder."

Maude was being careful to give only as much information as she deemed necessary for her husband and Sir Guy to understand the gravity of her uncle's death, but to keep secret her own role in the events that had led up to it. Her husband might be willing to turn a blind eye to her part in the conspiracy, but Sir Guy had no reason to do so. But sober reflection had convinced her that if Abbot Robert had had the audacity to strike at Sir Hugh, his own partner in this business, he wouldn't blink at doing away with Sir Hugh's accomplice either. So something must be done about Sir Hugh's murder in order to protect her from the abbot's treachery, without putting her into legal difficulty with Sir Guy. So she needed to walk a fine line with her revelations.

"Sir Guy," she began, "the murder victim is…or was…my uncle, Sir Hugh, Lord Peveril of Codnor Castle…"

"Codnor? But that is close by—that's certainly in your jurisdiction, sheriff!"

"No, no," the sheriff said. "The murder took place in Peveril Castle, where Sir Hugh was visiting."

"Yes," Lady Maude continued, miffed at being interrupted when she'd had her performance so carefully rehearsed. "My uncle had gone to Peveril on a mission of mercy, to visit his own dying uncle, Lord Ranulph, the Earl of Chesterfield, to be a comfort to him in his last days. But alas, it was not to be. No sooner had he arrived than he was offered a carafe of wine by Earl Ranulph's attendants and, as it happened, the wine was poisoned. Deadly nightshade, I believe, was the diagnosis. It is not known who poisoned the drink…"

"And what of Earl Ranulph?" Sir Guy pounced before she could continue. "As lord of the manor, has he set out to investigate the matter, or does his ill health prevent him?"

"The earl died that same night," Maude told him. "No investigation has been conducted."

Sir Guy's eyebrows raised at that. "And was Sir Hugh to have been the earl's heir? Is that the problem?"

"Not exactly, Sir Guy," Maude answered. "Earl Ranulph's granddaughter, the lady Lydia Peveril, has already been named Countess of Chesterfield as the earl's heir."

"But she is a woman! What an eccentric bloke this Earl Ranulph must have been! Is the lady to be married?"

"I believe her marriage arrangements are a matter of some

debate within the family," Maude continued. "I myself am too distantly related to be party to these negotiations, but suffice it to say that Countess Lydia is not at Peveril right now. The castle seems to be in the hands of one of the countess's ladies-in-waiting, or so my sources tell me. A certain Lady Mary of Winchester."

Sir Guy pursed his lips and wrinkled the brow of his hatchet-like face. "Lady Mary…hmm. I don't believe I know of her. Is she of a very wealthy family?"

Becoming a little frustrated with Sir Guy's habit of continually steering her away from her intended target, Lady Maude hissed, "Noble but not wealthy, as I believe. In any case, she is hardly up to the task of finding the killer of my uncle. But what I must tell you now I do in the strictest confidence. It comes from my suspicions, based only on hints dropped in my correspondence with my uncle and those in his household over the past year or so."

The sheriff, as she expected, looked up at this, since she hadn't revealed any of her suspicions when she first broached the subject with him. But he had been, as usual, only a means to an end for her in this situation. It was really Sir Guy she was hoping to convince with this charade.

"Wha…?" John of Oxenford babbled. "What are these suspicions?"

"My lord," she said, addressing Sir Guy. "You have asked about the marriage prospects for my cousin, the Countess of Chesterfield. I know that my uncle had a strong interest in securing a marriage that would be most advantageous to the family. And I know as well that Robert Longchamp, the Abbot of Saint Mary's Abbey in York, also took a personal interest in that marriage. I believe that those interests came into conflict —so much so, I suspect, that the abbot himself may have found it in his own interests to eliminate my uncle, whom he may have seen as an obstacle to his plans for that marriage."

John of Oxenford scoffed. "The Abbot of Saint Mary's? The most powerful prelate in the north? You think he'd get his hands dirty with the murder of, let's face it my dear, a fairly petty lord like Sir Hugh? Why would he stoop so low? How's a one such as your uncle going to get in his way?"

"Let's not be too hasty to reject the notion," Sir Guy mused, more open to the idea. "There's a good deal of power and influence, not to mention a wealth of land, attached to this earldom of Chesterfield. And with this Sir Hugh gone, I assume that his Codnor Castle and estate would come under the influence of the earldom as well, would it not mistress Maude?"

Maude felt the slight like a slap to her face, but kept her expression fixed as she said in a low voice, "*Lady* Maude, if you don't mind, Sir Guy."

Gisbourne closed his eyes and waved his hand, brushing away such trivialities. "Yes, yes, *Lady* Maude, of course. But is it true that the estates of this Countess Lydia are increased by your uncle's death? And would in fact be increased as well if a suitable marriage is found? It seems to me there is enough here to pique the strong interest of the abbot. But enough to cause him to suborn murder? I don't know..."

"This Abbot Robert is as unscrupulous a schemer as any in Britain," Maude blurted out, exasperated. Then, realizing she might be acting somewhat more vehement, and more familiar with the abbot's character, than her supposed tangential relationship to the conspiracy called for, she added, appropriately subdued, "At least that is what my uncle implied to me on the occasion he confided to me the abbot's interest in the situation."

Her husband shrugged and raised his eyebrows in a gesture of vacillation. "All the more reason for us to tread carefully in this matter. If the abbot is so skilled in political maneuvering, in examining this case we could be stepping into deep water without knowing it."

Sir Guy seemed willing to follow where the sheriff was leading. "And I am new to this position in this territory. Surely the abbot has far more powerful friends than I have been able to cultivate since being sent here."

"But..." Lady Maude sputtered, bewildered at the response she was getting from these two officers of the king's peace. "This fat monk may be responsible for the cold-blooded murder of a castellan from a noble house. He flaunts the law. Isn't it your duty to arrest him if he is guilty?"

"My dear Lady Maude," Sir Guy patronized her. "This Abbot Robert has power, wealth, and reputation. People from here to Yorkshire respect and fear him for his extensive influence. If I am going to spend my time chasing wealthy barons and prelates for their peccadilloes, I shall make powerful enemies, and accomplish nothing, while at the same time allowing upstart ruffians like your Robin Hood and his outlaws to harass their betters on the public roads. I know my priorities, as, I take it, does your husband."

"Indeed," John of Oxenford acceded. "Abbot Robert is no one to be taken lightly. We should be studying how to ingratiate ourselves with him, not alienate him."

"But my uncle is *dead*," the exasperated Maude asserted.

"Exactly," Sir Guy said. "All the more reason to stay out of this business and give the abbot his head. We don't want to be next on his list. We would do much better to court his favor, it seems to me."

"Right," the sheriff nodded in agreement. "Come, then Maude, I'm sure Sir Guy has other more important matters to attend to," and with that he rose and took Maude by the arm to encourage her to come along.

Sir Guy stood and motioned them out, blustering, "Yes, yes, always a pleasure, do feel free to come and see me any time sheriff, Madame Maude."

Her face bright red with what Sir Guy and her husband took to be embarrassment and humility—but which she knew herself to be rage—Maude took on the role of the humble little woman, murmuring, "Yes, thank you Sir Guy, sorry to have bothered you..." while her mind spun with schemes of putting this oily "Sir" Guy in his place, and her husband for going along with it. "Madame" Maude· indeed. Just who did this little whipper snapper think he was? And how could John of Oxenford have the gall to think she would go home and be quiet about this murder? It was time he found out just who he was married to. She would have her revenge and she would get to the bottom of this murder and she would have the help of a much truer man than either of them. She was on her way to Sherwood.

* * *

She sat astride a handsome chestnut palfrey, her blue linen skirts arranged so as to keep her saddle covered and expose her yellow hosen below her knees. She was dressed light for summer, with a fashionably tight-laced bodice and a wimple with an expensive silk veil. She wore no cape or hood because of the warm June weather. From her saddle hung two large heavy-looking leather purses.

Two of the sheriff's recently appointed deputies rode on either side of Lady Maude, armed in black leather armor and carrying swords as well as crossbows. John of Oxenford had been lashed roughly by his wife's angry tongue for having given up so quickly her desire to send Sir Guy to investigate the murder of her uncle, and so had quickly said yes when she expressed her desire to ride north to Peveril Castle herself, to offer her support and guidance to those tasked with picking up the pieces after the earl's demise and the poisoning of the last remaining male heir in the Peveril family. Among other things, the sheriff was just happy to get her out of the house. But he made sure to send her with an armed escort. The outlaws of Sherwood had been relatively quiet of late, but there was no telling when or where Robin Hood might strike next. He also made Maude promise to send him word, via one of the deputies, when she had safely arrived at Peveril Castle.

It was a steady ride of at least two days from Nottingham to Peveril, but the truth was that Lady Maude did not expect to be on the road that long. She wore bright garments and a rich veil, and bore two heavy purses, with the object of making herself as conspicuous a target for highwaymen as she possibly could. Since her warning to Robin's men to beware of Sir Guy's patrolling guards, she knew they had been avoiding the Blue Boar or any other pub in or near Nottingham. In fact, she suspected they had moved deeper into Sherwood, the better to stay clear of the knights under Gisbourne's command. Thus there was no way that Maude could think of to get a message to Robin or any of his men. So she was trying the next best thing: let *him* find *her*. And what better way to do that than by putting herself in his way like a plump morsel in a baited trap.

But things weren't working out as she had planned. All day they had seen only six other travelers, all heading south, and they'd been as unmolested as a prioress treading the Nottingham streets on her way to church on a Sunday morning. Shadows were beginning to grow long on the road, and she was going to have to consider stopping for the evening, perhaps at Chesterfield if they could make it that far. What kind of bandits *were* these Sherwood outlaws, anyway? How were they going to make anything of themselves if this was as good as they could do?

So she was relieved rather than startled when a figure clad in Lincoln green dropped from the branches of a tree to stand directly in front of her in the road, holding up his hands. She bit her tongue to avoid crying out, "Well it's about time!" to the woodsman as he shouted, "I'm going to have to stop you right there my lady! I have the honor of inviting you and yer escort to a fine venison dinner at the camp of Sherwood Forest's most hospitable outlaws. And believe me when I say we won't take no for an answer. Now you lads might want to put down those swords, ya see, because right now we've got a half dozen archers with arrows trained right at ya, and I know from experience that those leather hauberks of yers just won't stand up to an arrow shot from this close a range."

The two deputies, who to Maude's dumbfounded disdain seemed to have been taken completely off guard, held up their hands as more green-clad foresters moved in on them and relieved them of swords and bows, and two of the outlaws took the deputies' horses by their bridles and began leading them into the forest to what Maude knew must be Robin Hood's new camp.

The bandits' spokesman took her own palfrey's bridle and followed his colleagues, chattering to her about what fine weather they'd been having, and about what a lovely horse she had, and about how fat her purses looked. He had a round face and a pug nose overspread with dark freckles, and his broad smile flashed a sparse set of teeth at her when he peered back at her over his shoulder. But his expression changed suddenly to puzzled surprise when she said, "You're Much the miller's son, aren't you?"

Much stopped and looked back. Too startled to make a coherent answer, he let his mouth hang open until Maude continued, "I recognize you from our meeting in the Blue Boar Inn in Nottingham."

The half-toothed smile returned, and Much continued his jovial escort of Maude and her horse to the outlaw camp. "So, my lady, you've surprised us again, haven't ya? Looking a good deal more presentable than you did that night, if ya don't mind my saying so. Now why is it I get the feeling that our encounter this time is no more coincidental than it was that night? You have some business yer wanting to conduct with our Robin, do ya?"

Lady Maude could not help smiling herself at the outlaw's manner and his quick perception of the situation. "I do indeed. I've got a favor to ask of him. And I expect to reward him handsomely if he's willing to help me with it." And she was, too. Though the reward she had in mind was not necessarily a monetary one.

"Only the problem right now is, Robin is away from home. Turns out somebody *else* wanted his help." Much looked back over his shoulder and shrugged, as if to say, "What can you do with someone so much in demand?"

This was a development Maude had not really foreseen. Recalculating, she prepared herself to make some quick assessments during this evening "banquet" she was being led to: She must determine who best to leave a message for Robin with, and how long it might take to reach him, and how long Robin would take to come to her aid.

She remained in these thoughts as they arrived at a clearing in the woods where the outlaws had made a temporary camp to which they now brought their invited guests. It was closer to the road, and using it as their daytime headquarters kept outsiders from ever seeing their permanent camp at the caves of Creswell: Robin had realized that bringing Lady Mary and her companions there had been a mistake the moment he'd received Marion's request for help addressed to him at Creswell

Crags. Before he'd set off for Peveril Castle, he'd ordered that this new routine be followed when the outlaws waylaid any new paying customers on the Great North Road.

Lady Maude was pleasantly surprised when Much led her to a comfortable seat on the grass beneath a spreading elm tree and courteously asked her to be seated while he saw to it she was served a fine helping of venison with some bread and cheese and ale, and while he sent a few gentlemen along to keep her company. Glancing around the camp, she recognized David of Doncaster and Arthur Bland from her evening at the Blue Boar, and was surprised to see the tonsured head and portly frame of a friar bustling about self-importantly, and the dark visage of a tall, dignified Moor turning the spit as venison roasted over an open campfire. A dwarf was leading her horse off to the edge of the camp, while two of the other foresters—one with a long blond braid like a Viking—welcomed the two guards from her escort.

When her eyes shifted back in the direction Much had gone, she saw two of the green-clad woodsmen coming toward her purposefully. The one leading the way was quite young, but there was a quiet confidence in him that was well beyond his years. He was slight of build and deep-tanned from the sun, which had also brought out a sprinkling of freckles across his well-formed nose. Indeed, his whole face was well-formed, with large, deep brown eyes that locked on to hers as he approached with a smile. He was quite the handsomest lad Maude had seen in some time. Maude considered that she may have to rethink her infatuation with Robin Hood if this boy was on the menu. The other fellow was more mature, a huge, brawny slab of a man with blue eyes and a face that seemed carved out of stone and that too, like his tawny beard and hair, had been well colored by the sun.

"My dear lady," the charming young man said, bowing courteously as he approached her. "I understand from my colleague Much that it is you we have to thank for your warning to us regarding Sir Guy of Gisbourne's threat to our company. It was a timely and welcome alert, and we are quite grateful for it—I would even say in your debt, my lady. Please, allow me to name to you my companion, Mr. Naylor, whom we all call 'Little John' because, as you see, he is such a diminutive, inconsequential fellow."

John nodded briskly and forced a polite smile and a guttural, "My lady." Maude let a high note of pleasure escape, and held out her hand graciously to the big man. "Little John himself!" she cried. "Your reputation precedes you, sir. You are hated and feared among the rich in Nottingham nearly as much as Robin Hood himself! A pleasure, sir!"

Little John, scoffing modestly, took her proffered hand and bowed again perfunctorily, mumbling, "The pleasure is all mine, my lady…uh…my lady…?"

Noting the question in his voice, Maude said, "I am called Lady Maude Peveril." She thought it prudent not to volunteer the fact that she was married to the band's most hated rival.

"And my name is Will Stutely, my lady," the handsome young man declared, taking her outstretched hand himself and bowing again. "May my companion and I join you for dinner? We want to discuss with you your request to speak with our master Robin."

"Please do, Mr. Stutely, Mr. Naylor," she replied as the two foresters sat, one on each side of her, and Much, Alan a Dale, and Will Scathelock brought each of them a bread trencher with venison and cheese and a flagon of ale.

"So, then," Stutely continued. "Would you care to confide to us the purpose of your seeking Robin? You need his help with some personal issue, we've been led to believe?"

"That's right," Maude began. "I can't really share all the details now, but I want Robin's help finding out who killed my uncle. He was a fairly influential nobleman around here, and he was poisoned just over a week ago."

Will and John said nothing, but looked at one another with intimate expressions she could not read, until at last she burst out with exasperation, "What?"

"Uh, Lady Maude," Little John said with a tense edge to his voice. "This kinsman of yours…wouldn't be a certain Lord Hugh Peveril, would it? Lord of Codnor Castle and killed up here at Peveril?"

Now it was Maude's turn to stare in surprise. "Why yes! How did you know? What do you know of this murder?"

"We know little of the murder itself," Stutely admitted. "But it may surprise you to know that Robin Hood is even now at Peveril Castle, where he has gone to see if he can be of any help to Lady Mary of Winchester."

"Lady…who?" Maude asked, confused.

"The Countess of Chesterfield's chief lady-in-waiting, an old friend of Robin's from the time of the last king," Will explained. "She found herself suddenly in command of the castle when Lord Peveril and the old earl both died at the same time, and no one knew where the countess was. They still don't know that. But Robin and I rode together to Peveril several days ago, and when he saw the situation he sent me back here to bring a few good men to the castle to support Lady Mary. It's difficult to know who she can trust in her current situation, and I am to bring Little John here, and our good Sir Palomides," and at that Will gestured to the Moor, just now sitting down after his endeavors with the venison. "We leave in the morning."

Maude was much taken aback by these revelations, and began silently to filter through her involvement in this conspiracy and to weigh just what aspects of it she should reveal and what she must keep hidden. First of all, she was definitely not going to give away anything to these two woodsmen, no matter how courteous and charming this Will Stutely was, or how intimidating the big fellow, Naylor, could be. Only let her get to Peveril, and she would see. She was sure Robin would help her. And though she didn't know about this Lady Mary of Winchester, she was certain she could handle *her*.

"Mr. Stutely," Maude began, her calculations over for the moment. "I am gratified to know that Robin Hood is already doing precisely what I had been planning to ask of him. And I and my escort are even now traveling to Peveril Castle ourselves to see what might be done about this vile murder. The evening is coming on now, and it is another day's ride to Peveril. Would it be possible…"

Now Little John was doing some calculating himself. Lady Maude seemed to him to be holding something back, perhaps only because she was slow to trust anyone but Robin himself, but he was not ready to trust her completely, and bringing her to the caves, especially with her two guards, was not a safe choice, in his opinion. So before Stutely could extend an invitation, John made an offer of his own. "My Lady," he said, "you're welcome to stay around our campfire overnight. We have a few tents, or perhaps your men would prefer to sleep under the stars—it promises to be a fair night."

Will scowled at John, anticipating an uncomfortable rest, but he realized what John was doing. "Indeed," he said, "most of our band have other lodgings for the evening, but John, Sir Palomides, and I will keep our horses here, and they have tents in their packs, the better to sleep out here and be off quickly in the morning. You are welcome to stay here overnight, and ride with us tomorrow to Peveril Castle. The six of us riding together will be a more formidable party, which any of the highwaymen who trouble these parts will think twice about attacking!"

Lady Maude saw that irony for what it was, but replied, "We readily accept your courtesy, such as it is. I'll let my escort know the situation."

"Little John!" Came Thorvald's voice, shouted over the chatter of the forest banquet. He was standing across the clearing and holding up one of the purses Lady Maude had carried on her saddle. "Not a bad exchange for a fine supper. Looks like the lady 'as some sixty nobles in 'er purse!"

"That ain't bad at all," John replied.

"The usual tax then, Little John?" the dwarf asked. "Twenty for us, twenty for the poor, and twenty for the lady to carry on with?"

Lady Maude, shaken from her misconception that she was merely a guest of the outlaws, began to sputter. "B…but…what was all that you said about being in my debt and all? Doesn't that count for something?"

"Precisely, madame," John concurred. "Thorvald! Just take twenty nobles. Leave her the rest!"

Crossing her arms with indignation, Maude did not appreciate her tax break, but Will began to cajole her. "Cheer up, my lady, we live in an uncertain, transient world, where all things must pass as soon as flowers fair. Enjoy your evening here with us—look, our Alan a Dale is tuning his lute and will soon be singing us some ditty to take our minds off our troubles."

And as the jongleur struck up a chord, Maude let herself be swept up in the music, and settled into the ambiance of the forest.

CHAPTER ELEVEN

Will Stutely was on his way back from Peveril Castle to the outlaw encampment at Creswell Crags. To get to the castle one branched off from the Great North Road and rode west for several miles, and he was just returning from that direction to catch the Great Road south, where after a short ride he would turn off again to the east, toward the caves. He'd made this trip back and forth twice now in five days, and he knew his way better than anyone in Robin's crew. But the fact was he was feeling stiff and sore in places he had forgotten he could even feel, and he was beginning to regret his earlier snatching from Gisbourne's troops this big, brown stallion he was riding—whom he had named "Sir Guy" in honor of its donor.

Will dismounted when he pulled into the Great Road, and decided to give his horse, and his backside, a rest by walking for a few miles. He was in no great hurry. He'd left Little John and Palomides with Robin, along with Lady Maude and her escort, having chatted up the pair of deputies on the ride and, he thought, put a bug in their ear about possibly quitting their unprofitable, and underappreciated, work for the sheriff and taking up a forester's life in Sherwood. Robin and Marion seemed to have the situation at Peveril Castle well in hand, though he wasn't sure anybody had an idea who had killed that Maude lady's uncle, but he'd been sent back to the campsite—again—to talk to Friar Tuck about working up a plan to go back to follow up on the strangely empty grave of Sir Walter of Horsley. Robin and Little John had got to talking soon after their arrival about that particular mystery, and Marion had mentioned that it was quite strange, since Sir Walter had been one of the suitors for the hand of the Countess Lydia, and how there might be some connection between the two mysteries, since both involved the countess somehow. And since Robin couldn't focus on Horsley while he was still at Peveril, he wanted the friar to spend some time considering the matter. But that was not exactly news of the moment, so Will was sure a few hours one way or the other was not going to make a difference.

And so Will was strolling along at a leisurely pace, leading Sir Guy by his bridle and singing to himself a ballad he'd heard Alan a Dale sing many times (about a young lad who complains to his mother about his shrewish wife who, it turns out, has poisoned him). Will liked to sing, but his companions were usually annoyed when he did. Little John always told him he had a voice that could sour milk. It was made to be employed at the bottom of a well, or on a boat let loose alone in the middle of the sea. But by himself on the road, Will could sing as loudly as he liked.

So when he suddenly came over a slight rise and ran directly into four armed and mounted men coming straight for him, their swords drawn and pointing in his direction, his first thought was that they didn't like his singing. For a split second Will considered athletically swinging into his saddle and spurring his horse to gallop in the opposite direction and leading the soldiers on a merry chase—he could even see it in his mind's eye—but at the same instant he heard two more horses closing in behind him. No chance at escape that way, then. So, he decided: brazen it out?

"Well," he called to the advancing knights, in lieu of a greeting. "There's a lesson for me then: Never sing so loudly to yourself on the road that you can't hear riders coming straight at you! Well learned, I would say, well learned. And who might you lads be, eh? Not thinking of molesting a lonely traveler on the road, are you? I assure you I'm not carrying but a few pence in cash, so if you lot are part of that notorious band of Sherwood outlaws I've heard so much about, you'll not get much profit from the likes of me, that I can tell you!"

"I thought so," said a gruff voice from behind him, ignoring Will's cheery greeting. "I'd recognize this tall mount anywhere, by his dark brown coat and these dappled back legs. This here horse was one of the ones those bandits stole from us when we were trying to sniff 'em out south of here, 'bout a month ago, wasn't it Jack?"

"It was," said a tall, black-bearded horseman who seemed to be the leader of the group in front of Will. "And I think you're right about this here horse. We just might have run into a bit of luck, boys. Take a look at how this little chatterbox is dressed. Lincoln green, right? That's their livery, ain't it? Robin Hood's men, green as the forest itself."

"Oh, this old thing?" Will said. "My other clothes were burned this morning when I was…uh, shoeing this horse. I'm a blacksmith by trade, you see, and a fellow came to me earlier today saying his horse had thrown a shoe, and left me with the animal. So, I finished the job, but singed my work clothes, and since I promised to bring the horse to where the fellow lives, here in Sherwood, I…looked in the pack he had left on the animal's back and found these fine Lincoln green garments. So, that's my story. And what's yours—Jack is it? What brings you and your companions out here on this lonely road this fine afternoon?"

"Funny him being out here by himself," said another of the

horsemen blocking the road, scratching the stubble of beard under his greasy blond locks. "Don't they usually travel in bunches? Is Sir Guy going to be satisfied if we just bring in the one?"

"Sir Guy is gonna be overjoyed that we finally got one of those outlaws. We been looking for a month and've got nothing to show for it yet. One's a whole sight better than none!" Jack opined.

"And besides," said one of the other guards, a brutal looking rider with a weathered face, an eyepatch, and a wide, feral mouth, "Sir Guy promised hangings. When he strings this one up, that'll send a message to all the rest of that outlaw crew."

"He *said* he'd hang *Robin Hood*," Jack corrected.

"Maybe the little blighter *is* Robin Hood," Eyepatch returned.

"Who me?" Will exclaimed. "I'm way too young. This Robin Hood is a middle-aged chap. In his thirties, at least. No, no, I'm much younger. And much better looking, too, as I'm sure you'd agree if you saw us together." And that gave Will an idea. "In fact," he said, elaborating on the story that no one in his audience had for one second believed, "that's the fellow who brought me this horse to shoe! No wonder you mistook me, since these clothes are, of course, his. What with me finding them on his horse, and all. Right? But since I'm going now to his camp to deliver this horse back to him, maybe you'd all like to come along with me so that you can meet him, if you've a mind to. Eh? How does that sound?"

It was an offer, Will reasoned, that he'd jump at himself if *he* were one of these ruffians. A chance to capture Robin himself? How could they resist? And they'd make so much noise approaching the camp that Much and Scarlet and Alan a Dale and the good friar would have them surrounded by a score of the best archers in Britain before they got halfway there. And he'd be saved. He was quite fond of his neck, and would prefer to keep it as it was, without the inconvenience of stretching. But Sir Guy's boys were not having it.

"Shut him up," Jack commanded, and the first speaker, whom Will had still not seen, struck him a savage blow on the back of his head with the broadside of his sword, and that was the last thing Will was aware of for a good many hours.

"Throw him over the horse, then, and tie his hands and feet together, to keep him from falling off," Jack commanded, as the two horsemen who had been behind Will dismounted to carry out the order. They lifted the unconscious Will, threw him over the horse, with his belly on the saddle and his head and feet hanging over either side of the stallion, and tied his hands and feet with leather thongs. "We'll take him to our quarters in Chesterfield, rendezvous with our lads there, and move back south tomorrow with the prisoner. These outlaws won't dare to attack a score of armed men. And Sir Guy will want to rush our friend here to the scaffold, the sooner to make a statement to the people of this region that this kind of lawlessness will not be tolerated." And with that, the contingent started off on the road toward Chesterfield.

In the branches of one of the taller oak trees along the Great North Road squatted a figure whose Lincoln green doublet and hose kept him well camouflaged, with his face in the shadows. The patch of sunlight that broke at that instant through the branches and lit the figure's face revealed the freckled snub nose of Much, the miller's son. By himself, he could do nothing. He ran his hands over his face in frustration as he tried to consider the best course of action. Follow them, to see where they would be holding Will? Go back to Creswell Crags to get reinforcements? Ride to Peveril Castle to inform Robin and John what had happened? That last option was the least appealing, since Much knew that the news would probably send Little John into an uncontrollable rage. On the other hand, if he wasn't the first to know of this abduction, it would almost certainly send Little John into an uncontrollable rage. But if he didn't get back to the outlaw camp before nightfall, they'd be sending out a search party for Much himself. And he didn't want his friends stumbling around Sherwood in the dark with Gisbourne's troops in the area and out for blood. All right, Much decided. Back to camp first, but after that he was taking a horse and heading for Peveril Castle. He'd ride through the night to get there. Alone, if necessary.

* * *

The sun beat down on Stutely's face, and his hat had been lost somewhere in the struggles of the past night and morning. His hands were tied behind him as he rode precariously on Sir Guy's back, so he could not put up his hood to keep the morning rays from his face and very tender head. And the warm June day promised to get a lot warmer as it moved into the afternoon, so he anticipated getting quite thirsty as the day went on.

His captors, riding two by two, ten of them in front of him and ten behind, did not seem overly concerned with his comfort. In fact, he thought it would not be an exaggeration to say that they really didn't care whether he lived or died—it was even possible that they'd prefer it if he did die, since they considered him more burdensome than he was worth. The only thing keeping him alive at all, he reasoned, was that Sir Guy wanted very, very much to entertain the burghers of Nottingham with a showcase hanging of one of the Sherwood outlaws.

Will had no delusion, though, that his captors would shrink from any means they might have of tormenting him—they had done so that morning when they refused to give him any breakfast before embarking on the day-long ride to Nottingham Castle. Indeed, their entire attitude toward him since the moment he had met them on the road was to ignore him. Not one of them had responded to anything he'd said, or had directly addressed him at any time, during the length of his captivity. They seemed unwilling to extend him the recognition of his humanity. And that was probably a deliberate strategy. So he had no intention of asking anyone for water. He just hoped that they might have enough decency to let him eat and drink something when they stopped for a midday meal, as he knew they must.

But despite his discomfort, his thirst, and his weakness, Will had no intention of letting Gisbourne's minions think of him as abject and broken. Not as long as he still had a voice with which to annoy them.

"I say, you there," he called to the rider directly in front of him. "You with the arse bigger than your horse's. Are you planning to give that horse of yours any kind of a rest soon? Poor thing looks like it's ready to give up the ghost if she doesn't get something to drink soon. Or are you planning to ride her till she drops?"

"Shut yer mouth, or I'll shut it fer ya," came the growled response from the rotund fellow on the gray rouncy who didn't bother looking back.

"Ride her till she drops, then, is that it? Funny, that's what your wife told me she wanted me to do when I visited her the other day…" Will continued, expecting to have to dodge a backhanded swing from the heavy fellow's right hand.

But to his surprise the guardsman turned around in has saddle and glared at him, with a rough red face that reminded Will of an angry boar, and snarled, "Ha! The joke's on you, funny boy! I ain't even *got* a wife!"

"Wow," Stutely replied. "I'm truly shocked. What a great loss to the fair sex of England!"

Pig-face turned back and kept riding, apparently unaware he was being insulted. Lord, thought Will, how do you insult people too stupid to know when they're being abused? But he did feel a personal sense of victory at that moment: He had forced one of the buggers actually to speak to him, to acknowledge his existence. Now for his neighbor, Will thought, eyeing the guard riding next to Pig-face. It was, he noticed, his old friend Eyepatch from last night. Surely he could find a way to get under this grisly fellow's skin.

"How about you, Eyepatch?" Will began, goading the other rider. "Have you got a wife? Surely the gentle ladies of Nottingham will not have left one with so fair a visage as yours to remain single for long."

Nothing but silence came from the stoic man with rugged face. He merely kept his eyes forward and his jaw clenched. Stutely took another tack.

"Or are those gentle dames of the town too mild for your tastes? Ah, yes, I see it now. Frequent the stews of Nottingham when you're feeling the urge, do you? Wear the harlots out with your unquenchable lust, do you? Two or three or four at a time, until you've run through the house?"

A red tint was climbing up from Eyepatch's neck and into his cheeks, and his jaw muscles seemed to bulge, but still he made no reply—though Pig-face seemed to be stifling a laugh at his fellow's expense. Will shifted tactics again.

"No," he admitted, "I'm just having you on. I mean, I'm sure that you do frequent the stews, but only because no woman will have you—at least not without getting paid for her trouble. I imagine you have to pay them double, don't you? They see that face coming and run for cover leaving only the ugliest strumpets for you, and even they won't do it without getting paid twice."

Crickets.

"Wait!" Will called out suddenly. "I've got it figured out! *Now* I know how you lost that eye! You were getting so desperate you tried to have your way with your own horse, right? But even she wouldn't have you, and she kicked you in the face, so the nail of her horseshoe caught you in the eye, and *that's* why..."

The blow came quickly and without warning, catching Stutely on the right side of his head and sending him tumbling from his saddle. Without his hands to protect him, all he could do was pray inwardly not to hit his head. Fortunately he was able to hunch himself together and land on his side, taking the brunt of his fall on his left shoulder and hip. It hurt, and he'd definitely feel it in the morning, but he was conscious and pretty sure he hadn't broken anything when Eyepatch, having leapt down from his own horse, came rushing toward him with fists flailing, and shouting as he landed blow after blow, "You bastard villein, you'll be lucky if you've got any eyes at all when I get done with you! I'll string you up here and leave you till the crows pick your bones and peck out your eyes!"

"Hunter!" Jack's voice bellowed over the man's ravings. "Get away from that prisoner! If you spoil the goods before we get him to Gisbourne, then you'll take his place on the scaffold yourself, you hear me? And that goes for all of you!" Jack reeled his horse around, taking the whole column into his purview. "Leave the prisoner alone! Do not engage with him!"

Eyepatch paused in mid blow, glared back at Jack with the look of a small boy interrupted in his favorite pastime of pulling the wings off flies, then turned again and glowered at Will, and climbed back on his horse.

The two guards who had been riding behind Will had dismounted and were now lifting him back onto Sir Guy, still keeping his hands tied. One of the guards whispered into his ear, with what Will could only assume was a charitable intent, "You need to keep quiet, boy, or you're not going to make Nottingham in your own skin!" But Stutely smiled grimly, mainly to himself. Another of the guards had spoken to him. Little by little, he was forcing them to see him.

The whispering guard had been correct, though. Will was bruised, beaten, and much the worse for wear, and his approach so far promised to get him more of the same, so unless he was so devoted to disappointing Gisbourne that he was willing to sacrifice his life in order to deprive Sir Guy of the satisfaction of taking it himself, Stutely needed a new strategy: one that continued to annoy the guards, but refrained from insulting them. At least not in ways they could understand.

Then he recalled what he'd been doing when he was first captured by these bullies. And he smiled. He considered a wide range of ballads he'd heard time and again from Sir Palomides or from Alan a Dale, and chose one that he thought particularly appropriate, given his situation, and one that might be especially grating for soldiers riding through mile after mile of mind-numbing road.

"Oh good Lord Judge, and sweet Lord Judge," Stutely sang, and went on

Peace for a little while!
Methinks I see my own father,
Come riding by the stile.

"Oh father, oh father, a little of your gold,
And likewise of your fee!
To keep my body from yonder grave,
And my neck from the gallows-tree."

"None of my gold now you shall have,
Nor likewise of my fee;

For I am come to see you hanged,
And hanged you shall be."

"Oh good Lord Judge, and sweet Lord Judge,
Peace for a little while!
Methinks I see my own mother,
Come riding by the stile.

"Oh mother, oh mother, a little of your gold,
And likewise of your fee!
To keep my body from yonder grave,
And my neck from the gallows-tree."

"None of my gold now you shall have,
Nor likewise of my fee;
For I am come to see you hanged,
And hanged you shall be."

"O good Lord Judge, and sweet Lord Judge,
Peace for a little while!
Methinks I see my own brother,
Come riding by the stile..."

"His brother!" moaned Pig-face. "What's next? Sisters? Aunts and uncles? My ears are aching with this." Several of the other guards began grumbling as well, but Will continued to sing out loudly and clearly, if not especially sweetly. And he smiled to himself. He had a big, big family, all of them ready to do their musical part.

CHAPTER TWELVE

Around a large circular table in the lesser hall of Peveril Castle, Lady Mary had assembled all interested parties now within the castle's confines to meet and exchange whatever they knew that might have any bearing on the murder of Lord Peveril. As the de facto castellan, she felt a great weight on her shoulders, and had welcomed Robin as someone she had known of old and so trusted, and he'd brought these others to the summit: the Moorish knight, the big forester Little John, and the rather pushy shirttail Peveril relation named "Lady" Maude, that title being, to Marion's mind, a bit dubious, what with her marriage to the burgher Sheriff of Nottingham. But then, if Lord Peveril had accepted her claim, who was Marion to look askance, particularly since her own aristocratic claims were based solely on her father's bankrupt noble house and her relation to two of the old king's knights.

Lady Maude had not trusted her own guards to be anywhere near the room in which these matters were to be discussed, and Lady Mary, still without a clue as to who may have put the nightshade in Sir Hugh's drink, was loath to trust anybody—even her own companions from Countess Lydia's household or Codnor Castle—who had been in Peveril at the time of the murder. Even Giles, the young squire she had sent to fetch Robin Hood, she would not trust to be in the room, though she did post him outside the door to keep out any unwanted visitors. Thus there were only five at the table.

Sir Palomides broke the silence with an amused observation. "A round table," he remarked. "It puts me in mind of those feast days under the old king, when the knights would meet together."

"Well," Robin said, looking around doubtfully. "The table's a bit smaller. That one sat a hundred and fifty knights, as I recall."

"And no women," Palomides said, adding gallantly, "a reduction in scale, then, but a significant increase in courtesy."

Lady Maude let loose a derisive snort. "The Moor has a honeyed tongue," she said. "How sincere is he?"

"Sir Palomides embodies all that is left of the honor and chivalric code of that body of knights who formed the Round Table in the days of its glory," Robin responded. "He does not engage in frivolous or discourteous speech. Which may be more than can be said of anybody else at this table. Myself included."

"Yes, yes," Little John said, trying to bring the meeting to order. "But this ain't what we're here for. Lady Mary, you've assembled us. You start us off."

Marion nodded at the big man with quiet gratitude, and then addressed the group. "I thank you all for being here, and it might be apparent to everyone that, while I've always been close to women in power, from the old queen to the new countess, I've never really had the role of leader, in charge of anything. And here I am in charge of a castle, purely by default. I don't know where the countess is, and that's one thing I need to find out. And then I need to figure out how to get to her and bring her back here to take over her rightful estate. But at the same time, I don't know who killed Sir Hugh or why, and that's the most pressing problem that I need to solve. And in solving it, I need to figure out how it affects my lady, the countess, and if it's even safe for her to come to Peveril Castle, or if she's going to be in danger here as her cousin, Sir Hugh, was. And you're all here because you know something that might help, or because you're among the few people I think I can trust."

"But there's more," Little John said. "We also have the business of Sir Richard at the Lee, whose lands were very nearly forfeit to the Abbot of Saint Mary's Abbey in York. His son Sir Peter of Verysdale was forced to travel to the Holy Land to try to make his fortune when it appeared he was about to lose his ancestral lands. And now we learn that this Sir Peter was a suitor for the hand of the Countess Lydia of Chesterfield, the murdered lord's kinswoman."

"And," Robin added, warming to the mystery and its many strands, "Sir Richard's lands were nearly forfeit because his son had, supposedly, unintentionally killed Sir Walter of Horsley in a tournament. And this is where the abbot comes into it: It was his judgment that imposed the crippling fine on Sir Peter that nearly lost his father his ancestral estate. It seemed clear to us at the time that the abbot's aim in imposing the fine was to gain control of Sir Richard's lands. But let me reveal to those of you who don't yet know. I and some of my men were compelled to make a close investigation of the grave of this Sir Walter one night when Horsley Castle was asleep. And what we found was a shock to us all: There is no body in Sir Walter's grave."

There was a gasp from Marion and Maude, and Marion asked with some confusion, "But…but where did the body go?"

There was silence for a moment, until Robin said quietly, "We think Sir Walter's death may have been faked."

"Faked!" Marion exclaimed. "But why on earth…"

"It was necessary, so as to allow the abbot to impose the fine," Sir Palomides said, just now realizing the truth of that statement. "Which means, Sir Walter and his mother, the lady Abigail of Derby, must have conspired in all of this with the abbot as well."

"But how does Sir Hugh come into it?" Little John asked.

"I'm not sure," Lady Mary said thoughtfully, "but I know how Countess Lydia does. I told you that Sir Peter was a suitor for her hand. Well, Sir Walter was another. Both of them had been vying for her favors since long before she was named sole heir by the old Earl of Chesterfield. It was a rivalry that had become pretty heated, I believe, before that deadly tournament at Sheffield."

"Of course," Robin said. "Sir Richard told us that his son and Walter had been great friends in their youth, but had a falling out before that tournament. Obviously, it was occasioned by their rivalry over this girl."

"It's always safe to blame the woman," Maude muttered. It was her first contribution to the discussion and not, she would freely admit, a very constructive one. She had been hanging back, wondering how much these others knew, and how much she ought to reveal once they got to the point where they didn't know any more.

"Everything seems to revolve around this countess and her inheritance, and her marriage," Robin said. "And around the abbot, who for some reason is taking an unprecedentedly strong interest in Lady Lydia's marriage; doesn't that seem to be the case?"

"I don't think we can doubt it," Little John said. "Remember I went to York with Sir Richard and confronted the abbot. A less Christian monk I never hope to meet. Proud, covetous, avaricious—I'd say most of the Seven Deadly Sins he counts as character traits. And I was told by Nicholas, one of the lads that worked in his kitchen, that he was overheard complaining about Sir Richard's paying off his loan and so saving his estate, since it meant 'the young woman ain't going to get as big an inheritance as we planned' or words to that effect. The girl with the inheritance has got to be the countess, wouldn't you say?

And somehow Sir Richard's lands were going to be made part of this Lady Lydia's estates, and not the abbey's once the abbot had stolen them from their rightful owners. Mind you, I'm still not sure how that benefits the abbot."

"More to the point, none of this tells us anything about why Sir Hugh would be targeted for murder," Sir Palomides put in.

"Wait a minute," Marion said, a thoughtful frown on her face. "A kitchen boy named Nicholas you said, Little John?"

"Yes," John replied, squinting and cocking his head inquisitively. "Older teenager I'd say. Red face. Long dark hair, kind of greasy. Why? That mean something to you?"

"You'd know this boy if you saw him again?" Marion asked.

"Dare say I would. What are you getting at, my lady?"

"Maybe it's just a coincidence," Marion said. "But then again, maybe not. Oh Giles!" she called out to the young squire outside the door.

The youth swung through the door and into the room, standing at attention like a boy playing soldier. "Yes, my lady?" he said. "You need something?"

"Yes, Giles. I want you to run down to the kitchen for me. Ask Oswald, the cook, to send his boy Nicholas back up here with you. We need to speak with him."

"As you wish, my lady," Giles said, and dashed off to do her bidding.

"You think, what, that this kitchen boy is the same one Little John spoke to at Saint Mary's Abbey?" Robin asked.

"Why not?" Marion answered. "He was the one that brought in the wine that poisoned Sir Hugh. We questioned him at the time but he pleaded ignorance, and we had no reason to suspect he had any motive for killing Lord Peveril. He didn't know Sir Hugh and gained nothing from his death. I mean, it wasn't as if he were going to rob him or anything with me in the room..."

With that she paused for a moment and went pale, as if suddenly struck by something. "Of course, I suppose I might easily have had some of that wine myself, and ended up just as dead as Sir Hugh." She shook her head at that, though, after a moment, and said, "I suppose I was saved because we'd had so much ale to drink at dear Robin's feast earlier that day that I had no desire for wine." Lady Maude's head came up at that. "Dear Robin" is it? So more was going on between Robin and this Lady Mary Sunshine with the golden hair and prissy air than she had first suspected. Or at least Lady Mary thought there was. She'd have to watch the little minx.

"But Sir Hugh was clearly the target of the poison," Marion went on, "since he was the one who had asked for the wine to be brought, and even if Nicholas had succeeded in killing both of us and then robbed us, the castle was full of guards and attendants who would have found us straightaway, and the lad wouldn't have got away with it. But if he was working for someone else, if he was an agent of the abbot, then he was simply a tool of someone else's motive."

"But what would be the *abbot's* motive?" Sir Palomides asked, returning to the question at issue.

At last Maude cleared her throat. The time had come for her to add what she knew to the mix. Not all of what she knew, certainly, but she might as well reveal to these people what she had already let fall on Sir Guy's deaf ears. "I think I may be able to clarify something there," she began. When all eyes had turned to her, she went on. "As I've told you, Sir Hugh was my uncle. He was the one member of my family who did not treat me as a poor relation and consign me to the dustbin of society. In fact, he became my foster father and raised me at Codnor Castle, well before you were there, my dear," and she glanced down at Marion. "We did keep up a fairly regular correspondence over the years since my banishment to the sheriff's household in Nottingham, and in his latest letters he hinted at a three-way agreement he had entered into with the abbot and with Lady Abigail of Derby…"

"That would be the mother of the disappeared Sir Walter," Robin clarified.

"The same," Maude agreed. "Now as far as I understand the business, the agreement was that my uncle would use all his influence to put pressure on Lady Lydia to wed her son Walter. The abbot would transfer the lands bordering on Lady Abigail's to Walter and Lydia's control, and together with the Codnor and the Horsley estates, and the lands already gathered under the Earl of Chesterfield's jurisdiction, the countess and her spouse would command the greatest fiefdom anywhere in the midlands or the north."

"And Sir Richard's lands were to be added to these," Little John mused. "Indeed, they are a bit of an impediment, since they stand between Horsley's grounds and the abbey's holdings, so without them the large estate would not be contiguous. Hard to believe the abbot would give up on owning those lands."

"Well, I know nothing about that," Maude said innocently. "But I do believe that the three conspirators planned that, once the marriage had been concluded, the three of them would serve as the real power behind the countess and her consort, whom they believed they could control as mere figureheads. I'm sure they believed this scheme would make them extremely wealthy. I believe," and here Lady Maude was going beyond what she had revealed to Sir Guy and her husband, but it was information that would help make her case, "that the abbot and Lady Abigail have secreted Lady Lydia away someplace known only to them—in fact, secreted her away with Sir Walter as well, perhaps even forced their marriage—so that with the countess secured and Sir Peter out of the way in Palestine or wherever he's gone, my uncle's influence was no longer needed. And riches split two ways are much more desirable than riches divided three ways. The abbot found my uncle superfluous, I believe, and killed him."

At that point Giles came through the door, followed by someone who was definitely not the youth Nicholas. He was a portly, middle-aged servant with a spherical head that glistened with sweat, small pig-like eyes staring out of a large pudding of a face with no beard but three or four days of brown and gray stubble on his cheeks and chin. He was dressed in a drab green tunic and faded brown hosen and wore a once-white apron stained with grease, blood, and other foodstuffs. He could barely restrain himself while Giles kept up the courteous ambience of the room, nodding deferentially to Lady Mary and announcing him: "M'lady, the household cook, Oswald, has come to speak with you," he said.

"Yes ma'am, uh, my lady, I had to come," Oswald burst out. "This boy Nicholas, he's gone. Hasn't worked here since that morning after the earl died. And that other bloke. I mean, that other lord." There were sighs and murmurs all around the table at that bit of news.

"Gone?" Marion said, glaring in Oswald's direction. "Do you mean you dismissed him, or did he run away?"

"He was just gone, ma'am, uh, your ladyship. I went to get him up that morning to help with getting the breakfast on, and he was nowhere to be found. None of the other lads saw him go to bed at all that night, but Caleb, the boy that takes care of the kennels, told me there was a horseman who was waiting outside the gates with a spare mount shortly before the guards closed the portcullis for the night, and somebody, he thought it looked like Nicholas, left by the gate and rode off with him. Anyway, by morning this Nicholas had taken all his belongings and buggered off. Uh…sorry ma'am, took off."

"Bolted before being found out," Robin guessed. "Must have been right after you questioned him."

"This Nicholas," Marion pressed. "How long had he been working in the kitchen here?"

"Not long at all," Oswald said. "No more than three weeks, I'd say. He came looking for work, said he'd had experience working in the kitchens at a big abbey in York, but he had family in Chesterfield and wanted to be closer to 'em. Seemed as good a recommendation as any to me, so I took him on. He wasn't a bad worker at all. But then this. Here one minute, gone the next. Ya just can't get reliable help no more." And with that Oswald shook his round head ruefully, and Marion thanked him for the information and told him he could return to his kitchen. Giles went back to his post outside the door.

"Well," said Little John. "If there was any doubt that Abbot Robert is behind the murder of Sir Hugh, I think that pretty well clinches it. And the motive, like Lady Maude here says, is pretty clear as well: greed and power."

"Well, this is outrageous!" Lady Mary exclaimed. "There is enough evidence here to bring this wicked abbot to justice, isn't there?"

"I have brought the murder and my suspicions to the attention of my husband, the sheriff, and to Sir Guy of Gisbourne, the king's representative in this area," Lady Maude said. "Neither of them would lift a finger. I don't think this additional evidence, convincing as it is to us, would make any difference to them. The abbot is too powerful an enemy to make. None of the secular powers in York would be any more eager to take action against him. And he *is* the religious power in these parts."

"Is there nothing we can do about this?" Marion asked, her face flushing with righteous anger, and a feeling of helplessness in the face of these revelations.

"Beard the lion in his den!" Sir Palomides cried. "By God, I'll storm his abbey's gates myself, and call him out! The man is a disgrace to his habit."

Little John looked skeptical. "The abbey seems well guarded," he said. "And it isn't as if we—any of us—have any legal authority. Who does have authority over the abbot? Only the pope?"

Sir Palomides, a bit calmer now, knew the answer. "The archbishop, if I remember my catechism correctly, must approve the appointment of an abbot. But he is supposed to be elected by the monks themselves. Perhaps we could speak to the Archbishop of York?"

"Perhaps," Robin said. "But more immediately, we need to make sure that the abbot's scheme is foiled."

"Absolutely!" Marion agreed. "And to do that, the first step is to find Lady Lydia." With that she looked across the table at Lady Maude. "Did Sir Hugh know where they were keeping the countess? Did he ever say anything to you that might have been a clue?"

Maude swallowed hard. Things were getting very tricky here, and she needed to tread carefully. Perhaps she'd been a fool to try to bring her uncle's killer to justice while keeping her own part in the affair hidden. But she could answer this question truthfully. "I do not believe they told my uncle where they were holding Lady Lydia. At least he never indicated to me that he knew. They wanted to keep it a well-guarded secret."

"So only the abbot knows?" Sir Palomides asked. "Then we really *must* confront him in his own abbey!"

"No, no, no," Robin said thoughtfully. "If Sir Walter is one of the keys to this, then I'm betting he is with the countess. And if that's true, then his mother, Lady Abigail, surely knows where they are. I would say it may be more profitable to approach *her*, wouldn't you think?"

"But how?" Little John asked. "Do we break into her castle and threaten her? Do we approach her as a delegation and tell her we know who murdered Sir Hugh and that we will have her arrested as an accomplice?"

"Let me think about it," Robin said. "I know something about that castle by now. I think I can come up with a plan to get her to reveal the secret. Give me some time."

"But if the countess has already married Sir Walter, then our efforts will be in vain," Sir Palomides pointed out.

"If the countess had married Sir Walter, they would be here already and established in authority," Marion pointed out. "Surely they'd want a public and open wedding, so that the legitimacy of the marriage is unquestioned. No, I think if we find Lady Lydia, and rescue her if need be, we'll have cut the head off this snake of a conspiracy."

"But I'd feel more confident if we could bring back Sir Peter," Little John said. "If he was the suitor the lady preferred, it would be safer to see her married to him. Safer, too, for Sir Richard and his estates, since it would put them out of reach of the abbot's grasp."

"Well," Sir Palomides sighed. "At least he is out of the country, and safe from this treachery."

By now, Lady Maude was squirming uncomfortably on her chair, and she was beginning to feel that she was perspiring enough that her forehead could rival the recently departed Oswald's. Her uncle was dead, so any profit she had hoped to reap from this grand conspiracy was lost. These people had uncovered the most important details of the plot and were prepared to expose the abbot's part in it, so she probably had nothing to fear from that quarter. And worst of all for her, this Little John kept insisting that the whole plot against Sir Richard at the Lee be examined and set right. It was certainly possible that her role might be revealed at some point in the future despite her attempts to conceal it. It seemed the decision was made for her: If she came clean now, she must ultimately be viewed as one of those who defeated the abbot's schemes, rather than as just another one of the failed conspirators. It made sense to join the winning side.

"I can tell you something of Sir Peter," she finally said, completely without emotion.

Four sets of eyes looked at her with confused surprise.

"Yes," Maude said, lowering her eyes so as not to have to look anyone directly in the face, and to compose a story in her head that would enable her to come out looking virtuous…or, at least, not a downright villain. "My uncle did let me in on one part of this scheme. He told me he would make sure that I would share in the prosperity to be enjoyed by the Peveril family if I would help in what he called 'one small matter.' He would send me, he said—and this was at the abbot's bidding—two villeins, former mercenaries, and I was to pay them five hundred gold nobles for a task they were being hired to perform, for the abbot and my uncle."

"Five hundred?" Little John echoed. "Sounds like this was a bit more than 'a small matter.' And you just happened to have that much cash lying about did you?"

"I had saved it over the years of my marriage," Maude said, shrugging. "To tell the truth, I was saving it against the day I might be able to leave my husband and set up my own household somewhere far from Nottingham."

"But how do you accumulate that much cash in your position?" Marion was curious to know.

"Oh, my husband accumulates a *lot* of cash, make no mistake," Maude informed her. "He collects city taxes from all the residents in the town for the city council, for instance, and keeps the lion's share for himself. He also takes a toll from anyone moving up or down the Great North Road through Nottingham. Not unlike Robin Hood himself," and with that she nodded across the table. "But his way is considered legal. Anyway, he is not miserly, I'll give him that, and whenever I ask for money for household expenses, or for clothing or to give to the church or whatever I think of, he gives it to me. And I always ask for two or three times what I actually intend to spend. So yes, I steal from my husband just as he steals from everyone else. And thus the world goes round."

"But this is getting us off the subject," Little John said. "You were to pay these mercenaries five hundred gold nobles—to do what?"

"I did not know at first. My uncle would not tell me," Maude lied. "But they were not secretive when I paid them. They kept speaking of tracking down a knight who'd gone to the Holy Land. They even mentioned a letter they had been given, purporting to be from my cousin the countess herself, that would get them into the knight's circle of trust, thus making it easier for them to murder him. For that was what the money was for, I won't lie to you." At least not about that, she thought. "From everything you've all said around this table, I now believe it must have been this Sir Peter of Verysdale. No doubt the abbot still plans to incorporate this Sir Richard's estate into his vast holdings once the rest of his scheme falls into place."

"To be clear, you say that two mercenary assassins have been dispatched to follow Sir Peter to the Holy Land and slay him there?" Sir Palomides said, his brow lowering like a thundercloud.

A little frightened at his demeanor, Lady Maude simply nodded.

"Then the knight must be saved!" Sir Palomides exploded in righteous anger. "And I must save him!"

"Well," Robin began cautiously. "Maybe we ought to consider

the practical difficulties of attempting such a task. I mean, aren't you looking for a needle in a haystack, for one thing? And for another, these assassins are already at least a couple weeks ahead of you, aren't they?"

He looked at Maude, who answered quietly, "A month."

"A month, then!" Robin threw up his hands. "How can you hope to catch up to them? Track them down? Stop them? And all by yourself, at that?"

"Listen to me," the Moor said decisively. "I can move more quickly by myself. I grew up in that part of the world. I know these places, and know how to get around them. If anybody can find Sir Peter, it will be me more easily than those mercenaries. As for their head start, if they are moving overland, I can still get there ahead of them by sea. If I can get a ship from Southampton bound for Lisbon or Cadiz, I can find passage from there to Genoa. Then perhaps cross Italy to Venice, where I can certainly find a ship bound for the Holy Land. It can be done, and I can cut at least a month off the travel time. So you see, I am not going blindly into this endeavor.

"But listen to me now," and here Sir Palomides became deadly serious. "This is the task I have been waiting for. This outlaw life is not what I am used to or what I am comfortable with. It's true that after the old king died, I tried for many months to find a new lord to whom I could pledge my loyalty, and in the fallen world that now grinds from day to day, I find little on which to expend my chivalric instincts. But this—this search for an innocent knight in danger of assassination by brigands, the chance to save a truly courteous soul—this is a quest of honor worthy of the name. An adventure worthy of the oath I swore when I became a knight: to defend the right, to succor the weak and needy, to take arms only in a just cause. I will do this, Robin, Little John. I leave it to the two of you to set things right here while I am gone."

There was no arguing with that. Sir Palomides had made up his mind, and he was going. There was some talk about expenses he would encounter on such a voyage, and he was not averse to taking some gold that Lady Mary knew of in the castle, and Robin and Little John contributed generously from their own purses, while Palomides carried some money of his own, and allowed that, if he became short of funds, he could always earn cash by playing his lute and singing his own compositions in any courts or inns he passed through on the way. But he was anxious to leave, for he had a long and dangerous road ahead of him. Robin and Little John put their heads together with Marion and decided that no more time should be wasted before rescuing the countess, and decided to go directly from Peveril to Horsley Castle, by some means to force from Lady Abigail the location where Countess Lydia was being held. Marion, of course, needed to stay at the castle and hold it for the countess. And in the morning, she would send Giles back to Creswell Crags to tell the outlaw band where Robin and John were off to.

As for Maude, she had accomplished what she'd set out to do: She had found proof that Abbot Robert was behind the murder of her uncle, and had found allies in her hope of avenging Sir Hugh's death upon the abbot. True, she'd also found that she had a rival for Robin's affections, but that did not surprise her, nor did it worry her much. She didn't see Robin as a one-woman man anyway, and Lady Mary was a young inexperienced little thing he'd probably lose interest in before long. And if not, well, there were other fish in the sea. That Little John was a manly man, wasn't he?

So it was that when Much the miller's son arrived at Peveril the next day with the dire news of Will Stutely's capture by Gisbourne's ruffians, he found that Little John had already left for Horsley, and began to despair for Stutely's life.

CHAPTER THIRTEEN

Robin, riding his fine white palfrey Daisy, and Little John, on the broad brown rouncy Bishop, had made up their minds to avoid the Great North Road and to cut cross-country south toward Horsley Castle, believing it would be a shorter route, and knowing that it would probably be safer. It would also make it easier for them to avoid the persistent troops of Guy of Gisbourne, who now patrolled the length of the road from Nottingham to Chesterfield.

Even on this more direct route, it would still take them the better part of two days to make the trek, and Little John was happy to have Robin for his traveling companion, since Mr. Kempe, a.k.a. Hood, was the greatest bowman he had ever seen, and could bag them a dinner of rabbit or partridge or black grouse with his eyes closed. And aside from that, Robin loved to hear himself talk, which complemented John's natural reticence fairly well. The outlaw leader chattered most of their first travel day of little things, moving from the special turn of Lady Mary's upturned lip, to the astonishing courage Sir Palomides had shown in taking on the individual quest for Sir Peter's assassins, to the bright sparkle in Lady Mary's azure-colored eyes, to the audacity of the abbot in sending his own kitchen boy to murder Sir Hugh, to the flawless sheen of Marion's skin. Considering the tricky and dangerous game they were playing against the abbot and his fellow conspirators on the one hand, and Sir Guy and the sheriff on the other, it seemed to Little John that Robin was spending an inordinate amount of energy concentrating on the lady Mary of Winchester. And John let his thoughts wander to the dashing and indomitable youth Will Stutely, and let out a sigh.

It wasn't until evening, as they sat on either side of the small campfire over which they were roasting the fat partridge Robin had bagged with a single bowshot, that Little John broached the subject that seemed most pressing. "So you've been to Horsley Castle twice now in recent weeks. You said you'd have a plan to get the location of this Countess of Chesterfield out of Lady Abigail. Well, we're going to be there by this time tomorrow, you know. Tell me you've got a foolproof plan. Or are you thinking we'll make it up as we go along?"

Robin grinned, sinking his teeth into a juicy drumstick. "It's coming together. Just a few details need working out."

"A few small details like the who, what, when and how of the plan?" Little John demanded. He'd seen Robin engage in some seat-of-the-pants maneuvers before, and wasn't looking forward to taking part in any more of those any time soon.

"Why, John Naylor, you cut me to the quick," Robin returned. "When have you ever known me to move without a carefully considered strategy? Listen, all we need is the assistance of somebody in the castle that the lady trusts…"

"Well that ain't going to be easy!"

"Maybe easier than you think, my lad," Robin came back. "I've got a young kitchen wench I think might be game. Now, how are you at playing the part of a priest?"

"Me a priest?" John said. "Never had a call to that vocation, I'm afraid. How many priests you know wearing Lincoln green, anyway?"

"Yes, that is a bit of a problem. But maybe we can get my friend

Agnes to loan us a black hooded cloak from somewhere in the castle too."

"Oh Agnes is it?" John asked. "Sure you can trust her?"

"Pure as the virgin martyr she's named for. Told me so herself. She'll help us out," Robin guessed, "for the fun of it, if nothing else, or I'm a lousy judge of character."

"Well," John said, stroking his beard, "I haven't known you to be one hundred percent infallible in that area, now that I think of it."

"What?" Robin seemed deeply affronted. "When has my judgment every been impaired? Except that one time, when I invited a certain oversized footbridge bully to join our band."

"Well, there's that Lady Maude who just attended our war council," John suggested. "The Sheriff of Nottingham's wife? Arranging the murder of Sir Richard at the Lee's son and heir? She held that back until the last minute, didn't she? What else ain't she telling us?"

Robin shrugged. "She came through in the end, though, didn't she? I swear, inside that conniving virago there's a good woman struggling to come out. Anyway, she implicated the abbot and told us who we needed to lean on to find the whereabouts of Lady Lydia, didn't she? And she was right when she warned us about Gisbourne's troops."

"Maybe so," Little John answered grudgingly. "I wouldn't turn my back on her. But back to this role-playing. Why do I need to pretend to be a priest? Why can't you do it? You're more the silver-tongued orator than I am."

"Because," Robin said with a grim smile. "I've got to be Robert of Boltby."

"You…what? Who?"

"Enough, now, just listen…" Robin said, and began to explain his plan to Little John in detail.

* * *

Much the miller's son overtook Lady Maude on the road shortly after she had left Peveril Castle with her two accompanying deputies, and he wasted no time in revealing to them the extent of his concern. He had seen Will Stutely in the clutches of Gisbourne's goons, and being dragged off to Nottingham under the threat of hanging. And he'd been too late to bring Robin or Little John to lead the rescue.

Maude was genuinely distressed at the news. She would not deny that she'd been charmed by the young man's gallant if cheeky manner, and the thought of him in the clutches of that axe-faced bureaucrat Gisbourne gave her heartburn. As for her companions, they too had been drawn to the young man's persuasive praise of the free life of the Sherwood outlaws. But what was to be done?

"I can help," Maude said decisively. "Sir Guy will see me, and if I plead for Stutely's life..." but she broke off, remembering how Gisbourne had put her off in the matter of her uncle's murder. "No," she said with a sigh. "He won't listen to pleas. But he is vain and wants Robin Hood more than anything. Perhaps I can convince him that if he delays the execution long enough, it will force Robin to try to rescue his fellow outlaw. And maybe that will give you and your mates time to stage an actual rescue?"

"Any delay will be some help," Much admitted. "I'm to meet Friar Tuck, Will Scarlet, and several of the other boys at the fork of the road that turns east toward our camp just ahead here. Can you get to Nottingham in time to delay things, even for a day or two?"

"You collect your comrades and make your plans," Maude said grimly. "We will ride!" And with that she turned her horse and began to gallop, and her two companions followed her at their best speed. Much watched her go and sighed. At that rate, he thought to himself, she'll kill her horse before she gets halfway to Nottingham. But at least her heart was in the right place.

* * *

Agnes's hair was shining with grease and sweat and her apron streaked with the drippings of various stews that Henry, Horsley Castle's cook, had concocted for the household's afternoon meal. She was carrying the leavings of that meal in a large bucket to scatter to a small family of hogs the cook was keeping in a pen behind the kitchen, to slaughter for a Sunday feast coming up in three days. Agnes was just turning to head back toward the kitchen when an arm came from behind her to encircle her neck and a strong hand clasped over her mouth. Another strong hand grasped the startled girl by the left arm and a soft voice murmured in her ear, "Promise me you won't cry out and I'll let you go!"

With a brief, tight nod, Agnes answered in the affirmative, and just as the hand loosened from around her mouth, she lunged after it and bit the little finger of the right hand with a vicious chomp.

Grimacing in pain as he tried to stifle his agonized cry, Robin held his injured paw in his other hand, hopping up and down, while Agnes put her hands on her hips and said, "Promise not to grab me and I won't bite you again!"

"All right," Robin said, shaking his sore hand while grunting again in pain. "But please keep your voice down. I'm trying to keep from being noticed here."

"I don't care," Agnes told him. "How'd you get in here then? You trying to rob the place or what? So you left that tinker you were traveling with, eh? Didn't seem like such a good fit to me either. But what are you doing back here?"

"I came in with a group of farmers looking to sell some produce. Look, I took your advice and decided to become a wandering player. But for my first show I decided I'd come back and see you, my saucy Agnes, because I haven't been able to get you out of my mind!"

"Oh right, I was born yesterday and I'll definitely fall for that one," Agnes retorted. "Well don't for a minute think I won't have a much easier time keeping you out of my skirts than you have keeping me out of your tiny little mind, if that's what you're thinking."

"No, no, come now, Agnes, you liked me well enough when I was here before. Why such a rough welcome now?"

"Well I didn't know you'd be coming back to rape and pillage, did I?" Agnes said. Then, softening, she added, "Not that you're not cute enough, standing there all forlorn and that. But I don't like anybody scaring the pants off me, all right? I much prefer to take them off myself." And with that she shot him a sly half-smile.

"Ah," Robin said, giving his hand one last shake. "Now that's the Agnes I remember so fondly. Listen, I know you're going to think this is pretty strange, and you're going to think I'm a little bit crazy, but there's a long complicated story behind it that I don't really have time to tell you. Let me just talk about the part that most concerns you."

"So you really *aren't* here because you can't stop thinking about me."

"Well, it's certainly true that I've thought of you a few times since we met," Robin began diplomatically, "but I was really looking for your help in a little masque one of my fellow wandering players and I are planning to put on here tonight!"

Agnes narrowed her eyes and put her hands on her hips. "Here now, what are you on about? Lady Abigail hasn't said anything to anybody about no players coming here tonight. And you're no more a player than you are a tinker. What exactly are you, anyway? Robin you said your name was. And here you are all in Lincoln green, just like they say Robin Hood himself wears, and those Sherwood bandits we hear so much about lately. Now I wonder what my lady's reaction would be to the news that she's got a notorious outlaw sneaking around her castle accosting her innocent kitchen maids?"

Robin was out of ploys and realized he was going to have to fall back on the truth with this young girl—but without admitting that he was, indeed, the notorious Robin Hood. "All right Agnes," he said, blowing out a frustrated sigh. "Here's the truth. You told me when I was here before that you were unhappy at the way Sir Walter's burial had been handled, and you were suspicious of the part that Abbot Robert played in the affair, isn't that right?"

Agnes's left eyebrow shot up and her brown eyes took on a curious sparkle. "I sure did. You're going to tell me that you're here about that business? Why?"

"Let's just say I and some friends of mine have a vested interested in the affair. Now listen, because this is the absolute truth I'm telling you: I happen to know for a certainty that Sir Walter is not buried in that grave they dug for him. Nobody is."

"But I saw his coffin buried there…" Agnes contended.

"The coffin is filled with stones," Robin told her, and as she let out a *'coo'* of surprise, he went on: "We believe that Sir Walter is still alive, and that he and the Countess Lydia of Chesterfield are being held at some common site in order to force her to marry him. He himself may be innocent of wrongdoing in this affair, but the abbot and Lady Abigail are definitely behind it. They have already committed one murder—Lord Peveril of Codnor Castle—and there may be others in danger. I and my friend John, who's waiting outside, are here to try to force

Lady Abigail to tell us where they are holding Sir Walter and the countess."

"Well, why didn't you say so in the first place?" Agnes said, clenching her jaw in determination. "I don't trust that abbot. And I want to see Sir Walter back here. What do you need me to do?"

Robin, taken slightly aback by how well the truth actually worked in this case, told her, "First, my friend needs to disguise himself as a priest. Is there anywhere in the castle we can borrow a black hood or some such item or cape for his disguise?"

To his surprise Agnes gave a conspiratorial snicker, and said, "The chapel! That dodgy abbot has been here pretty regularly, maybe once a month since Sir Walter's funeral. He actually keeps a spare cassock in the chapel so he doesn't have to dirty his best robes on the road! I can sneak in there without anybody seeing—the chaplain's an old man who sleeps most of the time and he won't notice even if he *is* there."

"But how will you get it to us?"

"There's a small door that goes straight out from the chapel through the rear wall of the castle into the graveyard. There'll be nobody watching there. If you come to that back wall, I can get the robe to you and nobody inside the castle will know about it."

"That's perfect!" Robin said. "Can you get it to me now, if I leave the castle and come around the back way up into the churchyard?"

"I can, but don't keep me waiting. I don't want to get locked out. But that's all you need?"

"Oh no," Robin said. "That's the easy part! We need you to do one more thing. How good an actress are you?" And when Agnes allowed as how she could lie her way out of almost anything, much like Robin himself, he proceeded to tell her what exactly he and

Little John had planned for the Horsley graveyard at midnight.

* * *

After letting Lady Maude and her companions hurry off toward Nottingham, Much waited at the crossroads until he was met by a good sized party coming into the road from Creswell Crags. Thorvald was driving his cart, in which rode Friar Tuck, Will Scarlet, Alan a Dale, and David of Doncaster. Following on horseback were the robust Arthur Bland and Alan of Winchester, Robin's former corporal from the king's guard and a crack shot with a bow. They had left Will Scathelock, as usual, in charge of the camp in Robin's absence, and were determined to find some way to free Stutely from the gallows. Much had to admit that he had come too late to Peveril Castle to catch Little John, who had the most personal interest in Stutely's rescue, and to the general despondency over that, Much added that John and Robin had gone on their own quest to Horsley Castle. A few of the group grumbled at the news, but Friar Tuck pursed his lips in thought. When Much told them that Lady Maude had vowed to stall Will's execution if she possibly could, they were a bit relieved. Thorvald's cart was a useful form of transport, but it was not going to get to Nottingham any time within the next two days.

When Much fell in with them and rode beside the cart, he noticed it held a number of weapons and also several tents and sleeping pallets, the assumption being that the group would camp by night and travel openly during daylight hours. Gisbourne's entire contingent had been seen on the road heading south, guarding their one prisoner, so it occurred to the outlaws that they could very likely take the Great Road south with impunity, without the likelihood of running into any guards unless it be a single sheriff's deputy or a very small party of them, and the outlaws had a large enough contingent to scare off any such trouble.

"So," Much began tentatively, speaking to Friar Tuck in the cart, whom he saw as the natural leader of this particular group. "I'm not sure how much thought you've been able to give to this rescue, but I'm wondering if we've got a plan? Because I've actually spent a few days in one of the cells there at Nottingham Castle. The previous sheriff locked me up as a vagrant when I first arrived in town after fleeing the estate where my father was miller. So I can tell you from personal experience that Nottingham Castle is well guarded, and the cells are in the bowels of the building, below ground with heavy locked doors. And Gisbourne will have forty of his mercenaries guarding the place. Plus the sheriff will be there with his deputies. Even with the best archers in the realm—and I freely concede that Will and the two Alans here rank in that class—we'd need a whole army of them to force our way into that fortress. And even then we wouldn't be able to do it without severe losses. So what I'm saying is that unless we are planning on sacrificing four or five men in order to save one, we need to have a plan that does not involve storming the castle walls."

"Your point is well taken," the friar replied. "I must admit, our first response was to try to hurry after them in order to catch them on the road. That would have been a lot easier than trying to assault a castle. But we soon realized that Gisbourne's men just had too great a head start on us. We'd never catch them and would wear our horses out in the attempt. So we had to rule that out, and also rule out any notion of taking the castle by force."

"So what's the alternative?" Much asked.

"Stealth, of course," the friar replied, with a broad smile, "and cunning. For doesn't our Lord say, 'I am sending you out like sheep among wolves. So be as cunning as serpents and as innocent as doves'?"

The friar paused and Much, at a loss, answered, "Well, you'd know better than I would. But how do you mean? Have you got a plan or not?"

"What we do depends on how Gisbourne and the sheriff decide to stage poor Will's execution: whether they build the gallows inside the castle itself or in a more accessible place outside," said Friar Tuck.

Thorvald, listening in from his seat at the front of the wagon, snorted. "That Gisbourne's out to make a big splash," he asserted. "'E'll want to make the 'angin' as public as possible."

"I'm sure you're right," the friar said, nodding. "And that's the better for us. Say they build the gallows in the very center of town, near Saint Nicholas's Church off Castlegate Road, where the whole city can gather unmolested to watch the execution. We leave our cart and horses somewhere safe. Then say we spread ourselves out in the crowd, robed and hooded but with bows and swords ready to hand. And say we find a way to slip Will a weapon—he springs on his captors and runs away into the crowd. The rest of us fire some arrows at any guards around. One of us throws a cloak and hood over Will, we all sneak away, and at night we meet up secretly with the horses and ride back to Sherwood."

Much looked at the friar in disbelief. "That's it?" he said. "How do you expect to sneak away in the crowd? Those people will know who used their bows. They'll turn on us!"

"Not them," the friar responded confidently. "Robin Hood's reputation is a charitable one. They all know him as the outlaw who robs from the rich and gives to the poor. They'll not turn his men in to the greedy sheriff."

"Sounds to me like there's an awful lot of 'playing it by ear' in that plan. I can't say I'm bursting with confidence after hearing it."

"Well, it's all we can do until we see exactly what things look like on Gisbourne's end," the friar conceded. "But have faith, my friend. God provided manna in the wilderness for the wandering Jews, why would he let *us* down?"

"Doesn't have a good record of keeping people from being hanged, though, does he?" Alan a Dale said gloomily from the cart. Thorvald grunted in agreement.

"But I am concerned that Little John still knows nothing about this situation," the friar said. "You say he and Robin are at Horsley?"

"They probably aren't there yet, but that was their destination," Much replied.

"I'd feel a lot better if they were able to join us in this endeavor," Friar Tuck admitted. "But time is of the essence, and even though we'll pass right by the road leading to Horsley, I think it would be wrong to take the time to turn off there. It could be the difference between saving Stutely and being too late."

Much sighed. "I guess I could take that road and ride to Horsley, and try to get them to follow me to Nottingham. Maybe we'll only be three or four hours behind."

"Brilliant!" the friar agreed. "Without you, we're one man down, but if you get to the city in time, we're two men up! Worth the risk, I'd say."

"We're still outnumbered ten to one, at least," Much said. "I wish the odds were a bit less in their favor."

"Never fear," the friar answered. "God gave Gideon victory over a whole army of Midianites with just three hundred men!"

Much looked down and muttered to himself, "Yeah. I sure wish *we* had three hundred men."

* * *

Little John wore a large crucifix and a black Benedictine habit with the hood over his head, which he was keeping bowed as if in prayer, his hands folded before him, as he stood in the dark in the churchyard outside Horsley Castle's back wall. The robe was too short for him and revealed more of his dark green hosen than he would have liked, and the sleeves were too short as well, but he had pushed them up to his elbows where they could hang down regally. In the dark, he felt, he could pass for one of the clergy. And besides, he was fairly certain that, if things went as planned, *he* was not the one that Lady Abigail would be looking at.

But he was becoming impatient. It was spooky enough out here in a graveyard all by himself, even without the shenanigans that were about to begin, and he would just as soon get it over with. He didn't expect to hear any bells from the chapel to announce matins or any other hour—Agnes had made it clear that the country chaplain here was not the most zealous of rectors—but he could estimate by the visible stars that it must be about midnight. Where was the silly kitchen wench anyway? He wondered if Robin was getting as impatient as he, and looked out toward the edge of the churchyard. They had made good use of the tunnel that had previously been dug through the side of the hill under Sir Walter's spurious grave. But it was too dark to see anything there, though he knew that where Robin was it was even darker than here.

Suddenly the small door from the chapel opened out into the churchyard and John knew the masque had begun. He heard the voice of an older woman that he knew must be Lady Abigail, who was holding out a lighted candelabra and skeptically chiding her younger companion, "There's nothing out here but the darkness, you foolish girl, just as I told you, you see? Now stop your inane prattle and take yourself to bed."

"No, no, my Lady," Agnes shrieked (a little over the top, Little

John thought to himself), "look, here's a…a local priest who's come up to see for himself! All the country round is talking of it!"

"What?" Lady Abigail held up her candelabra to see what she could of John's face, which he still held hooded and bowed. "Who are you, priest? What are you doing here in our churchyard in the middle of the night?"

"I'm, uh, Brother Reynold Greenleaf from Nottingham Friary, my Lady. Some of the local folk have told me about the dead who walk in your graveyard at night, and have begged me to come to see about exorcising the place."

"What kind of nonsense is this?" the lady of the castle said. "I haven't heard anything out here before!"

"But he's been rising from his grave and terrorizing the local village folk," John insisted. "You know, howling and spooking their dogs and what not, so they can't sleep for the noise and for the shaking with fear. It's been going on for at least three nights now. I've come to see what I can do."

Lady Abigail scoffed and was about to speak when a blood-curdling scream split the night and her face froze. The scream had seemed to come from the far end of the churchyard—and from underground.

"It's him! It's the ghost!" Agnes screamed in her turn, and followed it up with a shriek of her own as she put her hands to her face in what Little John had to admit was a fairly decent simulation of terror.

"There!" John pointed toward the supposed grave of Sir Walter. "See! He rises!"

On that cue a figure pushed out from under the earth, and as Lady Abigail waved her shaky candelabra in that direction, they could see by the dim light a bloody head pushing up from one of the graves, followed by a body covered in a shroud caked with dirt. Robin's face was unrecognizable, smeared as it was with dirt and blood, It was pig's blood, as it happened, which Agnes had provided after a slaughter in the kitchens. But Lady Abigail had no way of knowing that, and all she could see was a risen corpse—and all she could hear was the berserk ghost screaming as if in agony.

"Speak to it, Brother Reynold!" cried Agnes. "Ask who it is, and why it's haunting us!"

"Be soothed, spirit," Little John spoke softly. "We want only to help you! Tell us who you are that have risen from your narrow cell."

"Ohh! Aaargh!" the figure moaned inarticulately like a spirit in torment. "One who once held this castle—with that woman there!" And with that the ghost pointed directly at Lady Abigail.

Her eyes grew wide and her face twisted in fear. But this woman was not an easy mark. "William? Sir William of Horsley? Can that be you, husband? But…why is your voice so different than it used to be?"

Little John, who as the representative of the clergy present naturally assumed the role as expert on the walking dead, assuaged the lady's doubts, saying, "Well, actually, he's been in the ground rotting for what, a year my lady? It's a miracle he has any voice box left at all!" Then, turning to the writhing corpse, who was still groaning painfully, asked, "What has disturbed your peaceful slumber, Sir William? Has some demon possessed your corpse? Is there some great sin you regret in life that you need to atone for before your spirit can have rest? Or…is there some great wrong that threatens your legacy that you walk the earth to decry and to set right?"

"Gaaah!" the ghost howled at John's last suggestion, as if he'd hit the nail on the head with that one. "My dear friend! Sir Richard at the Lee!"

Now Lady Abigail stiffened, and she began to see that there

was something to this beyond its being simply a charade. "What of this Sir Richard?" Little John asked.

"His lands!" Robin yelped. "They want to steal his lands! Traitors in my own castle! They shall die with me before that happens! Oh *vi-i-ile*!" He let that long vowel rise like a screeching hawk into the air.

Lady Abigail pursed her lips. This was frightening, but she was still not completely convinced that this was a true ghost. But she did not know how it could know about her plot against Sir Richard. John followed up: "And that is why you are walking the night? You are concerned for your old friend?"

"*Noooo*..." the ghost groaned at length. "It is a new sorrow, but it is not what has driven me mad!"

"Then what has caused this?" John pressed.

"My *son*!" Sir William's supposed corpse cried. "*Where is he*?"

Now Lady Abigail quavered. This was something completely unexpected. Nobody could possibly know about that, she told herself, as she leaned for support against the castle wall. Now Agnes, playing her part to the hilt, cried out, "He's there in his grave, Sir William! Right next to your own!'

"Noooo!" Now Sir William's ghost bellowed out in sheer anguish. "That grave is a sham!"

Now Lady Abigail slumped to the ground, shaking, her back against the wall. Agnes took the candelabra from her with one hand and patted her shoulder with the other. "What is it, my lady?" she asked in mock concern.

The ghost continued, "That grave is filled with stones!"

"How could he know that? Nobody can know that!" Lady Abigail began to mutter, but the ghost resumed his demand:

"Where is my son? Where is he? I will raze this castle to the ground and search for him stone by stone!"

"He's not here! How can you know this?" Lady Abigail screeched, panting and putting her hands over her ears, closing her eyes.

Robin, sensing they might be getting close to the answer, began to stalk toward her, the more to frighten her, his hands outstretched, moving his head from side to side and repeating, "Where? Where? Where?" while Agnes moved the candelabra down and away to ensure that Abigail could not get a close look at him.

"*He is at Skipsea Castle on the Yorkshire coast*!" the lady Abigail finally shrieked, after which she fainted dead away against the castle wall.

Robin, now standing directly over Lady Abigail, looked at Agnes and then at Little John, who had come over to see what had happened. Sensing their cue to escape the premises, Little John said, just in case Lady Abigail could still hear them, "Well, you have your answer, ghost, now go and haunt the people of Yorkshire and leave this place alone!"

"Right, I'm off!" Robin said, before reaching for Agnes with a "Thank you, my dear girl," and kissing her full on the lips before dashing off, followed by Little John, who, having quickly doffed his priestly habit, was waving a grateful goodbye to Agnes.

Agnes, armed with the new knowledge of what had happened to Sir Walter, smiled to herself. What Lady Abigail would say once she'd come to, Agnes didn't know, but she was pretty sure that having that secret knowledge was going to make Agnes a much more important member of the Horsley Castle household than she had been heretofore.

* * *

"Where exactly is Skipsea, anyway?" Robin was asking as he and Little John rode their mounts back in the direction of Nottingham.

"All the way up on the northeast coast of Yorkshire," Little John said grimly. "Days away. Maybe close to a week. I've never been there, and obviously neither have you. But if we're going to get the girl back, that has to be where she is."

Robin sighed. He was trying to wipe the mud and blood off his face while balancing on Daisy's back as they ambled along the well-worn path leading back to the main road. "This mess just keeps getting more and more complicated. We've got to cover territory from Nottingham all the way to the Yorkshire coast."

"All the way to Jerusalem," Little John corrected. "Don't forget the plot against young Sir Peter."

Robin let out a deep breath. "No, I'm not forgetting. But Palomides has gone on that little journey. Maybe we need to do the same with the other parts of this thing: split our men up and send some to York to confront and depose Abbot Robert, some to Skipsea to rescue the countess."

"We've got another rescue to do first," came a familiar voice from the darkness in front of them. As Robin and Little John held up their horses and peered ahead, Robin asked cautiously, "Much? Is that you?"

Much the miller's son came toward them on an ambling horse. "I see you two weren't trying to keep your presence quiet in any way," he said as he pulled in to ride beside them. "I've been hearing you for at least two furlongs."

"We didn't think anyone else would be crazy enough to be out this late on this deserted road," Robin said. "What on earth are you doing here? I'm guessing this isn't just an incredible coincidence."

"No," Much said slowly. We heard from Lady Mary that you had come this way, and Friar Tuck sent me to find you. He...he and several of the other fellows are in Nottingham."

"What?" Little John said. "We leave for a few days and everyone goes crazy? What are they doing there? Are they *trying* to let Sir Guy capture them?"

At that Much took a deep breath. He knew what he said next was going to wake the sleeping bear in Little John's breast.

CHAPTER FOURTEEN

Will Stutely sat on a small pile of dirty straw, on the dirt floor of a cell deep in Nottingham Castle's dungeon. His arms were chained to the wall and his legs stretched out in front of him. It was not by any means comfortable, and the thought flashed through Will's head that when he got back home to Sherwood, he would write Sir Guy of Gisbourne a letter complaining of the accommodations. But it only flashed for an instant, because Will was becoming more and more convinced that he was never going to get back to Sherwood.

Nor, he thought reasonably, was it fair to complain about being uncomfortable sitting there by himself, when these were the least painful moments of his captivity. It had been a day and a half since he'd arrived at the castle with his entourage of twenty guards, and in that time he'd had three long and brutal interrogations, first by Sir Guy himself, then by the sheriff, then by Sir Guy again. In his first interrogation, Sir Guy had lamented the fact that the previous castellan at Nottingham Castle, being an appointee of the old king, had failed to equip the castle with a rack or wheel or other instruments of torture. How, Sir Guy had wondered, did they ever get their prisoners to talk? At any rate, Gisbourne had the two guards Will thought of as "Jack" and "Eyepatch" in the cell with him as he questioned Will, pressing him to know where Robin Hood's camp was located, how many men he had with him, how much money they had stored away, whether they had any spies or allies in Nottingham, and whenever he failed to get a satisfactory answer, Jack and Eyepatch would take turns beating him—Jack with a whip to the back, and Eyepatch with fist blows to the face and body.

The sheriff had his own methods, and came in with one of his deputies, who burned Will's feet with a hot iron when he failed to give the sheriff acceptable answers. Will tried to space out the punishment by giving short half-answers or lies in response to their questions, but when his lies to the sheriff turned out not to match the lies he'd told Sir Guy, Gisbourne came back into his cell once more, and this time did not really seem interested in getting answers at all, but only in causing Will pain. Recognizing that this was what his captor had in mind, Will came up with the impulse to sing once more, the more to annoy his captors and so get them to knock him into unconsciousness, where he would no longer feel pain. All it took was one more verse of "*I am come to see you hanged, / And hanged you shall be*," and Eyepatch fetched him such a blow to the jaw that he was dead to the world.

He wasn't sure now just how long he had been out, but he was not sure he wouldn't still rather be in that condition than the one he was in. His head and face throbbed, his back felt raw from whiplashes and his feet blistered from several burns. His ribs were pained, and he was sure some were cracked. His eyes were blackened and swollen nearly shut, his lips were split and bleeding, he had lost a few teeth, and he was afraid that his jaw might be broken. Well, he thought, if Little John could see him now, he might not think Will was quite so handsome as he had been.

But that thought, too, was going to have to go under the "not bloody likely" heading in Stutely's fuzzy brain. The only way he was going to get out of this alive, he was now convinced, was if Robin and all his meinie came into Nottingham with their longbows raining down deadly shafts on this castle guard and snatched him away from his jailers. And that seemed unlikely, since it would be madness to try to storm a castle with just two dozen men. And even if they did rescue him, they were likely to lose half their number in the process. It would be foolhardy to take such a risk, and Robin was never foolhardy. Now if John were in charge of the band...but no. Will couldn't even conceive of Little John taking that chance with so many other lives. Though he wouldn't put it past John trying something on his own. And inwardly, Will prayed that John didn't. He would almost certainly just end up dying along with Will. Stutely would much rather die alone than be the cause of his partner's demise.

What Will had no way of knowing was that the lady Maude had been lobbying tirelessly for the past twenty-four hours, with her husband and, when possible, with Sir Guy, to preserve Will Stutely's life for as long as she could. As predicted, she and her companions had worn their horses out, but, being the wife of so great a personage as the Sheriff of Nottingham, she had been able to trade them for fresh horses in Doncaster and, as a result, rode into Nottingham less than an hour after Gisbourne's troops had arrived with Stutely.

And that was when she began her harangue. They could not execute Will Stutely, she argued, because he was too small a fish. They should hold him until Robin Hood himself knew of his retainer's capture and was lured to attempt a rescue. Wouldn't it be a much better show for the town to send Robin himself to the scaffold? When that argument lost its appeal with Sir Guy, she changed course completely and argued that the common people of Nottingham thought of Robin and his men as heroes, robbing from the oppressive landlords and prelates and giving valuables to the poor who were in most dire need. A public hanging might cause a riot, she suggested.

Lady Maude's arguments did have the effect of prolonging Stutely's interrogation sessions and, ultimately, his beatings. On the other hand, they also staved off his execution, and in the long run preserved his life, until Friar Tuck and his small party appeared, cloaked and hooded, on the streets of Nottingham. Here they heard the sawing and hammering of workmen hurriedly putting up a wooden scaffold near Saint Nicholas's Church off Castlegate Road—precisely where the good friar had hoped it would be erected. And while his companions scattered themselves among the gathering crowd in the public square, Friar Tuck made his way to Nottingham Castle, where he insisted in a loud voice and quite publicly that he be allowed to see the condemned man in order to hear his last confession.

The crowd that had already gathered around the gates of the castle began shouting their support for the friar's demand. Was this Gisbourne some kind of heathen, that he would deny a condemned prisoner access to spiritual comfort before taking him off to execution? Gisbourne himself, standing on the wall and hearing the crowd's disapproval, called down to his guard and told him to bring the friar to the prisoner. He had never given any order forbidding such a visit, he clarified, for the sake of both the guard and the crowd. So Jack, for he was the guard in charge, let Friar Tuck into the castle and down to the dungeon. And the friar, beyond suspicion because of his clerical robes, carried beneath them two short swords—one for Will Stutely and one for himself—in case they had to fight their way out of the town square.

When the door to his cell was opened and the light poured in, Will lifted his head and squinted at the faces entering the dungeon. He recognized Jack, at the sight of whom the pain in his scarred back grew more intense. Jack's words barely registered in Will's groggy brain, but they did not really surprise him: "The captain has allowed you a visit from this friar, to hear your last confession. You've been found guilty of theft and poaching, and have been condemned to death."

A wry smile crossed Stutely's shattered face. "Found guilty?" he rasped hoarsely. "I don't remember coming before any judge…"

"You were tried in absentia," Jack replied. "I'll be guarding the door," he added, more to the friar than to Will. "When you're done, I will escort the prisoner to the scaffold. You're welcome to follow, if you like, and do your praying, if *that's* any good to you." And with that the guard stepped around the door frame and shut the door behind him.

Stutely looked up at the face of the clergyman looming over him, who was moving his hand in the pattern of a cross and murmuring something in Latin. Will blinked a few times. His mind must still be dazed from his trauma, he thought, for he was almost convinced that the face he was glimpsing through his swollen eyelids was that of Friar Tuck.

"Will!" he was saying. "Will Stutely, I barely recognize you! Ah, those devils have battered you bloody, by all the saints."

"Friar Tuck?" Will whispered in disbelief. "It's really you? I can't believe it. Oh, friar, then they're going to hang me after all? I wish they'd given me a little more time to get used to the idea. I thank God you've come to be with me. Look, tell Little John he was in my heart when they hanged me, will you?" And tears, which he'd held out against through all the pain of the past two days, welled in his eyes when he thought of leaving his world, his band, and his John.

"Buck up, Will! You're not going to hang today, not if I can help it," the friar chided him. "I'm not alone. We've got several of our best bowmen amongst the crowd, and we've got horses waiting. And look here!" the friar lifted his robe to reveal his two swords, at which a spark of hope was kindled somewhere deep in Will's swollen, bleary eyes.

But he remained pessimistic. "I'm so weak and battered I don't know if I could swing a sword," he rasped. "And they'll have my hands tied, too, I'm sure."

"They will, you can be sure," Tuck agreed. "But don't forget I'm going to be with you the whole way. The first opportunity that presents itself, I'll have a sword out and cut your bonds, and put it in your hands. And don't worry about your strength. You'll just need to hold the sword out to ward off any of the unarmed crowd. I'll take care of the one guarding you. Alan a Dale will be standing close to foot of the scaffold—he'll be cloaked and hooded, and he'll have an extra cloak to throw over you so you and he can disappear into the crowd."

"But the guards," Will objected. "There'll be a whole group of them..."

"They'll be confused by the arrows coming at them from every direction," Friar Tuck said. "You see, we've thought of everything! Now buck up and be ready for this, my boy. You'll have to be on your toes, and not have your brains scrambled the way you do now."

Will scoffed and tried to recover a bit of his old bravado. "Just see how well your brain is working after some one-eyed brute pounds on it for the better part of a day! Well, if we're going to pray, we'd better do so, Friar Tuck, because with your plan we're sure to need it."

"Amen," the friar agreed. "How about the twenty-third psalm? The one about the valley of the shadow of death...that might be appropriate."

* * *

It was not long before the door to the cell opened again and Jack entered, along with Eyepatch and Will's old friend with the fat arse. "Pig-face!" Stutely managed to croak out. "I've been wondering where you'd got to!" At that Jack raised an arm to give Will a backhanded smack across the face, but thought better of it with the friar watching, and merely gave Eyepatch and Pig-face the order to take off Will's shackles and tie his hands behind him, and get him up on his feet.

This latter proved difficult, chiefly because the blistered burns on Stutely's feet made it painful for him to stand, let alone walk. And Will would not only have to walk up the steps into the castle bailey, but out the gate and another two hundred yards at least to the scaffold itself. By the time Will's hands had been bound behind him, even Jack could see the futility of trying to make Will walk all the way to the gallows. "You're going to have to brace him up between you," he told Eyepatch and Pig-face, "and pretty much carry him all the way." The friar could see the necessity of this, but at the same time began to despair of having a chance to cut Will's bonds and slip him the sword, with those two brutes holding onto him from either side.

"Let's go then," Jack commanded, and he led the way out of the dungeon, with Eyepatch and Pig-face walking slowly behind, holding up Will between them, who occasionally placed his bare feet on the floor, only to wince in pain when he did. Friar Tuck paced behind them soberly, leaning forward to speak slowly and clearly into Stutely's ear as they moved.

"Be strong, my lad, be strong. Remember, this is not your home. This is only a temporary prison, this earthly life. Think of Our Lord, boy, as he carried his cross toward Calvary. You are on the way to your own Calvary, but remember what he said when he raised Lazarus: 'I am the resurrection and the life, and he that believes in me, though he were dead, yet shall he live.' And you, my boy, are one of those who is going to live. Just keep believing, listen to me and do as I say."

The small party became the center of attention as they moved through the bailey and out the gate into the streets of the city. Borne by rumor and gossip, news of the morning's scheduled execution had spread throughout the city and into villages close enough to draw the interested and the ghoulish. The crowd along the street and around the scaffold had swelled into the hundreds which was, the friar considered, good news in one way, since it would make it very difficult for the guard to track down any of the outlaw band scattered among them, but it could also be bad news since it could make it more difficult to find Alan a Dale to pass Will off to among the crowd. Oh well, the friar reasoned. Only so much can be planned. The rest we have to make up as we go, reacting to the changing environment around us. And pray God doesn't have any disasters planned for you.

Will's mind was finally starting to clear, which also meant that his aching head, back and feet were making their presence known all the more insistently. But as his mind cleared it also began to focus. And as he floated above the ground between the strong if unsympathetic arms of Pig-face and Eyepatch, listening to Friar Tuck's ramblings that kept telling him to have faith and insisting he was going to live, he let his swollen eyes scan the crowd looking for familiar faces. He saw a few that seemed amused by his plight and apparently eager to watch his execution as if it were grand public entertainment—which it was. But most of the people seemed saddened by the spectacle, and looked him in the face with concern and sympathy. As the friar had said, he would have supporters in the crowd, who would ease his escape, if only he could get away from the guards. What he had not seen among the throng were the faces of his comrades. But the friar had assured him they were about. What about Little John? Was he out there somewhere?

Friar Tuck was beginning to second-guess himself. When

would he get an opportunity to use the swords he had smuggled in and to pass one to Stutely? If it didn't happen soon it would never happen, and the friar would have to take the sword and attack both of the guards holding Will by himself, hoping that the third guard would not simply turn around and run Will through before setting upon Tuck. And now the friar realized another problem with the crowd—his friends, scattered among this mass of bodies, would hardly be able to loose an arrow safely or accurately if he and Will started anything on the street, surrounded by that host of bodies. And now the scaffold was in sight.

And now Friar Tuck revised his plan.

He could see that the twenty steep steps leading up to the scaffold were narrow and could only accommodate one person at a time, which meant that for those last steps, Will would have to climb by himself—there was no other way. The head guard, Jack, would no doubt mount the steps ahead of him but Tuck would make sure that he was allowed to accompany the prisoner onto the scaffold, and would follow close behind him—during which time he should be able to reach under his tunic and produce a sword.

Once on the scaffold, they would all be high enough to make easy targets for the likes of Alan of Winchester or Will Scarlet, who could be relied upon to put Jack and the hangman himself out of commission. This rescue might come off after all. Tuck smiled to himself.

But how to let Stutely know what he was planning, without alerting the guards as well? The friar searched his mind for appropriate scraps of scripture, until he finally said, as they approached the scaffold, "Pray with me now, my son: 'I lift up my eyes to the hills, from whence cometh my help.' Oh, lift them up my son. There is your salvation." And as he said this he noticed a black-cowled figure in the very front of the crowd surging in front of the gallows. It was Alan a Dale. "Just as Our Lord on his way to Calvary had many watching his steps, so you, my son, have your friends among the throng. This black hooded figure in front of the crowd, perhaps he is your own Simon of Cyrene, willing to suffer with you as he takes up your cross…"

Will glanced to his right into the crowd and spotted Alan a Dale, and for the first time in days he let himself smile. It hurt.

"We can't carry him up those steps," Eyepatch complained to Jack, who had already begun mounting the ladder.

"He'll have to come up them himself," Jack said.

"Not a lot of incentive for me to do that, is there Jack?" Will managed to croak out, getting in one last dig. The head guard glowered at him, then turned to Friar Tuck. "You come up behind him and push on him, brother friar. If I pull him up, which I've half a mind to, it won't be any too comfortable for him." And he turned to climb up.

This was working out just as the friar had hoped. He let Will struggle up the first two steps on his own, then climbed behind him, positioning himself one rung below Stutely, where his bound hands would be perfectly in position for the friar's bare sword. He called his comfort out to Will loudly as the two of them inched up the ladder. "Remember what Our Lord told his disciples: 'Be alert at all times, praying that you may have strength to escape all these things that will take place, and to stand before the Son of Man.'" After which he whispered so that only Will could hear: "At least I'm pretty sure Alan a Dale's father was a man."

Will had glimpsed the black-hooded figure in the front ranks of the crowd, and grunted an acknowledgment to the friar as Tuck followed close behind him up the ladder, pushing him from behind, nudging him with his shoulder so that he could brace himself to negotiate the narrow steps slowly, painfully, one at a time as Jack, his arms crossed, looked down from the scaffold where he now waited. Annoyed at the delay but realizing there was no way for Will to move his broken body any faster, Jack turned his back and, arms folded, strutted over to the executioner who stood, a black mask over his face, next to the trap door that would fall from beneath Will's feet, allowing him to drop until the rope jerked, stopping his fall and snapping his neck.

But with no one watching—with the exception of the hundreds of spectators—Friar Tuck reached under his robe and pulled out a short sword with which he severed Will's bonds and then placed the pommel in the prisoner's hands. Will, still holding his hands behind him so that neither Jack or the executioner would see that he was free and possessed a weapon, took the final step onto the scaffold, and stood on his aching feet, waiting for the friar to join him. The crowd surrounding them began to cry out, some in surprise and excitement at having seen the prisoner obtain a weapon, some in dismay, who were trying to shout to the guards that something was amiss.

Tuck stepped onto the scaffold himself, his hand inside his robe clutching the handle of his own short sword, and now, at the foot of the ladder, Eyepatch and Pig-face were realizing that something had gone wrong, and drawing their own weapons, were beginning to climb up the steps to the scaffold. At that point Friar Tuck realized the one flaw in his brilliant plan: Even if he managed to save Will from the hangman's rope, how were they going to get down from the scaffold, as several more of the castle guard now began making their way to the foot of the ladder?

First things first: Will Stutely had brought his sword out, holding it before him in both hands and pointing it toward Jack, who finally had realized what was happening and had drawn his own sword and begun inching cautiously toward Will. Friar

Tuck was striding confidently toward the executioner, who was backing away, armed only with a small dagger. But Eyepatch was almost to the top of the steps.

At that moment, whistling through the air like a darting falcon, an arrow fell from the sky and planted itself in Jack's shoulder, piercing his leather armor and forcing him to drop his sword and cry out in pain. At the same time, another arrow from a different part of the surrounding throng swooped in, and with a sickening smack, entered Eyepatch's neck and lodged there, its point jutting out the other side. A look of unpleasant surprise came into Eyepatch's visible eye, and he fell down the steps, taking Pig-face with him all the way to the ground.

Several of Gisbourne's guards had rushed to congregate at the foot of the ladder and Will, seeing instantly that he could not escape that way, surprised everyone, including himself, by stepping up to the rope hanging from the gallows, grabbing the noose in both hands after shoving the short sword into his belt, leaning back and swinging as far as he could, his legs stretching out over the crowd, and letting go.

Stutely might easily have broken an arm or a leg in the fall, but Friar Tuck had been right in gauging the temper of the multitude, and ten men in the mob, sympathetic to the outlaw's cause, stepped forward to break Will's fall and then shove him into the crowd behind them. But Will had not leaped blindly from the scaffold: He had seen where Alan a Dale stood, and had aimed toward his black-cloaked comrade as he soared from the precipice edge. Now Alan stepped forth, a spare cloak and hood in his hands, which he draped over Stutely and sped him away, as fast as his blistered feet could carry him, through the crowd toward safety.

That left Friar Tuck on the scaffold with the badly wounded Jack, who lay moaning in his own blood on the scaffold floor, tended to by the executioner, who was ignoring the friar as somebody else's problem. The portly Tuck took one look at the swinging noose and abandoned any notion of following Stutely's example. Before he had a chance to consider how he might get down safely, there was a terrible commotion among the crowd, and a giant of a man in Lincoln green, a blond bearded berserker with fierce blue eyes in a dark tanned face, came roaring toward the scaffold, swinging in fury a long wooden staff.

Little John had arrived with Robin and Much just as Will Stutely had completed his climb up the scaffold steps, and seeing his partner's dilemma, had leaped off his horse, grabbed his staff, and pushed through the gathered throng. He'd missed Will's desperate leap, and had just come close enough to the scaffold to zero in on the guards at the ladder's base. Robin himself, still mounted farther up the street, had sent Much to confer with Thorvald, whom they could see two streets away waiting in his cart. All the outlaws should meet up behind the Blue Boar Inn once they had made their way discreetly out of this chaos. But Robin, being so visible alone on Daisy, made a perfect target for Alan a Dale to make for, dragging Will Stutely as best he could through the crowd.

Little John, having reached the knot of guards below the scaffold, was swinging his staff deftly and dangerously. It was far longer than any swords the guards had, so that John was able to whap several guards across the nose or ears and send them reeling before anyone would really get a good stroke at him with their own weapons. Several arrows had also come swooping in from the sky to help scatter those guards still standing, and when Friar Tuck saw his way was clear, at least for the moment, he tucked his sword back under his robes and skittered down the ladder as quickly as he could.

When Tuck reached him, Little John was leaning on his staff, breathing heavily in the momentary respite he'd earned with the help of his archer friends. The guards had scattered, but they were sure to return, and Tuck pulled at the big man's sleeve. "Come on, John! Will's safe, look!"

And with that the friar pointed toward Robin, who, sweeping Will out of Alan's hands and onto the back of Daisy, galloped away with the rescued prisoner. Alan a Dale leaped onto Bishop's back and rode after him, and John nodded, his chest still heaving. You go, friar! I'll watch your back and follow as quickly as I can!" And with that Friar Tuck sped off through the crowd, which closed around him protectively, as John took one more gasp of breath and started to follow.

But by this time, the guards Little John had driven off had returned with reinforcements, and what had been half a dozen originally had now swelled to twenty, and they were approaching him from all sides. Under threat of the guards, the crowd now parted and allowed the surrounding ruffians to close in on John from all sides. Most had their swords at the ready, and at least seven of them had armed crossbows pointed directly at his chest. Once more John planted his staff on the ground and leaned on it, looking around at the company and saying, "Well, you've got me. What are you going to do with me?"

* * *

In a small grove of maples behind the Blue Boar Inn north of Nottingham, well off the Great North Road so that they could not be seen by casual travelers or visitors to the tavern, Robin had met up with Alan a Dale and with Much the miller's son, who had also picked up Friar Tuck as the friar had exited through the crowd. Arthur Bland and Alan of Winchester, several arrows lighter than when they'd arrived in Nottingham, were quick to join them on their own horses. They had not been waiting long when Thorvald's cart came slowly up from town and veered off the road to join them in the grove. David of Doncaster and Will Scarlet were lying down in the bed of the wagon, covered with several black cloaks and cowls. "Some of the guard stopped us once," Thorvald told the others, "but I just convinced 'em I was a merchant, sellin' cloaks and cowls ya see. So they let us go."

"Well, make a bed out of those clothes," Friar Tuck told them. "Will Stutely is in no shape to ride a horse. Let him lie there as comfortably as he can."

Indeed, Will had spent the last of his strength swinging on that rope, and he was now in a good deal of pain and feeling weaker than ever. When they had reached the grove and Robin had got his first chance to look at Will closely, he nearly despaired of the young man's life, he looked so beaten and wretched. Now David, Will Scarlet and the two Alans were placing him gingerly in the cart, and he could only give out a low moan. Stutely had borne up under torture and had made as gallant an escape as Robin had ever seen, but if he did not recover from this ordeal, it would have all been for naught. And what would Little John say?

And where was Little John anyway?

"He said he would be following right behind me as I made my way from the scaffold," Tuck said when Robin pressed him. "Didn't anyone else see him?"

"I shot a few arrows toward those guards, and then I turned and made my way out of there when I saw Will being carried out," Arthur Bland said to Tuck. "I never saw John after that. I thought he was following you."

"Well, this is a fine mess," Robin complained. "We go in to save one man, and we just trade him for another! What kind of ragtag outfit would we be without Little John?"

The men looked at their feet, and some began to pace about. "If John's taken, then our work here's not through," Much pronounced. "We've got to go in after him as well."

It was the thought on everyone's mind that nobody had wanted to utter. The friar asked, "And what if we go back to rescue him and just get him killed, as almost happened with Will Stutely, and, in fact, could finally be the case after all? Or if he's not killed, what if it's Alan a Dale, or you, Much, or even Robin himself?"

"Do we really have a choice?" Thorvald asked realistically. "If the men of this 'ere brotherhood don't truly believe that their mates will stick their necks out for 'em if they're ever nabbed by the law, then it ain't gonna last long, I promise ya."

"By the same token," the friar shrugged, "every man in this group has vowed to lay down his life for his friends. Which means that John might very well rather die himself than be the cause of death for any of his comrades—in particular Will Stutely, whose life he had come like a raging bull to save."

"Enough debate," Robin said. He'd stopped pacing and had his hands on his hips. "There is no question. I will be going back after John. Anyone else who is willing to can come with me."

"I, for one, will be coming with you," his nephew Will Scarlet said, laying a hand on Robin's shoulder while the others all murmured their assent—even, from the bed of the cart, Stutely himself. "But hold off for now. We do not even know whether Little John is taken. He is barely late at this point. We know he was in the midst of the crowd and would have been on foot, since Alan a Dale came here on John's horse."

The young jongleur blushed a bit and said, "I did, it's true. We were all scampering to get away from there as fast as possible, and I jumped on the back of the first animal I saw…"

"Oh, no one's blaming you, boy," Friar Tuck said. "Of course you had to take the horse. But Will Scarlet is right. We're jumping before we've been bit. We need to sit tight for now."

"But for how long?" Robin asked, folding his arms and looking back towards Nottingham, as if he could see at any moment Little John striding up the Great North Road. "We can't leave him in Gisbourne's hands overnight. Look at what they did to Stutely."

Arthur Bland spoke up. "You know, we've got to have a new plan to get John out. We can't use the friar again, they know his face. And they won't make it a public execution this time, 'cause they know that just exposes them to rabble like us."

"Right," Robin agreed. "They'll kill him in private, inside the castle. Which means…"

"Which means," Will Scarlet added, "that we've got to find a way to infiltrate the castle. And we've got to do it today. …Any ideas?"

"I've got one idea that nobody's gonna like," Thorvald said. "My idea is that our poor Will Stutely 'ere in my cart needs to get to some place where 'e can get 'is wounds looked to by someone what knows 'ow, or I won't answer for 'im in the future."

"Will he even survive the trip all the way back to Creswell Crags?" Alan of Winchester asked.

"He needn't have to," Friar Tuck answered. "We should take him to our old camping spot at the Great Oak. We can shelter there for the night. There is fresh water and I know from our tenure there where all the healing herbs grow. I can nurse him there as well as they could here at the inn, or at any other secret house in Nottingham. When he's a bit stronger we can cart him to the caves."

"My wife Ellen can nurse him when we get him to Creswell Crags," Alan a Dale added. "She's as cunning as any witch with her herb knowledge."

The friar nodded in agreement and added, "But somebody needs to nurse him now, whether we wait to try to rescue John, or go now to the Great Oak."

"You've made it clear that you should go now to the old campsite to tend Will Stutely's wounds. Thorvald should drive you and Will there now, while the rest of us come up with a plan to get into the castle." There was assent all around to that suggestion, except from within the cart, where Stutely groaned his objections. "Now," Robin said. "Any ideas?"

"We…could…say we're a wandering troupe of players and jugglers. Have Alan a Dale sing to them while the rest of us search for John?" Much offered.

When Robin squinted doubtfully, Will Scarlet made another suggestion: "Let's say we're mercenary archers who've heard Sir Guy of Gisbourne is trying to hunt down the outlaws of Sherwood, and we've come to volunteer to join his guard."

"And we won't look at all suspicious, showing up dressed in Lincoln green?" Robin asked.

"How about we say that we're a bevy of devils let loose from Hell to plague Gisbourne for taking the Lord's name in vain?" said the booming voice moving toward them from the road.

"Little John!" Robin cried, nearly collapsing in relief. "Thank God! We feared that Gisbourne or the sheriff had got you!"

"Oh, they had," Little John told them.

"What? But you escaped?" the friar asked.

"Well, I persuaded them to let me go," the big man said.

"What? How?" Much asked, laughing, as all the men gathered around Little John to welcome him.

"I would tell you," John said, stretching lackadaisically and sitting down under one of the larger maple trees. "But it's a long story and I'm pretty parched right now."

Taking the hint, Thorvald reached back into the supplies he

kept in his cart and brought out a skin of red wine, tossing it to John, who smiled in acknowledgment and swigged a good mouthful of the sweet liquor. "It was like this," the big man began.

"That ring of toughs had me surrounded, and several of them had their loaded crossbows aimed at me. Nothing I could do then but surrender. But I had it in my head that nobody was gonna beat me to a pulp the way they did Will. I'd go down fighting and take some of the bastards with me, if it came to that. But I did let those pissant guards tie my hands—in *front* of me, I made sure of that—and take me to see the big man himself, Gisbourne, who by the way was hopping mad those guards had let Will escape. And two of those thugs stayed behind me, holding my shoulders like I might try to run away any second.

"It was in a small room on the ground floor of the castle, probably a room that led straight down into the dungeon. He was seated at a table along with that dumb ox of a sheriff and, to my surprise, our friend Lady Maude, the sheriff's wife, who it seems had been giving advice to Sir Guy. He was berating her when I came in, telling her they'd waited too long to hang Stutely because she said that'd give them a chance to capture Robin Hood trying to rescue him. And she yelling back that she'd been right, they had had a chance to catch Robin and they botched the job."

"That's just what she said she'd do," Much the miller's son declared. "She said she'd try to get them to put Will's hanging off as long as she could stall them, in the hopes we'd get there in time to rescue him."

Little John nodded at this, and went on. "This time, though, they weren't going to make *that* mistake again. 'Now we've got the legendary Little John himself,' the slimy sheriff gloated. 'No public execution for him! He ain't leaving our dungeons. Not alive, anyway.' And Maude herself keeps trying, I've got to give her credit, and she says, 'But this is the most famous of all the

Sherwood outlaws, except Robin Hood himself. Think of what a coup it would be to hang him before the whole city! Or even make a bigger splash—take him to York! Or London!'"

"Ha! Good girl," Robin said. "Think how many chances we'd have to set you free if they made that long a trek with you!"

"Unfortunately, that's just how Gisbourne was thinking. 'No,' he says. 'We ain't letting this one slip through our fingers. When we hang him, it's going to be right here in the castle bailey, right outside this window, where I can enjoy the show without worrying about interruptions.'

"'I agree,' says the sheriff, wringing his hands like he's got some new toy. And all the while I'm looking at his wife, and thinking, 'How'd a woman as impressive as her end up with a puffed up windbag like that?' And then I remembered what she'd said about how both her husband and this Sir Guy had backed off looking into her uncle Lord Peveril's murder, for fear of crossing that scoundrel, the Abbot Robert. And that got me to thinking about something I'd forgotten about completely."

"And what was that?" Friar Tuck asked.

"Well, I told you I had my hands tied in front of me, and I was pretty happy about that just then, because I started patting around my tunic, where I remembered I had an inside pocket. So just as Gisbourne is about to order his two stooges to throw me down into the dungeon, he glances up at me for a second and says, kind of like a rote legal formality that he expects no answer to, 'Does the prisoner have anything to say in his own defense before we send him to his cell?'

"And at that moment I pull out of the inside pocket of my tunic this sealed parchment I had stuck in there weeks ago and forgotten, and I tell him 'I just have this, my Lord.' And what it says is this long Latin phrase which means nothing to me, but I remember Sir Richard's laughing about it, and Sir Guy reads it and translates: 'the bearer of this certificate is to be held free of any debt or penalty previously incurred in my jurisdiction.' And the seal hanging from it Sir Guy recognizes as that belonging to that same Abbot of York they were so awed by.

"And that's how I got free."

CHAPTER FIFTEEN

She stood on the highest platform of the castle keep, looking to the east to where the waves of the North Sea broke over the narrow beach, and the bloody sun was giving birth to a new day. "Seventy-five," she whispered to herself.

Lady Lydia Peveril, Countess of Chesterfield, surveyed the land for miles about while her dark, untamed tresses danced on the wind like waves on the North Sea. The wind always blew strong on this coast. Her piercing brown eyes glared into the sea as if she expected her deliverance to come from that direction, though in truth, it was much more likely that Danish Viking invaders would be coming from that quarter, since Skipsea Castle had been built largely for the purpose of protecting that coast from the Danes—and to provide a safe port for peaceful merchant ships who might use the natural harbor that lay inside the protection of the castle. The castle's builder, Drogo de la Beauvriére, first Lord of Holderness, had constructed an earthen dam to trap more water from the marshy land surrounding the castle, thereby creating Skipsea Mere, a shallow inland lake that connected to the sea by a navigable waterway, through which ships might enter the lake to dock at the castle's long bailey. Despite the danger of Danish attacks, help was more likely to come from the sea than through the marshes, which were hard to navigate by those unfamiliar with the area.

The young woman heaved a long sigh, made up of three parts gloom and seven of boredom. There was so little to do in this remote backwater that she was given to spending long hours here on the castle keep imagining other lives—lives in which she was carried off by a tall blond Viking prince over the seas to Thule where the sun never rose in winter, or in which she captained her own ship dressed in armor like a man, and set fire to coastal towns that resisted her demand for tribute. And sometimes Sir Peter of Verysdale played a part in her fantasies riding in at the head of a company of crusading knights to snatch her from her imprisonment. And sometimes she imagined the scarred face of Sir Walter of Horsley, abject and at her mercy as he knelt on the deck of her ship and awaited her command that he be made to walk the plank. That, she had to admit, was the most satisfying of all her daydreams, though it seemed by far the most unlikely.

There were times she debated in her soul the wisdom of keeping to her stubborn vow never to yield to her captors' demands that she agree to marry Sir Walter. She was of an age to be married—past it even, at twenty-one—and a woman in her position was typically wed by this time to some nobleman of her father's choosing who could be relied upon to protect her lands and fortune, and get upon her sons to whom she could pass those lands and fortune on. But her own father was long since dead, and her grandfather had wished her to make her own choice of a husband and had left everything to her. Now he, too, had died—as, mysteriously, had her kinsman, Sir Hugh. Skipsea had learned this news a few short days ago, from a messenger sent by the Abbot of Saint Mary's Abbey. Now she truly had no man to give his consent and blessing to her choice of spouse. Consequently, she knew Sir Walter and his allies, the Aumerle family who now commanded the castle, expected her to consent much more readily to pressure to marry him.

Well, Lady Lydia mused, if that's what they thought, they had another think coming.

A shuffle on the stairway behind her made her look back over her shoulder to see the long, thin face and greasy brown hair of Sir Walter emerge from below. She turned back to look again at the sea as her captor and suitor stepped onto the unprotected top floor of the timber-built castle keep. He was dressed in a light blue tunic that reached to his knees and was slit up the front and back, belted with a leather girdle, and covered by a darker blue surcoat. He wore, as well, light tan boots that reached nearly to his knees and dark brown hosen beneath them. No doubt, Lydia mused, he thought of himself as highly fashionable. She merely thought of him as vain and ridiculous.

"My lady," he addressed her with a slight bow, "you persist in gazing out from these walls as if you were a prisoner. Why do you not enjoy the company of the ladies who are here to wait on you? Do some embroidery. Listen to the reading of some romance or other. Have the castle fool sing you some song or ditty. Go hear a Mass at the castle church. Or do whatever else you women do with your time."

"This *is* what some women do with their time," Lydia responded without taking her eyes off the breakers that beat against the shore. "Particularly when they *are* in fact prisoners."

Walter scoffed. "This is simple hysteria," he responded.

"Do I seem hysterical to you?" she asked, turning and looking him coldly in his one good eye. She quickly shifted her gaze to the black patch he wore over his left eye, which did not quite cover the red scar stretching from his eyebrow to his cheek, the result of a splintered lance that had struck him through his helmet in a freak jousting accident. She preferred to look on this side of his face, since it meant she did not have to see into the soul behind his true eye, a soul that recognized the futility of this charade they played day after day. By now he must realize that she would never consent to this coerced marriage they were trying to force on her, particularly now that she had no close male relatives with a legitimate say in who she was to marry. For her kinsman Lord Peveril of Codnor Castle had also died, and she thought of herself as free.

"Certainly," Walter said, looking away. It unnerved him when she wouldn't meet his eye, and he became self-conscious when he thought anyone was looking at his eyepatch. "All you are saying is that you are a woman. Is marriage a prison?"

She considered answering that, but then let it go. "I am not married, as I think you must be aware. And I believe I have made it clear enough, for the past seventy-five days, that if I ever do get married, it will not be to you. And yet you and your Aumerle allies persist in keeping me here against my will. Ergo, prison. QED."

Walter let out a deep sigh of frustration, cursing under his breath Lydia's indulgent grandfather, the late earl, who'd had the cockeyed notion that women ought to be educated, and had indulged her with clerical tutors when she was growing up. Why couldn't he have left well enough alone and just married her off to the highest bidder when she was twelve or so, instead of letting her grow up to become a pawn in this game of marriage and dynasty that his mother and the abbot were playing—and in which he, too, was just another pawn. "You're here because your guardian, Sir Hugh Peveril, negotiated a betrothal with my mother and Abbot Robert, and it only remains for you to agree to the terms," he recited half-heartedly, as if by rote.

"And who said that Sir Hugh was my guardian?"

"Well, *he* did, of course."

"Well, he *lied*," Lydia retorted, certainly not for the first time in the past seventy-five days. "My grandfather was my guardian and he certainly never agreed to any kind of betrothal with anyone, nor would he ever have agreed to anything with that hedge-born liver-eater, which is what he always called the abbot. And even granting the falsehood that Sir Hugh could in any way speak for me, may I remind you that he is now dead as well. I am now the only person who can speak in my own interest, and I am the bloody *Countess of Chesterfield*!"

Sir Walter swallowed, but gamely pushed on. He knew that his mother would want him to do so. "A woman cannot be responsible for herself. The church has made it clear."

"Oh really?" Lydia answered with some verve, swinging her head about to look him in the eyepatch again. "What about this precious mother you're always yammering on about?"

"Well, she's a widow. Having had a husband to advise her makes her more capable of looking after her own affairs. And besides, she relies on the abbot to guide her in her responsibilities. Which reminds me," he added, coming to a point he'd never put to her before, because he'd just thought of it recently. And by *thought of it* that is to say he'd just received the proposal in that same recent message from the abbot. "Abbot Robert has suggested that you become his ward. An orphaned woman like you needs a man's protection, and he expects to get the blessing of the Archbishop of York to take you on as his Christian duty."

Now it was Lydia's turn to heave a great sigh of frustration. She looked away and replied in a calm voice, to ensure she could not be accused again of hysteria: "I am of age. I must consent to any such arrangement, and rest assured that will never happen. Just as I must consent to any marriage contract, and I swear by my grandfather's blessed bones that, even if I am forced bound and gagged to the church door, I will refuse to utter assent to any marriage vows with you. Ever."

Sir Walter cleared his throat, thought for a moment, and then answered drily, "Well, if you were indeed gagged, you couldn't utter anything at all."

"We're done talking now," Lady Lydia muttered, turning again to the sea. "I'm sick of looking at you. Go away and let me watch the waves. They're much better company."

* * *

It was from the waves that salvation came. It came in the unexpected form of a ballinger, or small boat, making its way along the coast from the south. It had a single square sail and was manned by a Norse-looking skipper and about eight oarsmen, though the boat was large enough to have used a good dozen more. It did seem to be carrying a cargo of clothing or other fabric, and at first Lydia thought it was a merchant vessel. Such boats were often used in coastal trade, and she had seen a score of similar vessels come in and out of the castle's harbor in her imprisonment, so at first she had paid no particular attention to the passengers as they docked their boat in Skipsea Mere. They did look rather curious to her, though, as she gazed down at the group from her tower. Only the captain seemed like a seaman. There was a little person, a dwarf she thought, with a white beard. There was a giant of a man with huge shoulders, and a well-fed cleric of some kind. And it looked like they had a blonde woman with them, a young woman of some noble bearing. Their leader, a man dressed in a Lincoln green tunic and brown hosen, was calling up at the main gate that led into the castle's living quarters, a set of low timber buildings ranged around a central courtyard. He was a man of some confidence, Lydia noted. Perhaps even brazenness.

It was no great surprise to her when one of the Aumerle servants, a woman who had always treated Lydia with kindness, came up to tell her that a troupe of players had arrived, and that the castellan, William de Forz, lord of Holderness, had engaged them to put on an entertainment in the castle courtyard, in exchange, the servant said, for dinner and lodging for the night. There was in such offers, Lydia knew, a tacit promise of monetary reward as well if the performance was to the castellan's liking. In any case, the servant told her, the company was setting up an acting platform even now, and Sir Walter had asked that the lady Lydia be expressly invited to attend the entertainment—knowing, he had said, how tedious life at Skipsea had become with so little to amuse her. Lydia smiled inwardly, and thought that perhaps Walter actually *did* occasionally listen when she talked. But that, she reminded herself, was no reason to change her mind about marrying him. He was still a kidnapper, a bully and a misogynist. And those were his good points.

"The players are expectin' to start their little entertainment within the hour, I was to tell you, ma'am," the servant said, with a curtsy. Lydia didn't bother to correct her. Properly, as Countess of Chesterfield, she was entitled to be addressed as "Lady Courtesy." At least the servant might have said "My Lady." But no matter, Lydia thought to herself. She was hardly in her own castle now. The servant continued, "If you'd like to start makin' your way down to the courtyard now, you'd be sure not to miss anythin'."

"Yes, Nancy, I would very much like to see these players. You go ahead. I will come down directly." And as Nancy left with another bob up and down, Lydia sighed. Finally, she thought, something to break the monotony of her captivity. She wondered, as she started down the tower steps, how many more weeks it would have to last her.

The courtyard was bustling with industry and anticipation as she entered. Everyone in the castle had apparently turned out for this unusual and unexpected treat. Directly within the castle's main gate, a low, makeshift wooden platform had been quickly pounded together from boards and trestles generally used for dining, and a sort of scaffold had been jerry rigged at the back of the stage holding a long, wide curtain, behind which the players were now gathered in the space between the stage and the open gate, apparently getting into costume and making last-minute plans. Servants, pages, and members of the castle guard were finding places to stand all about the yard, while several benches, also used for dining, had been set up close to the stage for members of the Aumerle family and other notables. As she entered the courtyard, Lydia noticed that Walter had kept a space open next to him at the end of the bench directly in front of the stage.

Lady Lydia immediately began glancing about to see whether there was another open space on one of the benches and, spotting none, considered just how uncomfortable it might be to stand throughout the players' entire performance. But as she was debating inwardly, the young lady she had noticed from the tower stepped out from behind the curtain and began walking toward the well that stood in the middle of the courtyard. At the sight of her, Lydia's eyes bulged, and she began to turn a bright shade of red. The lady caught her eye, as no doubt she had intended, and with a furtive shift of her eyes and surreptitious motion of her head, she beckoned Lydia to meet her at the well. Lydia, having recognized her chief lady-in-waiting, the lady Mary of Winchester, lowered her eyes demurely and stepped toward the well, clutching her hands together to keep them from betraying the violent trembling that was threatening to overwhelm her entire body.

"My God, Mary, is it really you, or has my long captivity here finally driven me mad?" Lydia whispered, suppressing the urge to throw her arms around her closest living ally.

Mary, pulling the bucket up from the well to drink some water from the dipper, and casually offering the same to Lady Lydia, answered very quietly, "Easy, my lady, do not betray me to the castle guard. Softly and calmly, that's the way. We're just a couple of thirsty wenches meeting by chance at the local well..."

"Speak for yourself, wench!" Lydia answered with a soft chuckle, falling into her old habit of speech with her friend. "I assume you're here to rescue me?"

"To carry you off in our ship, yes," Mary said.

Lydia raised an eyebrow. "That's no ship," she told Mary.

"But it's fast and they'll never catch us," Mary told her.

"But how are you planning to get me out of here without raising the whole castle against you?" Mary answered her with the plan.

* * *

On the improvised stage, Thorvald had come out to quiet the audience, which was beginning to show some impatience. A fair number of little people made a rather comfortable life for themselves in the courts of English nobles as entertainers, jugglers, jesters, or licensed fools, and so Thorvald figured he could amuse the crowd for a few moments while the rest of the troupe made their last-minute strategies. Looking down into the first row, he saw seated in the center of the bench the richly attired and self-important man with the well-groomed beard and ermine cloak that he knew to be the castellan Sir William de Forz. He also noted that the small, dark-haired lady in the blue samite gown, whom he assumed must be Lady Lydia, had taken her seat at the end of the bench next to the man with the eyepatch, whom he guessed must be the wounded-but-far-from-dead Sir Walter. Assuring himself of their presence had been his main purpose in coming onto the stage. Any entertainment he might provide would strictly be an afterthought.

"Sirs and madams and all you worthies standing about, we are an 'umble troupe of players what begs your attention this afternoon to our play. Our fine actors are even now gettin' into their costumes and their characters. I 'ave but one request afore we begin our play: We'd like a young volunteer from the audience to play one small part in this 'ere production. Ya don't 'ave to learn any speeches or sing any songs, just stand on the stage an' look pretty is all we ask."

There were a few quick hands that shot into the air from various spots in the crowd, but Thorvald never looked anywhere but the end of the front bench. "You, my lady," he said to Lydia, "please come this way, if you'd please go behind the curtain and they will explain your part and get you into a costume!" And with that Thorvald held out his hand, helped the countess onto the stage and led her to where the curtain parted and she joined the players backstage, all the while noting that Sir Walter watched with a sincere smile on his face, glad that Lady Lydia had finally found something that seemed to please and interest her. "An' now, your honors," the dwarf continued, "we'll be gettin' under way in just a moment or two."

But by now some of the crowd was truly impatient, and a few of the servants standing in the rear called to Thorvald to do some cartwheels since that, in their experience, was what entertaining dwarfs did. Thorvald looked back at them with some scorn and pointed to his beard. "You see these white whiskers?" He called back to them. "I ain't done a cartwheel in thirty years, an' I ain't about to start now. *You* come up 'ere and do a cartwheel."

Now others in the audience were calling on Thorvald to juggle, or to dance, or to sing, but the dwarf held out his hands to quiet them and said, "Look, the best singer you'll 'ave 'eard in years'll be right out 'ere in 'arf a minute. For now, may'ap I can just dazzle you with my wit. 'Ow's this? Just before we set up the stage 'ere, your lord Sir William 'ere was complainin' to me as 'ow 'e's lost a few of 'is teeth lately, ya see, an' 'e 'as a couple more that's so loose as' e's afraid they might fall out too!"

The crowd had grown very quiet at this, and all were looking at Sir William, who was lowering his brows at the dwarf with an expression that could hardly be called amused. But Thorvald seemed oblivious, and continued: "'Don't you give it another thought,' I told 'im. 'An' why not,' 'e says. 'Because,' I told 'im, 'my testicles 'ave been 'angin' loose for sixty years, an' they ain't fallen yet!'"

Sir William's explosion of laughter at the joke gave the rest of the audience permission to laugh as well, and they did, riotously. Thorvald looked back toward the curtain to see the face of Will Scarlet peeking out, whispering to the dwarf to keep the crowd occupied just a wee bit longer, and Thorvald sighed and thought up another joke. "So on the way 'ere, I was talkin' to my good friend, what plays the portly friar in our troupe." Thorvald had decided not to press his luck with Sir William, and to make one of his own friends the butt of the next joke. "Now we was a lot later than we thought we was gonna be, and the friar, worryin' about the time of day, says to me, 'Do you think I'll be able to get through the castle gate?' And me, lookin' at 'is ample girth, I says to' im, 'I wouldn't worry, friar. If a cartload o' hay can make it through, I reckon you'll be able to squeeze in.'"

Amid the renewed laughter, Thorvald looked around again and this time saw Alan a' Dale's face peeking out at him through the curtain, and turning again to the crowd, he proclaimed, "An' now, gentles all, I give you our renowned minstrel, the golden-tongued Alan a...uh...of the hill!" Alan gave him a questioning look as they passed on the stage and Thorvald shrugged, whispering, "probably shouldn't tell 'em our real names, eh?"

Alan stuck the strings of his lute and began to sing in his pleasant tenor:

Lords and Ladies, hearken to me
For we'll show you this day a yarn:
One of Father Abraham
And the two sons to him born.

At this point Robin, wearing a fake white beard and long white robes, walked out on stage. He was bent over, pretending, unconvincingly, to be an old man. Alan continued,

This all occurred long years ago
Now his wife Sarah was so old,
In the Holy Land it was,
She could never have a child.

Now it was Will Scarlet's turn to step out on stage. He, too, was acting like an old person, but his long white wig and woman's gown made it clear he was intended to represent an old woman. Alan a Dale went on:

She sent her servant in to him
Hagar she was called,
And Abraham knew that concubine
And she bore him a child.

While Alan was delivering this verse, Lady Lydia was pushed onstage, her expensive samite gown removed and replaced with a simple brown tunic that a servant girl might wear. As she stepped out and faced the crowd, Robin-as-Abraham stepped behind her, held her by the shoulders and made a thrusting motion with his hips, which, though never touching her, was a close enough simulation of sexual congress that the audience roared with laughter, some in a kind of shocked surprise, some with a bit of satisfaction at seeing the aloof woman who had considered herself apart from and, as they saw it, superior to the castle folk, humbled to some extent. Only Sir Walter looked out of sorts over this bawdiness directed at the woman he still subconsciously thought of as his promised wife, even if he'd consciously given up on her weeks ago. But despite all this furor, Lydia/Hagar seemed scarcely aware that anything had happened when Alan sang his next verse:

Nine months later she bore a son
Ishmael was his name.
He didn't much like any man,
And every man's hand was against him.

At these words Alan of Winchester sprang out from behind the curtain and danced around the stage in a kind of wild frenzy. Grinning from ear to ear and showing off his semi-toothless gums, Winchester seemed to be having a great time playing an uncontrollable adolescent, his leathery brown face rearranged into a happy cluster of wrinkles. "*I'm Ishmael and I'm a wild, wild man*," he sang out

And I don't wanna listen to my mom or dad!
Just give me all the property my pop has got,
And then maybe I'll be glad!"

The audience clearly liked Winchester's clowning, but Will

Scarlet-as-Sarah soon put a stop to it, pointed in mock anger at Hagar and her son and singing out

This slave and her son are getting uppity!
Husband, I want them gone!
Get that concubine out of my sight
And tell her to take her son!

Now Robin and Will moved to the back of the stage while Lydia and Ishmael/Winchester moved front and center, and sat down, looking tired and hungry. Alan a Dale narrated,

Abraham was sick of Sarah's nagging
So he threw out Hagar and her child.
And so they wandered all alone,
Out in the desert wild.

And Alan of Winchester, rearranging his wrinkles into a mask of sorrow, moaned out his own sad verse:

No food, no drink, no dear old dad,
He threw us out, but why?
Oh pray to God my mother dear,
I'm afraid I'm gonna die!

Now the audience was on the verge of tears, so fond had they been of Alan's Ishmael. Even Lady Lydia tried her best to look sad, feeling the pressure of her role. Then suddenly, to everyone's delight, an angel appeared, with wire wings and a halo over his white robes. It was Friar Tuck himself, carrying a jar held up carefully. He delivered his lines with true Thespian fervor:

I'm Raphael, an angel sent from heaven,
Through Hagar's prayer so true!
So stop your tears and start to smile,
I'm here to rescue you!

At that word Tuck dumped his water-filled jar right over Alan/Ishmael's head, at which the lad started up with a cry, shaking himself off, and the good angel took Lydia/Hagar by the hand and led her off through the curtain, followed by a muttering, still shaking Ishmael. The audience, delighted by the horseplay, cheered appreciatively, but grew more silent as Robin and Will moved sadly to the center of the stage, and Alan a Dale continued:

Now Abraham had no more son,
He was a hundred years old,
And Sarah, ninety winters gone,
Her womb was mighty cold.

At that word, Robin went down on his knees and turned his eyes heavenward, and pronounced this lament:

Here I've got all this wealth,
Servants and flocks and rents,
And no child of my blood to inherit it,
Just the slave who guards my tents.

To which Alan responded,

Then God called down, "You! Abraham!
I'm giving you a son of your loins.
Your Sarah, she will soon be blest
With a child, by Him who bought our sins!"

Now Will Scarlet, who'd been waiting for his big moment, stepped forward and belted out his solo part:

Me bear a child? Don't make me laugh!
It's been fifty years since my time of the month.
As for my husband's role as the siring stud,
Well, I think maybe I'll just shut my mouth.

The audience exploded again, and Alan a Dale, who had written all of the parts, smiled. If there was one thing he'd learned in his time as a traveling minstrel and entertainer, it was that any class of audience—nobles, burgers, or villeins, or even clergy—would fly into hysterics at the bawdy and the scatological, so if you wanted to make them laugh you had to hit them below the belt. But he was also smiling at the crowd because he knew something they didn't know. He knew that Skipper Haakon who'd been acting as sailing master of the ballinger on which they'd all arrived, had stayed on board and by now had the sail up and the ship ready to embark at a moment's notice. And he knew that every character leaving the stage—and that included Thorvald, Alan of Winchester, Friar Tuck, and most importantly Lady Lydia, accompanied by Maid Marion—had passed through the gate and down to the port to board the ship, unobserved by the guards who had abandoned the barbican to watch the show. They simply had to finish the play, get everyone safely off, and pull on those oars before anyone in the castle was the wiser. But as Alan turned again to strike up his lute and face the audience, he noticed something that did not look quite right. There were now two empty seats in the front row, not just one. Where had Sir Walter wandered off to? Well, Alan thought, nothing he could do about that right now. The show must go on. He delivered a few verses describing Isaac's birth and Abraham's joy. Alan had actually briefly considered depicting Isaac's circumcision, but had skipped it for the sake of brevity. He didn't want to draw the play out too long while everyone was itching to be gone. But oh, the audience would have loved it. But now Sarah was done, and as Will Scarlet passed behind the curtain he threw off his dress and wig and ran full speed through the gate toward the waiting boat. Now Much the miller's son stepped on stage in his role as Isaac, whom Alan a Dale had conceived as a great contrast to Ishmael. As Isaac, Much walked meekly onto the stage, a bundle of wood strapped to his back for reasons unknown at this point in the story. His hands were steepled before him, and he said,

I'm the son of Abraham's old age,
Gentle Isaac, meek and mild.
I'm the apple of my father's eye,
I'm never rough and never wild.

Then Much put the bundle of wood on the ground, and after some mawkish embracing of father and son, Alan broke in with this verse:

Now God called "Abraham! Take your son
Your only son, the one you love,
And burn him as an offering to me, your God!
Your only God, in Heaven above.

Don't question me! Don't hesitate!
You've got to learn obedience!
Wife, parent, or child are nothing to you
Next to my love and your faithfulness.

Alan could feel the tension as the audience suddenly had become deathly quiet. Surely they knew this story, he thought as he looked into their eyes, but seeing it acted out before them was something different. Robin, hunched over like the hundred-year-old patriarch, turned his eyes to the sky in mock anguish, saying,

Son of my old age, Isaac has been
A most dear child to me,
But yet I love my God much more
And must follow his decree.

Then, moving in a slow shuffle across the stage, as if beginning a journey, he called to Much/Isaac:

Come my child, my son so dear,
My child obedient and wise,
The Lord commands that we go thither
And make to Him a sacrifice.

Much, picking up the bundle and bearing it conspicuously on his back, answered,

Right! I'll carry the wood for the fire!
But father, why do you look so sad?
And by the way, where is the lamb
We should kill on the altar of God?

Much, looking wary and fearful, kept following Robin around the stage, while Alan sang a few verses about climbing a hill to the altar, during which the pair stopped and Much/Isaac put down his burden, and Robin/Abraham pretended to tie the boy to the wood for his sacrificial pyre, and pulled from under his robes a long, sharp-looking dagger. Now Isaac made his most pathetic appeal:

If I've trespassed, father, I sore repent
And submit to your authority.
Only father, hold off a space—
I'm awfully young to die!

Mock tears were flowing from Much's eyes and Robin was working some up himself. Many in the audience were being carried away by real tears as Robin held up his knife and pulled Much's head back by the hair to expose his vulnerable neck, at which point Much, in a mischievous whisper, muttered, "Don't shave me too close, Dad!" Robin, stifling a laugh, momentarily buried his face in his shoulder as if fighting with a devastating sorrow. Recovering, he raised the knife again and spoke

The heart in my breast will break in two
But I cannot stay my hand.
Sarah hearing this shall die,
But I obey my Lord's command.

And just as Robin/Abraham seemed about to sweep the knife across Isaac's innocent throat, Little John burst through the curtain and grabbed Robin's hand, wrenching the knife out of it, so much to the delight of the audience that they actually cheered. John, unlike Friar Tuck as the earlier angel, was not robed in white, nor was he sporting wings or a halo. In fact, he wore only his brown hosen and boots, and was stripped bare to the waist, showing off his considerable muscles, and he proclaimed in a booming voice, to Robin and Much as well as to the assembled crowd,

I'm the angel Michael! I command God's host,
And I'm here to command you:
You're not to sacrifice your boy.
Instead, cook up this Ewe!

With that, in a somewhat unlooked-for finish, the angel Michael gestured to Alan a Dale far to stage right, and Alan fell onto his hands and knees, pulling from under his tunic a crude hat that had quite obviously been made of sheep's wool. John stepped to him, grabbed him by the collar, and led him baaing over to Robin and Much. The three of them scooted off through the curtain, and Little John took center stage to pronounce the moral of the story, and to give the other three ample time to disrobe and scamper through the gate and into the waiting ballinger.

Gentles all, our play is done,
Much it may teach you and me:
Know first that, however dire your plight,
God may yet rescue thee.

And gentles, if that lore suffices not
Then learn you this as well:
Submit you to the Lord's mild yoke:
In the end, God has his will.

The castle's populace, in this out of the way corner of York, were an audience appreciative of any sort of outside entertainment, and let Little John feel their appreciation with raucous cheers and hoots at his concluding remarks, and John let the ovation go on long enough, he felt, for all the others to have climbed into the boat. Now, of course, he had to get himself away as best he could, and this time he had no letter of exoneration from Abbot Robert to place in anyone's hands. But he, Robin, Friar Tuck and Alan a Dale, who together had planned this farce, had come up with a tentative scheme for getting John away, though it did involve a certain element of improvisation.

"My friends," John began, holding up his hands to stop the applause. "We like to end our revels with one final marvel: I happen to be, I make the claim, the strongest man in England. See my muscles if you doubt it!" And with that he flexed his arms, making his biceps dance, much to the admiration of the female members of the audience, and the envy of the men and boys. Little John, meanwhile, was looking around the courtyard until his eyes rested on a large four-wheeled wagon standing in the far corner, unhitched to any horses. He continued, "Now as our parting caper, I will perform for you an astounding feat of strength, one of your own choosing!" But before anyone in the crowd had a chance to suggest anything, John seemed to just catch sight of the wagon, and pointed to it as if a thought had just struck him. "Aha! I see you have a large wagon there in the corner! What would you think of my taking hold of it and pulling it, single handedly like a team of horses, across this courtyard?" The audience thought that sounded fine, and gave John cheers of encouragement. And at their shouts he nodded, leaped down from the platform of the stage, and strode confidently toward the wagon. The crowd parted for him, and as he approached the wagon he noticed that it was not empty, as he'd thought, but bore a heavy load of farm implements. He felt sweat forming on his brow and wondered whether he might have bitten off too large a mouthful.

The crowd began to murmur as John inspected the wagon, pushing a bit on the wheels to make sure they were not stuck or weighed down heavily into the earth of the courtyard. They seemed free, and John walked to the front of the wagon, placing himself between the shafts that would have gone around the horse under normal circumstances. He held one of the shafts in each hand and lifted up on them tentatively, just giving them a little test. Oh yes, he thought to himself. That is one heavy wagon.

But John knew one thing that his admiring audience didn't: The big feat of strength in this case would be the very first instant. The wagon was very heavy, it was true, but once it started moving, once the wheels started going around, those wheels became his allies, and it was much easier to *keep* the wagon moving than to *start* it moving. John even noticed that the courtyard slanted ever so gently downward toward the bank of the harbor, and that would help even more. So everything depended on that first powerful jerk. So grasping a horse shaft in each hand, John planted his feet, took a deep breath, and gave one mighty yank.

Nothing happened.

The audience began to murmur more audibly, and Little John even thought he heard a few wagers being laid among the crowd as to whether he would indeed be able to make good his boast and pull this heavy burden across the castle grounds. John let go the shafts, spit on his hands, took up the shafts again and with a prodigious groan surged forward.

The wagon jerked forward slightly for an instant, then fell back into its original position.

Now the crowd's noise became bolder and more heckling. There were cries of "He can't do it!" and "Strongest man in what country?" and the wagers were becoming louder as some that had first supported John now tried to hedge their bets. But John just smiled. He wished he had a little money on it. He was pretty sure he could get really good odds, and he was certain that this third try would be successful. The first two had just been for show.

With another deep breath and a gritting of his teeth, Little John let out a cry and gave one powerful heave, and the wagon broke from its stasis and slowly began to roll. Once he had it moving, he strained to keep it going, and the wagon picked up speed as it rolled through the assembled crowd, which was now nearly silent with awe and, as John pulled his load closer and closer to the gateway out of the courtyard, built up its response into an appreciative roar. Just as I predicted, John thought to himself. This is the easiest part, and this is getting the biggest cheer!

"He's going to take it right out the gate!" Someone in the crowd shouted, and that inspired laughter and more cheers as the crowd followed John and the wagon around the back of the stage and toward the open gate.

But Little John did not pull the wagon out of the gate. Instead, he came at the gate from the side, pulling the wagon into the space until he had actually wedged the heavy wagon into the castle gate. Ducking under the outside shaft, Little John turned to his admiring onlookers and waved with a wide smile. "Adieu, my friends!" he called, and then dashed off toward the docked boat.

The crowd kept cheering and laughing, pounding one another on the back, and the few who had been steadfast in their wagers were happily collecting their winnings. Then a few people started to notice that the entire troupe had left the castle, and for some curious reason had left all their costumes and their large curtain behind. A few others began to wonder how they were going to get that wagon dislodged from their gate, realizing that, as it was, nothing else could move through the exit, unless a person climbed over it. And then a high-toned screech sounded above the crowd's tumult, and the servant Nancy cried out, "Lady Lydia! She was with them players! She's never come back! I think they've gone off with her!"

* * *

As Little John approached the ballinger, the rest of the crew were all aboard, with sail raised and oars at the ready, and they were shouting to him to climb aboard so they could get a fast start, fast enough to make futile any chase the lord William de Forz might send in their wake.

But before John could undo the dock line and leap into the boat, a figure emerged from where he had been crouched out of sight near the neighboring boat and put himself between John and the outlaws' ballinger. He was clearly a wealthy young man, dressed in a fashionable blue tunic and darker blue surcoat and tan boots, and he had a thin face and long oily brown hair, and had one deep-set lively brown eye. His other eye was covered with a black patch that obscured most, but not all, of a raw scar. Several voices called from the boat, urging Little John to throw the intruder into the mere and get in the boat so they could get away quickly. The Countess of Chesterfield herself called from the boat that this intruder was none other than Sir Walter of Horsley, who had kept her in Skipsea Castle against her will for three months, and whom John ought to flatten with one great punch to the head and think no more about it.

There is little doubt that John would have had no difficulty in doing just that, and given how pressed for time the group was, it probably would have been expedient to do so. But there was something in the intruder's face, a kind of pleading expression in his single eye, that made Little John hold his fists, though he kept them clenched as he demanded, "Well? You are Sir Walter, as she says? Can you give me any reason not to do as she suggests?"

"He's got five seconds to tell you," Robin called from the stern of the boat. "After that, we put the dock line around you and you can swim back to Scarsborough behind the boat!"

"Take me with you!" Sir Walter pleaded without preamble.

That John had not expected. "But…you…" he babbled in surprise.

"This whole thing was my mother's idea, not mine. Well, hers and the abbot's. Lady Lydia obviously doesn't want me, and I'm fine with that. Take me with you and nobody can blame *me* that she got away!"

"Time's up!" Robin called from the boat. "All on board who are coming on board."

And after a beat Lady Lydia's voice called out, "I guess that means you too, Walter."

And with a broad smile, Sir Walter of Horsley joined Little John in leaping aboard the ballinger just as her oars struck the water, the wind puffed her sail, and she scooted down the mere to enter the North Sea and speed down the coast to the harbor in Scarsborough.

* * *

Back inside the castle, Sir William's guards were scurrying about, some trying to dislodge the wagon from the gate, others running to get a strong horse to pull it away, and still others preparing to climb over the wagon to rush down to the dock and get a boat prepared to set off in pursuit of the outlaws' craft, already beating oars out of the harbor to the sea. One of the officers of the guard was barking orders as he tried to assemble a crew to man one of the castle's own cogs currently moored nearby, but at the same time the commander of the castle guard was explaining to Sir William that it would take some time to prepare the sails and get the ship out of the harbor, by which time the ballinger would be well ahead of them and, unfortunately, the smaller boat would move much faster than their cog in these coastal waters.

Sir William de Forz stood glaring out into the sea after the escaping boat and thought to himself, well, he'd done what the Abbot of Saint Mary's Abbey of York had asked him to do. He had a good deal of land of his own in Yorkshire, and the abbot was an influential friend to have. But this business of keeping the young girl against her will to try to force her into an unwanted marriage left a bad taste in his mouth. He'd done what he could, someone had stolen her back despite his best efforts, so there it was. He thought about the entertainment he'd just witnessed. Sometimes God steps in to rescue someone at the last moment when you least expect it, wasn't that what saved Isaac, and Ishmael too? Saved Lady Lydia as well, it seemed. And who was he to question God's plans? Better to be like Abraham, and accept God's will in this matter.

"If there's no way to catch them, then there's no point trying, is there?" Sir William said to the commander of his guard. "Let them go. The abbot won't be pleased but he can go whistle for all I care." And with a little smile, he turned into the courtyard to look for his wife in the confusion.

CHAPTER SIXTEEN

The sail up the coast was brisk and bracing, but otherwise uneventful, and the ship they had anticipated chasing them never materialized from Skipsea. The journey to Scarborough was about thirty sea miles. Since their average speed was six knots—more if they all rowed together, but with no ship giving chase they did not feel compelled to do so—they should get to the old harbor just south of the castle in around five or six hours, as Haakon figured it.

It was time enough for Lady Lydia and her favorite lady-in-waiting to catch up as they sat huddled together in the stern of the boat. Lady Mary explained just who Robin Hood and his cohorts were, and how they had become entangled in the countess's saga by their friendship with Sir Richard at the Lee. She broke the news to Lydia of her kinsman Sir Hugh's murder, only to learn that the countess had already heard the news. But the charge that it was the Abbot of Saint Mary's Abbey who'd been behind the murder was news to her, and not welcome news. And while Lady Lydia fumed, Marion told her about the summit she had held at Peveril Castle with Robin, Little John, Sir Palomides, and the countess's own cousin Maude. At that name Lady Lydia scoffed. She'd never known Maude to be interested in supporting anyone's interests but her own, but when Marion told her how it had been Lady Maude who worked out the abbot's likely part in Sir Hugh's murder, and how she had revealed the plot to kill Sir Peter overseas, Lady Lydia shrugged and admitted, "Well, maybe there's something noble in my cousin after all. I wonder if I ought to do something for her, now I've come into my inheritance."

Lady Mary continued, relating how Sir Palomides had taken on the task of rescuing Sir Peter from his assassins, and how Robin and Little John had coaxed the whereabouts of the countess and Sir Walter from Walter's mother. Lydia laughed heartily at the image of Lady Abigail frightened into confession by the supposed ghost of her late husband. Then Marion went on to explain how the countess's own rescue had been executed. Emboldened by their successful stratagem at Codnor Castle, Robin had suggested an all-out theatrical smokescreen to rescue Lydia from the well-guarded fortress at Skipsea. And with Alan a Dale's talents it had worked. But the most important piece in the rescue puzzle had been acquiring the boat they would arrive on and escape in. That had been the work of Skipper Haakon.

Haakon made no secret that he had in the past been on Viking expeditions, which the unenlightened people of Yorkshire thought of as pirate raids. When he'd grown weary of risking his life constantly on the high seas, he'd decided to retire here in the north of England, where a good number of the folk had Norse roots. But Haakon would never make a farmer and joining Robin's band was as close to being a pirate on land as was possible. But he did, of course, have a lot of experience with the sea, and he still knew a number of his old Viking comrades, a few of whom he knew frequented the port at Scarborough, where their Norse forbears had established a fishing village that they had named *Skarðaborg*. One of these old mates had been willing to loan Robin and his crew the fleet little ballinger that he used as a fishing vessel—for the small fee of thirty gold nobles—and agreed to keep their horses and Thorvald's cart as collateral. And Haakon's seamanship had been a huge boon to this adventure.

"And now," said Robin, who'd been listening to the two women's exchange, "the time has come to beard the lion in his den. From Scarsborough, we go to York to confront the abbot himself."

The Countess Lydia's eyes widened into globes until, clinking her jaws shut after gaping for an instant, she choked out, "York is somewhat larger than Skipsea." Then she advised, "and the abbot's guards are not all peaceful monks. How do you expect to get to him, or to bring him to justice even if you get that far? He is not just the most powerful prelate, he is the most powerful *man* in Yorkshire. You have what, nine men? Plus us two women, who aren't likely to be of much use in a pitched battle."

"Heavens, let's hope it doesn't come to any pitched battle," Robin said. "But we do have the Countess of Chesterfield, assuming you'll come with us to confront him. And we've got the Lord of Horsley Castle, assuming you'll do the same, Sir Walter."

Lydia and Walter looked at each other in surprise, then Walter shrugged and said, "Why not? It's time I stood up for myself, right?"

"You're telling me," Lady Lydia shot back at him. "As for me, I think it's time I let my enemies know that I am capable of making my own decisions—something my grandfather the earl recognized and encouraged. This abbot doesn't have the right to decide my future for me."

"But these things will barely ruffle the proud abbot's feathers," Little John said. "He's behind the murder of Sir Hugh Peveril, and he's guilty of ordering the murder of Sir Peter. Those crimes should topple him from power."

"But we have no way of connecting him with the threat to Sir Peter—not without Lady Maude as a witness, and she's in Nottingham," Robin said.

"But for Sir Hugh's death there is the kitchen lad, Nicholas," insisted Little John. "I know him, and I can find him, and trust me, I can convince him to testify."

"Testify?" the countess echoed. "You think you'll be able to bring the abbot into a court? You must be insane."

Little John shrugged. "There are a number of opinions about that. And I must admit, worse things have been said about me. But no, I have no illusions about bringing him into a court of justice, either civil or ecclesiastic. But if we can confront him where Sir Richard and I confronted him on our earlier visit to the monastery, in the chapter before his entire community, I believe he may have some difficulty evading the judgment of his fellow Benedictines."

"Trust the monks," Friar Tuck put in from farther forward in the boat. "'For the time is come for judgment to begin at the house of God,' as Saint Peter says in his letter. Trust the monks."

"At least we hope so," Robin said. "Because they're all we've got."

* * *

"My name is Robert fitz Ooth of Locksley, my good man," Robin intoned in an affected voice he reserved for times he wanted to sound more aristocratic. "I have come straight from Sir William de Forz, lord of Skipsea Castle, with an urgent message for Abbot Robert."

The guard at the tall gatehouse, a gruff looking veteran in worn leather armor, looked at the rather ragtag group that he'd been watching as they came along York's western wall and crossed the Ouse for the monastery. Here was a supposed messenger along with a giant of a man, a rotund friar, four more blokes on horseback, all accompanied by a dwarf driving a cart in which rode a muscular fellow with long blonde hair in braids, and three figures—two women and a man—whose faces were obscured by black hoods. "And it takes, what, twelve of you to bring this message?"

"Indeed!" Robin agreed, undeterred. "It's a complicated message." He paused as the guard looked at him quizzically. "In many parts," Robin added lamely. "And besides," he continued, "several of my companions are simply members of the guard Sir William sent with us, to protect us on the road. There are outlaws all about us on the open roads, you must know that!"

Now the guard nodded, somewhat convinced—and anyway, it was the abbot's problem, not his. "Well, talk to the Benedictine porter when you get inside. But you'll have to leave your weapons here at the gate. Can't go into the abbey armed."

Robin nodded and said, "We'll leave our cart here just within the gate, and leave all our weapons inside, will that be all right?"

"It will," the guard replied, and proceeded to watch them do it. Little John left his staff and sword, while Much, Alan of Winchester, Haakon, and Will Scarlet all left swords and bows. Robin's bow was already in the cart, as was Thorvald's, while the friar, who kept a sword concealed in his habit, did not care to reveal that fact. And Robin knew that Sir Walter had at least a short sword under his black cloak, which he did not deign to part with.

While the boys staffing the abbey's stables saw to their horses, the company's next obstacle was the Benedictine porter inside the gate. "Sir Robert fitz Ooth of Locksley," Robin introduced himself with a flourish, giving himself a noble promotion. "Here to see the Lord Abbot with an urgent communication from Skipsea Castle…uh, and in company with important members of the court of William de Forz, castellan at Skipsea," Robin added, to head off any objections.

The porter, a frail elderly monk with a pronounced stoop, was a trifle flustered at the sight of so many visitors bursting into the monastery at one time. He tried first to put them off. "The brothers are all in the chapter house," he said, "about their daily business meeting. I doubt the abbot would want to be disturbed just now. Perhaps if you would return at a later time…"

But it was, of course, precisely Robin's intention to disturb the abbot in his chapter house, with all his fellow monks around him. Little John had not forgotten that the meeting took place every day directly after the office of terce and had made sure that the company had arrived in the abbey at just that time. "Brother Porter," Robin said condescendingly, "I understand your concerns, but my lord's message cannot wait. It is, after all, on business that we are here, so it seems perfectly reasonable that we should bring it before the abbot at a business meeting. Bear in mind as well," Robin now adopted a threatening tone, "this is a message of extreme interest to the abbot and he must receive it without further delay. Abbot Robert will not look kindly on any who delay its delivery. Now have I made myself clear?" Robin hoped he'd struck just the right note in imitating the superior, arrogant manner in which the nobility bullied those they considered beneath them, and sure enough the porter was cowed.

"Right," he said. "Let me show you the way to the chapter house then, shall I?"

"That's a good fellow," Robin replied. "And my guard? We've been on the road for some time, and they have not broken their fast today. Might they be shown the way to the kitchen for a bit of bread or cheese, for your charity?"

"Of course," the gray-tonsured Benedictine answered, looking around the yard for someone who might guide that part of the group to the kitchen.

But Little John was quick to speak up, "Oh I know the way, Brother Porter, don't bother!" And with that he started off as if well acquainted with the abbey, followed by Thorvald, Haakon, Alan of Winchester, Much the miller's son, and Will Scarlet, as the outlaws had prearranged.

"Um, yes, well, good," the porter said. "Follow me then, my lord," and he led Robin, with Friar Tuck, Alan a Dale, and the three hooded figures under the stone arches of the cloister, until they had reached the grand stone archway that led into the great room from which the buzz of monastic voices could be heard.

Robin admired the carved archivolt at the entrance to the chamber, as well as the frescos on the walls of the octagon-shaped room where he and the others waited at the entrance as the porter stepped forward to meet Abbot Robert's bellowed challenge, "What is the meaning of this disturbance?"

"My Lord Abbot," the porter said, bowing his head slightly in deference. "This is Sir Robert fitz Ooth of Locksley, an emissary from your devoted servant Sir William de Forz, lord of Holderness. He has an urgent message for you, Father Abbot, from this Sir William, and begs audience with you now."

Robin could see the abbot reddening visibly as his face took on a dangerous combination of discomfiture and ire. "This is certainly not the place to be receiving messages from Sir William. Leave us, Sir Robert, and I will meet with you in my private chambers after chapter."

Robin looked at the mitered abbot, sitting on his dais as on a throne of state, so ironically situated beneath the stained glass depiction of the Good Shepherd, and the sunlight through the glass lighting up his head like a halo, and could not stomach the hypocrisy of it all. He stepped forward with a determination that it was time to remove this bloated leech from the body of the church.

* * *

The abbey's kitchen was a large, dark, and smoky wing of the building with easy access to the brothers' refectory, and from the other side to a pen in which several goats and cattle were kept. Little John had found it easily, having eaten in the servants' dining area adjacent to the kitchen itself on his last visit. Stepping into the dark, close space where the ovens blazed away and the smell of baking bread and roasting meat met them with the heat of a dozen fires, John and his companions could be forgiven if they felt momentarily as if they were entering the gates of Hell itself.

The chief cook, a tall ruddy Yorkshireman with blond hair and a neatly trimmed beard, wielding a ladle as if it were a jousting lance, met them at the door and tried to shoo them off. "Here now," he cautioned, displaying a Scandinavian accent, "if you're looking for a meal, you must needs go to the dining area. Around this way, yah?" he added, pointing his ladle.

"That's fine," John told him. "We'll be quite happy to avail ourselves of your hospitality later, but just at present we're looking for a particular kitchen boy. Skinny lad, long brown greasy hair, standing around this tall…" Little John held his hand about level with his shoulders. "Goes by the name of Nicholas."

The chief cook squinted suspiciously at John and shifted his eyes to the big man's companions, alighting on the kindred Norse face of Haakon in the group, to whom he directed a questioning glance. "*Ingen grunn til bekymring, bror*," Haakon told him (i.e., "No need to worry, brother"), and the cook relaxed, but still challenged Little John:

"And who might you be, then, to be questioning me about this?"

John drew himself up to his full height, stating, "My name is Reynold Greenleaf. I met this Nicholas lad on my last visit here. He is wanted for questioning in the murder of Sir Hugh Peveril, Lord of Codnor Castle, which I am investigating at the behest of Countess Lydia of Chesterfield. Now where is the boy?"

The cook raised his eyebrows, but then simply shrugged. "There's little I can tell you, Master Greenleaf," he admitted. "This Nicholas fellow worked here in my kitchen for several months. Then a few weeks ago, he vanished. The cellarer, Brother Simon, told me that he had been sent away on the abbot's business, but gave me no information as to when he would return to work, if ever. And I have not seen the lad since. That's all I can tell you."

Little John glared at the cook as if he might be able to frighten more information out of him with a look. But it seemed clear even to John that this was all the fellow knew. A glance at his companions told John that they were as much at a loss as he was how to proceed from here. "Well, then, we…uh…thank you for that information, and we'll be on our way for now." He turned and his five companions followed him out the door, where they stood in a cluster in the shadow of the kitchen walls.

"Well, at least we know that this Nicholas was indeed sent off on this murder mission," Will Scarlet said.

But Little John was less sanguine. "We know he was sent on *a* mission. We're going to need more than that to really convince the monks that their abbot is a murderer."

"Well what about this cellarer?" Much asked. "Can we get him to admit where he sent the lad?"

"I remember him," Little John replied. "Weaselly-looking fellow with a pointy nose and a face pale as death, always hunched over and agreeing with the abbot, no matter what rubbish he was talking. Yes, I remember him. If he gave any orders, it was with the abbot's blessing, you can be sure of that. But he ain't never gonna admit to anything if it's going to look bad for the abbot. He's counting on the abbot to make his fortune for him, or I'm a Turk."

"Then, what?" Thorvald asked. "We just expose the abbot's part in coercin' Lady Lydia to marry this Sir Walter? That won't be enough to get the monks to turn against Abbot Robert, will it?"

"They might censure him somehow, but it ain't the kind of thing he'd be removed from office for," Little John conceded. "It's a common enough practice among noble families, from what I've heard."

The little group stood silent for a while, considering what options they might have. Robin, Friar Tuck and the others were stalling right now, bringing the lesser charges against the abbot before the entire chapter of fifty monks. They were just waiting for John and the others to drag young Nicholas into the chapter house for the *coup de gras*. And now they could only bring suppositions. Little John gnawed on his lower lip as he watched students and their servants cross to and fro through the abbey's yard.

A few of the servants were making their way toward the kitchen. Among them was a thin teenaged boy with long, wavy brown hair, dancing green eyes, and the beginnings of a thin mustache on his upper lip. He walked with a kind of smug assurance that only the young are able to pull off, and it took a moment before Little John, lost in thought, recognized the lad. Then he snapped to and reached out. "You!" he called. "Downy mustache! Wait!"

The boy turned on his heel, saw the giant yeoman approaching him, and made as if to run off, but then turned back in recognition. "You!" he said. "Master...Greentree...Greenwood?"

"Greenleaf," John corrected his phony name.

"Yeah, that's it! I remember you, from what? A month or so ago, we had a dinner here, it was when the bishop was visiting.

And we were talking about why God made women, wasn't it?"

"Indeed it was, lad, but listen. I need your help now."

The boy started in surprise. "My help? For what? Why me?"

"Because," John said, placing a beefy hand upon the boy's shoulder as his fellows all gathered around the lad. "You were closest of the boys to the kitchen lad, Nicholas. It was you he'd gossiped with about what was said at the abbot's table, as I recall."

Wispy moustache swallowed nervously, his eyes shifting from face to face. "Nicholas?" he said warily. "I haven't seen him in weeks."

"No one has," Little John assured him. "That's why I'm talking to you. I want to know what you talked to him about the last time you saw him. And I'm betting it was not about God. Or the creation of women."

* * *

Robin bowed in feigned deference to the abbot, then spoke with loud authority, his voice filling the large octagon in which the abbey's fifty monks sat all around him, many fidgeting and muttering their indignation at being so impertinently interrupted: "My Lord Abbot, and you gathered Benedictines," and with this he nodded particularly to Prior Stephen and brother cellarer Simon, on the abbot's right and left hand. Though he did not know their names or titles, he recognized they must be important officers of the abbey. "I do apologize for this interruption, but this message really could not wait. And it must be delivered here in this chapter, not in your private chambers, Father Abbot."

Abbot Robert scowled with impatience and answered, "Very well, what is it that is so important Sir William insists on its being delivered here in open meeting?"

"Sir William?" Robin said. "Oh, I think there may be some

mistake, my lord. I did not say that my message was *from* Sir William directly. I said it was a message from Skipsea Castle."

His scowl growing deeper, the abbot snarled, "Don't bandy words with me, you churl. Sir William holds Skipsea Castle, so the message comes from him then..."

"Well," Robin answered, "the *countess* comes from him, and it is she who delivers the message."

With that word, Robin stepped away as Countess Lydia moved forward and threw off the cowl that had shrouded her face. "And that message is this!" she cried. "You, Father Abbot, did kidnap me and falsely imprison me at Skipsea Castle, keeping me from my friends and family in order to coerce me into agreeing to marry a man of your own choosing!"

The abbot was momentarily stunned by this sudden revelation of Countess Lydia and her bold accusation, but he quickly recovered, and without skipping a beat he laughed derisively, flapped his hand as if waving her away, and spoke in his most unctuous tones, "Young lady, you are sadly mistaken. I fear someone has been feeding you lies, perhaps for their own devious purposes. I know nothing of any kidnapping. And as for marriage—why, I don't even know who you are. Why should I care who you marry? No, no, my dear, if you've been imprisoned at Skipsea then you must deal with Sir William de Forz. He is, I understand, the castellan there and can probably tell you who is behind this if any wrong has actually been perpetrated against you."

He held his hand up, signaling he was finished with the matter. "Now we've had enough of these interruptions. Guards, show these intruders out of the chapter house, if you will," and with that the abbot lowered his eyes and waved to the two burly monks who stood at the door, indicating they should expel these visitors forthwith.

But that was the cue for another black hood to be thrown off, and Sir Walter of Horsley bared his face before the abbot. "I hate to call you a liar, my Lord Abbot, and I wouldn't have to if you hadn't just lied so outrageously." At the sight of Sir Walter, Abbot Robert could no longer keep his composure, but turned a bright crimson and threw a hand up to his face, his eyes popping. That the two pawns in his game should actually join forces against him was something he had not foreseen.

"Perhaps it slipped your mind that you and my mother—Lady Abigail of Derby, in case you've also forgotten her name—conspired to force me into marriage with this lady, after first giving out that I had been killed by my dear friend Sir Peter of Verysdale, in order to force his father to yield you his land!"

"This is preposterous," the cellarer, Brother Simon, declared, seeing that the abbot was too shocked even to defend himself from these charges. "What on earth had the abbot to gain by trying to force a marriage between the two of you—whoever you are!"

Robin, well aware that, while the abbot certainly knew Lady Lydia and Sir Walter on sight, they were quite unfamiliar to the other fifty monks in the room, who were growing ever more restless at this strange interruption, and at the obscure charges being brought against their master, and so he stepped forward boldly: "He had a huge territory to gain, to be ruled according to his own will. He assumed that he would add Sir Richard at the Lee's lands to his own holdings in Nottinghamshire, and cede them as a wedding gift to these two, so that they would own those lands, the lands of Horsley Castle, which are Sir Walter's, the lands of the Countess of Chesterfield, and the lands belonging to *her* family, the Peverils, which include Peveril Castle as well as Codnor Castle and its environs. And this would make this couple the greatest landowners in the north—with vast holdings that the abbot himself could control."

"This hardly seems like a nefarious scheme. It looks to me like a great act of Christian charity, helping these two young people to a great fortune. What was the abbot to get from it, other than the satisfaction of a deed well done? How was he to *control* it, as you say?" The drooping, cadaverous Brother Simon demanded.

"Through his influence over Sir Walter's mother," Robin asserted, though this particular aspect of the plan had never been especially clear to him.

"Influence?" the cellarer scoffed. "What sort of undue influence could our abbot possibly hold over this Lady Abigail?"

"She is my daughter," Abbot Robert broke in, and cleared his throat. And that silenced the room. No one had seen that coming, least of all Sir Walter.

"Your…daughter, Father Abbot?" Sir Walter said, blinking his good eye rapidly. "So you are saying that you are…"

"Your grandfather, yes." Abbot Robert admitted, shrugging. He paused a moment, sighed, and then continued: "I had just taken holy orders. I was young and foolish. I was drawn to a young maiden whose father was a supporter of our house. Perhaps you will understand when I say I was carried away by an irresistible passion. Perhaps you will not credit it. But as I say, I was very young. And very foolish. I thought it was a small indiscretion. But the wench conceived and in time was delivered of a girl child. The mother died. I could have left it at that—I don't think she had ever revealed I was the father, but I felt an obligation to the child. I had her brought up in a Benedictine convent and she actually did consider a vocation with the nuns, but I was her father and I thought it would be to her advantage to marry, and an opportunity arose to wed her to Sir William of Horsley when she was fourteen. I arranged that marriage and, well, here you see Sir Walter, the fruit of that."

Sir Walter squinted his eye at the abbot. "You're saying my mother wanted to give her life to God, but you decided that she was more valuable as chattel to marry off to someone with a title and land? To gain property that you could control yourself? You used my mother just as you planned to use me?"

"So…" Lady Lydia whispered to him. "Maybe there is hope for you yet, Sir Walter."

Walter looked abashed, but the abbot was unmoved. "What kind of drivel are you speaking? Did my daughter beget an idiot? I don't 'use' people, I make their lives better…"

"You made better the lives of Sir Richard at the Lee and his son Sir Peter, did you?" Alan a Dale spoke up. "You plotted to steal their land."

"They were not my family!" the abbot shouted, now clearly losing his temper. The monks watching him were beginning to squirm, and the prior at his right hand was pursing his lips with concern. "My responsibility is to my own family first, and ensuring they become one of the great houses in the land."

"And where is that written in the Rule?" Prior Stephen broke in, his round face and placid features in an unwonted frown. "By your own admission, Father Abbot, you have broken your vows of poverty and chastity. And you've not expressed any regrets for these lapses."

Brother Simon was quick to rise to his abbot's defense. "He says he is responsible for the well-being of his family. As our abbot, do we not call him Father? Are we not the abbot's dear family as well? Are not these lands he covets his means of attaining wealth for our great house?"

"Are they?" Brother Stephen responded. "I heard nothing of that in anything the abbot has said here. Not a word about his spiritual family, we in this great house. No, in fact, he suggests that lands held in common by the abbey he was planning to make over to this countess and her consort upon their marriage. Where is his responsibility to his brethren of this house?"

"You said you cared not for any harm you did to Sir Richard," the Countess Lydia pursued. "And what about me? Trying to coerce me into a marriage for the benefit of yourself and your family? Like Sir Richard, my wishes are not to be considered, is that it? Is this your Christian charity?"

"I had the support of your own kinsman!" Abbot Robert cried in his defense. "Sir Hugh, Lord Peveril of Codnor Castle, was our ally from the beginning in this."

"An ally whom you never told where his cousin was hidden away," Maid Marion now stepped forward, throwing off her own black cowl. "And just how did Sir Hugh's part in this conspiracy turn out, eh, Lord Abbot? Where is he now?"

"What are you saying?" The abbot now looked unsure of himself for the first time. "How can you say he was unaware? Who are you? What do you know about it?"

"I am the countess's lady, Lord Abbot, and I was the person who was with Sir Hugh when he died. When he was poisoned, I should say. He foreswore knowledge of her whereabouts with his last words."

"Poisoned? I was not aware of any poison."

"A bald-faced lie," the abbot's newly revealed grandson exclaimed. "You sent a messenger to me at Skipsea, telling me the Earl of Chesterfield had died and that his kinsman Sir Hugh had been murdered." Now the angry murmurings among the brethren rose in volume.

"And we have good evidence that it was a servant of your own that did the poisoning," Robin added.

"Oh, now you go too far!" The abbot exclaimed. "I? Suborn murder? You're mad, all of you! Guards, I say, throw these ruffians out of my chamber!" At that, the two beefy monks at the door came forward aggressively, but as they laid hands on Alan a Dale, Sir Walter produced his sword from beneath his cloak and brandished it at the monks, who held up their hands in an appeasing gesture.

"Hold!" Prior Stephen called out with a voice of authority. "No one is being ejected from this room, which *is*," he emphasized as he turned a stern face toward the abbot, "*our* chamber, not *yours*, Father Abbot. And as for you, young hooligan, you dare to draw a weapon in this sacred place? Put it away, and keep it sheathed."

"Not until this disgrace of a grandfather admits his part in these murders!" Sir Walter shouted, now provoked beyond reason.

"Murders?" Abbot Robert responded, beginning to recover from the initial shock. "Now you're saying I murdered more than just this Sir Hugh? My, my, I seem to have been very busy."

"You have, you bloody bastard," Robin asserted. "But sheath your weapon, young poltroon," he told Walter from the side of his mouth. Somewhat chagrinned, Walter put away his sword as Robin continued. "You may not have known, Lord Abbot, that Sir Hugh communicated everything he knew to his former ward, the lady Maude Peveril. It was on your orders that Sir Hugh contracted with Lady Maude to hire two assassins to follow Sir Peter, Sir Richard's son, on his crusade in order to end his life in a foreign land where it could not be traced back to you. You can deny it all you want," he continued as the abbot began to sputter, "but we can bring Lady Maude here at any time with the letters from Sir Hugh that will condemn you out of hand. It was all part of your obsession with attaining the lands of Verysdale to be part of your imagined Midlands empire."

Abbot Robert scoffed. "His idea then, this Sir Hugh. The letters would be in his own hand, not mine."

"Doubtlessly one of the reasons you had him killed," Robin said. "He can never testify against you now. But tell me, Lord

Abbot, where is the young kitchen boy Nicholas, whom you sent to Peveril Castle to murder Sir Hugh?"

That question caught the abbot off guard, and most of those present also noticed the cellarer on the abbot's left turn an even paler shade of green at that point.

"Kitchen boy?" Abbot Robert asked scornfully. "What do I know of kitchen boys?"

"The boy who brought Sir Hugh his poisoned wine," Maid Marion spat out angrily. "He was the same boy employed here in your kitchens until just before the murder."

"Probably some lad we dismissed for poor work habits," the abbot rejected the thought. "We have no responsibility for what such a lad does when no longer in our employ. If he poisoned this Sir Hugh it was his own doing. Nothing to do with us."

"Yes," said Brother Simon, who as cellarer would have been in charge of the kitchen. "I remember that particular lad now. A surly villein. We could not even beat the sloth out of him. Had to dismiss him oh, perhaps a month past."

"Liar!" came the cry from the doorway, through which Little John was coming, dragging by the arm a young scholar's servant with a wispy growth on his adolescent lip. Followed by his own entourage of Thorvald, Haakon, Alan of Winchester, Will Scarlet and Much the miller's son, John burst into the chapter house, swinging the boy before him, and continued, "this boy is Ned of Pickering, servant to one of the students who attends the minster school here. More important, he was best mates with Nicholas, the kitchen lad whose name you've been bandying about. Tell these assembled worthies what you told me just now, Ned!" He flung the boy to the front of the crowd that now stood before the abbot's chair.

With the furious eyes of the abbot, not to mention the enraged eyes of Brother Simon glaring down at him, young

Ned seemed to lose his courage, stammering, "Well I…I…I daren't say, for I vowed to Nicholas that I'd never reveal what he told me, and…and…I need to honor that pledge, don't I? You understand, don't you?"

"Don't be afraid of any of these great men you see in this room," Little John boomed at the lad. "They will not harm you as long as we are here to protect you. But I promise you this, lad: If you don't spit it out right now, what you told me earlier, I'll smack you so hard your mother will feel it back in Pickering!"

Ned shook with anxiety, looking first up at the abbot and then back at Little John, as if trying to weigh who had the power to hurt him the most. At that point help came from another source. Friar Tuck stepped toward the boy, laying his hands upon his shoulders, and said, "Fear not if you speak the truth, my boy. Your friend is lost, it seems, and breaking your pledge to him can no longer harm him. Nor will we allow any man in this room, lay or clergy, to harm a hair on your head if you tell us this truth. And if what you say condemns any of these great men in their black robes, it is God's will that their crimes be exposed. Though they wear black, they are only whited sepulchers: beautiful on the outside, but full of filth and corruption inside."

"Yes, sir," Ned murmured, still hesitant but willing to go ahead with his story. "For Nicholas," he clarified. "He came to me the night before he left."

"When was this?" Prior Stephen asked. "Do you recall precisely?"

The lad shrugged. "A month ago? Perhaps five weeks? He told me he was being sent away for a while. He said old Walking Dead…I mean, uh, brother cellarer there…" at that Brother Simon looked furious, while several of the other monks snickered behind their hands. "The cellarer told him he needed to go to Peveril Castle, get himself a job in the kitchen there, and wait for the old earl to die."

“This is hardly proof of murder,” Abbot Robert interrupted.

“I ain’t done yet!” Ned snapped back, then, chagrined, repeated a bit more calmly, “I ain’t done yet, yer honor. The cellarer told him that Sir Hugh Peveril was sure to come to that castle, either while the earl was dying or right after. And he gave Nicholas a vial of some sort of potion, he didn’t know what, but he was supposed to put this in Sir Hugh’s drink when he got the chance. I told him it was most likely some kind of poison, and maybe he should chuck that vial and just take off somewhere where nobody from here can ever find him. And he says no, the cellarer has got some guard going with him, who’s going to wait outside Peveril Castle and bring him back here when the job is done. And if he botches the job this guard is going to make him regret it before he comes back.”

“Obviously this boy is just making up a story,” the abbot scoffed. “These brigands who’ve broken in here have put him up to it.”

“No sir,” Ned insisted, his courage building as he warmed to his topic. “I’m giving you the Gospel truth. And Nicholas left the next morning, and he has not come back. If this Sir Hugh *was* murdered, and this John Greenpoint here tells me he has…”

“Greenleaf,” Little John murmured automatically.

“Then the only thing I can think of is that this guard of the cellarer’s killed poor Nicholas as well, so he couldn’t come back and tell anybody that the cellarer was behind it.”

Now there was an uproar from the company of monks. Many were on their feet, some calling for the cellarer to respond, some chiding the boy for lying, some asking whether this was to be laid at the abbot’s door. The abbot himself stood up, raised his hands for silence, and turned to the cellarer, asking, “Well, Brother Simon? These are serious charges. What have you to say to this? What would you possibly have against this Sir Peveril?”

The cellarer's jaw dropped, and he stared at his abbot, sputtering in disbelief. His face grew redder and redder until he burst out, "You great pompous hypocrite! Ingrate! You're going to pretend I didn't do all these things on your orders?" Now every monk in the room was on his feet shouting, and most were shouting against Abbot Robert.

But once again the abbot calmed them, and asked innocently, "I ask you, any of you, what sense do these charges make? What possible reason would I have to want Sir Hugh Peveril dead? First these people accuse me of conspiring with Sir Hugh to wed these two, against their wills as they would have it, and then they accuse me of wanting him dead. So he was my ally and my enemy? Make up your minds, you ruffians. Get your lies straight!"

"You murdered Sir Hugh because you thought once the old earl had died, your scheme was sure to succeed. You didn't want to share your new empire with anybody outside your own family," Maid Marion answered. "And your own sycophant, the cellarer, has just told us you did it."

"He did! He did!" Brother Simon, now fully committed, was insisting.

"So what we have here," Robin summed up, "is three murders: Sir Hugh, the unfortunate lad Nicholas, and Sir Peter of Verysdale, the target of those assassins that were sent to the Holy Land. You have much to answer for, Lord Abbot."

But Abbot Robert was still not cowed and thought to brazen it out. "None of these charges can be brought against me in a court of law," he scoffed. "You have nothing but hearsay, no real evidence. Even the testimony of this fellow here," he indicated the cellarer, "is nothing but his word against mine. The boy's testimony convicts Brother Simon, if anyone, not me! And anyway, who would presume to put me on trial? I answer to no one but the pope himself."

Now there was near pandemonium in the chapter house. The monks were angry, and while there were a few who were even now still willing to give the abbot the benefit of the doubt, by far the majority were calling for the abbot to admit his guilt. But in the midst of the furor, Prior Stephen stood up and called for order.

"We have had enough disorder here in our chapter house," Prior Stephen said, with a quiet dignity that silenced the room. "And you, Brother Robert," he blatantly dropped the abbot's title in addressing him. "You seem not to be familiar with the Rule of Saint Benedict. While it is true, indeed, that you are answerable to the Holy Father, you might recall that you hold your office through the election of the members of your house—that is, the brothers here gathered. For us, this is not a matter to bring before a court of law. This is a matter for us to decide. By your own admission here, Brother Robert, you have disregarded our Rule: through your voracious greed you have violated our rule of poverty; through your admitted lust you have broken our rule of chastity. Brother Simon!" The cellarer snapped to attention as his name was called. "Do you take your oath that what you have told us here is the truth?"

"I do," the pallid monk replied. "I arranged for the deaths of Sir Hugh and of the boy Nicholas on the orders of the abbot."

"Your oath is noted," Prior Stephen said. "My brothers," the prior now addressed the entire chapter house. "How many of you will give your voice now for Brother Robert?"

Not a single monk made a sound. Abbot Robert made an exasperated snort, and then actually jeered, "Who do you all think you are?"

"We think we are your brothers, and we think you have your office by our authority," Prior Stephen explained patiently. "Now, all who favor stripping Brother Robert of his office as abbot, stand up." Every monk in the house then stood. Abbot, now Brother, Robert fumed visibly. "Brother Robert," the prior continued. "You've displayed lust and greed, now you appear to be consumed by the sin of wrath. You have violated our vows of poverty and chastity, let us see now whether you can learn obedience. If not, there may be other disciplinary actions we will need to take, as we most certainly will be doing with Brother Simon as well." The former cellarer hung his head. "And it goes without saying that any private property you have accumulated or held on to as abbot will be forfeit to the house itself."

The former abbot, now completely deflated, sat back in his chair and sighed. Brother Simon slouched next to him, arms folded and head bowed low. Prior Stephen continued, "For the immediate future, as your prior, I will take on the supervision of Saint Mary's Abbey, but only for the time being. We will set a specific date for the formal election of a new abbot very shortly, which we will need to have approved by the archbishop next door. He will also need to formally approve our removal of Brother Robert from his position as abbot. But that," Brother Stephen allowed himself a grim half smile, "I don't anticipate will be a problem. As for you ladies and gentlemen," he now addressed Robin, Marion, and the others, "we thank you for bringing all of this to our attention, and for giving us the opportunity to cleanse this house—something that I believe has long been necessary. We invite you to be our guests and share dinner with us directly after this chapter house session, where we shall express our sincere gratitude to you."

"We thank you, Brother Prior," Robin replied, bowing courteously.

Friar Tuck, beaming brightly as the outlaw group drifted out of the room, poked Robin and Little John in the ribs and kept repeating, "Told you, didn't I? Trust the monks I said. Trust the monks."

CHAPTER SEVENTEEN

Friar Tuck, who made regular rounds to various hospitals and orphans' homes in the towns around Sherwood, was returning from one of these visits when he had stopped for refreshment at the sign of the Blue Boar north of Nottingham, and there the proprietor had passed the friar a letter he had been holding for a few weeks that had been brought by a returning pilgrim and was addressed to Robin Hood care of that particular tavern. Little John, Much, Alan a Dale, and Thorvald were all crowding around when Robin opened the letter, which he read with wonder and then laughed out loud, handing it to Alan to read out to the entire assemblage. Alan, too, laughed, and then read:

By my hand, written from Calais,
the third week of September

My greetings to Robin and to all the merry men Blessing on you!

You will scarcely credit the speed with which I have completed my quest, but rest assured it is finished, and finished to all our advantages. For I have found Sir Peter of Verysdale and have confounded his would-be assassins. Sir Peter is with me here in Calais, and we await transport to Dover on a ship across the Narrow Sea. I have entrusted this letter to an honest pilgrim who goes before us and hope that it may reach you before we do, which I hope will be some time before the end of October. Sir Peter has been ill, and so cannot travel as quickly as we might like, but he is mending fast, and I trust we will be in Sherwood in time to see the trees in full color.

Do not be amazed. Of course, I could not possibly have been to the Holy Land and back in the brief interval since I left Sherwood. As Fortune would have it, it turned out Sir Peter had never reached the Holy Land. He sailed first to Lisbon, and decided to rest awhile there, thinking that after all he need not travel all the way to Jerusalem to battle infidels: The men of Portugal and Spain were mounting their own crusade of reconquest from the Moors, and he looked to join them, fired with the crusading spirit. By the way, we have since had a long discussion of the precise meaning of the term "infidel" and of the relative merits of those same Moors, and I think by the end I had taught him a thing or two.

But I digress. For the assassins, we need fear them no more. I will tell you all the whole story when I get back to Sherwood. If you do receive this letter, please try to get word to Sir Peter's father, Sir Richard at the Lee, to ease his anxiety over his son.

Adieu for the moment, until we see each other again, far sooner than expected,

Sir Palomides

Sir Palomides' unlooked-for letter came close on the heels of another welcome message Robin had just received from Peveril

Castle. It was now two months since the showdown at Saint Mary's Abbey in York, and nothing more had been heard of the former abbot's machinations. It appeared he had reformed, and had become a model monk, obedient to his new master—Prior Stephen had, of course, been elected the monastery's new abbot and been approved wholeheartedly by the Archbishop of York. Brother Robert, outwardly at least, was a pious Benedictine, and for Robin and his friends it was enough that he could do them no more mischief.

Now autumn had come to Sherwood. The woods were alive with coppery brown oak leaves, fiery red maples, sunny yellow elms and birches and golden orange beeches. Robin and his men were busy buying up barrels of grain and ale from area towns and farms, but also hunting more urgently than ever the king's deer, for the herd needed to be thinned before the snow flew to prevent too many deer from starving in the bleak midwinter. The caves at Creswell Crags promised to be a much more comfortable winter headquarters than their earlier camp had been, though many of the band still missed the old oak clearing and talked about returning there for next year's summer months, if Sir Guy of Gisbourne's troops remained dormant as they had been since the day of Will Stutely's rescue.

Traffic on the Great North Road was not so busy in the fall and would dwindle to next to nothing in the wet, icy winter months, so the outlaws' revenue was not what it might have been. For Robin, the four hundred gold nobles he had given Sir Richard at the Lee to save his estate were beginning to look more and more like a foolish extravagance, and day by day the time for his admitting his reckless generosity to the rest of his meinie seemed to loom closer and closer.

As for Will Stutely, it had been a slow process, but his wounds had gradually healed, with the help of Friar Tuck's knowledge of herb lore and the ministrations of a physician sent from Peveril Castle, who was escorted blindfolded to Creswell Crags once a fortnight by Much the miller's son. Will's jaw had taken longest to heal, and he would always have a crooked smile now. He had a scar on his forehead from that last blow that had knocked him unconscious in his cell, and he still walked gingerly, with some pain from the burns on his feet. But he was in good spirits, and Little John claimed that Will was even better looking now than he'd been before his capture: "Your face has got some character now, like a man who's seen something of life. Not like some callow lad who's never had to grow up."

Doctor Phineas, that physician from the castle, usually brought a letter from Maid Marion, who had settled in comfortably as chief lady-in-waiting to the new Countess of Chesterfield, and Robin's heart leapt up when he received these letters, though they contained only the daily gossip of the countess's court, and nothing more personal. But one day Doctor Phineas brought Robin a letter with exciting news and with an invitation. The lady Lydia, Marion wrote, had decided to host a celebration of her formal ascension to the position of countess, and wanted to invite those friends who had been most active in securing her freedom from captivity to celebrate her good fortune with her. Robin was to come, along with Little John, Friar Tuck, and any others who might liven up the proceedings. The countess had also invited her kinswoman, the lady Maude, to attend—though without her husband the sheriff, since under the circumstances that could be rather awkward for all involved. She had even invited Sir Walter of Horsley, having softened to him somewhat after their mutual confrontation of Walter's sinister grandfather. Lady Mary seemed ebullient in anticipation of this celebration—at least, Robin seemed to read that emotion into her written words—because, she hinted, it would give her a chance to see

Robin Hood once again. Robin sighed, letting the pages of the letter sag in his hand.

The festival was to take place three weeks hence, on All Hallows Eve, and anticipation of the event would have filled all of Robin's thoughts in the interim had not Palomides' news followed so soon. Instructions must be left, he thought, for Palomides and Sir Peter to join the party at Peveril if they arrived in the interim. And at that, he must also get the welcome word to Verysdale, the sooner to set Sir Richard's mind at rest.

* * *

"Robin! Little John! And the good friar, you are all welcome. Truly, I would not be in this position if it were not for you and your chivalry in the interest of my honor! And this? Who is your companion?"

"Ah, Lady Lydia, this is my particular friend, Will Stutely," Little John said as he bowed courteously to the countess. "Though he was not part of your rescue party, he suffered mightily for our cause, and we deemed it only fair that he might come and enjoy this festival with you."

"My dear countess," Stutely said, placing his right foot before him and bowing humbly until his chin virtually touched his right knee. "I feel I already know you, so much I have heard of your praise since my fellow foresters returned from their adventure at Skipsea and York. But I fault them for this: They fell far short in their praise of your beauty and charm. If they even came within one tenth of your actual deserts, then chop me up for firewood."

Countess Lydia smiled graciously, saying, "Robin, you must keep this one hidden away in your forest camp, or he will charm all my ladies-in-waiting out of their maidenly virtue." Will smirked and John rolled his eyes. The countess sat on a dais in

Peveril Castle's great hall, clothed in a gown of white samite with long bell-shaped sleeves reaching to the floor from where she rested her wrists on the arms of her carved wooden chair. Her hair was held loosely in place by a golden crespine, and over her shoulders was draped a white silk pelisson lined with ermine. The gown itself was closely fitted to her body from shoulder to waist, with a fuller skirt hanging from the bodice, and she wore a girdle of the same white material, but with dozens of pearls stitched into the fabric, matching the white of the samite. From the girdle dangled a purse, which Robin eyed with a barely disguised longing.

Noting the direction of his gaze, the lady gave a brief close-mouthed smile and made a signal to Lady Mary of Winchester, who was standing to the right of the dais with her other ladies and who now stepped forward, carrying a small wooden chest. "Robin Hood of Sherwood," Lady Lydia announced in her most formal of voices, "the purse on which you rest your eyes is far too little a prize for your great service. And I will not be a peer insensitive to *noblesse oblige*. In this chest are five hundred gold nobles, a reward for you and your men, whom I name my own designated foresters of any part of Sherwood Forest that lies within my domains!"

Maid Marion, now standing next to Robin with a beaming smile, opened the chest to reveal the shining stacked coins inside, and Robin, his breath stifled by the shocked exultation rising in his heart, fell to his knees at the foot of the countess's dais. John, Tuck and Will followed suit, and when Robin could speak again, he breathed huskily, "My lady, this is too much! This is so far beyond generosity..."

"Oh, never mind all that," Lady Lydia waved away his protestations. "It's not as generous as you think. You should see all the wealth I've inherited now! Well, maybe not, considering what a thief you are. But the fact is I wouldn't have any of it if it hadn't been for you and your men. Take it with my good wishes."

Robin rose and, taking the chest from Marion's outstretched hands, gave her a nod and a wink, and stepped back with his men and away from the front of the dais. The countess's appointing of his band as foresters was truly, he knew, a name-only appointment, since Sherwood Forest was a royal preserve, and none of the forest proper was actually on the countess's estate. But the title did give him, and his men, a certain legal standing within the countess's domain, which could prove useful in future encounters with Sir Guy's troops.

One of Lady Lydia's household pages came forward and announced that another visitor had arrived for the banquet: Lady Maude Peveril of Nottingham. And upon the announcement, Lady Maude strode in, accompanied by the two sheriff's deputies who had protected her on her previous excursion to Peveril the past summer. Dodging her way among the many servants who were setting up a large banquet table in the hall in preparation for the festivities, Maude made her way to the dais. Her two deputies, recognizing Little John and Will, beamed and slapped them on the back with renewed camaraderie as Maude curtsied low before her kinswoman.

"Lady Maude, dearest cousin, I'm so glad you have come," the countess cooed in sincere delight. "It's so long since I've seen you. The last time was, I think, years ago at Codnor Castle, was it not?"

"Indeed my lady, that would have been it. We were children then, and Sir Hugh had taken me in there as his ward."

"Yes, I remember you were several years older than I. If I remember right, you and one of the pages tired of my tagging after you and threw me into the moat to see if I could swim."

Lady Maude colored and then shrugged sheepishly. "Ah, who

can fathom the vagaries of childhood fancies?" Then, more frankly, she admitted, "You were always the favorite, always with the best dresses and the fawning adults making much of you. I was too young to realize your position as the earl's heiress at the time. I hope we can put those days behind us. Please think of me as your servant and your advocate in your new role."

"Aha, that is precisely why I invited you here to this celebration of my assuming the title of Countess. My close advisor and chief lady-in-waiting, the lady Mary of Winchester, who governed this castle competently in my absence, informs me that your help was invaluable in exposing the villainies of Abbot Robert. I want to show you my gratitude, but I want to be sure that your reward is not only commensurate with your contribution, but also suitable for your temperament—that it be something you will feel comfortable with."

Maude's ears pricked up. Reward? Social advance? Money? She could be *comfortable* with a lot of things. "I'm sure my lady is too kind," she answered, discretely looking down at her feet and waiting to hear just how kind she might be.

But the countess was clearly unsure how best to reward her cousin. "I have thought that one possibility, if you wanted to be around my court, would be to bring you here as one of my ladies-in-waiting. I know that traditionally this would not be a role for a married lady, unless perhaps in a royal court where your husband might be a courtier as well. But if you have an interest in such a post, it might be yours."

Maude continued to look at her feet, merely murmuring, "I see" noncommittally.

Countess Lydia, undeterred, proposed another option: "It also occurs to me that, since I am now governess of Codnor Castle as well, which my late kinsman Sir Hugh held in fealty to my grandfather, that I should have someone act as steward there to administer the estate in my stead, under my guidance, given that I plan to make my court here at Peveril Castle. Who better to do so than one of my own kinswomen—particularly one who, like yourself, grew up to some extent in the castle's environs. That, too, is a post I have considered for you."

Again, Maude thought to herself, a position that would take her away from John of Oxenford, Sheriff of Nottingham and her wedded husband. Without lifting her eyes, she said again, "I see, my lady. A responsible post."

The countess sighed and pushed on. "The last option is that I grant you an annuity. On the first day of each new year, I would send you an annual gift of, let us say, fifty gold nobles, in perpetuity. These you would receive with the expectation only that you would defend my interests when you may, and that if I am forced to send to you for your support, you will come in your own person. And that is my last suggestion. Are you content to choose one of these as an expression of my appreciation?"

Without raising her eyes, Maude was thinking hard about the three possibilities. She had longed to leave her uninspiring marriage behind, and two of her choices presented a lifeline that would lift her from John of Oxenford's stifling and unappreciated authority in her life. But as the countess's lady-in-waiting, her every minute must needs be spent pleasing her sovereign lady. Her time and her life would not be her own. And though she thought she might have more chances to sport with Robin, the fact that this new interest of his, this Maid Marion, was in the countess's service as well would rankle her on a daily basis. Codnor Castle, on the other hand, would offer her more of a chance to make decisions on her own, but frankly it was not nearly the comfortable place that the larger and more opulent Peveril was, and despite her being nominally in charge, she would be only a deputy, and her every decision would be scrutinized by her mistress. When she thought about it, the sheriff had now twice let her ride forth to visit Peveril Castle for an unspecified time. She ran her own household with virtually no input from him. She had, it might be said, broken him in so well that he almost never imposed his will on her anymore, nor did he ask her to pay the marriage debt on more than a semi-annual basis, familiarity having bred contempt on his part as well. She would, she admitted to herself, be more of her own woman staying where she was and would have fifty gold nobles a year to boot, to do with what she would. No reason the sheriff should have to know anything about that little nest egg. She smiled to herself. "My lady," she said, lifting her eyes, "I would be very pleased to accept the generous annuity you offer. Thank you, my lady countess!" And with that Lady Maude curtsied low again and moved to the side of the dais where Robin and Marion were standing.

At that point the same young page who had stepped forward earlier came up to the dais and announced, "My lady, I am pleased to announce the arrival of Sir Palomides, now of Sherwood as he says, along with Sir Peter of Verysdale." At that announcement Robin and Little John whooped for joy, and Countess Lydia gave a maidenly simper and reddened visibly.

* * *

The banquet was winding down, the guests having devoured the harvest feast that Lady Lydia's bounty had provided for them. Even the gourmet Sir Palomides found little fault with the roast pork, the boiled pike with Galantine sauce, or the roasted goose in savory almond milk and flavored with onions and hot, spicy pellitory, and he was holding forth during the fruit and nuts course, entertaining the spellbound listeners with his account of having saved Sir Peter from his would-be assassins. Lady Maude lowered her eyes to hide her face from the rest of the dinner guests. She had, of course, sent those assassins herself, but she reasoned that nobody else needed to be reminded of that particular detail.

"Like me, Sir Peter had taken ship first to Lisbon, and had learned there about the siege of Lisbon more than a generation ago. At that time, English knights on their way to the Second Crusade halted in Portugal and laid siege to the city, having been guaranteed by the Pope that their service against the Moors of Iberia was as holy as the service in Palestine would have been. Both, of course, are mere church-sanctioned slaughter, but I digress. They allied with the Portuguese King Alfonso and succeeded in returning the city of Lisbon to Christian hands. I arrived in the port of Lisbon less than a fortnight after I left this castle, thinking from there to take ship for Genoa or Venice, and thence to Constantinople or direct to Palestine. But I made it my business, while waiting for passage to Italy, to make inquiries in Lisbon itself about a certain Sir Peter of Verysdale. I soon became convinced that I might find him in that very city, because everywhere I went I was hearing rumors of a new crusade, to be waged against the resurgent Almohad Moors from North Africa."

Sir Peter interrupted to add a point of clarification. "I had heard that combined armies from Portugal, Castile, Aragon, and Navarre were planning to unite and move into Andalusia in southern Spain where they expected to fight a great battle against the Almohads, and I had taken a room in the city until I could join forces with the Portuguese troops when they came down from Coimbra," he said, looking across the table at his father, Sir Richard at the Lee. Sir Richard had arrived shortly before the banquet started, having had word from Will Scathelock in Robin's camp that his son was returned, and where he was bound. "It was there that Sir Palomides found me."

"Mind you, it was not easy for me to make my way around that city. I was constantly being waylaid by members of the local garrison, or by civic-minded citizens conscious and wary of the Almohad threat to the city, so lately reconquered. They could see I was a Moor and thought I may be a spy or perhaps a saboteur. I had in my possession papers dating back to our former king and bearing his seal. And these usually were enough to allay their suspicions, and if they were not, I would recite the *Pater Noster* or the Creed to show them I was a Christian convert. When they were assuaged, seeing that I was a knight of some puissance, the more martial among them tried to enlist my aid in their upcoming campaign against the Almohads. Be assured, though I have converted, I would never make war upon the faith I grew up in. But I excused myself on the grounds that I had pressing business back in England and always inquired thereafter if any knew where Sir Peter of Verysdale might be lodged. And finally a local Portuguese knight, a certain Dom Álvaro to whose military contingent Sir Peter had apparently applied earlier, told me where he could be found, lodged in a few small rooms in the labyrinthine streets of the Alfama, the old part of town below the Castle of Saint George."

"Even there, though, Sir Palomides had some difficulties," Sir Peter put in again, "with the master of the house chasing him off, telling him his kind wasn't needed there and that I had already hired two of my own countrymen to serve me, so I wasn't looking for any valets or squires. How the good Sir Palomides bore that without skewering the fellow I still don't know, but I know it made him suspicious."

"Indeed," the Moor said, his face now taking on a serious expression as shadows danced across it, flickering from the candles inside the seasonal face-carved turnips that lit the table for All Hallows Eve. "I had no doubts as to who those two Englishmen were that now served Sir Peter. I waited in the shadows of a house across from his on the street of Saint Michael until I saw two men dressed as pilgrims make their way surreptitiously into the house. They were dressed simply, with broad hats and pilgrim scrips, and they were carrying a wineskin. One was tall with popping eyes, the other stockier and blond. But they were obviously English, and I'd venture of peasant stock. And I knew for a certainty that they were the assassins sent by the abbot."

"I had no reason to be suspicious of them," Sir Peter asserted in a plea of self-justification. "They had a letter that they showed me, one that bore the seal of the Peveril family and that purported to be written by my lady Lydia herself, telling me they came on her recommendation and that I could be sure of her love." These words were delivered very quietly, Sir Peter keeping his eyes fixed on the bread trencher still unconsumed on the table before him. It was a sore point with him that he had not understood and had determined to bring up when he came before the countess, and he had kept it back until this moment. He had no desire to embarrass the countess in front of her guests, but he wanted to see her reaction to this information.

Countess Lydia was astonished. "From me, you say? But I never wrote you aught. That is not to say," she backed up, not wishing to seem callous, "that I did not think of you, Sir Peter, once you had left the country, but I knew of no way to contact you. I wrote no letter, and I certainly never sent any country clowns to seek you out in your exile."

"So odd," Peter shook his head. "The hand was so like yours. And it bore the Peveril seal."

Lady Maude, who had visibly shrunk into herself as this

conversation ensued, now ventured in a quiet voice, "We know that Abbot Robert had contrived this entire plot with the aid of our kinsman, Sir Hugh. He'd have had no difficulty getting Hugh to seal the letter. For that matter, Sir Hugh would have been very familiar with your hand, my lady, and could have easily found some lady in his household to counterfeit it. This letter is not so much of a mystery."

Maude's explanation seemed to satisfy everyone, Sir Peter apologized to Lady Lydia for ever doubting her, and Sir Palomides continued his story. "I had seen enough," he said scowling angrily. "I was certain those men were the hired assassins. I drew my sword and burst into those rooms—you can be sure the master of the house made no more difficulty about it when he saw my naked blade. When Sir Peter saw me—he was just drinking some of the wine those men had brought—he looked up and saw my sword, and he thought at first that *I* had been sent to kill him. But I told him quickly to put down the wine, for I believed these men were assassins hired to do away with him. He scoffed at first, but at least he stopped drinking the wine. At my sword point he handed me his cup and when I sniffed it, I recognized immediately the smell of belladonna."

"Deadly nightshade!" Maid Marion cried. "The abbot's favorite weapon. It's what killed Sir Hugh."

"That seems fitting somehow," Friar Tuck commented, "since Sir Hugh was the one who apparently sent these men after Sir Peter to administer the same poison."

"Fortunately," Sir Palomides said with false modesty, "as a gourmet chef, I am familiar with herbs and seasonings of all sorts, and I quickly recognized that the wine had been poisoned. I snatched his cup from his hand and told the assassins to drink it themselves if they wished to prove they had not just tried to poison him. After a few half-hearted denials, they actually turned tail and fled without a backward glance. As assassins, they were a pretty pathetic pair."

"Don't I know it," Lady Maude muttered, her head leaning morosely on one hand.

"The strangest thing is," Sir Peter added, "the tall one grabbed my sword as they fled out the door. I thought at first that he was going to put up a fight against Sir Palomides, but that wasn't it at all. He apparently just wanted the sword. I can't see why if they were too cowardly to use it."

"Maybe they just wanted to sell it," Little John suggested.

Lady Maude gave a tight smile but said nothing. She knew exactly why they had taken the sword. She had demanded that they bring back proof of Sir Peter's death, and the tall villein was counting on the sword to be proof enough—if they'd been able to steal his sword, they reasoned, Lady Maude would believe him to be dead, since he'd have had to be defenseless for them to make him give up his one weapon. Well, Maude thought, she would look forward to the two of them calling on her and handing her the sword as proof of their accomplished task. They'd ask her for an additional two hundred and fifty nobles, and she'd show them the door. Or better yet, perhaps she'd hand them over to the authorities. Sometimes it was actually a good thing to be married to a sheriff.

"I believed I had saved Sir Peter's life," Sir Palomides continued. "But as it happened, though he had drunk only a small portion of the wine, he had ingested enough of the poison to become quite ill. I thought little of it and booked passage on a ship for Calais that was leaving the next day, but once we were under way the movement of the ship made the illness even worse. When we reached Calais, we had to take lodgings and wait for the poison to run its course. A physician there recommended bleeding him, but that I would not allow." At that there were some raised eyebrows around the table, particularly from Sir Richard, but Sir Palomides said, "In my study of herbs, I often consulted with physicians in my own country, and they were adamant that bleeding was a barbaric practice and did more harm than good, so when that Calais physician brought a knife to open a vein, I unsheathed my sword and chased him."

"That made me laugh for the first time in many days," Sir Peter said. "I think I began to feel better after that moment."

"And that is our story," Sir Palomides concluded. "Once I was certain Sir Peter was healed, we crossed the Narrow Sea to Dover and made our way on horseback the length of Britain. When we reached our forest camp and Will Scathelock told us where you had come, Sir Peter was quite eager to get here, once again to meet his beloved Lady Lydia."

There was a general murmur of appreciation around the board at that, and a few smaller conversations began on the other end of the table as Sir Richard, deeply moved by Sir Palomides' account, left his bench and knelt down before the Moor. "My Lord Palomides," his voice quavered. "You have restored my son unto me, having preserved his life when no other man could have done it. I fear I owe you a heartfelt apology. When first we met, I found your presence in our English forest…I don't know…unnatural perhaps I should say. Uncanny. And in my ignorance, I insulted you and your nation. I now know how wrong I was: I know you now to be a paragon of chivalry."

Sir Palomides smiled, accepted the compliment with the grace with which it was intended, but then added with an ironic smile, "I thank you for your good will, Sir Richard. And do you find me less barbaric because I conform to your English Christian sense of courtesy? I wonder if you could find in the people of my homeland a virtue and a wisdom in their own customs and religion. Different from yours but not without merit in the eyes of

God." When Sir Richard's face displayed so profound a blankness that he was aware such a way of thinking was as foreign to the old man as the Saharan sands, Sir Palomides pursued it no more and only smiled and nodded at him.

Then Sir Richard rose and, turning toward Robin, caught him by the shoulder, saying, "And you, good yeoman, I have come with a surprise for you. In my saddle bags I have brought four hundred gold nobles, with which I shall repay you the loan your band so generously advanced me to save my estate from being lost to that nefarious abbot! You will always have my thanks and my good will for coming to my aid in my darkest hour."

"Wait. What?" Will Stutely chirped, and Friar Tuck's eyes bulged in astonishment. "Our band…"

"Check yourself there, Will," Little John spoke low in his ear. "Don't interrupt Sir Richard when he's talking, especially about Robin's business."

"*Robin's* business, right," Stutely said, and pursed his lips.

"Sir Richard, the lady Lydia has already repaid us for that loan," Robin answered. "We want only your good will now. Say we will be faithful friends from this point forward. And put that money to some good work instead."

"Faithful friends with all my heart," Sir Richard replied. "And I shall give some thought to some good I might do with such a sum."

"Put it toward improving the lots of your tenants, the villeins on your estate!" Little John proposed. "Remit their rents, or their required manorial services for the next year. You have the money to cover those losses to your estate, and you cannot imagine what such relief will do to improve the lives of those peasants. They will sing your praises for years for such an act."

Sir Richard was just as bewildered by this suggestion as he had been by Sir Palomides', it being similarly outside of his world view, but he did recognize that this idea was apparently in line with the radical ideas John had been spouting on their earlier journey to York, and to please the big man, who'd been a significant part of his salvation, he agreed to do it for Little John's sake. And that was good enough for John.

"But as to the repayment coming from Countess Lydia, that news makes my heart glad!" Sir Richard said. "For it may presage a great joy. Perhaps she is about to announce her acceptance of my son's suit!"

"Sh!" Friar Tuck said. "Listen—I think what she's discussing right now is her marriage status!"

It was actually Sir Walter of Horsley who was speaking. He'd been invited to this celebration more or less as an afterthought, given his active role in the events that had culminated in Lady Lydia's inheritance, but he did not see it that way. Perhaps his mother and grandfather had gone about it the wrong way, but Walter was still not willing to abandon the idea of wedding himself to the new countess. True, their relationship had been rocky while he had held her in captivity, and, if he was being completely honest, he didn't like Lady Lydia all that much. Or at all. But none of that really mattered when it came to marriage. What mattered was family alliance and property. And Countess Lydia offered great opportunities in both areas.

"My lady countess," Sir Walter began. "Permit me to congratulate you on your inheritance and on your escape from the position you had been put in by my own greedy relatives. Please know that I regret that affair and renounce the nefarious motives behind it. Let me say that, having been made aware of my own mother's forced marriage, I am completely in sympathy with your declared resolve not to be forced into a marriage you find unacceptable. But I hope you will now freely reconsider my own suit. I am the son of an honest and doughty lord, Sir William of Horesly, whose heir I am, and with all due modesty I can say that I hold my inheritance with a not inconsiderable puissance of my own. You need a husband of some wealth and prowess to keep and protect your own estate, and marriage to me will bring you a greater estate and a solid defender of your title. Countess Lydia, I am asking for your hand."

Sir Peter gasped at that word, and made as if to protest, but his father put a restraining hand upon his arm. Everyone else at the table went completely silent, keen to hear how the countess would respond. Lady Lydia took a moment, briefly taken aback by such a bald proposal and in such a public space but having dealt with Sir Walter's pleadings daily for almost three months, she was not really surprised at his manner.

"Sir Walter," she began. "Be assured I am gratified by your assertion, at long last, that I am free to choose my own future. I do understand and do not deny your own fitness as a husband for any noble lady. At least for any noble lady who finds you desirable as a mate. And if I were looking for, as you say, a man with lands to increase my estate, and with the kind of martial prowess able to defend it, then I might think of you." Sir Walter, a light coming into his eye, began to feel a twinge of hope.

"However," Lady Lydia continued, and Sir Walter's hopes flagged, "I believe I have made it clear day after day for weeks at a time that I am not in the market for such a husband, and that I do not find you a desirable prospect as a spouse. I apologize for being so frank, but your proposal here, before so many witnesses, leaves me no choice but to speak my mind freely. No, Sir Walter, I will not give you my hand. That is my last word on the subject."

Sir Walter, utterly deflated and feeling shamed before the dinner company, slumped in his seat and would say no more. Robin could not help but feel for the rejected suitor and made a mental note to waylay Sir Walter when the feast was ended and commend to him the simple charms and virtues of a certain kitchen wench in his own castle. Agnes already admired Walter far beyond his deserts. Perhaps the boy might find some solace there, if his aristocratic outlook would bend enough to let him find a mate in so unlooked for a position.

Taking the countess's definitive rejection of Walter as his cue, Sir Peter left his seat on the bench and rushed to the head of the table where he threw himself to his knees at Lady Lydia's feet. "My lady," he gushed. "Forgive my audacity but having witnessed your rejection of Sir Walter I am emboldened to put forward my own suit in like manner. You must know, my dearest heart, how I have worshiped you, how your image sustained me through my exile and my illness. On my journey back here to you, with Sir Palomides' help I have put all my love into a love lyric that he has agreed to sing for you. Good Palomides, if you would please?"

Without giving the startled countess a chance to respond, Sir Palomides stood and backed away from the table. He hadn't hauled his lute along with him on this journey, but he did carry a small gittern, and striking a chord, began to sing in his mellow baritone:

Across the seas far from my home
I sailed far from my love,
But all the while on sea or foam
Your face I see
For you shall be
My angel from above.

I am your prisoner—set me free!
I shiver in my cell.
Your true love is the only key!

I weep and wail
To no avail.
Only your medicine makes me well.

I see your eyes shine like gemstones bright
I see your hair so gold.
I see your neck so long and white
So like a swan…

"Stop!" the countess cried, standing and waving her arms. "Enough! Stop please!" Sir Palomides, taken aback, gaped at the lady and stilled his gittern. "Sir Palomides, your voice and playing are wondrously entertaining, I'm not denying that. But Sir Peter! Truly! I rejected Sir Walter, but at least he implied he would protect and defend my lands. You, Sir Peter, present yourself as a suffering servant, crucified for my love? What good does that do me? And what is this about my eyes like gemstones? My eyes are dark brown, in case you haven't noticed. How many brown gemstones do you know of? And I'm a brunette, so how does my hair shine like gold?"

"Well," Sir Peter ventured, "I've seen you wear it bound with a gold crespine, as you're doing right now. That certainly shines, doesn't it?"

Ignoring him, Lady Lydia continued her tirade. "And what's this about a long white neck? I look like a swan to you?"

"A swan is a beautiful bird…"

"I'd look like a freak if my head bounced around on the end of a swan's neck. Besides, I am not as fair as all that. I've been on a tower looking out over the sea for three months."

"But my lady, these are the conventions of love poetry…" Sir Peter argued.

"Exactly!" Lady Lydia answered. "By your poetry, and by

your bewilderment right now, it seems to me that it isn't me that you love, but some idealized image of womanhood that you want to force me into. An angel from above your song says. But do you know what? That's not who I am. At all. And I have no intention of marrying somebody who doesn't have any idea who I am."

"But my lady countess," Sir Richard at the Lee ventured. "You must marry *someone*. You can't govern this earldom on your own. Your castles and lands must have a lord."

"Exactly what I've been saying all along!" Sir Walter piped up, blinking his one eye excitedly.

"Why?" the countess asked. "Where is it written that a woman cannot govern? Was not Zenobia a great ruler in antiquity? Did not Cleopatra rule Egypt in her own right? What about the Amazons and their Hyppolita? I've even heard of an Olga of Kiev ruling the Russians not so many centuries ago."

Sir Walter, rolling his eye, muttered, "This is what comes of educating women."

"Therefore, I hereby resolve, before this company as witnesses, that I will perform the duties and responsibilities as Countess of Chesterfield as a single woman. If I ever do marry, it will be in my own time, and to a person of my own choosing. I ask only the support and good will of my neighbors in governing my lands. History shows us that an intelligent, decisive and independent woman can rule on her own. I am an intelligent, decisive and independent woman. Therefore, I can rule on my own." And looking with a self-satisfied smile toward Sir Walter, she added, "QED."

Sir Walter threw up his hands in exasperation. Sir Richard frowned and, confronted at this same banquet by a third and even more basic challenge to his entire world view, shook his head in doubt and disbelief. But Robin Hood, inspired by the lady's courage and resolve, called out, "You will have my support whenever you need it, my lady!"

"And that of the other foresters of Sherwood!" cried Will Stutely, loudly seconded by Little John, Tuck, and Sir Palomides as well.

Sir Peter, scorned but smiling, rose from his knees and bowed respectfully to the countess. "I am chastened, my lady, but will live in hope that someday I may be that person that you choose. Meanwhile, I shall of course support you in whatever you may need." Maid Marion and Lady Maude, inspired by the countess's words, gave a short cheer and clapped their hands.

"Our banquet is ended," Sir Palomides said, "and it ends on a note of celebration." He lifted a cup of the countess's fine mulled wine and raised it up. "Drink to our noble countess and to her staunch resolve! And drink, too, to Robin Hood and his men, through whom all these marvels were wrought. Now, my love song was interrupted, but let me knit up all this affair with a ballad—if my lady assents…" He glanced up at Countess Lydia and she nodded in reply, and Sir Palomides stuck up his gittern and sang out:

Let us be thankful for these times
Of plenty, truth and peace.
And leave our great and horrid crimes,
Lest they cause this to cease.

I know there's many a feignéd tale
Of Robin Hood and his crew;
But chronicles, which seldom fail
Report this to be true.

If any listener please to try,
This story I tell now,
The truth of this brave history,
He'll find it true, I know.

And I shall think my labor well
Bestowed to purpose good.
When it shall be said that I did tell
True tales of Robin Hood.

CAST OF CHARACTERS

Abigail of Derby: Lady Abigail of Derby is the widow of Sir William and the mother of Sir Walter. An imperious woman, Lady Abigail rules Horsley Castle with a strong hand, and has conspired with Abbot Robert of York to force the marriage of her son Sir William to Lady Lydia Peveril, Countess of Chesterfield.

Abbot Robert of Saint Mark's Abbey: The abbot of this large abbey in the city of York, Abbot Robert de Harpham is the most powerful churchman in the north of England, and the richest. Called upon by Lady Abigail of Horsley Castle to mediate in the case of her son Walter's accidental death in a tournament at the hands of Sir Peter of Verysdale, the abbot imposed a 600 noble fine upon Sir Peter, which forces Peter's father Sir Richard at the Lee to borrow most of the money from the abbot himself. When this loan appears about to force Sir Richard to forfeit his ancestral lands, Robin and his men suspect that the abbot's plan all along was to steal Richard's land by extortion.

Agnes: Agnes ("like the virgin martyr") is a flirtatious kitchen wench at Horsley Castle who helps out Robin in his machinations there, and who has a soft spot in her heart for Sir Walter.

Alan a Dale: A member of Robin Hood's band, Alan a Dale is best known as a jongleur or minstrel who entertains the men with ballads of his own composition, or that he has learned from others. He is also one of Robin's younger followers, and one of his better archers. He is one of the married outlaws, living with his wife Ellen in Sherwood after being married by Friar Tuck.

Alan of Winchester: Formerly a corporal under Robin Kempe in the king's guard, Alan followed his old commander into a life in the forest after Camelot fell, and now is one of the outlaw band of Sherwood. As a former well-trained soldier, Alan is one of the most skilled archers in Robin's band.

Arthur Bland: Arthur is a very large and muscular man who had formerly made his living as a tanner. Upon meeting Little John, the huge tanner wanted to test his mettle against the equally large woodsman, and when Little John bested him, he decided he'd rather join Robin's band than keep his former profession, and joined the Sherwood bandits, a few teeth lighter after his skirmish with John.

Bishop of Hereford: The bishop is one of the wealthiest prelates in England, and proves an easy mark for Robin Hood and his men when he makes his way along the Great North Road through Sherwood. He does not hold back in letting others, particularly the Sheriff of Nottingham, know how badly he believes he was treated by Robin and his men, who relieved him of a thousand gold marks when they entertained him for dinner.

Brother Simon: Brother Simon is the cellarer, or chief steward, of Saint Mary's Abbey in York. Brother Simon is the sycophantic accomplice of the Machiavellian Abbot Robert.

David of Doncaster: David is the youngest of Robin's band, and turns sixteen during the course of the novel. An orphan, David has found a home with the outlaws of Sherwood. Tradition says that David of Doncaster was a yeoman wrestler.

Ellen: Ellen is the wife of Alan a Dale, and lives with him among Robin's outlaws in Sherwood. She is one of the youngest and most outspoken of the women who live with Robin's men, and is very knowledgeable in herbal lore.

Friar Tuck: Tuck is a Franciscan, though he belongs to no house and lives with Robin and his men in the forest. He does see to the outlaws' spiritual needs, and is licensed to hear confessions, though he does fight at their sides if need be. He is in charge of most of the outlaws' charitable ventures, taking half of all they take from their rich marks to give it to the poor.

Guy of Gisbourne: Sir Guy of Gisbourne is the newly appointed commander of the royal fortress of Nottingham Castle. Determined to enforce royal authority in Nottinghamshire, he vows to track down the outlaws of Sherwood and hang them.

Haakon: "Skipper" Haakon is a Norseman and former Viking who, having given up the sea, still manages to keep his hand in the robbing and looting trade as a member of Robin's outlaw band. His seaman skills occasionally come in handy, if any of the outlaws need a boat.

Hugh Peveril: Sir Hugh is the castellan of Codnor Castle, a nobleman whose uncle, Ranulph Peveril, was the Earl of Chesterfield. He was first cousin to Lady Lydia Peveril's father Stephen, making the countess Lydia his first cousin once removed. Sir Hugh did raise Lady Maude, his niece born out of wedlock, and she has remained loyal to him.

John Naylor: See "Little John."

John of Oxenford: See "Sheriff of Nottingham."

Little John: Little John is Robin Hood's right hand man. Born a villein on a manor belonging to a monastery, John fled his servitude and became an outlaw in Sherwood. He is tall, strong and imposing, and is in a committed relationship with Will Stutely. When necessary, John goes by the pseudonym "Reynold Greenleaf."

Lydia Peveril, Countess of Chesterfield: Lady Lydia was the daughter and only child of Sir Stephen Peveril and his noble wife, Lady Margaret Le Strange. Her father being deceased, she is the only direct descendant of Earl Ranulph of Chesterfield, and so is his heir. As such, she is the target of several noble families who want to marry their sons to her and so control her inheritance.

Maid Marion: Robin's nickname for Lady Mary of Winchester. Former lady-in-waiting to the old queen (i.e., Guinevere), Marion is now chief lady in the entourage of Lady Lydia Peveril, Countess of Chesterfield. Still unmarried at twenty and without prospects, her fellow ladies all call her "maid."

Mary of Winchester: See "Maid Marion."

Maude Peveril: Lady Maude Peveril is the wife of the Sheriff of Nottingham. She is a by-blow of Sir Aubrey Peveril, younger son of the powerful Peveril family, recognized and raised by her uncle Sir Hugh Peveril, lord of Codnor Castle. She is a love interest of Robin Hood.

Nicholas: Nicholas is a kitchen knave at Saint Mary's Abbey in York, and, later, briefly serves in the kitchen at Peveril Castle as well.

Palomides: Sir Palomides was a knight in the court of the old king (Arthur) before his kingdom's demise. A Moor born in the Middle East, Palomides became a Christian when he joined the Round Table. After that table fell, he could find no other lord in Britain who would take him on as a knight, and chose to join his old friend Robin in his outlaw band. Palomides is known for his culinary skills, as well as his skill in music and poetry.

Peter of Verysdale: Sir Peter is the young son of Sir Richard of the Lee, who accidentally kills his former friend Sir Walter of Horsley in a tournament, and is subsequently fined 600 nobles by the Abbot of Saint Mary's Abbey. The fine destroys his father's estate, and Peter is forced to go on a crusade to restore his good name and find a living for himself.

Prior Stephen: Prior Stephen of Saint Mary's Abbey is an honest and hospitable Benedictine who serves under the less than saintly Abbot Robert.

Richard at the Lee: Sir Richard at the Lee, lord of Verysdale, has a large estate around the village of Lee that has been in his family for seven generations, but which he is in danger of losing through a debt he owes the Abbot of Saint Mary's Abbey in York. Robin and his men stop him on the road, but he has no money to steal, and they vow to help him.

Robin Hood: Leader of a band of outlaws in Sherwood Forest. Of yeoman status, Robin's real name is Robin Kempe, and he is the former captain of the guard under the old king (King Arthur). Now he poaches the king's deer and robs rich nobles and prelates on the Great North road through Sherwood. When necessary, he goes by the alias "Robert fitz Ooth of Locksley."

Robin Kempe: See "Robin Hood."

Sheriff of Nottingham: Robin Hood's oldest and most persistent enemy, the sheriff, John of Oxenford, is a corrupt royal official who rakes in a good deal of money through bribery and the illegal seizure and taxation of goods that come through Nottingham. He is married to the far from pliable Lady Maude Peveril, and tends to give her a good deal of freedom.

Thorvald: Thorvald is an old dwarf with a white beard, who formerly drove a cart in which he carried prisoners to execution or other punishment. Later he gave up that trade to become a merchant under the old king, but since the king's fall he has taken to the forest with his old acquaintance, Robin.

Walter of Horsley: Sir Walter of Horsley, former friend of Sir Peter of Verysdale, had a falling out with Sir Peter over their rivalry for the favors of Lady Lydia Peveril. In a tournament, Sir Peter accidentally grievously wounded Sir Walter, and is accused of his murder.

Wat o' the Crabstaff: Wat is a part of Robin's outlaw band who was once a tinker, but was convinced by Robin to give up that trade and join the outlaws of Sherwood. In the early ballad "Robin Hood and the Tinker," it is told that he had vowed to capture

Robin and turn him in for the reward, but Robin gave him a reward of his own to join his band. A crabstaff is a quarterstaff, which is Wat's favorite weapon. Wat also brought along his horse Genevieve, who has an easier time in Sherwood than she did pulling the heavy tinker's wagon.

Will Scarlet: Everyone knows that one of the most popular figures in Robin's band is Will. However, the early ballads do not seem to agree on his last name. Thus, if you read the early ballads, there seem to be three different Wills in Robin's band: Will Scarlet, Will Scathelock, and Will Stutely, unless of course, they are all referring to the same character. I've made them all different. Will Scarlet is Robin's nephew, one of his younger followers. He wears a scarlet hood over his Lincoln green livery, and has blond hair and blue eyes. He's one of Robin's most loyal men, and one of his best archers.

Will Scathelock: Scathelock, the un-Scarlet, is a tall, lanky, middle-aged member of Robin's crew, known as a reliable and experienced woodsman. He is often left in charge of the outlaw camp when Robin and Little John are away, because of his stalwart trustworthiness.

Will Stutely: Stutely, even younger than Will Scarlet, is generally considered the handsomest of Robin's crew. He is a slight young man with a freckled and tanned face and sparkling brown eyes. He is deferential to Robin and courteous to ladies and others, but has a particularly caustic wit when he wants to annoy an enemy. And, he is a terrible singer. Will is Little John's particular friend, and the two share a tent together.

William de Forz: Sir William de Forz, Lord of Holderness, is castellan of Skipsea Castle where Lady Lydia is held against her will. As a large landowner in Yorkshire, he does what he is asked to do by the influential Abbot of St. Mary's Abbey, but is unenthusiastic about it.

William of Derby: Sir William of Derby, also known as Sir William of Horsley, the name of his castle, was a close friend of Sir Richard at the Lee, and had lands bordering Sir Richard's. Sir William fostered Sir Richard's son Peter, and made him squire to his own son, Sir Walter. Eventually Sir William knighted the lad Peter. He has died by the time this story begins, and is buried in the churchyard at Horsley Castle.

ABOUT THE AUTHOR

JAY RUUD is a retired professor of English at the University of Central Arkansas, now devoting much of his time to fiction writing. He has retold the traditional legend of King Arthur for modern readers as a series of Merlin Mysteries, the final volume of which, *To the Great Deep*, was published by Encircle in the fall of 2020. He's also written scholarly books, including an *Encyclopedia of Medieval Literature* (2006), *A Critical Companion to Dante* (2008), and *A Critical Companion to Tolkien* (2011), as well as the first full-length study of Chaucer's short poems, *"Many a Song and Many a Lecherous Lay": Tradition and Individuality in Chaucer Lyric Poetry* (1992), a book that was reissued by Routledge in October 2019 after 27 years.

He taught at UCA and chaired the English department for 13 years, prior to which he was Dean of the College of Arts and Sciences at Northern State University in Aberdeen, South Dakota. He has a Ph.D. in Medieval Literature from the University of Wisconsin-Milwaukee, and is married to the thoroughly awesome poet and novelist Stacey Margaret Jones. He has two more or less adult children, and as many spectacular dogs as grandchildren (four). He has been to all seven continents, is a lifetime Chicago Cubs fan, and dabbles in community theater, where he once played his own daughter's mother. Follow Jay Ruud on Facebook and @GildasOfCornwall on Instagram.

If you enjoyed reading this book,
please consider writing your honest review
and sharing it with other readers.

Many of our Authors are happy to participate in
Book Club and Reader Group discussions.
For more information, contact us at info@encirclepub.com.

Thank you,
Encircle Publications

For news about more exciting new fiction, join us at:

Facebook: www.facebook.com/encirclepub

Instagram: www.instagram.com/encirclepublications

Twitter: twitter.com/encirclepub

Sign up for Encircle Publications newsletter and specials:
eepurl.com/cs8taP

www.ingramcontent.com/pod-product-compliance
Lightning Source LLC
Chambersburg PA
CBHW050527110726
47899CB00005B/1618

9781645993728